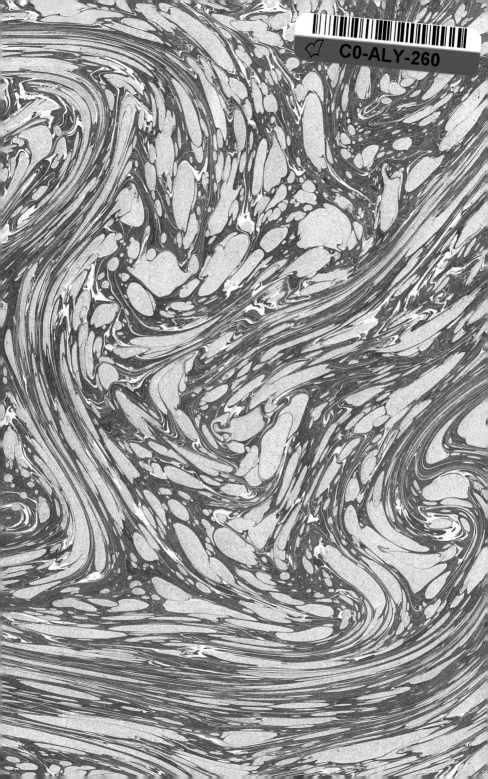

PÈRE GORIOT

Honoré de Balzac equaled his prodigious literary output with his energetic zest for life. Although he remained essentially insolvent, in his fifty-one years he wrote more than ninety novels and tales, traveled frequently and extensively, and pursued wealthy older women and get-rich schemes with like fervor.

Born in Tours on May 20, 1799, Balzac spent his first four years in the care of a wet nurse. At age eight he was sent to boarding school where he remained unhappily for seven years. Reading was his only escape. He never forgave his parents, particularly his mother, for what he felt to be this early neglect.

Nonetheless, Balzac went to law school to please his parents; but at the age of twenty, he announced his intention to become a writer. Surprisingly, his family agreed to finance him for two years. While he had no success in his own name, he wrote successful potboilers under a pseudonym. Realizing that the publishers were keeping most of the income from these books, he launched the first of many projects to get rich by starting his own firm to publish inexpensive editions of the classics. The firm failed. He next bought a printing business which also foundered, leaving him deeply in debt.

In 1829, at the age of thirty, Balzac published his first novel, *Les Chouans*, under his own name, to which he hoped to give a more distinguished ring by adding the aristocratic *de*. Although *Les Chouans* was only modestly successful, Balzac continued writing novels at an exhausting pace and began to develop an avid following. As his fame increased, his lifestyle became more extravagant than the considerable income from his writing could support.

In 1833, Balzac fell in love with a wealthy, married Polish aristocrat, Evelina Hanska, and pursued her relentlessly. In March, 1850, the widowed Mme. Hanska finally agreed to marry her persistent suitor, who was by then ailing, and who was to die five months later. By the end of his life, Balzac had become an easily recognizable figure throughout Europe. Few authors have been so immortalized in sculpture, portraits, and caricature.

Le Père Goriot appeared in serial form beginning in December, 1834. It was an instant success and is considered by many to be the best realized novel of Balzac's genius. Its plot is simple: a retired flour merchant is victimized by his love for his two ruthless daughters, who reject his love but take all his money in their effort to elevate themselves in society. They leave him destitute and dying, alone in his boardinghouse room attended only by Rastignac, a young law student who lives there but who also moves in fashionable circles. Rastignac, a pivotal character in the book, observes the heartless treatment of Père Goriot as well as the hypocrisy of the "fashionable world."

In 1842, Balzac gave the title *La Comédie Humaine* to his novels, both those he had completed and those he planned to write. At his death, this massive, unfinished life's work contained some 3000 characters from all walks of life, many reappearing in various novels at different points in their lives. Rastignac, for example, appears in no less than twenty-two novels and stories. Although Balzac sought out the rich and famous and was thought to be a shameless snob, his novels make clear that he was a keen observer and recorder of the whole social fabric.

The Editors

This Special Edition of
PÈRE GORIOT
was prepared for
subscribers to
The Oxford Library of
the World's Great Books

THE OXFORD LIBRARY OF
THE WORLD'S GREAT BOOKS

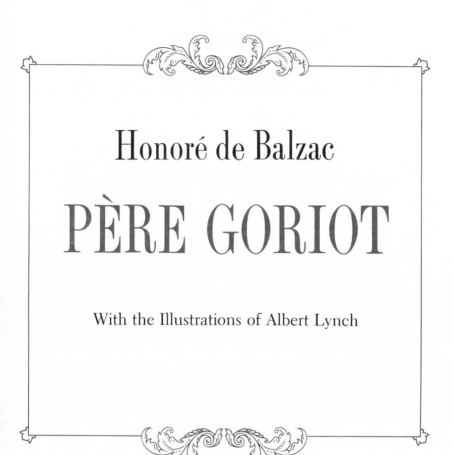

Honoré de Balzac

PÈRE GORIOT

With the Illustrations of Albert Lynch

OXFORD UNIVERSITY PRESS

THE FRANKLIN LIBRARY
has been selected by the
OXFORD UNIVERSITY PRESS
as publishers of
THE OXFORD LIBRARY OF THE WORLD'S GREAT BOOKS

To the great and illustrious
Geoffroy Saint-Hilaire
as a tribute of admiration for
his labors and his genius

BALZAC

 Contents

PART ONE

The Vauquer House

1

M ME. VAUQUER, whose maiden name was De Conflans, is an old woman who for forty years has kept, in Paris, a family boardinghouse situated in the rue Neuve-Ste-Geneviève between the Latin Quarter and the faubourg St-Marcel. This boardinghouse, known as the Vauquer House, is open to men and women, and to young and old; yet, so great is its respectability that it has never been assailed by slander. Still, for the last thirty years, no young woman has been seen there, and if a young man should board with Mme. Vauquer, it is certain that he receives but a meager allowance from his family. However, in 1819, the year in which this drama begins, a poor young girl was living there. Though the word drama has fallen into discredit by the lavish and violent manner in which it has been abused in the present time of sensational literature, I must use it here; not that my story is dramatic in the strict sense of the word, but before the end, some tears may be shed *intra* and *extra muros.*

It is doubtful whether it will be understood outside of Paris. Its details, gathered from observation and tinged with local color, can be appreciated only between the hill of Montmartre and the heights of Montrouge, in that famous valley full of tottering plaster and black and muddy gutters, where the miseries are real and the joys too often false, and where the excitement of life is so terrible that something extraordinary is required to produce a lasting sensation. Nevertheless, some sorrows loom up in great and solemn proportions on account of the accumulated mass of vices and virtues of which they are composed; at the sight of them, even egotism and self-interest stop to pity, but the impression received is as transient as that of a luscious fruit that is greedily devoured. The chariot of civilization, like that of the idol of the Juggernaut, though it may be delayed for a moment by some heart harder to crush than the others that checks its wheel, soon grinds it to powder and continues its triumphant progress. And you too will do the same, you who hold this book in your white hand, as you lounge in your soft armchair thinking, perhaps it will amuse me. After having read the secret sorrows of père Goriot, you will eat your dinner with a good appetite, laying your insensibility to the charge of the author, whom you will accuse of poetic exaggeration. But, believe me, this drama is neither fiction nor romance. It is all true, so true that each one of you may recognize its elements in your own family—perhaps in your own heart.

The family boardinghouse I speak of belongs to Mme. Vauquer. It stands at the foot of the rue Neuve-Ste-Geneviève, just where the ground slopes toward the rue de l'Arbalète so steeply and abruptly that horses are seldom driven past, either up or down the hill. This circumstance is favorable to the silence that reigns in the streets crowded between the dome of the Val-de-Grâce and the dome of the Panthéon—those two buildings that change the conditions of the atmosphere, tinging it with yellow and darkening it by the heavy shadows thrown by their cupolas. The pavement there is dry, there is no muddy water running in the gutters, and grass is growing along the walls. All the passersby, even the most lighthearted, are touched with melancholy; the noise of a carriage is an event; the houses are gloomy and the walls like those of a prison. A Parisian straying in this direction would see nothing but family boardinghouses or institutions, poverty or depression, decrepit old age or joyous youth bound to toil. No quarter of Paris is more unpleasant or, I might say, more unfamiliar. The rue Neuve-Ste-Geneviève is like a bronze frame, the only one in keeping with my tale, for which the minds of my readers cannot be too well prepared by somber colors and solemn thoughts, just as, step by step, the daylight wanes and the song of the guide grows hollow as the pilgrim descends to the Catacombs. This is a true comparison, for who can say which is the more horrible to look upon, a withered heart or an empty skull?

The front of the boardinghouse overlooks a little garden, so that the building stands at right angles with the rue Neuve-Ste-Geneviève, from which you can see the whole width of it. Along the front of the house, separating it from the garden, there runs a pebbled channel six feet wide, beyond which there is a graveled pathway bordered with geraniums, oleanders, and pomegranate trees planted in large pots of blue and white crockery. The entrance to this pathway is made through a small door surmounted with a placard on which is inscribed: THE VAUQUER HOUSE, and underneath: FAMILY BOARDINGHOUSE FOR LADIES AND GENTLEMEN. During the daytime a latticed door furnished with a jangling bell allows you to see at the other end of the path, on the wall opposite the street, an arch painted by some artist of the district to imitate green marble. Under this counterfeit arch there stands a statue representing Love. The coat of varnish that covers it is scaling off, and lovers of symbols might accept it as a myth of Parisian love, the cure for which is to be found at no great distance. Upon the pedestal, a half-obliterated inscription recalls the date of the decoration by the enthusiasm it shows for Voltaire on his return to Paris in 1777:

Whoe'er thou art, thy master see,
Who is, or was, or is to be.

At nightfall the latticed door is replaced by a paneled one. The garden is as wide as the facade is long and is shut in by the street wall on one side and on the other by the party wall of the next house, which is overgrown and completely hidden by a mantle of ivy that draws the attention of passersby by a picturesqueness of effect unusual in Paris. Both walls are covered with vines and fruit trees that have been trained against them, whose slight and dusty produce is the subject of Mme. Vauquer's yearly fears and of her conversations with her boarders. Along each wall runs a narrow path leading to a group of lime trees whose name Mme. Vauquer, though born a De Conflans, obstinately mispronounces, in spite of the grammatical remonstrances of her guests. Between these two side alleys there is a bed of artichokes flanked by fruit trees cut in the shape of pyramids and bordered with sorrel, lettuce, and parsley. Under the shade of the lime trees is placed a round table, painted green and surrounded with seats. There, in the dog days, though the heat is intense enough to hatch an egg, those boarders who can afford the luxury come to enjoy their coffee.

The facade, three stories high and surmounted by attics, is built of rough stone and is washed with the yellow color that lends an ignoble character to most of the houses in Paris. The five windows on each story are filled with small panes of glass and are supplied with blinds, no two of which have been drawn up to the same height, so that the lines of all are out of harmony. The width of the house admits of two windows on each story, and those on the ground floor are ornamented with iron bars and gratings. Behind the building there is a courtyard about twenty feet broad, where pigs, chickens, and rabbits live peaceably together, and at the end of which stands a woodshed. Between the woodshed and the kitchen window hangs the safe for provisions, and underneath it the greasy water from the sink flows into the courtyard. The court opens into the rue Neuve-Ste-Geneviève by a narrow door through which the cook sweeps the refuse of the house, when, under penalty of contagion, she cleans the gutter by flooding it with water.

The ground floor, which seems naturally destined for the purposes of a bourgeois boardinghouse, is composed, in the first place, of a room lighted by the two windows that look on the street, and is entered by a glass door. This parlor communicates with the dining room which is separated from the kitchen by a staircase whose steps are of wood, painted with a check pattern and waxed. Nothing can be more melancholy than this parlor with its sofas and chairs covered with horsehair, striped alternately with dull and glossy lines. In the middle stands a round table with a top of Sainte-Anne marble, on which rests one of those tea services that are so common nowadays, of white china with gilt decorations half worn away. The floor of the room is somewhat badly laid; the wainscoting is breast-high, and the remainder of the walls is hung with a glazed paper representing the principal scenes of *Telemachus,* whose classic personages are in color. The panel between the grated windows presents to the boarders a view of the banquet given by Calypso to the son of Ulysses. For forty years this picture has provoked the jests of young boarders, who fancy they show their superiority to their position by ridiculing the dinner to which their poverty condemns them. It is evident from the cleanliness of the hearth that a fire is built there only on great occasions, and the chimneypiece is ornamented with two vases of shabby artificial flowers under glass cases, between which stands a clock of bluish marble in the worst possible taste. This first room exhales a smell that has no name in the language and must be called a *boardinghouse* smell. It is a close, musty, rancid smell; it chills you; it is damp to breathe; it permeates your clothing; it tastes like a room where dinner has been going on; it reeks of the kitchen, the pantry, and the hospital. Perhaps it might be described, if a process were invented by which it were possible to estimate the elementary and nauseous quantities emitted by the catarrhal and *sui generis* atmosphere of each boarder, young or old. Still, in spite of these depressing horrors, if you compared the parlor to the dining room, which adjoins it, you would find it elegant and fragrant as a boudoir.

The dining room is paneled to the ceiling and was once painted a color that has now grown dim and makes a background for the different layers of dirt that have settled upon it and grouped themselves into fantastic patterns. The walls are lined with sticky sideboards covered with cloudy, cracked decanters, basins of tin, and piles of thick, blue-bordered china plates that were manufactured at Tournai. In one corner there is a box with numbered compartments that serves to hold the boarders' napkins, spotted with grease and wine. Indestructible articles of furniture banished from other places are to be met with here, just as the ruins of civilization are gathered together in a home for incurables. You will find here a barometer furnished with a Capuchin that comes out when it rains; some execrable engravings that take away your appetite, framed in varnished black wood ornamented with gilt moldings; a clock of tortoiseshell inlaid with copper, a green stove, and some Argand lamps coated with oil and dust; a long table covered with oilcloth on which the grease lies thick enough for a facetious boarder to write his name in it with his finger; mutilated chairs and forlorn little straw mats that are always coming to pieces and yet are never wholly destroyed; and wretched, charred foot warmers with broken tops and loosened hinges. In order to explain in how great a degree this furniture is old, cracked, rotten, rickety, corroded, shabby, disabled, crippled, and ruinous, I would be obliged to write a description that would diminish the interest of my readers and that busy people could never forgive. The red floor is full of valleys produced by waxing and various coats of paint. In short, here poverty without poetry reigns supreme—shabby, economical, concentrated poverty. If it has not as yet reached a condition of positive filth, it is squalidly dirty; if there are no absolute rags and tatters, everything will soon fall to pieces from rottenness.

This room is to be seen in all its glory just at the moment when, toward seven o'clock in the morning. Mme. Vauquer's cat precedes her mistress, and jumping along the sideboards, sniffs the milk that is contained in various bowls covered with saucers, and sets up her matutinal purr. The widow soon makes her appearance attired in a tulle cap, underneath which hangs a mass of ill-adjusted false hair; she comes in shuffling in her slippers full of wrinkles. Her round, elderly face, in which the salient feature is a nose shaped like the beak of a parrot; her little fat hands; her person, plump as a partridge; and her gown that hangs loosely about her—all are in harmony with the room reeking with squalor and infected with the love of sordid gain, whose close, warm air she can breathe without disgust. Her face is fresh as the first frost of autumn, and the expression of her wrinkled eyes passes rapidly from the forced smile of an opera dancer to the harsh scowl of a bill discounter; in short, her whole personality explains the boardinghouse, as the boardinghouse suggests her personality. The jail cannot exist without the jailer; you cannot imagine one without the other. The little woman's unwholesome plumpness is the product of her life, just as typhus is consequent upon the exhalations of a hospital. Her knitted wool underpetticoat sags below the outer one that is made from the stuff of an old gown and through whose rents the wadding is protruding; it sums up the parlor, dining room, and garden; it announces the kitchen and prepares us for the boarders.

When Mme. Vauquer is present, the spectacle is complete. She is about fifty years old and resembles all *women who have had many troubles*. She has the glassy eye and seemingly innocent expression of a procuress who will fly into a passion in order to obtain better terms but, at the same time, is ready for any deed that will turn to her advantage, even to betray Georges or Pichegru, if Georges or Pichegru were here to be betrayed. Still, her boarders, who believe her to have no money because they hear her moaning and groaning like themselves, declare her to be a *good creature at heart*. Who was M. Vauquer? She never spoke freely of him. How had he lost his fortune? She said he had been unlucky. He had treated her badly and had left her nothing but her eyes

to cry with, her house to live in, and the privilege of refusing her sympathy to all other unfortunate people, because, as she used to say, she had suffered everything that
it was possible to suffer. As big Sylvie, the cook, heard
her mistress's step, she made haste to serve the breakfast
of the regular boarders.

Generally, the dayboarders came only to dinner, for
which they paid thirty francs a month. At the time of
the beginning of this story, there were seven boarders
who lived in the house. The best two apartments in the
house were on the first floor; Mme. Vauquer lived in the
smaller one, and the other belonged to Mme. Couture,
widow of a commissary of the French republic. She had
with her a very young girl named Victorine Taillefer, to
whom she gave a mother's care. The sum paid by these
two ladies for their board amounted to eighteen hundred
francs. There were two apartments on the second floor,
one of which was occupied by an old man named Poiret,
and the other by a man about forty years old who gave
his name as M. Vautrin, wore a black wig, dyed his
whiskers, and called himself a retired merchant. Of the
four rooms on the third floor, two were let—one to an old
maid, Mlle. Michonneau by name, and the other to a
former manufacturer of macaroni, vermicelli, and starch
who was known as père Goriot. The two other rooms
were destined to birds of passage—those luckless students
—who, like père Goriot and Mlle. Michonneau, could
pay only forty-five francs a month for board and lodging.
But Mme. Vauquer did not care to have them and took
them only when she could do no better: they ate too

much bread. At the time of which I write, one of these two rooms belonged to a young man who had come from the environs of Angoulême to study law in Paris and whose large family was enduring every hardship at home to be able to send him twelve hundred francs a year. Eugène de Rastignac, for this was his name, was one of those young men inured to work by poverty who, in early youth understand the hopes reposed in them by their parents and create a distinguished career for themselves by calculating the aim of their studies and adapting them beforehand to the future developments of society, from which they mean to be first in exacting tribute. Without his power of shrewd observation and the adroitness with which he made his entrance into the salons of Paris, my tale could never acquire the true colors that it will henceforth owe to his acuteness and to his desire of unraveling the mystery of a situation as carefully hidden by the authors of it as by their victim.

Above the third story was a garret used for drying clothes and two attic rooms used by Christophe, the handyman, and big Sylvie, the cook. Besides the seven houseboarders, Mme. Vauquer had, on an average, eight students of law and medicine, and two or three inhabitants of the neighborhood who came to dinner only.

Eighteen persons took dinner in the dining room, which could hold twenty, but in the morning the seven lodgers alone met together and partook of what looked like a family meal. Each person came down in slippers and, with every appearance of intimacy, indulged in confidential remarks upon the dress or manner of the day boarders and upon the events of the preceding evening. These seven boarders were the spoiled children of Mme. Vauquer, who measured out to them her attentions according to the amount they paid her, with astronomical accuracy. One and the same consideration affected all these beings brought together by chance. The two lodgers on the second floor paid only seventy-two francs a month, Mme. Couture alone making an exception to the rule, and such cheapness, to be found only in the faubourg St-Marcel between the Bourbe and the Salpêtrière, indicates that the boarders were all oppressed by poverty more or less apparent.

The wretched spectacle offered by the interior of the house was repeated in the equally dilapidated dress of its inmates. The men wore frock coats whose color had become problematical and such shoes as in fashionable quarters are thrown into the gutter: threadbare linen and garments that were but ghosts of their former selves. The women had shabby, dyed, and faded gowns, old darned lace, gloves shiny with use, red collars, and frayed neckerchiefs. Such were their clothes, but they almost all had solidly built frames, constitutions that had resisted the storms of life, and cold, hard faces, worn and obliterated like coins that have lost their inscriptions; their withered mouths were armed with voracious teeth. These boarders suggested dramas that had been already completed or were still in action; not of the kind played before the footlights between the painted scenes, but mute and living dramas, ceaseless chilling dramas that sharply stir the heart.

The elderly Mlle. Michonneau wore over her tired eyes a dirty green silk shade edged with brass wire that would have frightened the Angel of Pity. Her body was so angular that her shawl, trimmed with a meager, stringy fringe, looked as if it were folded round a skeleton. What acid had destroyed this creature's feminine charms? She must once have been pretty and well shaped. Was it vice or grief or avarice? Had she loved too well? Had she bought and sold cast-off finery, or had she been simply a courtesan? Was she expiating the triumphs of her exultant youth with its throng of pleasures by an old age that was repellent to all who saw her? Her pale glance chilled you, and her shriveled face was threatening. She had a voice shrill as that of a grasshopper chirping in its bush at the approach of winter. She said she had taken care of an old gentleman afflicted with a catarrh of the bladder and abandoned by his children, who believed him to be without means. This old gentleman had bequeathed her a life annuity of a thousand francs, which was periodically disputed by his heirs to whose calumny she was exposed. Though her face was ravaged by the play of passions, there was still a certain fineness and whiteness in her complexion that showed some traces of former good looks.

M. Poiret was like a kind of machine. Often, as he crept along an alley in the zoological gardens like a dark shadow—a flimsy old cap on his head, an ivory-handled cane that he held with difficulty in his hand, his shabby coattails floating behind him, disclosing the loose trousers a world too wide for the blue-stockinged legs that shook like those of a drunken man, his white waistcoat, soiled and dingy, his cravat twisted round his flabby throat and imperfectly adjusted to the shrunken shirt-frill of coarse cotton—many people have wondered if this fantastic being belonged to that audacious race of the sons of Japheth who swarm upon the boulevard Italien. What toil had withered him, and what passion had yellowed his swollen face that would look unnatural even in a caricature? What had he been? Perhaps he had been employed in the Ministry of Justice, clerk of the office where the executioner sends the memorandums of his expenses, his bills for black veils furnished to criminals, for the sawdust in the basket, and cords for the guillotine. Perhaps he had been receiver at the gate of a slaughterhouse, or subinspector of the Board of Health. It was evident that this man had been one of the drudges in our great social mill, a Parisian Raton who did not even know his Bertrand, a pivot on which public mischance or impurity had turned; in short, one of those men of whom we say when we meet them, "Such creatures have their uses." The gay side of Paris ignores their faces blanched with moral or physical suffering, but Paris is like the sea. Try to sound it, but you will never know its depth. Study it, write of it; but with whatever zeal you may study it and write of it, however numerous and eager may be the explorers of its ocean, there will always be an untrodden shore, an undiscovered cave, strange flowers, pearls, and creatures unknown and forgotten to literary divers. The Vauquer establishment is one of these curious monstrosities.

Two figures formed a striking contrast to the crowd of other boarders. Though Mlle. Victorine Taillefer was pale and anemic and looked sickly, though she harmonized with the general misery that made up the background of the picture on account of her habitual depression, embarrassed manners, and poor wan looks, yet her face was not old, her movements were lithe, and her voice, fresh. The luckless young girl was like a shrub transplanted to unfavorable soil whose leaves are dying. Her blond cast of countenance, reddish hair, and too-slender waist realized the grace that modern poets recognize in the statues of the Middle Ages. Her gray eyes, deepening into black, expressed great sweetness and Christian resignation, and her simple inexpensive garments covered a youthful frame. She was pretty by juxtaposition. If she had been happy, she would have been lovely; a woman's happiness is her poetry just as clothes are her tinsel. If the excitement of a ball had reflected its rosy tints on her pallid face, if the pleasures of an easy life had rounded and reddened her cheek that was already slightly sunken, if love had kindled her melancholy eyes, Victorine might have rivaled the greatest beauties. She lacked that which creates a woman anew: her dress and her love letters. Her history might have furnished a subject for a novel. Her father, who thought he had reasons for refusing to acknowledge her, would not have her live with him, allowed her but six hundred francs a year, and had converted his estate into personal property so that he could bequeath it entire to his son.

Mme. Couture, a distant relation of Victorine's

mother, who had long ago died in her house, cared for the orphan as for her own child. Unfortunately, the widow of a commissary of the armies of the Republic owned nothing besides her marriage settlement and her pension; she might die any day and leave the poor girl, without experience or resources, to the mercy of the world. The good woman took Victorine to mass every Sunday and to confession every two weeks, determined at all events to make a pious girl of her. She was right, for a religious vocation alone offered a future to the disinherited child, who loved her father and made a yearly pilgrimage to his house, trying to induce him to pardon her mother; but every year she knocked in vain at the paternal door, which remained inexorably shut to her. Her brother, who was her only mediator, had not come to see her in four years and sent her no help. She implored God to unseal her father's eyes and soften her brother's heart, but she never accused them in her prayers. Mme. Couture and Mme. Vauquer could not find words enough in the dictionary of abuse to characterize such barbarous conduct. When they cursed the infamous millionaire, Victorine's voice arose, sweet as the song of the wounded dove, full of love and pain.

Eugène de Rastignac had a southern countenance, clear complexion, blue eyes, and black hair. His figure, manner, and habitual attitude marked him as the son of a noble family, from which he had received an education in accordance with the traditions of good taste. Though he was obliged to be careful of his wardrobe and wore his old clothes on ordinary days, he was sometimes able to walk out dressed like a young man of fashion. Ordinarily he wore an old coat, a shabby waistcoat, the ugly, black, crumpled, badly tied cravat of a student, trousers to match, and resoled boots.

Between these two persons and the others, Vautrin, who was forty years old, with dyed whiskers, served as a transition. He was the kind of man generally known as a jolly fellow. He had broad shoulders, a well-developed chest, and thick square hands strongly marked on the fingers with tufts of bright red hair. His face was lined with premature wrinkles and showed signs of hardness contradicted by his soft insinuating manners. His low-pitched voice, in harmony with his noisy mirth, was not disagreeable. He was cheerful and obliging. If a lock was out of order, he would instantly take it to pieces and, having repaired, filed, and oiled it, would put it back, saying that he understood all about that sort of thing. He seemed to be familiar with everything: with vessels, the sea, France, and foreign countries; with men, business, events, laws, hotels, and prisons. If anybody made much ado about his troubles, he was prompt to offer his services. He had lent money several times to Mme. Vauquer and to some of the boarders, but they would have died rather than not return what they had borrowed, for in spite of his apparent good humor, his inscrutable and determined look struck them with fear. Even the manner in which he expectorated revealed an imperturbable composure that would not recoil before a crime that was to free him from an equivocal position. Like a stern judge, his eye seemed to probe all questions, thoughts, and consciences.

It was his habit to go out after breakfast, come back for dinner, to disappear for the whole evening, and return toward midnight by the aid of a passkey, with which Mme. Vauquer had entrusted him. He alone enjoyed this indulgence, for he was on the best terms with the widow, whom he called Mamma and round whose waist he was in the habit of clasping his arms. The good woman hardly understood this piece of flattery, which she thought was an easy thing to do, whereas no one but Vautrin had arms long enough to enclose such a bulky circumference. It was characteristic of him that he generously paid fifteen francs a month for the coffee and brandy he took with his dessert. Persons less superficial than these young fellows who were swept before the whirlwind of Parisian life, or these old men who were indifferent to all that did not immediately concern them, would have been dissatisfied with the doubtful impression produced upon them by Vautrin. He knew or guessed the affairs of all who surrounded him, but nobody fathomed his thoughts or his occupations. Although his seeming good nature, his constant gaiety and disposition to oblige, raised a barrier between him and the others, there were sometimes glimpses to be had of the alarming depth of his character. Often a sally worthy of Juvenal, in which he apparently took pleasure in scoffing at the laws, in satirizing the upper classes and convicting them of inconsistency, made it evident that he nourished a grudge against society, and that there was at the root of his life a mystery carefully buried.

Mlle. Taillefer, who was attracted perhaps unconsciously by the strength of the one and the good looks of the other, divided her furtive glances and secret thoughts between the man of forty and the young student; but neither of them appeared to pay any attention to her, although at any time chance might change her position and make her an advantageous match. Besides, none of the boarders took the trouble to find out whether the misfortunes alleged by the others were true or false. They all maintained toward one another the indifference mingled with mistrust resulting from their respective situations. They knew they could not help one another and had confided their troubles so often that they had drained the cup of condolence. As with old married people, they had nothing more to say, and there remained between them only a mechanical intercourse, like the motion of unoiled wheels. They all walked straight past a blind beggar in the street, listened coldly to a tale of distress, and looked upon death as the only solution of the wretched problem that made them insensible to the misery of others. The happiest of these afflicted souls was Mme. Vauquer, who ruled in this free prison. To her alone the little garden, forlorn as a steppe because of the excess of silence and cold, of damp or draft that reigned there, was a shady bower; and to her the dingy, gloomy house, redolent of verdigris as a shop counter, was full of charms. The cells belonged to her; she fed the convicts condemned to eternal imprisonment, and exercised over them a respected authority. Where in Paris could those poor creatures have found, at the price at which she offered it, wholesome and sufficient food, and lodgings, which it was in their power to render, if not elegant or commodious, at least clean and salubrious? Had she been guilty of crying injustice, her victims would have borne it without complaint.

SUCH an assemblage must of necessity offer in miniature the elements of the whole of society, and in fact, among the eighteen guests, just as happens in schools or in the outside world, there was to be found a poor despised creature, the butt of all the jests of the boarders. At the beginning of his second year, this figure became to Eugène de Rastignac the most striking of all those among whom he was doomed to live for two years more. This common laughingstock was the retired manufacturer of macaroni, père Goriot, upon whose head a painter would, like a historian, have concentrated all the light of his picture. By what chance had a half-malicious contempt, a persecution mingled with pity, and an utter want of respect for misfortune fallen upon the oldest of all the boarders? Had he himself been the cause through some weakness or eccentricity harder to pardon than vice itself? These questions touch closely much of the injustice of society. Perhaps it is in human nature to torment anybody who endures everything in true humility or through weakness or indifference. Don't we, all of us, like to prove our strength at the expense of somebody or something? Even a wretched little street boy rings everybody's doorbell in cold weather and clambers up to write his name on a virgin monument.

Père Goriot, who was about sixty-nine years old, had retired from business in 1813 and established himself at Mme. Vauquer's. He had first engaged the apartment that Mme. Couture now occupied and had paid twelve hundred francs for his board with the air of a man for whom five louis more or less a month was a trifling sum. Mme. Vauquer had renewed the three rooms of this apartment in consideration of a preliminary indemnity, which defrayed, it was said, the expenses of a cheap set of furniture made up of varnished, plush-covered chairs, yellow cotton curtains, a few glazed pictures, and wallpaper that would have been rejected by every saloon in the suburbs. Perhaps the careless generosity with which père Goriot, then always respectfully called M. Goriot, allowed himself to be imposed upon made her think him a fool with no head for money matters. He had come to her provided with an ample wardrobe, an outfit like that of a shopkeeper who thinks nothing too good for him on retiring from business. Mme. Vauquer had admired his eighteen shirts of fine linen, whose delicate texture was rendered more conspicuous by the two pins set with large diamonds and connected with a little chain that the macaroni merchant stuck in his falling frill. He usually wore a light blue coat and put on daily a fresh white piqué waistcoat, under which his round protuberant paunch rose and fell, swinging his heavy gold chain and the trinkets attached to it. His snuffbox, also of gold, held a medallion with a lock of hair that looked as if he had had success with the fair sex. When his hostess accused him of being a *gallant,* he smiled in the pleased, fatuous way of a bourgeois whose vanity is flattered. His *armoires*—which he pronounced *ormoires* after the fashion of the common people—were filled with a quantity of silver that he had used in his housekeeping. The widow's eyes shone as she officiously helped him to unpack and arrange the spoons and forks, ladles, gravy spoons, cruets, sauceboats, a few dishes, and a breakfast service in silver—all more or less handsome and amounting to some marks in weight. He was unwilling to dispose of them. They were gifts that reminded him of the solemn occasions of his domestic life.

"This," he said to Mme. Vauquer, as he handled affectionately one of the dishes and a little porringer whose cover was ornamented with two billing turtledoves, "this is the first present I had from my wife on the anniversary of our marriage. Poor dear, she put into it all the savings of her girlhood. I tell you, madame, I would rather do anything in the world than let them go. Thank heavens I can take my coffee in this porringer every day for the rest of my life. I need not complain, for I have enough laid away for the future."

Then, Mme. Vauquer's lynx eyes had seen some cer-
tificates of the Register of Funds, which roughly com-
puted might bring this splendid Goriot an income of
eight to ten thousand francs a year. From that day on,
Mme. Vauquer conceived designs—she who had been
born a De Conflans and was forty-eight years old in
reality, although she owned to only thirty-nine. In spite
of the tear ducts of Goriot's eyes being swollen, drooping,
and turned outward so that he was obliged to wipe them
frequently, she thought him pleasing and gentlemanlike
in his appearance. Besides, his long square nose and the
large and salient calves of his legs prognosticated moral
qualities, whose existence was confirmed by the good old
fellow's moon-shaped and ingenuously foolish face. This
attracted the widow, who thought him a sturdy simpleton whose heart would govern his head. His hair was
daily powdered and dressed by the barber of the Ecole
Polytechnique to stick out on both sides; it was arranged
in five points on his low forehead and became him well.
Though a little rustic, he was so well fixed up and took
his snuff with so much air, sniffing it as if he were always
sure of filling his box with Macouba, that on the evening
of the day of his installment in her house, Mme. Vauquer
went to bed at night on fire, like a basted partridge, with
the longing that possessed her to emerge from the chrys-
alis of a Vauquer and be born anew a Goriot. She
dreamed of marrying, selling her boardinghouse, and
walking arm in arm with this flower of the bourgeoisie; of
becoming a lady of note in the neighborhood and collecting money for the poor; of making little excursions on

Sunday to Choisy, Sossy, and Gentilly; and of going to the theater whenever she chose, occupying a box without waiting for the complimentary tickets she occasionally received from some of her boarders in the month of July; in short, all the El Dorado of middle-class Parisian family life. She had never confided to anybody that she owned forty thousand francs, which she had hoarded penny by penny, and she fully believed herself a suitable match on the score of fortune.

"Besides, I am quite worthy of the old fellow!" she said, as she turned on her bed, trying to convince herself of her charms, whose hollow imprint was found every morning by big Sylvie when she came to make the beds.

For three months afterward, Widow Vauquer engaged the services of M. Goriot's hairdresser and was at some expense for her costume, under the plea that it was her duty to give her house an appearance of decorum in harmony with the distinguished persons who lived in it. She went to a great deal of trouble in her endeavors to change the class of boarders who came to her, announcing that, from then on, she meant to receive only those who were in every way desirable. If a stranger presented himself, she boasted to him of the preference shown to her house by M. Goriot, one of the best known and most worthy of Parisian merchants. She distributed circulars, at the top of which MAISON VAUQUER appeared in large letters. It was, she said, "one of the oldest and most valued family boardinghouses in the university quarter." It possessed a delightful view over the valley of the Gobelins—which could be seen from the third story—

and a "pretty" garden, at the end of which stretched an "alley" of lime trees. She enlarged upon the pure air and retired situation. This prospectus brought her the Comtesse de l'Ambermesnil, a woman of about thirty-six, who was waiting for the final settlement of a pension due to her as widow of a general, who had died, as she said, on "the" fields of battle. Mme. Vauquer paid particular attention to her table, lighted the fire in her parlors for six months, and so faithfully fulfilled the promises of her prospectus that *she was compelled to make a considerable outlay.* The Countess used to say to Mme. Vauquer, whom she called her dear friend, that she would procure her the Baroness de Vaumerland and the widow of Colonel Comte Picquoiseau, two friends of hers, who were finishing their three months' term in a boardinghouse at the Marais, which was more expensive than the Vauquer establishment. She assured her that these ladies would be very comfortably off when the War Office had settled their business.

"But," she would say, "the office is so slow."

The two widows went upstairs together after dinner to Mme. Vauquer's room, where they chatted amicably, drinking black currant cordial and eating such dainties as were reserved for the consumption of the mistress of the house. Mme. de l'Ambermesnil approved her hostess's views on the subject of M. Goriot; she thought the idea an excellent one, and indeed it had occurred to her the first day of her arrival; she considered him quite perfect.

"Oh, my dear," the widow said to her, "a man who

is as sound as my eye and so well preserved might still make a woman very happy."

The Countess generously added some remarks to Mme. Vauquer upon her dress, which she told her was not in harmony with her pretensions.

"You must prepare for war," she said.

After many calculations, the two widows went together to the Palais Royal, where they bought, in the Galeries de Bois, a bonnet and a hat trimmed with feathers. The Countess dragged her friend to the shop of La Petite Jeannette, where they selected a dress and scarf. When this ammunition was in operation and the widow under arms, she looked for all the world like the sign of the Boeuf à la mode. Nevertheless, she was so pleased with the change in her appearance and thought herself so indebted to the Countess that, although disinclined to making gifts, she begged her to accept a bonnet that cost twenty francs. To tell the truth, she expected to ask her friend to do her the favor of sounding Goriot and singing her praises to him. Mme. de l'Ambermesnil obligingly lent herself to this stratagem and beset the old flour dealer until she succeeded in having an interview with him; but she found him so backward, not to say refractory, in meeting the overtures suggested to her by her own desire of entrapping him for herself, that she left him, repelled by his rudeness.

"My angel," she said to her dear friend, "you will never get anything out of that man, who is so ridiculously distrustful! He is a skinflint, a fool, an idiot who will never give you anything but trouble."

In fact, matters had gone so far between Mme. de

l'Ambermesnil and M. Goriot that she was not willing
to see him any longer; so she went off the next day, for-
getting to pay for six months' board and leaving behind
her some cast-off things that were valued at five francs.
In spite of the eagerness of Mme. Vauquer's searches,
she could never succeed in receiving any intelligence in
Paris of the Comtesse de l'Ambermesnil. She often talked
of this deplorable affair and complained of her too-
confiding nature—she who was more suspicious than a
cat; but she was like many people who mistrust their
friends and throw themselves into the arms of the first
stranger who comes along. This is a moral fact, strange
yet true, and its root is easily found in every human heart.
It may be that some people have nothing more to gain
from those with whom they live. After having disclosed
the emptiness of their souls, they feel themselves secretly
judged with the severity they have deserved; but since
they experience an overpowering need of flattery or are
devoured by the desire of appearing to possess the qualities that they have not, they hope to take by storm the
esteem or the heart of persons who are unknown to them,
at the risk of losing it later on. Again, there are people
who are born mercenary and never do a kindness to their
friends or relations because it is their duty; whereas,
when they confer a favor upon strangers, they reap a
reward in their own self-conceit. The nearer home the
circle of their affection, the less they love, but the more
extended it is, the more obliging they are. Mme. Vauquer partook, doubtless, of these two natures, which are
both essentially mean, false, and detestable.

"If I had only been here," Vautrin said to her, "this

misfortune would never have happened! I would have stared down the little humbug; I know their *faces*."

Like all narrow-minded people, Mme. Vauquer never sought the causes of events or stepped out of the immediate sphere in which they occurred. She liked to lay her own mistakes at the door of others. After her loss, she looked upon the good flour dealer as the author of her misfortune and began from that time to cool off toward him, as she called it. When she saw the futility of her allurements and of the expense lavished upon her dress, she was not slow to guess the reason. She then perceived, she said, that he must be absorbed in his own intrigues. In short, it was clear to her that the hope she had so tenderly nursed rested upon chimerical foundations, and that she could never get anything out of the man, to use the energetic expression of the Countess, who seemed an adept in such matters. Her aversion was necessarily greater than her liking had been, for it was not the result of love but of disappointed hopes. If the human heart ever pauses in climbing the heights of affection, it seldom stops on the steep descent of hatred. Still, M. Goriot was her boarder, and like a monk enraged against his prior, the widow was obliged to stifle the explosions of her wounded vanity, to repress the sighs that her delusion cost her, and to restrain her desire for revenge. Little minds satisfy their good and evil impulses by constant acts of pettiness. All the widow's feminine malice was directed toward inventing a system of underhand persecution against her victim. She began by retrenching upon the superfluities she had introduced into her household.

"No more pickles or anchovies; that is all nonsense!" she said to Sylvie the morning on which she returned to her original program. M. Goriot was a frugal man, and the parsimony necessary to those people who make their own fortunes had become a second nature with him. His favorite dinner was always soup, boiled beef, and a course of vegetables, so it was very difficult for Mme. Vauquer to torment a boarder whose tastes she found it impossible to offend. In despair at finding him unassailable, she tried to bring him into discredit with the boarders, whom she inspired with her dislike of him so successfully that for their own amusement they served her purposes of vengeance. Toward the end of the first year, the widow reached such a degree of distrust that she wondered why a merchant with an income of seven or eight thousand francs, a magnificent set of silver, and jewels as fine as a courtesan's would come to live with her and spend for his board a sum so small in comparison with his fortune.

During the greater part of his first year with her, Goriot had dined out once or twice a week; then, little by little, it came to his dining out only twice a month, and M. Goriot's little outings were so much in Mme. Vauquer's interest that she could not help being displeased with the progressive exactness with which he took his meals at home. The change was attributed to a slow decrease in his income and to his desire of annoying his hostess; for one of the most hateful propensities of Lilliputian minds is to endow others with their own pettiness. Unfortunately, toward the end of the second year, M. Goriot justified the gossip about him by asking Mme. Vauquer to allow him to go up to the second story and to reduce his board to nine hundred francs. His economy was so strict that he had no fire all winter. Mme. Vauquer insisted upon being paid in advance; M. Goriot acquiesced, and from that time the widow called him père Goriot.

Then began a rivalry as to who would guess the causes of his decadence, and the task was a difficult one, for as the pseudocountess had said, père Goriot was sly and taciturn. According to the logic of empty-headed people who babble because they have nothing of importance to tell, those who keep silence about their affairs must surely be engaged in wrongdoing; so the distinguished merchant became a rogue, an old flirt, and an old reprobate. Vautrin, who came about this time to the Vauquer establishment, said that père Goriot had ruined himself at the Stock Exchange and still continued to speculate there in a small way. Another opinion was that he was a petty gambler and played every evening for the sum of ten francs. Again, they suspected him of being a spy in the employ of the police, although Vautrin declared that he was not clever enough for that. It might be that père Goriot was a miser who lent money for a short time at heavy interest, or a man who kept betting upon the same number at a lottery with constantly increasing stakes. All hateful mysteries that could possibly be engendered by weakness, vice, or shame were attributed to him. Only, however ignoble his conduct or his vices, the aversion he occasioned was not sufficient to cause his banishment: he paid for his board. Besides, he was useful; everybody whetted his good or ill humor upon him, in jest or rudely.

The most probable theory, and the one generally adopted, was Mme. Vauquer's. According to her, this man, who was so hale and hearty, so well preserved, and who might still make a woman very happy, was a libertine with strange tastes. Here are the facts upon which Mme. Vauquer based her slanders.

A few months after the departure of the disastrous Countess who had lived for six months at her expense, before getting up one morning, she heard upon the stair the rustle of a silk gown and the light, brisk step of a young woman who was making her way to Goriot's room, whose door opened to greet her. Big Sylvie came immediately to tell her mistress that a young woman, too pretty to be honest, *dressed like an angel* and shod in prunella boots on which there was not a particle of mud, had glided like a snake from the street into the kitchen and had asked her where M. Goriot's room was. Mme. Vauquer and her cook flew to the door to listen and overheard some tender words in the course of the interview, which lasted for some time. When M. Goriot went out with his *lady*, big Sylvie took her basket and pretended that she was on her way to market, so that she might follow the loving couple.

"Madame," she said to her mistress, on her return, "M. Goriot must be damned rich to keep her like that. Only think, there was a splendid carriage waiting at the corner of the Estrapade, which *she* got into."

At dinner, Mme. Vauquer rose to draw down a curtain to prevent Goriot's being inconvenienced by a ray of sunlight that shone in his eyes.

"A beautiful woman loves you, Monsieur Goriot, and the sun pursues you," she said, alluding to the visit he had received. "Dear me, you have good taste; she was very pretty."

"It was my daughter," he said, with a kind of pride that the boarders took to be the fatuity of an old man trying to save appearances.

A month after this visit, M. Goriot received another. His daughter had first come in morning costume, but this time she arrived after dinner, dressed for a ball. The boarders, who were busy talking in the salon, caught a glimpse of a pretty blonde, slender, graceful, and much too distinguished to be the daughter of a man like Goriot.

"Two of them already!" exclaimed big Sylvie, who did not recognize her.

A few days afterward, another girl, a brunette, with a tall, fine figure, black hair, and brilliant eyes, asked for M. Goriot.

"Three of them!" Sylvie said.

The second girl, who had come to see her father the first time in the morning, arrived a few days later in the evening. She was then in a ball dress and came in a carriage.

"Four of them!" exclaimed Mme. Vauquer and big Sylvie, who saw no resemblance between this great lady and the simply dressed girl who had made her first visit in the morning.

Goriot was still paying twelve hundred francs board. Mme. Vauquer thought it natural for a rich man to have four or five mistresses, and even admired his adroitness in passing them off as his daughters. She was not displeased with him for bringing them to her house, only, as these visits proved his indifference toward her, at the beginning of the second year she went as far as to speak of him as *an old baboon*. Later, when he only paid nine hundred francs for his board, she asked him insolently, on seeing one of these ladies going down stairs, what use he expected to make of her house. Père Goriot answered that the lady was his elder daughter.

"You have thirty-six daughters, then, have you?" Mme. Vauquer demanded sharply.

"I have only two," he replied with the gentleness of a ruined man to whom poverty has taught submission.

Toward the end of the third year, père Goriot again reduced his expenses and went up to the third story, where he paid only forty-five francs a month. He gave up his snuff, discharged his hairdresser and wore no more powder. When père Goriot appeared for the first time without his powder, his hostess uttered a cry of surprise as she saw the color of his hair. It was a dull greenish gray, and his face, which had grown imperceptibly sadder from day to day, was the most wretched of all those at the table. There was no longer any room for doubt; père Goriot was an old profligate who had required all the skill of a physician to preserve his eyes from the injurious influence of the drugs he used for his maladies. The repulsive color of his hair was the result of his excesses and of the medicines that he used in order to continue them. The moral and physical condition of the poor man seemed to warrant her wild suppositions. When his shirts were gone he bought some cotton at fourteen sous a yard to replace the fine linen he had previously worn, and his diamonds, his gold snuffbox, his chain, and his trinkets disappeared one by one. Instead of his light blue coat and rich clothes, he wore, summer and winter, a brown coat, a mohair waistcoat, and gray trousers of double-milled cloth. He became gradually thinner; his legs grew lean; his face, once expanded with the satisfaction of bourgeois happiness, became abnormally wrinkled; his brow was furrowed; and the outline of his jaw could be sharply seen.

In the fourth year of his establishment in the rue Neuve-Ste-Geneviève, he no longer bore any resemblance to himself. The good vermicelli-maker of sixty-two, who seemed less than forty, the fat, sleek, rosy, simple bourgeois, whose brisk looks cheered the passersby and whose smile was like that of a young person, had become a dull, wan, infirm septuagenarian. His bright, blue eyes had turned iron-gray and lost their luster; they had faded, and though they no longer overflowed, their red rims looked as if they had shed tears of blood. He inspired some of the boarders with horror; others with pity. Some young medical students, who had remarked the fall of his lower lip and measured the top of his facial angle, abused him for a long time without receiving any response and then declared that he was becoming idiotic. One evening after dinner, Mme. Vauquer said to him jestingly, "Your daughters don't come to see you anymore, do they?" just as if she did not believe in his having daughters. Père Goriot started as if she had stuck a needle into him.

"Yes, they come sometimes," he answered in a shaken voice.

"Oh, ho! You do see them sometimes then?" exclaimed the students. "Bravo, père Goriot!"

But the old man did not hear the jokes to which his answer had given rise; he had sunk back into a reverie that his superficial observers took for senile torpor owing to his want of intelligence. If they had understood him, they might have been deeply interested in the problem presented by his physical and moral state; but such knowledge was too difficult of attainment. Although it would have been easy to find out whether Goriot had really been a flour merchant and what the amount of his fortune was, the old people, whose curiosity he had roused, never went out of their own neighborhood and lived in their boardinghouse like oysters in their shells. As to other people, absorbed by the peculiar fascinations of Parisian life, as soon as they left the rue Neuve-Ste-Geneviève, they forgot all about the poor old man whom they ridiculed. To the narrow-minded elders and to the young and lighthearted alike, père Goriot's dull misery and stupid bearing seemed incompatible with fortune or capacity of any kind. With regard to the women whom he called his daughters, they all shared the opinion of Mme. Vauquer, who used to say, with the stern logic that gossiping old women learn from their constant habit of inquiring into other people's affairs:

"If père Goriot had daughters as rich as those ladies appear to be who come to see him, he would not be living on the third floor of my house at forty-five francs a month, nor would he go about dressed like a beggar."

There was nothing to contradict these assumptions, so, toward the end of the month of November, 1819, the time of the opening of this drama, everybody in the boardinghouse had settled opinions about the poor old man. He had never had either wife or daughter; the abuse of pleasures had converted him into a snail, into an anthropomorphical mollusk to be classed among the *casquettifères*, as a young man who was employed in the museum and dined in the boardinghouse used to say. Poiret might be called an eagle, for he was a gentleman compared to Goriot. Poiret spoke, conversed, and answered when he was addressed; it is true that he said nothing of consequence when he spoke, argued, and answered questions, for it was his habit to repeat what others said in other words; but he contributed to the conversation. He was alive and seemed capable of sensation whereas père Goriot, according to the museum employee, was always at a temperature of zero.

PART TWO

First Glimpses of Society

1

EUGÈNE de Rastignac had returned in a frame of
mind known to young men of superior intelligence
or to those to whom the difficulties of their situation
have momentarily imparted the qualities of refined men.
During his first year in Paris, the small amount of study
necessary for taking the lower degrees in the university
had left him leisure to enjoy the visible delights of material Paris. A student has none too much time on his
hands if he wishes to know the stock pieces of every
theater, to study the issues of the Parisian labyrinth, to
learn the habits and the language, and to become familiar with the pleasures peculiar to the capital; to explore all haunts, both good and evil, to follow those
courses he finds amusing, and to examine the treasures
of the museums. A student is sure to be enthusiastic
about trifles that appear to him of great moment. He has
his great man, one of the professors of the College of
France, who is paid to keep up to the level of his audi-
ence. The student pulls his cravat into place and poses
to attract the attention of a woman in the first gallery at
the Comic Opera. By successive initiations, he loses his
early greenness, widens the horizon of his life, and finally

understands how each stratum of human society is super-
imposed upon the one that lies beneath. If he has first
admired the carriages that drive past him in the Champs-
Elysées on a fine afternoon, he will end by coveting
them.

Eugène had unconsciously served this apprenticeship
by the time he went home for his vacation, after taking
his degrees of Bachelor of Letters and Bachelor of Laws.
His childish illusions and provincial ideas had disappeared. His altered conceptions and heightened ambition
enabled him to see his home and family in their true
light. His father and mother, his two brothers, his two
sisters, and an aunt whose fortune consisted of pensions
lived together on the little estate of Rastignac. This
estate, which brought in an income of about three thousand francs, was subject to the uncertainty incident to
the industrial product of the vine, and yet twelve hundred francs had to be yearly extracted from it for his use.
The sight of the grinding poverty that they generously
strove to hide from him; the comparison he was forced
to draw between his sisters, who had been so lovely in his
childish eyes, and the Parisian ladies, who realized the
type of a beauty he had dreamed of; the uncertain future
of his numerous family that trusted to his efforts; the
niggardly care that he saw bestowed upon the least produce of the farm; the wine made for the family from
the lees of the wine press—these and many other circumstances unnecessary to mention here increased tenfold
his longing for success and made him thirst for distinction.

Like all noble natures, he wished to owe everything to his own merit, but his temperament was eminently that of a southerner. In executing his projects, his will was sure to be subject to hesitation, such as besets a young man on the open sea when he does not know in what direction to steer his boat or to what wind to trim his sails. He was first inclined to throw himself heart and soul into his work, but he was soon impressed with the necessity of making friends, and observing the immense social influence of women he suddenly resolved to enter society in order to acquire patronesses. Why should he fail in such an achievement, since he was young, high-spirited, and clever; gifted, moreover, with a graceful figure and that sort of nervous beauty that is so attractive to women? These thoughts assailed him in the fields, where he had once walked so happily with his sisters, who now thought him sadly changed.

His aunt, Mme. de Marcillac, had long ago been presented at court and used to know the aristocratic celebrities there. All at once it occurred to the young aspirant that in the recollections with which his aunt had so often amused him there lay the elements of several social conquests quite as important as those he was seeking in the law school. He questioned her about the ties of relationship that could be renewed, and after shaking the branches of the genealogical tree, the old lady came to the conclusion that, of all those persons who could serve her nephew among the egotistical tribe of rich relations, the Vicomtesse de Beauséant would be the least recalcitrant. She wrote to that young lady a letter in old-fashioned style, which she gave to Eugène, telling him that if he succeeded with the Viscountess, she would help him to find his other relations. A few days after his arrival in Paris, Rastignac sent his aunt's letter to Mme. de Beauséant, who answered it by an invitation to a ball the next evening.

Such was the condition in which matters stood in the boardinghouse at the end of November 1819. A few days later, on the evening of Mme. de Beauséant's ball, Eugène did not return till two o'clock in the morning. In order to make up for lost time, the courageous student resolved, while dancing, to work till morning. He was going to sit up all night in that silent house for the first time, still under the spell of an illusive energy caught from the splendors of fashionable society. He had not dined at Mme. Vauquer's, so the boarders did not expect him to return till the next morning at dawn, as had happened before, sometimes, when he came home from entertainments at the Prado or balls at the Odéon, with mud on his silk stockings and his dancing shoes trodden out of shape. Before bolting the door, Christophe had opened it to look down the street, and Rastignac, who appeared at that very moment, ran upstairs to his room without making any noise, followed by the servant, who made a great deal. Eugène undressed, put on his slippers and an old coat, lighted his turf fire, and prepared so silently for work that his quiet preparations were drowned by the creaking of Christophe's heavy shoes.

Eugène sat thinking for a few minutes before plunging into his law books. He had just discovered that the

Vicomtesse de Beauséant was one of the queens of fashion in Paris and that her house was considered the most agreeable in the faubourg St-Germain. Moreover, her name and fortune made her one of the celebrities of the aristocratic world. Thanks to his aunt, the poor student had been well received at her house, although he was not as yet aware of the extent of the favor shown him. To be admitted to those gilded salons was equivalent to a certificate of high birth. By appearing in this, the most exclusive of all circles, he had acquired the right of going everywhere.

He had been dazzled by the brilliant assemblage and had scarcely exchanged a word with the Viscountess, but he had interested himself in picking out of the throng of Parisian divinities at the ball one of those women who are capable of inspiring love at first sight. The Comtesse Anastasie de Restaud was tall and well made and was thought to have one of the prettiest figures in Paris. She had great black eyes, lovely hands, delicately modeled feet, and spirited movements; she was a woman whom the Marquis de Ronquerolles would have called a thoroughbred. Her highly strung nerves robbed her of no possible charm, and although plump and well rounded, she could not be accused of being too stout. *Thoroughbred, woman of breeding*, and like phrases had begun to take the place of epithets such as "heavenly angels," "Ossianic figures," and the other metaphors of the old mythology of love rejected by modern dandies. But, to Rastignac, Mme. Anastasie de Restaud was the woman to be desired. He had managed to write down his name twice in the list of partners upon her fan and had been able to speak to her in the first quadrille.

"Where shall I see you again, madame?" he had asked abruptly with the passionate fervor that women like.

"In the Bois, at the Bouffons, or at my own house; wherever you like," she answered.

The adventurous southerner tried boldly and eagerly to make the acquaintance of the lovely Countess as successfully as a man can make a woman's acquaintance in the brief space of a quadrille or a waltz.

He told his partner, whom he took for a great lady, that he was Mme. de Beauséant's cousin; she immediately invited him to visit her at her house, and the last smile she gave him made him think that she expected a call from him.

He had also met a gentleman who had not laughed at his inexperience—a singular piece of good luck—for the love of ridicule was the fatal defect of the distinguished fops of the time, the Maulincourts, the Ronquerolles, the Maxime de Trailles, the De Marsays, the Ajuda-Pintos, and the Vandenesses, who had all been there in the glory of their folly. There too had been all the most fashionable women: Lady Grandon, the Duchesse de Langeais, the Comtesse de Kergarouët, Mme. de Serisy, the Duchesse de Carigliano, the Comtesse Ferraud, Mme. de Lanty, the Marquise d'Aiglemont, Mme. Firmiani, the Marquise de Listomère, the Marquise d'Espard, the Duchesse de Maufrigneuse, and the Grandlieus. So it was fortunate for the young student that he fell in with the Marquis de Montriveau, lover of the Duchesse de Langeais, a general, simple as a child, from whom he learned that the Comtesse de Restaud lived in the rue du Helder. To be young, to thirst for society and the love of woman, to see two houses open their doors to him, that of the Vicomtesse de Beauséant in the faubourg St-Germain and that of the Comtesse de Restaud in the Chausseé-d'Antin! To look through the salons of Paris, one by one, sure of finding a woman to help and protect him for the sake of his good looks! To feel ambitious enough to give a reckless kick to the tight-rope on which he must walk with the assurance of an experienced gymnast, and to have found in a charming woman the best of balancing poles!

With these thoughts in his mind, and before the image of this stately woman that rose beside his turf fire, between his law books and his poverty, who would not, like Eugène, have fathomed the coming years in his med-itations and fed them with success? His vagrant fancy discounted his future joys so quickly that he was already in imagination with Mme. de Restaud, when a plaintive sigh broke the silence of the night and reechoed so loudly in the young man's heart that it seemed to him like the last gasp of a dying person. He quietly opened his door and, as soon as he stepped into the corridor, perceived a line of light shining through the crack beneath père Goriot's door. Eugène feared that his neighbor was ill, and applying his eye to the keyhole, he looked into the room. There he saw père Goriot engaged in a task that appeared to him of a criminal nature, and he believed he would render a service to society by investigating the nightly labors of the old man who called himself a vermicelli dealer. Père Goriot had fastened to the bar of his table that he had turned upside down a richly embossed platter and porringer of silver, and having twisted a cord round them, he was pulling it violently, evidently trying to convert the plate into ingots.

Good heavens, what a man! thought Rastignac, as he looked at the nervous arm of the old man, who, with the aid of the cord was kneading the silver as if it had been dough. Is he a thief or a receiver of stolen goods who pretends to be harmless and stupid and lives like a beggar in order to carry on his business more safely? continued Eugène to himself as he rose for a moment from his stooping posture.

Then he put his eye again to the lock. Père Goriot had untwined his cord and, taking the mass of silver, placed it on the table, which he had already covered with a cloth, and then rolled it up and down until he had rounded it into a bar, an operation that he performed with marvelous facility.

He must be as strong as Augustus, King of Poland, thought Eugène when the round bar was nearly molded into shape.

Père Goriot looked sadly at his work, and tears fell from his eyes as he blew out the small taper by whose light he had welded his silver. After that, Eugène heard him sigh deeply as he got into bed.

He is mad, thought the student.

"My poor child," père Goriot said aloud.

After hearing this, Rastignac decided that it would be prudent for him to keep silent about what he had seen and not to condemn his neighbor too rashly. He was going back to his room, when suddenly he heard a noise, difficult to characterize, but which might be made by men coming upstairs in felt slippers. He listened and caught distinctly the sound of the alternate breathing of two men. He could not hear their steps nor did he hear the door open, but all at once he saw a faint light that came from M. Vautrin's room on the second story.

How many mysteries there are in this house! he thought. He descended a few steps, listening, and the clink of gold struck his ear. In a minute the light was put out, and though the door had not creaked, he heard again the double breathing, which grew fainter as the two men went downstairs.

"Who is there?" Mme. Vauquer cried, opening the window of her room.

"It is only I coming in, Mamma," Vautrin said in his deep voice.

That is strange! Christophe bolted the door, Eugène said to himself as he went back to his room. A man must sit up all night in Paris to find out all that is going on about him.

These trifling events broke up his dreams of love and ambition, and he set to work. Distracted by the suspicions he entertained of père Goriot, and still more by the vision of Mme. de Restaud that appeared to him from time to time as the harbinger of a brilliant destiny, he ended by going to bed and sleeping soundly. Young people are sure to spend in sleep seven out of ten nights consecrated to work, for a man must be more than twenty if he wishes to keep awake.

2

THE next morning Paris was enveloped in one of those dense fogs during which the atmosphere is so clouded and darkened that the most precise persons make mistakes about the hour. People miss their business appointments, and at midday everybody thinks it is only eight o'clock. It was half past nine, and Mme. Vauquer had not stirred from her bed. Christophe and big Sylvie, also late, were comfortably enjoying their coffee made with cream skimmed from the milk destined for the boarders, which Sylvie had boiled for a long time to prevent Mme. Vauquer's finding out about the tithe they had illegitimately levied.

"Sylvie," Christophe said, dipping his first slice of toast in his coffee, "M. Vautrin is a good fellow, but he had a visit from two men last night. If Madame has got wind of it, we must not let her know anything further."

"Did he give you anything?"

"He gave me five francs this month, just as if he were telling me to hold my tongue."

"He and Mme. Couture are not stingy, but the others would like to take back with one hand what they give us with the other on New Year's day," Sylvie said.

"And what is it they give us?" Christophe continued. "Only a dirty five-franc piece. Père Goriot has cleaned his boots himself for two years. That skinflint of a Poiret goes without blacking altogether and would rather drink it down than put it on his shoes. As to that miserly student, he only gives me two francs! Two francs don't even pay for my brushes, and he sells his old clothes in the bargain. What a hole this house is!"

"Oh, pooh!" Sylvie said, sipping her coffee. "Our places are the best in the neighborhood: we are well-off here. But, about Grandpapa Vautrin, Christophe, has anybody spoken to you about him?"

"Yes. I met a gentleman in the street the other day, and he said to me, 'Isn't there a big man with dyed whiskers living in the same house with you?' I said, 'No, monsieur, they are not dyed. A good fellow like him doesn't have time for such things.' I told it to M. Vautrin, and he said, 'You have done right, my boy! Always answer in that way, for nothing is more disagreeable than to have one's infirmities known. Besides, it might spoil a match for me.'"

"When I was at the market, they tried to coax me too into telling them whether I had ever seen him put on his shirt," Sylvie said. "What a joke! There," she added, interrupting herself, "the Val-de-Grâce is striking a quarter to ten, and nobody is stirring."

"Pshaw! They have all gone out. Mme. Couture and the young girl went at eight o'clock to receive the communion at St-Etienne. Père Goriot started out, carrying a bundle, and the student will not come back till ten

51

o'clock, after his lecture. I saw them go as I was sweeping the stairs, and père Goriot hit me with the thing he was carrying; it was hard as iron. What is the old fellow up to? The others drive him round like a top, but he is a nice man all the same and is worth more than all of them. He doesn't give much of anything, but the ladies to whom he sends me tip me famously, and they are very prettily fixed up."

"Those he calls his daughters? There are a dozen of them."

"I have gone to two only, the same who came here."

"There is Madame coming, and she is sure to give us a scolding; I must go to her. You must watch the milk, Christophe, and look out for the cat."

Sylvie went up to her mistress.

"How is this, Sylvie? It is a quarter to ten, and you have let me sleep like a dormouse! Such a thing has never happened before."

"It is all on account of the fog, which is so thick that you can cut it with a knife."

"But what about breakfast?"

"Oh! Your boarders are possessed with the devil, and they all left *des le patron-jacquette*—at peep o' day."

"Speak correctly then, Sylvie," Mme. Vauquer replied. "You should say, *le patron-minette*."

"Well, madame, I will say it as you like. However, you can have your breakfast at ten o'clock, and that is soon enough. Old Michonnette and Poireau have not budged. They are alone in the house and are sleeping like the blocks they are."

"But, Sylvie, you put those two together, as if—"

"As if what?" Sylvie asked with a burst of stupid laughter. "The two make a pair."

"It is very strange, Sylvie, that M. Vautrin came in last night after Christophe bolted the door. How did he do it?"

"You are mistaken, madame. Christophe heard M. Vautrin and went down to open the door for him. And you thought—"

"Give me my morning jacket and go see about breakfast. Warm up what is left of the cold mutton with some potatoes, and give us some stewed pears—the kind that cost two pennies apiece."

A few moments afterward, Mme. Vauquer came in to discover that her cat had upset with its paw the saucer that covered a bowl of milk, which it was lapping with avidity.

"Mistigris!" she cried.

The cat ran away and then came back and rubbed itself against her legs.

"Yes, you are trying to make your peace, old thief!" she said. "Sylvie! Sylvie!"

"What do you want, madame?"

"See what the cat has been drinking!"

"It is all the fault of that fool, Christophe, whom I told to set the table. Where has he gone? Never mind, madame; we can use it for père Goriot's coffee. I will put some water in it, and he will never notice. He pays attention to nothing, not even to what he eats."

"Where has the old rascal gone?" Mme. Vauquer asked as she put on the plates.

"How should I know? He is about some devil's errand or other."

"I slept too long," Mme. Vauquer said.

"But you are as fresh as a rose, madame—"

Just at this moment the bell rang, and Vautrin came into the salon, singing in his bass voice:

> "Long have I wandered here and there,
> And I've been seen in every clime . . ."

"Oh, good morning, Mme. Vauquer," he said on catching sight of his hostess, whose waist he gallantly encircled with his arm.

"Come!" she said. "Stop this nonsense."

"Call me an impudent fellow," he said. "Come, say that I am one, won't you? There, I am going to help you set the table. I am very obliging, don't you think so?

> "Courting the girls, brunette and fair,
> Loving and sighing . . .

"I have just seen something very odd.

> "By chance . . ."

"What?" the widow asked.

"At half past eight this morning, père Goriot was in the rue Dauphine, at the shop of the goldsmith who buys old silver and gold lace. He sold to him at a good price a household utensil of silver, very well twisted for a man who is not of the trade."

"No, really?"

"Yes. I was on my way home from accompanying one of my friends who is leaving the country by the royal mail-coach; I waited to see what père Goriot was up to. It is a ludicrous story. He returned in this direction to the rue des Grès, near here, and entered the house of a well-known usurer, Gobseck by name, a precious rascal who is quite equal to making dominoes out of his father's bones. He is a Jew, an Arab, a Greek, a Bohemian, and a man whom it would be very hard to get the better of, as he has a large bank account."

"But what is père Goriot doing?"

"He is doing nothing; he is undoing himself. He is an ass who is idiotic enough to spend all his substance on girls who—"

"There he is!" Sylvie cried.

"Christophe," père Goriot called out, "come upstairs with me."

Christophe followed père Goriot and soon came down again.

"Where are you going?" Madame inquired of her servant.

"I am going to do an errand for M. Goriot."

"What is that?" Vautrin said, snatching a letter from Christophe's hands and reading the address. "*Mme. la Comtesse Anastasie de Restaud.* Where are you to take this?" he asked, returning the letter to Christophe.

"To the rue du Helder. I have orders to deliver it to nobody but the Countess."

"What is in it?" Vautrin said, holding up the letter to the light. A banknote? No." He half opened the envelope. "A receipted bill," he cried. "The devil! He is a chivalrous old dotard. Go, simpleton," he continued, putting his large hand on Christophe's head and turning it round and round like a thimble, "you will get a good tip."

The table was set, and Sylvie was boiling the milk. Mme. Vauquer lighted the stove with the assistance of Vautrin, who kept on humming:

> "Long have I wandered here and there,
> And I've been seen in every clime."

When all was ready, Mme. Couture and Mlle. Taillefer came in.

"Where have you been so early, my dear lady?" Mme. Vauquer asked of Mme. Couture.

"We have been paying our devotions at St-Etienne du Mont, for we are to go today to M. Taillefer's. Poor girl, she is trembling like a leaf," Mme. Couture added, sitting down before the stove at whose door she held her steaming shoes.

"Warm yourself, Victorine," Mme. Vauquer said.

"You do well, mademoiselle, to pray the good God that your father's heart may be softened," Vautrin said, placing a chair for the orphan girl. "But that is not enough. You need a friend to tell the truth to that wretch, a barbarian, who is said to have three million and yet refuses to give you a dowry. Even a pretty girl needs a dowry, nowadays."

"Poor child!" Mme. Vauquer said. "My dear, your monster of a father is really tempting Providence."

At these words, Victorine's eyes filled with tears, and the widow stopped at a sign from Mme. Couture.

"If we could only see him, if I could speak with him and give him his wife's last letter," Mme. Couture went on. "I have never dared to risk it by mail, for he knows my writing, and—"

"*O innocent, persecuted, and most unhappy women!*" Vautrin exclaimed, interrupting her. "Is that as far as you have got? In a few days from now, I mean to attend to your affairs, and all will be well."

"Oh, monsieur," Victorine cried, looking with eyes that glowed through her tears at Vautrin, who remained unmoved, "if you know any means of reaching my father, tell him that his affection and my mother's honor are more precious to me than all the riches of the world. If you can succeed in mitigating his displeasure, I will pray for you. You may be sure of my eternal gratitude . . . "

"*Long have I wandered here and there,*" Vautrin sang in an ironical voice.

At that moment, Goriot, Mlle. Michonneau, and Poiret came down, attracted probably by the odor of the sauce Sylvie was preparing for the cold mutton. Ten o'clock struck as the seven guests sat down at the table; and the student's step was heard in the street.

"Oh, Monsieur Eugène," Sylvie said, "today you are going to breakfast with the others!"

The student bowed to the boarders and sat down beside père Goriot.

"I have just had a singular adventure," he said, as he helped himself generously to the mutton and cut a piece of bread that Mme. Vauquer measured with her eye.

"An adventure?" repeated Poiret.

"Certainly, and why should you think it so surprising, old goose?" Vautrin said to Poiret. "M. de Rastignac is just the person for adventures."

Mlle. Taillefer glanced timidly at the young student.

"Tell us your adventure," Mme. Vauquer demanded.

"Yesterday evening, I was at a ball given by the Vicomtesse de Beauséant, a cousin of mine, who has a magnificent house with rooms draped in silk. The entertainment was superb, and I was happy as a king—"

"Fisher," Vautrin said, interrupting him.

"Monsieur," Eugène said, warmly, "what do you mean?"

"I say fisher, because kingfishers are much happier than kings."

"That is true; I would rather be this little bird without any cares than a king, because—" said Poiret, who always repeated the sentiments of others.

"At all events," the student resumed, cutting him short, "I danced with one of the loveliest women at the ball, a beautiful Countess, the most exquisite creature I ever saw. Her hair was dressed with peach blossoms, and she wore in her gown a charming bunch of real flowers that had the most delicious perfume. But pshaw! You should have seen her, for it is impossible to describe how a woman looks when she is animated by dancing. Well, this morning I met the divine Countess, about nine o'clock, on foot in the rue des Grès. My heart beat fast, for I thought—"

"That she was coming here," Vautrin said, turning his inscrutable glance upon the student. "She was, no doubt, on her way to see Papa Gobseck, the usurer. If you ever explore the hearts of the women of Paris, you will find that a usurer occupies a more important place in them than a lover. Your Countess's name is Anastasie de Restaud; she lives in the rue de Helder."

Upon hearing this name, the student looked fixedly at Vautrin. Goriot raised his head abruptly and cast upon the two speakers an expressive, anxious glance that amazed the boarders.

"Then Christophe did not reach her in time and she must have gone there," Goriot cried, sorrowfully.

"I guessed rightly," Vautrin whispered in Mme. Vauquer's ear.

Goriot ate mechanically without knowing what he was eating. He had never seemed more dull or absorbed than at this moment.

"Who the devil told you her name, M. Vautrin?" Eugène asked.

"Ah, there it is," Vautrin answered. "Père Goriot knew her name, and why shouldn't I know it?"

"Monsieur Goriot?" the student exclaimed.

"What do you say?" the poor old man asked. "Was she looking lovely last night?"

"Who?"

"Mme. de Restaud."

"Do you see the old scamp?" Mme. Vauquer said to Vautrin. "How his eyes sparkle!"

"She must be his mistress, then," Mlle. Michonneau said to the student in a low voice.

"Oh, yes she was madly beautiful," resumed Eugène, who was eagerly observed by père Goriot. "If Mme. de Beauséant had not been there, my divine Countess would have been queen of the ball; the young men had eyes only for her. My name was the twelfth on her list; she danced every quadrille. The other women were furious. If anybody in the world was happy yesterday, it was she. It is a true saying that there is nothing more beautiful than a frigate under sail, a horse at a gallop, and a woman in the dance."

"Today, at the top of the ladder, at the house of a duchess," Vautrin said, "tomorrow at the bottom, in a discount-broker's office: so it goes with the ladies of Paris. If their husbands cannot satisfy their unbridled luxury, they sell themselves. If they could not sell themselves, they would tear their own mothers to pieces—if they could gain anything by so doing. They are up to a hundred thousand tricks; that is the truth of it."

Père Goriot's face, which had shone like the sun in a clear sky as he listened to Eugène, darkened after this cruel utterance by Vautrin.

"Well," Mme. Vauquer said, "where is your adventure? Did you speak to her? Did you ask her if she wanted to study law?"

"She did not see me," Eugène said. "But is it not

singular to meet one of the prettiest women of Paris in the rue des Grès at nine o'clock when you know that she did not go home from the ball till two o'clock in the morning? You could not have such an experience out of Paris."

"There are others stranger than yours," Vautrin cried.

Mlle. Taillefer had barely listened to the conversation, so preoccupied was she by the attempt she was to make. Mme. Couture beckoned to her to leave the table and go and dress herself. When the two ladies left the room, père Goriot followed their example.

"Did you see him?" Mme. Vauquer said to Vautrin and her other boarders. "It is clear that he has ruined himself for those women."

"You can never make me believe," the student cried, "that the lovely Comtesse de Restaud belongs to Goriot."

"But," Vautrin said, interrupting him, "we don't care whether you believe it or not. You are too young as yet to understand Paris; you will learn later that there are *men of passions* . . ."

At this, Mlle. Michonneau looked intelligently at Vautrin; it was like a war-horse starting at the sound of a trumpet.

"Ah," Vautrin said, stopping a moment to dart an obscure glance at her, "we have had our own little passions, haven't we?"

The old maid lowered her eyes, as a nun might before a statue.

"Such people," he went on, "are infatuated with a single idea of which they can never rid themselves. They will only quench their thirst at one fountain, though the water there is often stagnant. To drink of it, they would sell their wives or their children; they would sell their own souls to the devil. For some, this fountain is the gambling table or the stock exchange, a collection of pictures or insects, or it may be music; for others, it is the woman who happens to catch their fancy. You might offer such a man all the women in the world, and he would scoff at them; he only cares for the one who satisfies his passion. The woman may not care for him; she may maltreat him and make him pay dearly for any scrap of pleasure she affords him; but the fool will not give her up and will pawn his last shirt so that he may bring her his last penny. Père Goriot is such a man. The Countess makes him her tool because he keeps his own counsel; that is the way of the world. The poor old fellow thinks of nothing but her. Except for his passion, you see he is a stupid animal; but talk to him of her, and his eyes sparkle like diamonds.

"It is easy to guess this riddle. He carried some silver to be melted down this morning; I saw him going into Papa Gobseck's in the rue des Grès. Now listen to what I am going to say. On his return, he despatched that idiot Christophe to the Comtesse de Restaud, and the man showed us the address of the envelope that contained a receipted bill. It is certain there must have been urgent need, since the Countess also went to the old usurer; and père Goriot has gallantly advanced her the money. You can see it all clearly without putting two ideas together, and this may prove to you, my young fellow, that while your Countess was dancing, laughing, and flirting, playing with her dress, and tossing her head with its crown of peach blossoms, her shoe pinched all the time, as they say, and she was thinking of her own or her lover's protested bills of exchange."

"You make me wild to know the truth," Eugène cried. "I shall go to Mme. de Restaud's tomorrow."

"Yes," Poiret said, "you must go to Mme. de Restaud's tomorrow."

"Perhaps you may meet père Goriot there, come for the reward of his courtesy," Vautrin suggested.

"Paris must be a quagmire indeed," Eugène said, with an air of disgust.

"An odd sort of quagmire," Vautrin replied. "Those who drive through the mud in carriages are called honest, but those who go on foot with bespattered boots are rascals. If you have the bad luck to appropriate the slightest article belonging to somebody else, you are exhibited on the square of the Palais de Justice as a curiosity; but if you steal a million, you are labeled as a rarity in the salon. Yet you pay thirty million to the law and the police for upholding this system of morality. It is a pretty kind of thing!"

"What!" exclaimed Mme. Vauquer. "Has père Goriot had his silver breakfast set melted down?"

"Weren't there two turtledoves on the cover?" Eugène asked.

"Yes, it was that one."

"He prized it very much; he cried as he was crushing the dish and porringer. I saw him by accident," Eugène said,

"It was dear to him as life itself," the widow answered.

"See how infatuated he is," Vautrin cried. "That woman knows how to bewitch him."

The student went up to his room, and Vautrin left the house. A few moments afterward, Mme. Couture and Victorine got into a cab that Sylvie had called for them. Poiret offered his arm to Mlle. Michonneau, and they went out together for a walk in the Jardin des Plantes during the two pleasantest hours of the day.

"It is almost as if they were married," big Sylvie said. "They went out together today for the first time. They are both so hard that if they hit against each other, they will strike a spark like two flints."

"Mlle. Michonneau must take care of her shawl," Mme. Vauquer said, laughing, "for it will catch like tinder."

3

WHEN Goriot came in at four o'clock in the afternoon, he could see by the light of two smoky lamps that Victorine's eyes were red and Mme. Vauquer was listening to the account of the two ladies' fruitless visit to M. Taillefer that morning. Taillefer was tired of receiving calls from his daughter and her aunt and had consented to see them in order to clear things up with them.

"Dear lady," Mme. Couture said to Mme. Vauquer, "he never asked Victorine to sit down, so she was obliged to stand during the whole interview. He said to me, quite coldly and dispassionately, that we might spare ourselves the trouble of coming to see him; that the young lady, whom he would not call his daughter, only did herself harm by bothering him so often—only once a year, the monster!—that Victorine had no claims, as her mother had no money when she married him. In short, he spoke so bitterly that the poor little thing burst into tears. She threw herself at her father's feet and told him boldly that she persisted for her mother's sake alone, that she herself would submit to his will without a murmur, but she implored him to read the will of his poor dead wife. She took out the letter and gave it to him, speaking with great sweetness and true feeling; I cannot tell how she had learned such language. God prompted her, for the poor child was so inspired that I cried like a fool as I listened. Can you imagine what the wretched man was doing? He was cutting his nails. He took the letter stained with poor Mme. Taillefer's tears and threw it on the mantelpiece, saying, 'That will do.' He wanted to raise his daughter from her knees, but she tried to kiss his hands, and he pulled them away from her. Wasn't that a crime? His great ninny of a son came in without bowing to his sister."

"What monsters!" père Goriot said.

"Then," Mme. Couture went on, without noticing the old man's exclamation, "the father and son went away, bidding me good-bye and begging me to excuse them, as they said their business was pressing. That was our call. At least he saw his daughter. I don't know how he can refuse to acknowledge her—they are as much alike as two peas."

The boarders who lived in the house and those who came from outside dropped in one after another, said hello, and began to make some of those trifling remarks that constitute the kind of fun current with some classes of Parisians. Nonsense is its principal element, and its merit rests entirely upon some peculiarity of gesture or pronunciation. It consists of slang that is continually changing, and the jest that gives it point never lasts a month. A political event, a suit at the Court of Assizes, a street song, or the pranks of a comic actor may serve to keep alive a play of wit that depends mainly on seizing and returning words and ideas after the fashion of a game of battledore and shuttlecock. The recent invention of the diorama, which carried optical illusion to a far higher degree than had been done by the panorama, had introduced into some artists' studios the burlesque habit of adding the suffix *rama* to words, and this trick had been already brought into the Vauquer establishment by a young painter who took his meals there.

"Well, *Monsieurre* Poiret," the museum employee said, "how goes your little *healthorama?*"

Then without waiting for an answer he turned to say to Mme. Couture and Victorine:

"Ladies, I see you are in trouble."

"Are we going to have dinner?" cried Horace Bianchon, a medical student, who was a friend of Rastignac. "My poor stomach has sunk *usque ad talones*."

66

"The *coltorama* is terrible!" Vautrin said. "Get out of the way, père Goriot! What the devil do you mean by letting your foot fill up all the opening of the stove?"

"Illustrious Monsieur Vautrin," Bianchon said, "why do you say *coltorama*? That is a mistake; it is *coldorama*."

"No," the museum man said, "it is *coltorama*, by the rule: I have colt feet."

"Ah, ah!"

"Here comes His Excellency, the Marquis de Rastignac, Doctor of Lawless Law," exclaimed Bianchon, seizing Eugène by the neck and holding him so tightly as nearly to suffocate him. "Aren't the others coming?"

Mlle. Michonneau crept in noiselessly, bowed silently to the guests, and sat down beside the three women.

"That old bat always makes me shiver," Bianchon said to Vautrin in a low voice, speaking of Mlle. Michonneau. "I am studying Gall's phrenology system, and I think she has the bumps of a Judas."

'Pray, monsieur, have you seen him?" Vautrin asked.

"Who has not met him?" Bianchon answered. "On my word, that palefaced old maid makes me think of one of those long worms that gnaw through a beam."

"You are right, young man," Vautrin said, combing his whiskers.

> "A rose, she lived the life of a rose
> For one brief day."

"Ah, here comes some famous *souporama*," Poiret said, as he caught sight of Christophe respectfully bringing in the soup.

"Excuse me, monsieur," Mme. Vauquer said. "It is cabbage soup."

All the young men burst out laughing.

"You have put your foot in it, Poiret!"

"Poirrrrrette has put his foot in it!"

"Score two points for Mamma Vauquer," Vautrin said.

"Did anybody notice the fog we had this morning?" the museum employee asked.

"Yes," Bianchon said, "it was a crazy fog such as never was seen before—a lugubrious, melancholy, green, asthmatic fog, a Goriot fog."

"A *Goriorama* fog," added the painter, "because you could see nothing in it."

"Hey! Milord Gâôriotte, we are talking of you!"

Père Goriot was seated at the lower end of the table, near the door through which the food was served, and as he raised his head, he was sniffing the bit of bread he had under his napkin. It was an old trick of his trade that sometimes recurred.

"Well," Mme.. Vauquer cried to him sharply, in a voice that rose above the clash of plates and knives and forks and the buzz of conversation, "don't you think the bread is good?"

"On the contrary, madame," he replied. "It is made with the finest quality flour from Etampes."

"How can you tell?" Eugène asked.

"By its whiteness and by the taste."

"By the taste of the nose then, as you are smelling it," Mme. Vauquer said. "You are becoming so economical that you will wind up finding some means of feeding yourself by inhaling the air of the kitchen."

"Take out a patent for it," cried the museum employee. "You will make your fortune."

"Let him alone; he sniffs his bread to make us believe that he was a flour merchant," the painter said.

"Is your nose a cornucopia?" the museum employee continued.

"Corn-what?" Bianchon asked.

"Corn-el."

"Corn-et."

"Corn-elian."

"Corn-ice."

"Corn-icle."

"Corn-ea."

"Corn-ule."

"Corn-orama."

These eight replies were fired from every part of the room with the rapidity of a discharge of musketry and excited the more laughter because poor père Goriot looked about at the boarders in a dazed way, like a man who is trying to understand a foreign language.

"Corn . . . ?" he asked of Vautrin, who sat next to him.

"Corn on the foot, old man!" Vautrin said, clapping père Goriot's hat on his head with so much violence that it sank over his eyes.

The poor old man was bewildered by this unexpected attack and sat motionless for a moment. Christophe thought he had finished his soup and carried away his plate, so that when Goriot raised his hat and took his spoon, it struck upon the table. Everybody burst out laughing.

"Monsieur," the old man said, "that was a poor joke. If you ever attempt such another—"

"Very well, what would happen, Papa?" Vautrin said, interrupting him.

"You would pay dearly for it later."

"In Hell, I suppose you mean," the painter said, "in the little black cubbyhole where they put the naughty children."

"You're not eating, mademoiselle," Vautrin said to Victorine. "Did you find your papa recalcitrant?"

"He is a terror!" Mme. Couture ejaculated.

"We must make him hear reason," Vautrin said.

"But," Rastignac, who sat near Bianchon, said "Mademoiselle might bring an action on the ground of food, for you see she does not eat. Eh, eh, notice how père Goriot is staring at Mlle. Victorine."

The old man had forgotten to eat and was gazing at the poor young girl, in whose face real sorrow was plainly marked—such sorrow as a daughter feels when the father whom she loves disowns her.

"My dear fellow," Eugène said in a whisper to Bianchon, "we have all made a mistake about père Goriot. He is not idiotic, nor is his nervous system broken down. Try Gall's system on him and tell me what you think of him. Last night I saw him crushing a silver-plated dish as if it were wax, and at this moment, you can see from his expression that his thoughts are far from being common ones. His life seems to me so mysterious that I think it

would be worth studying. Yes, Bianchon, you may laugh
if you choose, but I am in earnest."

"I allow that the man is a fit subject for scientific investigation," Bianchon said, "and if he would let me, I
would like to dissect him."

"No, but feel the bumps on his head."

"If I did that, his stupidity might be contagious."

THE next afternoon Rastignac dressed himself in his
best and set out, toward three o'clock, to call on
Mme. de Restaud. On his way there, he indulged in
those wild and extravagant hopes that contribute so
many emotions to the lives of the young. They calculate
neither the obstacles nor dangers in their path but expect success on every side; their lives are touched with
romance by the mere play of the imagination, and they
are made miserably unhappy by the defeat of projects
that have never existed outside of their own unbridled
desires. If they were not ignorant and fainthearted, the
social world would be impossible. Eugène took great precaution not to splash his boots as he walked, but he was
thinking at the same time of what he should say to Mme.
de Restaud. He laid in a stock of ready wit for the occa-

sion, invented repartees for an imaginary conversation, prepared pretty speeches, and phrases à la Talleyrand, taking for granted that circumstances would prove favorable to his making the declaration on which he founded his future. He stepped into the mud and was obliged to have his boots blacked and his trousers brushed at the Palais Royal.

If I were only rich, he thought as he changed the five-franc piece he had brought with him to use *in case of need*, I would have taken a carriage and I could have thought as much as I pleased.

He finally reached the rue du Helder and asked for the Comtesse de Restaud. It was with the suppressed rage of a man who is sure of eventual success that he underwent the contemptuous scrutiny of the servants who had seen him crossing the courtyard on foot and had not heard a carriage drive up to the door. This scrutiny was the more disagreeable to him because on entering the courtyard, he was made aware of his own inferiority by the sight of a fine prancing horse, richly harnessed, and a smart equipage that proclaimed both the extravagant habits of its owner and his familiarity with all the pleasures of Paris. This, alone, put Eugène in a bad humor. The compartments that he had opened in his brain and expected to find full of ideas shut up of their own accord; he felt himself growing stupid. While waiting for the answer of the Countess, to whom a lackey had gone to announce the name of her visitor, Eugène stood carelessly in front of a window in the antechamber, leaning against the sash, and looked mechanically into the courtyard. The time seemed long to him, and he would have gone away had he not been endowed with the tenacity of a southerner, which accomplishes great things if it works along a straight line.

"Monsieur," the lackey said, "Madame is in her boudoir and is very much occupied; she did not answer me, but if you will walk into the salon, there is another gentleman waiting there."

Marveling at the appalling power of menials, who can accuse or sentence their masters with a single word, Rastignac deliberately opened the door through which the lackey had disappeared, apparently attempting to show the insolent servingmen that he knew his way about the house; but he burst heedlessly into a room that led to a dark passageway and back staircase and contained presses, lamps, and an apparatus for heating bathtowels. The stifled laughter he heard in the antechamber put the finishing touch to his confusion.

"The drawing room is this way, monsieur," the lackey said with a feigned respect that was covert ridicule.

Eugène retraced his steps with such precipitation that he stumbled against a bathtub, but he fortunately saved his hat from tumbling into the water. Just at this moment, a door opened at the end of the long corridor that was lighted by a dim lamp, and Rastignac could hear the voices of Mme. de Restaud and père Goriot and the sound of a kiss. He followed the lackey, entered the dining room, crossed it, and found himself in an antechamber. There he remained standing before a window that he observed looked into the courtyard, for he wished to make sure that this was the real père Goriot. His heart beat strangely, and he remembered Vautrin's alarming suggestions. The lackey was waiting for him at the door of the salon, when there unexpectedly appeared on the threshold a young man of fashion, who called out impatiently:

"I am going, Maurice. You may tell the Countess that I have waited more than half an hour for her."

This gentleman, who no doubt had the right to be rude, trilled some Italian air and walked toward the window where Eugène had taken up his position, evidently as much for the sake of seeing the student's face as of looking into the courtyard.

"You had better wait a moment longer, monsieur; Madame has finished her business," Maurice said, returning to the antechamber.

Just at this moment père Goriot issued through a little door that opened from the back staircase into the courtyard, near the carriage entrance. The good man had his umbrella in hand and was preparing to unfurl it without noticing that the great door was thrown open to give passage to a young man wearing a decoration, who was driving a tilbury. Père Goriot had just time to step out of the way to avoid being run over, for the umbrella had frightened the horse, which shied to one side and then rushed on toward the steps. The young man turned his head angrily, saw père Goriot, and before the old man left, made him a bow that represented either the strained politeness a man shows a usurer whose help he requires, or the respect he is forced to pay to an acquaintance of ill repute whom he will one day blush to acknowledge.

Père Goriot replied by a good-natured, friendly little nod. These events passed with the rapidity of lightning, and then Eugène, who had been too much engrossed to observe that he was not alone, heard the voice of the Countess.

"Ah, Maxime, are you going?" she said in a tone of mingled reproach and vexation.

The Countess had not noticed the entrance of the tilbury. Rastignac turned abruptly and saw the Countess coquettishly dressed in a loose gown of white cashmere trimmed with pink bows; her hair was carelessly arranged, as is the fashion in Paris for the morning. She was doubtless fresh from her bath and fragrant with perfume; her eyes were dewy, and her beauty softer and more voluptuous. A young man is quick to observe everything; his nature expands in the presence of a radiant woman as a plant breathes in its nourishment from the air; so Eugène had no need to touch the hand of the Countess in order to feel its blooming freshness. He saw through the cashmere the rosy tints of her neck, and his glances rested on her beauty, which her half-open gown at times exposed. The resources of the corset were not needed by the Countess to outline her flexible figure, which was clearly marked by a girdle. Her neck wooed love and her feet were enchanting in her slippers. When Maxime took her hand to kiss it, Eugène perceived Maxime, and the Countess noticed Eugène.

"Oh! It is you, Monsieur de Rastignac! I am delighted to see you," she said, but her manner was not to be mistaken by a person of any acuteness.

Maxime looked alternately from Eugène to the Countess, and his glance was sufficiently significant to drive away the intruder.

"Come, my dear, please send off this little fellow."

This phrase is a clear and intelligible translation of the arrogant expression of the young man, whom the Countess Anastasie had called Maxime and whose face she consulted with the submissive attention that betrays a woman's secrets in spite of herself. Rastignac was overcome with sudden hatred for this young man. In the first place, Maxime's blond hair was handsomely curled and made him conscious of how poorly done his own was; then, Maxime's boots were immaculate, whereas his own, notwithstanding the care he had taken of them in walking, were slightly spattered with mud. Then, Maxime wore a frock coat that fitted him closely and made his figure as graceful as a woman's, but Eugène had on a black coat though it was after half past two in the afternoon. The clever young southerner was keenly alive to the superiority that dress gave the tall, slender dandy with the clear eyes and pale complexion, who looked as if he were quite capable of ruining an orphan.

Without waiting for Eugène to answer, Mme. de Restaud flew into the next salon, the skirts of her gown floating behind her and fluttering up and down like the wings of a butterfly. Maxime followed her, and Eugène, in a fury, followed them both, so they all three found themselves standing together before the fireplace in the middle of the large salon. The student knew that he was annoying Maxime and was willing to annoy him, even at the risk of displeasing Mme. de Restaud. He suddenly recollected having seen the young man at Mme. de Beauséant's ball and guessed his relations with Mme. de Restaud; then, with one of those audacious impulses that inspire the young to do foolish things or achieve great ones, he said to himself, This is my rival, and I must triumph over him.

The heedless boy did not know that Comte Maxime de Trailles allowed himself to be insulted, took the first shot, and killed his man. Eugène was an adroit sportsman, but he had not hit twenty out of twenty-two puppets in a shooting gallery. The young Count threw himself into an armchair, seized the tongs, and poked the fire so violently and with such evident bad humor that Anastasie's lovely face clouded. She turned toward Eugène with one of those cold, questioning glances that ask a guest so plainly why he does not go, that if he has any knowledge of the world, he prepares forthwith to take his leave.

Eugène smiled pleasantly, and began:

"Madame, I was anxious to see you, because—"

He stopped short. A door opened and the gentleman whom he had seen driving the tilbury appeared, without his hat. He did not bow to the Countess and, looking annoyed at seeing Eugène, offered his hand to Maxime, saying good day, with a friendliness that was very surprising to Rastignac. Young men fresh from the provinces do not know the sweetness of life when shared by three.

"This is M. de Restaud," the Countess said, introducing her husband to Eugène.

Eugène bowed low.

"This is M. de Rastignac," she continued, presenting Eugène to the Comte de Restaud. "He is related to the Vicomtesse de Beausèant through the Marcillac family; I had the pleasure of meeting him at her last ball."

"Related to the Vicomtesse de Beausèant through the Marcillac family!" These words, which the Countess pronounced with a slight emphasis, and the pride she felt as mistress of her house in proving that she received none but people of distinction were magical in their effect; the Count dropped his cold, ceremonious manner and shook hands with the student.

"I am delighted, monsieur," he said, "to be able to make your acquaintance."

Even Comte Maxime de Trailles looked anxiously at Eugène and forgot to be impertinent. This tap of a magic wand, owing to the intervention of a powerful name, reopened the compartments in the student's brain, and he remembered the clever things he had meant to say. A sudden flash illuminated the atmosphere of fashionable Parisian society, still so obscure to him, and the Vauquer establishment and père Goriot were far from his thoughts.

"I thought all the Marcillacs were dead," the Comte de Restaud said to Eugène.

"Yes," he answered. "My great-uncle, the Chevalier de Rastignac, married an heiress of the house of Marcillac. He had only one daughter, who married Maréchal de Clarimbault, the maternal grandfather of Mme. de Beauséant. We belong to the younger branch and are very poor, as my great-uncle, the Vice-Admiral, lost everything in the service of the King. The Revolutionary Government refused to admit our claims when it settled the affairs of the India Company."

"Wasn't your great-uncle in command of the *Avenger* before 1789?"

"Certainly."

"Then he must have known my grandfather, who was in command of the *Warwick*."

Maxime shrugged his shoulders slightly and gave Mme. de Restaud a look that said, If he begins to discuss the navy with our friend, there will be no end to it.

Anastasie understood M. de Trailles's look, and with a woman's admirable sense of power, she said with a smile, "Come, Maxime, I have something to ask you about. Gentlemen, we leave you to sail the *Warwick* and *Avenger*, in company."

She rose and with a nod that was treacherously gay invited Maxime to follow her to her boudoir. This *morganatic* couple—to use a convenient German expression that has no equivalent in French—had scarcely reached the door, when the Count broke off his conversation with Eugène.

"Anastasie," he cried with some irritation, "stay, my dear. You know that—"

"I am coming back again directly," she said, interrupting him. "I only need a moment for what I have to say to Maxime."

She returned almost immediately, for like every woman who is forced to study her husband's character in order that she may behave herself as she pleases, she knew exactly how far she could go without losing his confidence that was so precious to her and never contradicted him in the little things of life. She had gathered from the inflection of the Count's voice that it would not be safe for her to stay long in the boudoir. Her disappointment was caused by Eugène, and her angry look and gesture directed Maxime's attention to him. Comte de Trailes immediately addressed them all three, saying epigrammatically:

"I see you are busy, and I do not wish to be in the way. Good-bye," and he ran off.

"Don't go, Maxime!" the Count called.

"Stay and dine," the Countess said, leaving Eugène alone with the Count for the second time and following Maxime into the antechamber, where they stayed together long enough to allow M. de Restaud time for dismissing Eugène.

Rastignac heard them as they laughed, talked, and kept silence alternately; but the mischievous student kept up the fun with M. de Restaud, flattered him, and started him on various subjects in order to have an opportunity of seeing the Countess again and finding out her relations with père Goriot. This woman, who was evidently in love with Maxime, who had her husband in her power, and who was secretly connected with the old vermicelli maker, was a complete mystery to him. He determined to solve it, for he hoped by so doing to become the master of a woman who seemed to him so eminently of the Parisian type.

"Anastasie!" the Count called again to his wife.

"Poor Maxime," she said to the young man, "we must resign ourselves. Until this evening . . . "

"I hope, *Nasie*," he whispered in her ear, "that you will send off that youth, whose eyes glowed like coals whenever the folds of your gown opened. He will make you a proposition and will compromise you, so that you will force me to kill him."

"Are you crazy, Maxime?" she asked. "Aren't these young students, on the contrary, excellent lightning rods? I shall certainly make Restaud take a dislike to him."

Maxime laughed and left the room; the Countess followed him and stood at the window, watching him as he got into his carriage and made his horse dance under the whip. She did not come back until the great door was closed.

"Know then, my dear," her Count said to her on her return, "that the place where this gentleman's family lives is not far from Verteuil, on the Charente. His great-uncle and my grandfather knew each other."

"I am delighted to find we have so much in common," the Countess said absently.

"More than you think," Eugène said in a low voice.

"What do you mean?" she asked quickly.

"I have just seen leaving this house," continued the student, "a gentleman whose room is opposite mine in the boardinghouse where I live. I mean père Goriot."

At this name embellished by the word *père*, the Count, who was stirring the fire, threw the tongs in the fire as if they burned his fingers and sprang to his feet.

"You might have said M. Goriot, monsieur!" he cried.

The Countess turned pale at first on seeing her husband's displeasure; then she blushed and was evidently embarrassed. Doing her best to appear unconstrained, she answered in a voice she tried to make sound natural:

"You could not mention anybody who is dearer to us—"

She stopped and, looking at her piano, added, as if at the dictate of some caprice:

"Are you fond of music, monsieur?"

"Extremely so," Eugène answered, reddening with the confused idea that he had been guilty of some stupid blunder.

"Can you sing?" she asked and, sitting down at the piano, ran her fingers quickly up and down the keys, from the lower C to high F. Rrrrah!

"No, madame."

The Comte de Restaud strode from one end of the room to the other.

"That is a pity, for you might have succeeded very well with it. *Ca-a-ro, ca-a-a-ro, ca-a-a-a-ro, non du-bi-ta-re,*" the Countess sang.

In giving père Goriot's name, Eugène had used the magic wand again, but its effect had been just the contrary to that he had produced when he said that he was a relation of Mme. de Beauséant. He was in the situation of a man admitted by special favor to see a collection of curiosities, who, on inadvertently hitting against a cupboard of statuettes, has knocked off a few heads that are insecurely glued. He wished that the earth would swallow him. Mme. de Restaud's face had grown hard and indifferent, and her cold eyes avoided meeting those of the unlucky student.

"Madame," he began, "you have something to talk over with M. de Restaud. Pray accept my compliments, and allow me to—"

"Whenever you come to see us," the Countess said hastily, detaining him with a gesture, "you are sure to give very great pleasure to M. de Restaud and myself."

Eugène bowed low to both the lady and gentleman and left the room, followed by M. de Restaud, who accompanied him to the antechamber in spite of his entreaties to the contrary.

"Whenever that gentleman comes to call," the Count said to Maurice, "neither the Countess nor I am at home."

5

WHEN Eugène set foot upon the steps, he saw that it was raining. I have just done one stupid thing, he thought, though I cannot as yet understand the cause or the extent of it. Now, I shall ruin my coat and hat in the bargain. I ought to stay in a corner and plug away at my books with no thought but that of becoming a hard-working lawyer. How can I go into society when, in order to keep up a decent appearance, I need carriages and patent leather boots and a lot of indispensable traps, such as gold chains, white deerskin gloves at six francs a pair for the daytime, and cream-colored kid ones for the evening. I've finished with you, Goriot, my old fellow.

A hack driver, who had just been employed for a wedding party and was only too glad to make a little money on his own account by smuggling a few trips from his master, caught sight of Eugène as he stood at the street door without any umbrella, in his black coat, white waistcoat, yellow gloves, and patent leather boots. Eugène was possessed by a blind rage that impelled him to plunge still deeper into the abyss into which he had fallen, as if there were any hope of finding a better way out of it. He nodded to the coachman and stepped into the carriage, where a few sprigs of orange blossom and scraps of tinsel bore witness to the journey of a bride and groom.

"Where are you going, monsieur?" the coachman asked, who had already divested himself of his white gloves.

Come, Eugène thought, since I am in for all this, it had better serve some purpose. "Drive to M. de Beauséant's house," he added aloud.

"Which?" the coachman asked.

Eugène was confounded by this unexpected inquiry, for, green youth that he was, he did not know there were two Beauséant houses nor how rich he was in relations who cared nothing about him.

"The Vicomte de Beauséant's, rue—"

"De Grenelle," the coachman said, with a toss of his head, interrupting him. "You know there is also the house of the Comte and Marquis de Beauséant in rue St-Dominique," he added, raising the steps.

"I know," Eugène answered dryly. Everybody is laughing at me today, he thought, throwing his hat on the seat in front of him. This little excursion of mine is going to cost me a king's ransom, but at least I shall make my call upon my so-called cousin in sufficiently aristocratic style. Père Goriot has already cost me ten francs, the old rascal, but I will tell the whole story to Mme. de Beauséant, and perhaps I shall make her laugh. She will no doubt know of the criminal and mysterious relations between that beautiful woman and that old rat without a tail. It is wiser for me to please my cousin than to try my strength against an immoral woman who, I think, would cost me too dear. If the name of the lovely Viscountess has so much weight, how powerful must she herself be? I must look higher, for when a man means to scale Heaven, he must aim at God Himself!

These words give a brief formula of the thousand and one thoughts floating in his mind. He became calmer and more assured as he saw how hard it was raining, and he said to himself that, since he was obliged to spend two of the precious five-franc pieces that remained to him, they could not be better employed than in saving his coat, hat, and boots. He was positively elated when he heard the coachman call, "Open the door there, please!" A porter in red and gold livery made the street door grate on its hinges, and it was with a pleasant feeling of satisfaction that Rastignac saw his carriage passing through the vestibule, turning into the courtyard, and stopping beneath the awning of the steps. The coachman, who wore a blue coat bordered with red, let down the carriage step for him. As he got out, he overheard smothered laughter that came from under the peristyle. Three or four lackeys were already cracking their jokes at the expense of the vulgar bridal equipage in which he had arrived, and their merriment enlightened the student, just as he was obliged to compare his own carriage with one of the most elegant coupés in Paris, drawn by two spirited horses with roses stuck behind their ears. They were champing their bits, and a powdered coachman in a high cravat had some difficulty in reining them in. In the courtyard of Mme. de Restaud in the Chaussée-d'Antin, Eugène had seen the handsome carriage of a man of twenty-six, but here in the faubourg St-Germain was the luxurious equipage of a great noble, which thirty thousand francs could not have paid for.

Who can be calling here? Eugène thought, who was slowly taking in the fact that he would find but few women disengaged in Paris and that the conquest of one of these queens would cost him more than his blood. "Damn it," he said, "I fear that my cousin has her Maxime too!"

He was quite crestfallen as he went up the steps. The glass door opened before him, and he found the lackeys solemn as judges. The ball at which he had been present had been given in the large reception rooms on the ground floor. Because he had had no time between the invitation and the ball to call upon his cousin, he had not as yet penetrated the apartments of Mme. de Beauséant. He was now to see for the first time the wonders of personal elegance that reflect the mind and habits of a lady of rank, and this investigation was the more interesting to him as the drawing room of Mme. de Restaud furnished him with a standard of comparison. The Viscountess was visible at half past four, but if it had been five minutes earlier, she would not have received her cousin. Eugène, who knew nothing of Parisian etiquette, was conducted up a broad white staircase with gilded banisters, carpeted in red and adorned with flowers, to Mme. de Beauséant's apartment. He had not as yet heard his cousin's biography, one of those changing stories that are whispered from ear to ear every evening in all the drawing rooms of Paris.

For three years the Viscountess had maintained a connection with one of the most distinguished of the Portuguese nobles, the Marquis d'Ajuda-Pinto. It was a bond so delightful to both that they were impatient of the intrusion of a third person, and the Vicomte de Beauséant had made himself a public example by respecting, willingly or unwillingly, their *morganatic* union. During the early days of this intimacy, those people who came to see the Viscountess at two o'clock were sure to find also the Marquis d'Ajuda-Pinto. Mme. de Beauséant was incapable of the indecorum of closing her doors, but she received her guests so coldly and gazed so persistently at the ceiling that they understood perfectly how much they were in the way. When it became known in Paris that it annoyed Mme. de Beauséant to have her friends call between the hours of two and four, she was left in complete solitude. She went to the opera or the theater in the company of M. de Beauséant and M. d'Ajuda-Pinto; but as M. de Beauséant was a man of tact, he always left them as soon as they were seated.

Now M. d'Ajuda was going to marry. His bride was a demoiselle de Rochefide. In all the fashionable world, only one person had not heard of his marriage, and that person was Mme. de Beauséant. A few of her friends had hinted to her of it, but she had laughed at them, for she believed that they envied her happiness and were trying to trouble it; nevertheless, the banns were about to be published. The handsome Portuguese had come to inform the Viscountess of his marriage, but he had not dared as yet to say a single word. Why? Certainly nothing is more difficult than to inform a woman of such an *ultimatum,* and a man may be more at ease in a duel with an adversary who holds a sword to his bosom than in the presence of a woman who bewails herself for an hour or two and then faints and calls for salts.

So it was that at this very moment M. d'Ajuda-Pinto was on pins and needles and longed to take his leave, telling himself that Mme. de Beauséant would be sure to hear his news; he would write her, for it would be easier to acquaint her with his act of refined treachery by letter than by word of mouth. When the lackey announced M. Eugène de Rastignac, the Marquis d'Ajuda-Pinto felt a thrill of joy. But, let me tell you that a woman who is in love is more ingenious in inventing doubts than she is in varying her charms, and when her lover is on the point of abandoning her, she is quicker to guess the meaning of his slightest gesture than was Virgil's steed to sniff the breeze that brought him tidings of his distant joys. For this reason, Mme. de Beauséant detected that slight, involuntary thrill that was so frankly alarming to her.

Eugène did not know as yet that it was never safe to call on anybody in Paris without first learning from the friends of the house the history of the husband, wife, and children, in order to avoid making those blunders of which they say so picturesquely in Poland, "Yoke five oxen to your cart!" meaning that you will require such aid to pull you out of the slough into which you have fallen. If there is no name in France for such mistakes, they are no doubt supposed to be impossible on account of the enormous publicity of slander. After having stuck in the mire at Mme. de Restaud's, who had not allowed him time to yoke the five oxen to his cart, Eugène alone was capable of coming to practice the art of ox driving again at Mme. de Beauséant's. Still, though he had been horribly in the way of Mme. de Restaud and M. de Trailles, he came to the relief of M. d'Ajuda.

"Good-bye," the Portuguese said, hastening toward the door, as Eugène entered the charming drawing room furnished in gray and rose, where luxury seemed no more than appropriate elegance.

"But I shall see you again this evening," Mme. de Beauséant said, turning her head to look at the Marquis. "Are you not going with us to the Bouffons?"

"I cannot," he said, taking hold of the door handle.

Mme. de Beauséant rose and called him back, without paying the slightest attention to Eugène, who was still standing, dazzled by the brilliant luxury about him. He was ready to believe in the reality of the *Arabian Nights* tales and did not know where to hide upon finding himself in the presence of a lady who had not observed his entrance. The Viscountess had raised the forefinger of her right hand and motioned prettily to the Marquis to take a seat in front of her. Her gesture was so full of the violent despotism of passion that the Marquis let go of the doorknob and obeyed her. Eugène looked at him with envy.

There, he thought, is the owner of the coupé. I see that in Paris a man must have handsome horses, footmen in livery, and piles of gold to make a woman look at him.

The demon of luxury gnawed at his heartstrings, and the lust of gain took possession of him; his throat was parched with the thirst for gold. He had but a hundred and thirty francs a quarter. His father, mother, brothers, sisters, and aunt together did not spend two hundred francs a month. The rapid comparison he drew between his present situation and the goal he meant to reach helped to bewilder his mind.

"Why," the Viscountess laughingly asked of the Portuguese, "why *can't* you come to the Opéra?"

"I have some business; I am to dine with the English ambassador."

"You must give that up."

When a man is deceiving, he is irresistibly driven to

tell one lie after another. M. d'Ajuda answered, with a smile:

"Do you insist upon it?"

"Certainly I do."

"That is what I have been trying to make you say," he answered, with a subtle look that would have assured any other woman.

He took the hand of the Viscountess, raised it to his lips, kissed it, and left her.

Eugène ran his fingers through his hair and put himself in position to bow, for he thought that Mme. de Beauséant would now acknowledge his presence; but she rushed out of the room into the corridor and ran to the window to see M. d'Ajuda get into his carriage. She listened to catch the order he gave his coachman and heard him say:

"Drive to M. de Rochefide's."

These words and the manner in which M. d'Ajuda sank into his carriage were like a stroke of lightning to the poor woman, who again fell prey to mortal apprehensions. Hers was the worst calamity possible in the fashionable world.

The Viscountess passed into her bedroom and selected a pretty sheet of notepaper.

"Since you are to dine at the Rochefides'," she wrote, "and not at the English embassy, you owe me an explanation, and I shall expect to see you."

Then, after straightening a few letters distorted by the convulsive trembling of her hand, she added a C that stood for Claire de Bourgogne and rang the bell.

"Jacques," she said to her lackey, who answered immediately, "go at half past seven to the house of M. de Rochefide and ask for the Marquis d'Ajuda. If he is there, you must be sure this note reaches him, but you need not wait for an answer. If he is not there, come and bring back my note to me."

"Madame, there is someone in the drawing room."

"Ah, yes," she said, opening the door. Eugène had begun to feel very ill at ease. Now at last he saw the Viscountess, who said to him in a tone so full of emotion that it stirred the fibers of his heart:

"Please excuse me, I had to write a line; but now I am quite at your service."

She did not know what she was saying, for she was thinking thus:

"Ah! He means to marry Mlle. de Rochefide. But is it in his power? Tonight the marriage shall be broken off, or I— There shall be no more talk of it tomorrow."

"Cousin—" Eugène began.

"What?" the Viscountess said, with a stare so icily cold that it froze the student.

Eugène understood her *what*. He had learned so many things in the last three hours that he was on the alert.

"Madame . . . " he resumed, blushing.

He hesitated and then went on:

"I beg your pardon. I am so much in need of encouragement that it is a relief to me to claim a relationship with you."

Mme. de Beauséant smiled sadly; she could not forget the storm that was lowering about her.

"If you only knew the sad situation of my family," he continued, "you would take pleasure in playing the part of one of those good fairies who love to banish obstacles from the path of their godchildren."

"Well, cousin," she said, laughing, "how can I be of use to you?"

"Can I myself tell? In the meantime, it is quite good fortune enough to be connected with you by the slightest tie of blood. You have embarrassed me, and I cannot remember what I came to say to you. You are the only person whom I know in Paris. . . . I meant to ask your advice and beg you to accept me as a poor boy who would like you to take him under your wing and who would die for you."

"Could you kill a man for me?"

"I could kill two," Eugène said.

"My poor child, for you are a child," she said, forcing back her tears, "I think that you would be capable of loving truly."

"You think so?" he said, with a toss of his head.

The Viscountess was eagerly expecting an ambitious answer. It was the young southerner's first venture, but he felt that, from Mme. de Restaud's blue boudoir to the rose-colored drawing room of Mme. de Beauséant, he had completed a three years' course of that unspoken *Parisian code*, which is yet of the highest importance as social jurisprudence and, when attentively studied and carefully applied, leads to all success.

"I understand," Eugène said. "I saw Mme. de Restaud

at your ball and admired her, so this afternoon I went to call on her."

"You must have been very much in the way," Mme. de Beauséant said with a smile.

"Yes. I am a fool, and I shall have all the world against me if you refuse to help me. I believe that it is almost impossible to find in all Paris a young, beautiful, rich, and fashionable woman who is disengaged, and I need such a one to teach me about life, which you ladies can explain so well. I know that I shall find a M. de Trailles in every house, so I came to ask you for the key of the riddle and to beg you to tell me the nature of the blunder I unwarily committed. I mentioned a certain père—"

"Mme. la Duchesse de Langeais," Jacques announced, interrupting the student, who plainly showed his vehement vexation.

"If you wish to succeed," the Viscountess said in a low voice, "you must, first of all, control your feelings."

"How do you do, my dear," she said, rising to meet the Duchess, whose hand she pressed with every demonstration of affection she could have shown to a sister and who returned her greeting with effusion.

Here are two good friends, Rastignac thought. From now on, I shall have two patronesses; these two ladies must have the same interests, and the Duchess will no doubt do her share for me.

"What happy thought prompted you to give me this pleasure, dear Antoinette?" Mme. de Beauséant asked.

"I saw M. d'Ajuda-Pinto going into M. de Rochefide's, so I thought I would find you alone."

Mme. de Beauséant did not compress her lips, nor did

she blush; her expression was the same, and she seemed to brighten as the Duchess pronounced the fatal words.

"If I had known that you were engaged . . . " the Duchess added, turning toward Eugène.

"This is M. Eugène de Rastignac, a cousin of mine," the Viscountess answered. "Have you any news to give me of General Montriveau?" she continued. "Sérizy told me yesterday that he was to be seen nowhere. Was he at your house today?"

It was generally supposed that the Duchess had been deserted by M. de Montriveau, with whom she was madly in love, so this question by the Viscountess pierced her to the quick, and she flushed as she replied:

"He was at the Elysée yesterday."

"On duty?" Mme. de Beauséant asked.

"I suppose you know, Clara," the Duchess said, infusing a world of malice in her glances, "that tomorrow the banns of M. d'Ajuda-Pinto and Mlle. de Rochefide are to be announced?"

This stab was too severe, and the Viscountess turned pale as she answered with a smile:

"That is a report that some idiot has set afloat. Why should M. d'Ajuda confer one of the distinguished names of Portugal upon a member of the Rochefide family? They are only nobles of yesterday's creation."

"But they say that Berthe will have two hundred thousand francs a year."

"M. d'Ajuda is too rich to make such calculations."

"Still, my dear, Mlle. de Rochefide is so attractive!"

"Ah!"

"Then, he is to dine there today, and everything is

settled. I am surprised that you know so little about it."

"What was the blunder you spoke of?" Mme. de Beauséant said, turning to Eugène. "This young fellow is so new to society, dear Antoinette," she continued, "that he cannot understand what we are talking about. Be so indulgent to him as to put off discussing this subject till tomorrow, for tomorrow, you see, it will be official, and you may be officious with certainty."

The Duchess stared rudely at Eugène from head to foot until he felt utterly crushed and reduced to the condition of a nonentity.

"Madame, unwittingly, I plunged a dagger into Mme. de Restaud's heart. It was done involuntarily, and that was my mistake," the student said, whose quickness had stood him in good stead and who had detected the stinging epigrams that lay concealed in the affectionate phrases of the two women. "You may continue to see and perhaps fear those people who are fully aware of the harm they do you, whereas the man who wounds without knowing the depth of the wound he inflicts is considered an awkward fool who can never learn better, and so everybody despises him."

Mme. de Beauséant turned her melting glance upon the student, and her look expressed both the gratitude and dignity of a noble nature. It was like balm to his heart that had been so deeply hurt by the manner of the Duchess, who had scrutinized him as if she were a sheriff's appraiser, trying to estimate his value.

"Only imagine," Eugène continued, "that I had just succeeded in winning the Comte de Restaud's goodwill, for you must know, madame," he said, turning to the Duchess in a manner that was both arch and humble, "I am only a poor devil of a student, very poor and very solitary . . . "

"Don't say that, Monsieur de Rastignac, for women never care for what nobody else cares for."

"No matter," Eugène said, "I am only twenty-two years old, and I must learn to bear those troubles that belong to my time of life. Besides, I am making a confession, and it would be impossible to kneel in a more charming confessional than this: one that might even tempt a man to commit those sins that he is obliged to confess elsewhere."

The Duchess frowned at this profane remark, the bad taste of which she condemned by observing to the Viscountess:

"Monsieur is succeeding . . . "

Mme. de Beauséant laughed outright at her cousin and the Duchess.

"He is succeeding, my dear, and is looking for someone to instruct him in good taste."

"Madame," Eugène said to the Duchess, "is it not natural to wish to be initiated into the secrets of that which charms us?" Come, he thought to himself, I am sure that I am talking like a hairdresser.

"But I thought that Mme. de Restaud was a pupil of M. de Trailles," the Duchess said.

"I knew nothing of it," the student replied, "so I rashly threw myself in between them. I had come to a good understanding with the husband and saw that I was not disagreeable to the lady herself, when I undertook to tell them that I had an acquaintance with a man whom I had just seen leaving their house by a private staircase and who had been kissing the Countess at the end of a dark corridor."

"Who was it?" the two ladies asked.

"An old man who lives at the other end of the faubourg St-Marceau, like me, poor student that I am; an unfortunate wretch, who is laughed at by everybody and dubbed père Goriot!"

"What a child you are," the Viscountess cried. "Mme. de Restaud's maiden name was Goriot."

"She is the daughter of a flour merchant," put in the Duchess. "A little person who was presented at court the same day as the daughter of a pastry cook. Don't you remember, Clara? The King laughed and made a Latin pun about flour. People—how did it go? People—"

"*Ejusdem farinae!*" Eugène said.

"That is it," the Duchess said.

"So it is her father!" the student exclaimed with a horrified gesture.

"Certainly it is. The old fellow had two daughters whom he was crazy about, but they have both pretty nearly disowned him."

Isn't the second daughter married to a banker with a German name, a Baron de Nucingen?" the Viscountess asked of Mme. de Langeais. "Isn't her name Delphine, and isn't she a blonde who has a side box at the Opéra, who goes to the Bouffons too and laughs very loud to attract attention?"

The Duchess smiled, as she answered:

"You really surprise me, my dear. Why do you notice such people? Restaud must have been infatuated to marry that vermicelli maker's daughter. But he has not made a good bargain of it, for she is under the thumb of M. de Trailles, who will be the ruin of her."

"They have disowned their father!" Eugene repeated.

"Yes, indeed, their father, their own father, the father, a father," the Viscountess reiterated. "A good father who gave them each five or six hundred thousand francs, so that he might ensure their marrying advantageously, and only reserved ten thousand francs a year for himself, believing that his daughters would always be the same to him and that each of them would offer him a home in which he would be loved and welcomed. In two years' time, his sons-in-law have banished him as if he were the last of the outcasts."

A few tears fell from Eugène's eyes, recently bathed in the pure and sacred spring of domestic affections and still under the charm of the faith of his youth; this was only his first day spent on the battlefield of Parisian civilization. True emotion is contagious, so for a moment the three gazed at one another in silence.

"Good heavens," Mme. de Langeais exclaimed, "it seems very dreadful, yet we see the same thing happening every day. Isn't there a cause for it? Tell me, my dear, have you never thought of what a son-in-law is? A son-in-law is a man for whose sake you or I bring up a dear little creature to whom we are bound by a thousand ties, who, for seventeen years is the joy of the family, its spotless soul, as Lamartine would say, but who will one day be its bane. When this man takes possession of the little

angel, he begins by using her love for him as a hatchet
with which to cut away from her heart every sentiment
that unites her to her family. Yesterday our daughter was
everything to us, and we were everything to her; today
she is our enemy. Don't we see this tragedy enacted every
day? In one case, a daughter-in-law is insolent to her
father-in-law, who has made every sacrifice for his son;
in another, a son-in-law turns his mother-in-law out of
the house. I hear people doubt whether there is anything
dramatic in modern society; but the son-in-law furnishes
a tremendous subject for a drama, not to speak of marriage, which has become a senseless thing. I can understand perfectly what has happened to the old vermicelli
maker. I think I remember that Foriot—"

"Goriot, madame."

"Yes, Moriot was president of his district during the
Revolution; he was in on the secret of the notorious
famine of that time and laid the foundation of his fortune by selling flour for ten times the sum it cost him.
He could buy all that he wanted; my grandmother's
steward sold him some for immense sums. No doubt,
Noriot, like all the others, shared the profits with the
Committee of Public Safety. I recollect that the steward
told my grandmother that she could remain without danger at Grandvilliers because her grain was an excellent
safeguard for her.

"Well, this Loriot, who sold corn to the cutthroats,
has had but one passion. He is said to adore his daughters. He made a nest for the elder in the Restaud family
and grafted the other upon Baron de Nucingen, a rich

banker, who pretends to be a Royalist. You can see that, under the Empire, it was not considered amiss for the two sons-in-law to have this old Revolutionist in their houses; the Buonapartes were not likely to object. But on the return of the Bourbons the poor fellow became inconvenient to M. de Restaud, and still more so to the banker. The daughters, who were possibly still fond of their father, tried to keep on good terms with him and their husbands at the same time. They invited old Toriot when they expected nobody else and invented some affectionate excuse for doing so. 'Come, Papa, it will be all the pleasanter, for we shall be quite alone!' And so on.

"I believe, my dear, that people of honest feeling are endowed with eyes and perceptive faculties, and the heart of the poor old Revolutionist must have bled. He saw that his daughters were ashamed of him, and if they loved their husbands, he knew they must think he stood in the way of his sons-in-law. It was his duty to sacrifice himself, and he did sacrifice himself because he was a father. He banished himself, and when he found how happy his daughters were, he knew that he had done right. Father and daughters were accomplices in this petty crime, but you may see the same thing everywhere.

"Père Doriot would have been out of place in his daughters' drawing rooms; he would have felt awkward and embarrassed there. And what happened to him might happen to a pretty woman with the man she loves best; if he wearies of her love, he leaves her and is capable of any baseness to rid himself of her. It is the same with all the affections. The heart is a treasure, but if you empty it too quickly, you are ruined. Nobody can forgive another for showing all his feelings any more than he can forgive a man for being without a penny. Père Goriot had given his all. For twenty years he had given his heart's love, and one day he gave his whole fortune. When the orange was well squeezed, his daughters threw the peel into the gutter."

"It is a wicked world," the Viscountess said. She had not lifted her eyes and was unraveling the edge of her shawl, cut to the heart by the words that Mme. de Langeais had inserted in her story for her special benefit.

"Wicked?" the Duchess repeated. "No. It goes its own pace, that is all. I am talking in this way to show that I am not the dupe of the world. I think as you do," she said, pressing the hand of the Viscountess. "The world is a quagmire; let us try to keep on the heights."

She rose and kissed Mme. de Beauséant on the forehead, saying:

"You are looking beautiful, my dear. I never saw such a lovely color as you have."

Then she nodded carelessly to the young man and left the room.

"It is very pathetic about père Goriot!" Eugene said, recalling how he had seen him welding his silver in the middle of the night.

Mme. de Beauséant did not hear him; she was lost in thought. A few minutes passed in silence, and the poor student, half-dazed with mortification, dared not go or stay or even speak.

"It is a wicked, cruel world," the Viscountess said at last. "You no sooner meet with a misfortune than a friend comes to tell you of it and pricks your heart with the point of a dagger, while forcing you to admire the handle. Sarcasm and ridicule, already! Ah, I shall know how to defend myself."

She raised her head like the great lady she was, and her proud eyes flashed.

"Ah, You are still here!" she exclaimed as she saw Eugène.

"Still here," he echoed ruefully.

"I tell you, Monsieur de Rastignac, you must treat the world as it deserves. You wish to succeed, and I will help you. You must sound the depths of feminine corruption and gauge the extent of the miserable vanity of men. I thought I was familiar with the book of the world, but there were pages in it that I had not read. Now I know all. The colder your calculations, the more effectual they will be. Strike without mercy, and you will be feared. Think of men and women only as post-horses that you are willing to work to death at every stage provided that you reach the goal of your desires. Let me tell you that you will be of no account here until some woman cares for you, and she must be young, rich, and fashionable. If you should feel any sincere emotion, hide it as you would a treasure and never allow it to be suspected, or you would be lost. You would be the victim instead of the tormentor. If you should ever love, keep your secret well and never betray it, unless you are sure of the person to whom you are opening your heart. Learn to mistrust the world if you wish to preserve in advance an affection that has, as yet, no existence.

"Listen to me, Miguel," she went on, inadvertently

calling him by another name, "if there can be anything
more dreadful than the desertion of the father by his
two daughters who would like to see him dead, it is the
rivalry between the two sisters. Restaud is of good family; his wife has been well received and presented at
court. But her sister, the rich and beautiful Mme. Delphine de Nucingen, married to a man of capital, is pining
with grief; she is devoured by jealousy and is entirely
alienated from her sister, who is no longer a sister to her.
The two women have disowned each other, just as they
have disowned their father.

"Mme. de Nucingen would crawl on her knees through
all the mud between the rue St-Lazare and the rue de
Grenelle to gain admittance to my house. She thought
that De Marsay would enable her to gain her object, so
she made herself his slave and talks of nothing but De
Marsay. But De Marsay cares very little about her. If
you introduce her to me, you will be her Benjamin and
she will adore you. Love her afterward if you can, but
if not, make use of her. I am willing to have her come
here once or twice when I give a large party and there
is a crowd, but I will not receive her in the morning. I
shall speak to her, and that is enough.

"The Countess's door is closed to you, because you
pronounced père Goriot's name. Yes, my dear young
fellow, you may go twenty times to Mme. de Restaud's,
but you will find her out every time. She has given orders
for you not to be admitted. Very well, get père Goriot to
introduce you to Mme. Delphine de Nucingen, and the
pretty Baroness will be your banner. If you are the man

she distinguishes with her attention, all the women will go crazy for you. Her rivals, her friends, even her best friends, will do their best to take you away from her. Some women love a man because he has been already chosen by another, just as those poor shopkeepers' wives buy hats like ours and expect to acquire our manners at the same time.

"You will succeed with women, and in Paris that means everything; it is the key to power. If women think you have cleverness and talent, men will think so too, if you do not undeceive them. No desire will be too ambitious for you; and every door will be open to you. Then you will know that the world is made up of dupes and rogues, but try yourself to be neither one nor the other. I give you my name to use, like the silken thread of Ariadne, in the labyrinth you are trying to enter. Do not compromise it," she added, arching her neck and looking haughtily at the student, "but return it to me unspotted. Come, leave me now; we women have our battles to fight too."

"If you should ever need a man willing to set fire to a mine for your sake—" Eugène began, interrupting her.

"What then?" she said.

He placed his hand on his heart, smiled as he saw his cousin smile and went out.

It was five o'clock, and Eugène was hungry; he was afraid of not reaching home in time for dinner, and this fear made him appreciate the pleasure of his rapid transit through Paris. This sensation, however, was purely mechanical and allowed free scope to his thoughts. Whenever a young man of his age has been treated with contempt, he forgets himself, flies into a rage, and shakes his fist in the face of society. He is mad for revenge, but he also loses his self-confidence. Rastignac was now overwhelmed by the words, *The Countess's door is closed to you.*

I shall go there, he said to himself, and if Mme. de Beausèant is right and I am not admitted . . . I . . . Mme. de Restaud will meet me in all the houses she visits. I mean to learn fencing and pistol shooting, and I will kill her Maxime!

How are you to get the money for it? an inner voice cried to him.

Suddenly the brilliant display he had seen at the Comtesse de Restaud's shone before his eyes. Hers was the luxury that must have been irresistible to a Mlle. Goriot —gilding and showy furniture, all the senseless extravagance of an upstart, the wasteful prodigality of a kept mistress. This fascinating picture was suddenly obliterated by that of the splendor of Mme. de Beauséant's house. His imagination, transported to the high levels of Parisian society, filled his heart with evil thoughts, while it rendered his brain and conscience more elastic. He saw the world as it is; he understood that law and morality have no power over the rich, and he knew that money is the *ultima ratio mundi*.

"Vautrin is right," he said. "Wealth is virtue."

6

AFTER reaching the rue Neuve-Ste-Geneviève, he ran quickly upstairs, came down again with ten francs to pay the coachman, and then went into the loathsome dining room, where he found the eighteen boarders in the act of feeding themselves, like so many cattle at a trough. The sight of the room and its squalor were horrible to him. The transition was so abrupt and the contrast so complete as to develop his ambition beyond all measure. On the one hand, he saw fresh and charming visions of social life among the higher classes, young and living faces framed by the marvels of art and luxury, passionate heads full of poetry; on the other, sinister pictures darkened with dust and grime, countenances in which the passions had left nothing but their cordage and mechanism. The lesson that Mme. de Beauséant had given him under the stress of her indignation at being deserted, her captious offers, recurred to his memory, and the penury of his surroundings helped him to comment upon it. Rastignac resolved to open upon fortune with two parallel lines of attack, to trust both to study and to love; to be at the same time a learned doctor and a man of fashion. He was still very young and ignorant, for these are lines that can never meet.

"You are in bad spirits, Monsieur le Marquis," Vautrin said to him with one of the looks with which he seemed to probe the hidden secrets of the heart.

"I am not in a mood to care for the jokes of anybody who addresses me as 'Monsieur le Marquis,' " he answered. "To be a real marquis, a man must have a hundred thousand francs a year, and if he lives in the Vauquer establishment he is not exactly Fortune's favorite."

Vautrin looked at Rastignac with a paternal and contemptuous air, as if he were saying, "Little monkey, I could swallow you in one mouthful."

Then he answered:

"Perhaps you are in a bad temper because you did not succeed with the beautiful Comtesse de Restaud."

"She has closed her doors against me because I mentioned that her father ate at our table," Rastignac exclaimed.

All the boarders exchanged glances. Père Goriot looked down and turned aside to wipe his eyes.

"You threw some of your snuff in my eye," he said to his neighbor.

"Hereafter, whoever torments père Goriot will have to deal with me," Eugène said, looking at the old man's neighbor. "He is worth more than any of us. I am not talking of the ladies, of course," he added, turning to Mlle. Taillefer.

This announcement produced a great effect. Eugène

had spoken in a way to impose silence upon the boarders. Vautrin alone said to him with a jeer:

"If you take père Goriot on your hands and make yourself responsible for him, you will need to know how to fence well and to use a pistol."

"And so I shall," Eugène said.

"Then you are prepared for war today."

"Perhaps," Rastignac replied, "but I do not owe an account of myself to anybody, especially as I don't try to find out what other people are doing in the middle of the night."

Vautrin looked at him askance.

"If you don't want to be deceived by the puppets, my young fellow, you must go inside the booth and not stop outside, looking through a hole in the curtain. That is enough," he added, as he saw Eugène was on the point of flying into a passion. "We can have a little talk together whenever you choose."

The dinner became a somber and silent affair. Père Goriot, who was absorbed by the deep sorrow the student's words had occasioned him, did not understand that the feelings of his companions had changed in regard to him or that a young man who was able to put an end to the persecution against him had stepped forward as his champion.

"Then M. Goriot is really the father of a countess?" Mme. Vauquer said in a low voice.

"Yes, and of a baroness too," Rastignac replied.

"That is all he is capable of," Bianchon said to Rastignac. "I have examined his head. He has but one bump, and that is the bump of paternity. He will be an *eternal father*."

Eugène was in too serious a mood to be amused at Bianchon's jest. He was anxious to profit by Mme. de Beauséant's advice and was considering how and where he should raise some money. He became lost in thought as he saw, in imagination, stretching before him the vast prairies of the world, at one and the same time bare and fruitful. Everybody went off after dinner and left him alone in the room.

"Then you saw my daughter?" Goriot asked in a voice full of emotion.

Eugène started from his reverie and, taking the old man's hand, contemplated him with some feeling.

"You are a kind, good man," he said. "We will talk about your daughters another time."

He rose without waiting to hear what père Goriot had to say and sought refuge in his own room, where he wrote to his mother the following letter:

Dear Mother:

Can't you open still another vein for me? I am in the way of making my fortune in a short time. I need twelve hundred francs, and I must have them at any price. Don't mention my request to my father, for he might oppose it, and if I did not receive this money, I would be ready to blow out my brains in despair. I shall explain my motives as soon as I see you again, for I would have to write volumes to make you understand my situation. I have not been gambling, dear Mother, and I am not in debt, but if you care to preserve the life that you gave me, you must procure the sum I want. I have been received by the Vicomtesse de Beauséant, and she has taken me under her wing. I must go into society, and I haven't a penny to buy clean gloves with. I can live on bread and water, and I can fast if necessary, but I cannot do without the implements needed for working in this vineyard. I must either make my own way or remain sticking in the mud.

I know the hopes you have placed in me and am anxious to realize them. Dear Mother, if you are willing to sell some of your old jewels, I will replace them before long. I know well how poor we all are, and I can appreciate such sacrifices. You must believe that I do not ask you to make them in vain; if I did, I would be a monster. You must consider my request as the cry of imperious necessity. The fortune of the whole family is contained in the subsidy I ask for and with which I must open the campaign, for this Parisian life is a perpetual battle. If my aunt is obliged to sell her lace in order to make up the sum I require, tell her that I shall send her some that is still finer, etc.

He wrote to each of his sisters to ask for their savings, entreating them not to tell anybody of the sacrifice he was sure they would be glad to make for him, and ensuring their secrecy by playing on those chords of honor that are so highly strung and so quick to vibrate in young hearts. After finishing his letters, however, he underwent some involuntary trepidation, his heart throbbed, and he trembled. This ambitious young man knew the noble nature of his two sisters, who lived buried in the solitude of the country; he knew the pains and also the joys he was about to cause them, and what pleasure they would take in hiding in the garden to talk of their dearly loved brother. By the light of his kindling conscience, he saw them secretly counting their little treasure; he imagined them as using some innocent artifice to send him the money incognito and blamelessly practicing this, their first deception.

"A sister's heart is a priceless gem, a well of tenderness!" he cried.

He was ashamed of what he had written. How powerful and pure would be the outpouring of the souls in prayer to Heaven! How happy they would be in their self-sacrifice, and how grieved his mother would be if she could not send the whole sum! Their noble affection and self-imposed hardships would be the ladder by which he was to reach Delphine de Nucingen. A few tears, the last grains of incense he threw on the family altar, dropped from his eyes, and jumping to his feet, he walked up and down the room in despairing agitation. Père Goriot, who had caught sight of him through the half-open door, came in and asked him what was the matter.

"Ah, my kind neighbor, I am still a son and a brother, as you are still a father. Your fears about the Countess Anastasie are well founded: she is in the hands of a M. Maxime de Trailles, who will be her ruin."

Père Goriot left the room, stammering a few words, whose meaning Eugène could not catch.

The next day Rastignac went out to mail his letters. He hesitated till the last moment and then flung them into the box, saying to himself, I shall succeed. This, the motto of the gambler and of the great general alike, has led more men to ruin than to success.

A few days later Eugène went to call upon Mme. de Restaud and was not admitted. Three times he returned to her door and three times he found it closed, although he was careful to go at an hour when Comte Maxime de Trailles was not there. The Viscountess had been right in what she had said. The student gave up studying altogether and only presented himself at his lectures in order to answer the roll call; after having shown himself, he disappeared. He had laid his plans after the fashion of most students and put off working until just before the examinations; he continued to enter his name for the terms of his second and third years but expected to wait till the very last moment before trying seriously to acquire a knowledge of the law. So he had fifteen months before him in which he was free to sail on the Parisian sea, to try to fish up a fortune from its depths, or to steer his boat in pursuit of any woman he chose.

Within a week he saw Mme. de Beauséant twice, having taken pains to call on her at the moment he saw the Marquis d'Ajuda's carriage drive from her door. This distinguished lady, the most interesting figure in the faubourg St-Germain, had gained a victory of a few days and had succeeded in putting off the marriage of the Marquis d'Ajuda-Pinto to Mlle. de Rochefide. But these very days, more passionately dear to her than all the rest because she knew herself on the brink of losing her happiness, were in fact hastening the catastrophe. The Marquis d'Ajuda, together with the Rochefide family, had regarded the quarrel and subsequent reconciliation as a fortunate circumstance, for they hoped that Mme. de Beauséant would accustom herself to the idea of the marriage and in the end be willing to sacrifice her afternoons in view of an occurrence to be foreseen in the life of every man. In spite of the most sacred promises, daily renewed, M. d'Ajuda was acting a farce, and the Viscountess was glad to be deceived by him. "Instead of nobly springing out of the window, she allowed herself to be rolled downstairs," her best friend, the Duchesse de Langeais said. Nevertheless, these last glimmerings of light lasted long enough to keep the Viscountess in Paris, where she was able to be of some service to her young cousin, for whom she felt a somewhat superstitious attachment. Eugène had been sympathetic and devoted to her at a time when she would otherwise have met with neither pity nor consolation, for if a man speaks a kind word to a woman under such circumstances, it is certain that he does so from interested motives.

As he was desirous of being perfectly familiar with his ground, before attempting to scale the house of Nucingen, Rastignac took pains to find out what he could of père Goriot's former life and succeeded in obtaining trustworthy information that may be given briefly, as follows:

Before the Revolution, Jean-Joachim Goriot had been in the employ of a macaroni maker. He was capable, economical, and so enterprising as to buy the business of his master, who as it happened fell an early victim to the Revolution of 1789. Goriot had established himself in the rue de Jussienne, near the corn market, and had had the good sense to accept the presidency of his district in order to obtain for his trade the protection of the most influential men of that dangerous time. His wisdom in this matter had laid the foundation of his fortune that began in the famine, whether real or pretended, in consequence of which grain commanded such enormous prices in Paris. Crowds of people were killing one another before the doors of the bakers' shops, while a few persons bought macaroni quietly at the grocers. During this year the citizen Goriot amassed the large sums that enabled him later to carry on his business with all the advantages that capital confers upon its owner. In his case, as with all those men who have but relative ability, his mediocrity saved him. Besides, as his fortune was not known until there was no more danger in being rich, he excited nobody's envy.

His traffic in grain seemed to absorb all his intelligence. If there was any question of wheat, flour, or refuse corn, and he was asked to tell of what quality they were or where they came from, to attend to their storage, to foretell the market prices, or to prophesy the abundance or scarcity of the crops, to buy cereals cheap, or to lay in a stock of them from Sicily or the Ukraine, Goriot had no equal. To see him carry on his business, to hear him discuss the laws of exportation and importation of grain, examining their principles and pointing out their defects, you would have thought him fit to be Minister of State.

He was patient, active, energetic, steady, and quick in his transactions; his eagle eye foresaw the future; he forestalled every contingency, knew everything, and kept his secrets: he was a diplomat in his plans, and a soldier in his execution of them.

Outside of his specialty and away from his obscure, unpretending shop, where he spent his leisure hours leaning against the doorpost, he again became a dull and ignorant man of the working class, incapable of understanding an argument and insensible to all intellectual pleasures, the kind of man who goes to sleep at the theater—in short, a Parisian Doliban whose only strong point is stupidity. There are many other men like him, and almost all of them are capable of some great emotion.

Two affections had exclusively filled Goriot's heart and had absorbed its vitality as his commerce in grain had engrossed all the capacity of his mind. His wife, the only daughter of a rich farmer of Brie, was the object of his religious admiration and boundless love. She was a delicate yet energetic woman, both pretty and sensible. If there is an innate sentiment in the heart of a man, it is the pride he takes in protecting a being weaker than himself, and if you add love to this which is the gratitude a candid soul feels toward the source of its happiness, you will understand many moral anomalies. After seven years of unclouded happiness, unfortunately for him, Goriot lost his wife. She had begun to gain ascendency over him, outside of the sphere of his affections, and might perhaps have educated his inert intelligence and trained it to some knowledge of life and things.

After his wife's death, Goriot's paternal instinct became immoderately developed, and he transferred his bereaved affections to his two daughters, who at first amply fulfilled his expectations. However brilliant the offers made him by shopkeepers or farmers who were anxious to have him marry their daughters, he persisted in remaining a widower. His father-in-law, who was the only man for whom he had shown a liking, confidently maintained that though Goriot's wife was dead, he had sworn never to be unfaithful to her. The men about the corn market, who were incapable of understanding such sublime folly, laughed at it and gave him a grotesque nickname. The first man among them who dared mention it to him, as they were drinking a glass of wine over the conclusion of a bargain, received from Goriot a blow that knocked him headfirst against the curbstone of the rue Oblin. Goriot's unreasonable devotion to his daughters and the reserved and delicate-minded affection he bore them were so well known that, one day when a competitor of his wished to send him away from the market in order to control the prices himself, he told him that Delphine had just been run over by a hack. Goriot, pale with fright, left the market immediately. He was ill for several days afterward, in consequence of the shock caused him by the contradictory emotions of this false alarm. Though he did not revenge himself by killing this man, he drove him from the corn market by forcing him into bankruptcy at a critical moment.

The education he gave his daughters was contrary to all reason. As he had sixty thousand francs a year and spent only twelve hundred on himself, it was Goriot's great pleasure to gratify the whims of his daughters, and the best masters were engaged to teach them those accomplishments that are considered necessary to a good education. They had a lady to live with them as a companion, and fortunately for them, she was a person of good sense and taste; they rode horseback and had carriages at their disposal; in short, they lived as extravagantly as if they had been the mistresses of a rich old nobleman. They had but to express the most expensive desires to have their father hasten to fulfill them; he asked for nothing more than a caress in return for all his gifts. Goriot ranked his daughters among the angels, so necessarily he thought them above his own head, poor man! He loved them even for the pain they gave him.

When his daughters were old enough to marry, he allowed them to follow their own tastes in the selection of their husbands. Each of them would have as dowry the half of her father's fortune. Anastasie was courted for her beauty by the Comte de Restaud, and her aristocratic inclinations disposed her to leave her father's house for a higher social sphere. Delphine cared for money, so married Nucingen, a banker of German extraction who had become a baron of the Holy Empire. Goriot remained in trade. His daughters and sons-in-law were soon scandalized by his continuing his business, although they knew it was his whole existence. After having resisted their entreaties for five years, he consented to retire upon the proceeds of his stock in trade and the profits of the last few years—a fortune that, according to the calculations of Mme. Vauquer at whose house he had established himself, brought him an income of from eight to ten thousand francs. He had buried himself in a boardinghouse in his despair at finding that his two daughters were deterred by their husbands not only from allowing him to live with them but also from receiving his visits openly.

These details were all that were known concerning père Goriot by a certain M. Muret who had purchased his stock in trade. The surmises Rastignac had heard expressed by the Duchesse de Langeais were thus confirmed. Here ends the narrative of an obscure but appalling Parisian tragedy.

PART THREE
The Debut

1

TOWARD the end of the first week in December, Rastignac received two letters, one from his mother and the other from his elder sister. The sight of their familiar handwriting made him thrill with both joy and fear, for he knew the two frail bits of paper contained the life or death warrant of his hopes. If he feared when he remembered the poverty of his relations, he was too confident of their love to doubt that they would shed their lifeblood for him. His mother's letter ran as follows:

My Dear Son:

I send you what you asked for. Make a careful use of this money, for even in a case of life and death, I could not send you such a large sum a second time without telling your father, and that would trouble our family peace, for we would be obliged to mortgage our land. It is impossible for me to judge plans which I know nothing about, but what can they be, since you are afraid to tell me of them? It was not necessary to write volumes in explanation, for a single line is all a mother needs, and that one line would have saved me from the anguish of suspense. My dear boy, I cannot hide from you the painful impression that your letter has caused. What is it that can have induced you to alarm me so much? You must have been unhappy as you wrote, for I was unhappy as I read. What career have you marked out for yourself? I fear that you have staked your life and happiness upon trying to appear what you are not, and upon entering society, which you cannot do without incurring expenses that you cannot afford and without wasting the precious time you owe to your studies. Dear Eugène, believe your mother when she tells you that crooked ways lead to no good end. A young man in your position should try to cultivate patience and resignation. I am not scolding, for I would not embitter the gift we send you. I only speak as a trusting but cautious mother. You know what you feel incumbent upon you to do, but I know how good your intentions are and how pure your heart. So I can say to you without fear, "Go your way, my dear one!" I only tremble because I am a mother; but every step of yours will be tenderly followed by our prayers and blessings. Be prudent, my dear son; you need to be wise as a man, now that you carry on your shoulders the destinies of five persons who are dear to you. Our fortunes depend on you, and your happiness is ours. We all pray God to keep you in your enterprise.

Your Aunt Marcillac has been wonderfully kind and even appreciated what you said about your gloves; she said, laughing, that she had a weakness for the eldest. Dear Eugène, you must be very grateful to her, but I shall not tell you what she has done for you until you have succeeded, for otherwise her money would burn your fingers. You children do not know what it is to sacrifice one's memories; but what would we not be willing to sacrifice for you? Your good kind aunt begs me to send you a kiss and wishes she could give it the power of bringing you good luck. She would have written you herself if she didn't have gout in her hand. Your father is well, and the harvest of 1819 surpasses our expectations. Good-bye, my dear boy; I shall not say anything about your sisters, for Laure is writing to you, and I leave her the pleasure of scribbling about the little family events. Heaven grant you success! Oh, I trust so, dear Eugène, for you have given me so much pain this time that I could not stand it again. I felt all the sting of poverty when I needed money to give to my child. Now, good-bye. Don't leave us long without news, and take here the kiss that your mother sends you.

Eugène was in tears after reading this letter. He thought of père Goriot crushing his silver dish and selling it to pay for his daughter's bill of exchange.

My mother has sold her jewels! he said to himself. My aunt must have wept when she parted with her old relics! What right have I to blame Anastasie? What she did for her lover, I have selfishly imitated for my own future! Who is worse, she or I?

The student felt an intolerable burning about his heart; he was ready to renounce the world and wished to send back the money. He experienced a noble, secret remorse, whose worth is rarely appreciated by men when they sit in judgment on their fellow creatures, but for whose sake the angels of Heaven are willing to absolve the criminal who has been condemned by an earthly court. Rastignac opened his sister's letter, the artless sweetness of which was most refreshing to him. It ran:

Dear Brother:
    Your letter came just in time. Agathe and I wanted to spend our money in so many different ways that we could not decide on any one purchase. You have played the part of the King of Spain's servant when he upset all his master's watches, for you have made us both agree. We were really constantly quarreling about which of our desires we should give the preference to, and we never guessed, dear Eugène, the one use of our money that would combine them all. Agathe jumped for joy, and we were like two mad creatures all day; in fact, we behaved with so much indecorum—to use one of my aunt's expressions— that my mother said to us severely, "What is the matter with you, young ladies?" If she had only scolded us the least particle, we would have been still better pleased, I think. How a woman must enjoy suffering for anybody she loves! But one thought troubled me in the midst of my joy. I know that I shall not make a good wife, for I am too extravagant. I had bought myself two sashes, a pretty stiletto to pierce the eyelet holes in my bodices, and some other trifles, so that I had less money than that big Agathe, who is very economical and hoards her savings like a miser. She had two hundred francs, while I, dear Eugène, had only a hundred and fifty. I was well punished for what I had done, and now I would like to

throw my sashes in the well, for I shall never take pleasure in wearing them. I feel as if I had stolen what was
yours. Agathe was very sweet and said to me, "Let's send
the three hundred and fifty francs from us both," but I
can't help telling you exactly how things are. Can you
imgaine how we arranged it in order to obey your direc-
tions? We took our wonderful money with us and went
out walking together; as soon as we reached the high
road, we hurried on to Ruffec, where we handed over the
sum to M. Grimbert, who keeps the Royal Mailcoach
office. We came home as lighthearted as swallows, and
Agathe asked me if it were happiness that made the way
so short to us. We said a great many things that I shall
not repeat to you, dear Parisian brother, for they were all
about you. We love you dearly, that is the main point.

As to your secret, such little witches as our aunt says
we are, are capable of anything, even of holding our
tongues. My mother and my aunt made a mysterious
expedition to Angoulême, observing strict silence on the
object of their journey, which took place after many long
talks from which both ourselves and the Baron were
banished. Great conjectures are rife in the State of Rastignac. The muslin gown with open-worked flowers that
the infantas are embroidering for her Majesty the Queen
is in secret progress, and there are only two more breadths
to finish. It has been decided to have a hedge instead of
a wall on the side toward Verteuil; the common people
will miss the fruit trees that would have been trained
against the wall, but distinguished strangers will enjoy
the beautiful view. If the Heir Presumptive needs hand-

kerchiefs, he is herewith informed that, as the Dowager of Marcillac was rummaging among the treasures of her trunks that we call Herculaneum and Pompeii, she discovered a fine piece of Holland linen, the existence of which she had forgotten, and the Princesses Agathe and Laure place their needles and thread and hands, always a little red, at his disposal. The two young princes, Don Henry and Don Gabriel, have kept up their unfortunate habits of gorging themselves upon preserves and of teasing their sisters; they continue to be disinclined toward study and amuse themselves by robbing birds' nests, romping violently, and violating the laws of the State by cutting willow branches to make switches. The Papal Nuncio, vulgarly called the parish priest, threatens to excommunicate them if they persist in abandoning the sacred canons of grammar for the bellicose cannons of elderwood. Good-bye, my dear brother; no letter ever carried so many wishes for your happiness or so much gratified affection. You will have much to tell us when you come again, and you must tell everything to me, for I am older than Agathe. My aunt dropped a hint that you had been making a success in society.

They speak of a fair lady, and drop the subject there.

But only to us, you may be sure. Dear Eugène, if you like better, we can give up the handkerchiefs and make you some shirts. Please let me know at once about this, because if you are in haste to have some fine, neatly sewed shirts, we would have to set to work immediately;

and if there are new fashions in Paris that have not as yet
reached us, you might send us a pattern, especially for
the cuffs. Now good-bye. I wish I could kiss you on the
left side of your forehead, the spot which belongs exclusively to me. I shall leave the other page for Agathe, who
has promised me not to read a word of what I have been
writing; still to make quite sure, I shall sit beside her as
she writes.

Your loving sister,
Laure de Rastignac

Yes, yes, Eugène said to himself. Success at any price.
There is no treasure great enough with which to repay
such devotion. I would like to give each one of them
every possible happiness. Fifteen hundred and fifty
francs, he added, after a pause. Every coin must tell to
the utmost advantage. Laure is right. Good heavens! I
have nothing but coarse, common shirts. A young girl is
as artful as a thief when she is planning for the happiness
of anybody she loves; guileless creature that she is, she
takes every precaution for me and is like the angels of
Heaven who forgive those sins of earth that they cannot
understand.

The world was his! His tailor had been already sum-
moned, sounded, and conciliated. On seeing M. de
Trailles, Rastignac had perceived the part a tailor plays
in a young man's life, for he must be either his mortal
enemy or else won over to friendship by means of the bill
that he presents. Alas, there is no middle course between
these two extremes. Eugène found his tailor to be a man

who understood the paternal nature of his trade and considered himself a connecting link between a young fellow's present and his future. So Rastignac, who was grateful for his services, made his fortune later by one of those pleasantries in which he grew to excel.

"I know that he has made two pairs of trousers," he used to say, "each of which was the occasion of a marriage worth twenty thousand francs a year."

Fifteen hundred francs and all the clothes he needed! At this point, the poor student's scruples deserted him, and he went down to breakfast with the indefinable air of a young man who has a certain sum of money in his possession. As the money slips into a student's pocket, he feels within him a strange column on which he leans. He walks with his head higher than before and knows that he has a fulcrum for his lever; his look is full and direct, and his movements, agile. The night before, he would have taken a beating with timid humility, but, the day after, he will be ready to give one to a prime minister. Strange phenomena occur in his consciousness; he longs for everything, believing everything within his reach; he is swayed by contradictory desires and is gay, generous, and unreserved. The unfledged bird has found its wings at last. Just as a dog dares a thousand perils to steal a bone, crunches it, sucks its marrow, and then distances all pursuit, so a penniless student snatches at a chance pleasure that falls in his way. But a young man who can jingle a few stray pieces of gold in his pocket tastes the full flavor of his joys; he tells them over one by one in ecstasy; he rises to the seventh heaven and forgets the meaning of the word *poverty*. All Paris belongs to him.

His is the age in which the world is all shining, glittering, and burning! The age of joyous faults by which neither man nor woman profits! The age of debts and sharp fears that lend a tenfold zest to pleasure! He who has never roamed along the left bank of the Seine, between the rue St-Jacques and the rue des Sts-Pères, knows nothing of human life!

Ah, if the ladies of Paris only knew, they would look this way for a lover! thought Rastignac, as he devoured the stewed pears that had cost two pennies apiece and were served at Mme. Vauquer's table.

A̲T THAT moment, a Royal Mail carrier who had been ringing at the street door appeared in the dining room. He asked for M. Eugène de Rastignac and handed him two bags and a book in which to sign his name.

Rastignac was conscious of a penetrating glance from Vautrin that cut like a knife.

"You will have enough now to pay for fencing lessons and visits to the shooting gallery," that gentleman said.

"Your ship has come in," Mme. Vauquer said, looking at the bags.

Mlle. Michonneau was afraid to turn her eyes in the

direction of the money, for fear that they should betray her covetousness.

"You have a good mother," Mme. Couture said.

"You have a very good mother," repeated Poiret.

"Yes, your mamma has drained herself," Vautrin said. "Now you can cut as many capers as you choose; you can go into society, fish for an heiress, and dance with countesses crowned with peach blossoms. Still, take my advice, young man, and don't neglect the shooting gallery."

Vautrin made a gesture as if he were aiming at an adversary.

Rastignac wanted to tip the carrier but found that his pockets were empty. Vautrin fumbled in his and tossed the man a franc.

"You have plenty of credit," he said, looking full at the student.

Rastignac was forced to thank him, although Vautrin was insupportable to him since the altercation they had had the day Eugène returned from his visit to Mme. de Beauséant. They had not spoken to each other for a week, but had studied each other closely when together, and Eugène idly wondered why it was he did so. Ideas are, no doubt, projected with a force in direct ratio to that with which they are conceived and strike wherever the brain sends them, in accordance with a mathematical law that may be compared to that which guides the ball shot from the cannon's mouth. Ideas are very different in the effects they produce; though some tender souls in which they lodge are devastated by them, other natures are strong to stand against them, and there are brains armed in triple brass from which the will of others falls flattened like a bullet from a wall; again, there are limp and flimsy minds into which other people's ideas drop slowly as a spent ball sinks into the soft earth of a redoubt. Rastignac's head was filled with explosive material ready to ignite at the least touch. He was too young and too much alive not to be sensitive to the ideas of others and to that contagion of thought, whose odd phenomena influence us so often without our knowledge. His inner vision was as clear and longsighted as that of his lynx eyes. All his senses, both mental and physical, had the mysterious sharpness and flexible adaptability that we admire in people of superior powers who are quick to see crevices in the armor of others.

In the space of a month, Eugène had developed an equal number of good and bad qualities. His defects had been necessarily engendered by his entrance into society and the accomplishment of his growing desires. One of his fortunate characteristics was that southern vivacity of temperament that drives a man on to grapple with a difficulty and never allows a moment of indecision to anyone born beyond the Loire. Northerners call this a defect and think that, although it was the origin of Murat's fortune, it was also the cause of his death. We may from this conclude that when a man succeeds in uniting the astuteness of the north and the audacity of the south, he will be a consummate person and will continue to reign King of Sweden. Rastignac could not long endure the fire of Vautrin's batteries without finding out whether the man was his friend or his enemy. From time to time, it seemed to him that this singular person saw through his passions and read his heart, though he had concealed his own affairs so perfectly that he appeared deep and immovable as the sphinx that knows and sees everything but says nothing. Now that his pockets were full, Eugène rebelled.

"Be so kind as to wait a moment," he said to Vautrin, who was rising to go out after having finished sipping his coffee.

"Why?" Vautrin asked, as he put on his broad-brimmed hat and took up the iron-tipped cane, which he was in the habit of swinging as if to show that he was not afraid of anybody.

"I want to return your money," Rastignac answered, and quickly untied one of his bags and counted out a hundred and forty francs to Mme. Vauquer. "Short reckonings make long friends," he said to the widow. "Now we are quits until Saint Sylvester's day. Please change me a five-franc piece."

"Long friends make short reckonings," Poiret repeated, with his eyes upon Vautrin.

"There is a franc," Rastignac said, holding out a coin to the sphinx in a wig who stood before him.

"You behave as if you were afraid of owing me anything," Vautrin cried, plunging his searching glance into the young man's soul and giving him the ironical and Diogenes-like smile that had a hundred times come near to making Eugène lose his temper.

"Well, I am," replied the student, who had the bags

in his hand and had risen to return to his own room.

Vautrin went out by the door leading into the salon, just as the student was preparing to leave the room by the door leading to the staircase.

"Do you know, Marquis de Rastignacorama, that what you have said is not exactly polite," Vautrin said, slamming the parlor door and advancing toward the student, who waited for him coldly.

Rastignac shut the dining room door and drew Vautrin with him to the foot of the stairs in the passageway between the dining room and kitchen, where there was a door opening into the garden, surmounted by a long grated window. Sylvie, who was just coming out of the kitchen, overheard the student say:

"*Monsieur* Vautrin, I am not a marquis, and my name is not Rastignacorama."

"They are going to fight a duel," Mlle. Michonneau said indifferently.

"To fight a duel," Poiret repeated.

"Oh, no," Mme. Vauquer answered, caressing her pile of gold.

"There they are under the lime trees," Mlle. Victorine exclaimed, springing up to look out into the garden. "Yet that poor young man had the right of it."

"Come upstairs, my dear child," Mme. Couture said. "Their affairs are none of ours."

As Mme. Couture and Victorine were about to leave the room, they met big Sylvie in the doorway, barring their passage.

"What is the matter?" she asked. "M. Vautrin said to

M. Eugène, 'Let's have a talk.' Then he took him by the arm, and there they are now walking among the artichokes."

At this juncture, Vautrin appeared.

"Mamma Vauquer," he said with a smile, "don't be frightened; nothing is the matter. I am going to try my pistols under the lime trees."

"Oh, monsieur," cried Victorine, clasping her hands, "why do you want to kill M. Eugène?"

Vautrin stepped back a little to take a good look at Victorine.

"That is another story," he exclaimed in a jeering tone that made the poor girl blush. "He is a nice young man, isn't he?" he continued. "You have put an idea into my head. I will make you both happy, my pretty girl."

Mme. Couture took her ward by the arm and dragged her away, saying in her ear:

"Victorine, your conduct this morning is incomprehensible."

"I do not want any pistol shots in my garden," Mme. Vauquer said. "Don't you know that you would alarm the neighborhood and bring the police directly?"

"Now be calm Mamma Vauquer," Vautrin replied. "There, there, don't worry, we will go to a shooting gallery."

He went out and rejoined Rastignac, whom he took familiarly by the arm.

"Even if I proved to you," he said, "that I could put a shot through the ace of spades five times running, at thirty-five paces, you would not lose courage. You look

to me as if you were in a passion and would be fool enough to let me kill you."

"You are trying to draw back," Eugène said.

"Don't irritate me," Vautrin answered. "It is not cold this morning. Come and let us sit down there," he added, pointing to the green-painted seats, "where nobody can overhear us. I have something to say to you. You are a good little fellow, and I wish you no harm. I like you, on the honor of Trompe—thunder and guns!— on the honor of Vautrin. I will tell you why I like you, but in the meantime, I know you as well as if I had made you myself and am going to prove it to you. Put down your bags," he said, pointing to the round table.

Rastignac placed his money upon the table and sat down, overcome by his curiosity that was now raised to the highest pitch by the sudden change in the manners of this man, who had just talked of killing him and was posing as his patron.

"You would like to know who I am, what I have done, or what I am doing now," Vautrin resumed. "You are too inquisitive, my young friend. Come, let us be calm. You will hear something much more remarkable! I have been unfortunate. Listen to me first, and answer me afterward. Here is my past life in a word. Who am I? Vautrin. What am I doing? Whatever I choose. That is enough. Do you wish to know my disposition? I am good to those who are good to me or to those with whom I feel in sympathy. To them I allow any liberty, and they may kick me as hard as they like, without my telling them to look out for themselves. But, by God! I am spiteful as the devil to the people who plague me or who are not to my liking. And I may as well let you know that I care as much about killing a man as I do about doing that!" he said, spitting into the air. "Only, when it is absolutely necessary, I like to make a neat piece of work of it. I am what you may call an artist. Such as you see me here, I have read the *Memoirs of Benvenuto Cellini*, and in Italian too. I learned from that man, who was a jolly good fellow, to imitate Providence, which kills us at random, and to love beauty wherever I find it. Besides, isn't it playing a fine game to be one against all the world and to have luck on your side?

"I have reflected a great deal on the actual state of social disorder, and I tell you, my dear fellow, dueling is mere childish nonsense. When one of two living men has got to disappear, a man is a great fool to leave it to chance. A duel? It is heads or tails, that is all. I can send five shots, one right after the other, into an ace of spades, and at a distance of thirty-five paces too; when a man is possessed of such a little accomplishment as that, he can be pretty sure of hitting his enemy. Well, I fired at a man twenty paces off, and I missed him. The fool had never handled a pistol before, yet look!" said the extraordinary man, undoing his waistcoat and displaying his chest, shaggy as a bear's back, but with hair that was of a reddish hue both repulsive and startling to behold. "The greenhorn scorched me here," he added, putting Rastignac's finger upon a scar that was on his breast. "But at that time, I was only a child; I was your age, twenty-one. I still believed in some things: in the love of a woman, and a whole quantity of rubbish that you are going to muddle your brains with. If we had fought, you might have killed me. Suppose that I were dead and buried, where would you be? You would have to make your escape, go to Switzerland, and spend your papa's money, which he has little enough of.

"I am going to enlighten you about your position, and I shall do so with the confidence of a man who has considered the things of this world and discovered that there are only two courses to take: either blind obedience or open revolt. I obey nothing; is that clear to you? Do you know how much you need at the rate at which you are going? You need a million, and right away too; or else with your small wits, you may go floating down to the nets of St-Cloud to find out whether there is a Supreme Being or not. I can give you a million."

He paused, keeping his eyes fixed on Eugène.

"Aha! That makes you a little more amiably disposed toward your friend Vautrin. As you listened, you reminded me of a young girl who expects a visit from her lover in the evening and tricks herself out in her finery, licking her lips like a cat lapping milk. So much the better. Now, between ourselves, here you are, young man. You have at home your papa, mamma, your great-aunt, two sisters, one eighteen and the other seventeen, and two little brothers, of fifteen and ten; that is the list of the family. Your aunt teaches your sisters, and the parish priest comes to give Latin lessons to your two brothers. The household consumes more boiled chestnuts than white bread, your papa has to be very careful of his trousers, your mamma can hardly get a new gown twice a year, and your sisters get along as they can. I know all about it, for I have been in the south. Such must be the state of things in your family, if they send you twelve hundred francs a year and your land only brings in three thousand francs. You have a cook and a servant, for appearances must be kept up, and your papa is a baron.

"As to you, you are ambitious; you are related to the Beauséants, and yet you are obliged to go on foot; you are crazy for money, and you don't have a penny; you have to eat Mme. Vauquer's stews and hashes, but you would prefer a fine dinner in the faubourg St-Germain; you sleep on a pallet, and you are longing for a palace. I am not blaming your desires. Everybody is not capable of feeling ambition, my dear fellow. Women care more for ambitious men than they do for the others. Ambitious men have more backbone; their blood is richer in iron, and their heart is warmer than that of other men. And a happy and beautiful woman in the fullness of her power prefers a strong man to any other, even though she is in danger of being crushed by him.

"I am taking the inventory of your desires in order to put a question to you. Here it is: you are as hungry as a wolf, and your teeth are as sharp as his; what are you going to do to stock your larder? You must first stuff yourself with the law; it is neither amusing nor instructive, but it is necessary. Very well. You must study it in order to become president of a Court of Assizes and send off to the galleys poor devils who are worth more than

you, branding them with T. F. on the shoulder, by way
of proving to the rich that they may sleep quietly. It is
dull work, and it takes a long time. First, you must wait
two years in Paris, looking at the *lollipops* you are greedy
for, with no chance of getting them. It is tiresome to be
always wishing and never satisfied. If you were palefaced
and made like a mollusk, there would be no harm in it;
but your blood is as hot as a lion's, and your appetite
would lead you into twenty blunders a day. You would
certainly succumb to this torment, which is the most
horrible in all God's hell.

"Suppose that you are well behaved, drink milk, and
write verses, in spite of your high spirit, you will have to
endure vexations and hardships enough to drive you mad
and then begin by filling some fool's place in a hole of
a town, where the government throws you a pittance of
a thousand francs, as you might throw a bone to a
butcher's dog. Raise a hue and cry after the thieves,
plead for the rich, and guillotine the brave men. Much
obliged! If you have no patronage, you may rot in your
provincial town. At thirty, you may be a judge with
twelve hundred francs a year, if you have not given up
the whole thing by that time. At forty, you may marry
a miller's daughter with an income of six thousand
francs. Thanks. If you have patronage, you may be a
crown solicitor at thirty, with a salary of three thousand
francs, and you may marry the daughter of the mayor.
If you can manage a few little political tricks, such as
reading on the bulletin 'Villèle' instead of 'Manuel'—
they rhyme, and that soothes your conscience—you may

hope, at forty, to be an attorney general, and you might become a deputy. Observe, my dear fellow, that you will have wounded your conscience a great many times, that you will have spent twenty years of worry and secret annoyance, and your sisters will have become old maids. Moreover, I have the honor to call to your attention that there are only twenty attorneys general in France and that you are one among twenty thousand aspirants to that honor, among whom there will be scamps who are ready to sell their souls to rise a peg in the world.

"If the trade is not to your taste, let us think of something else. Would the Baron de Rastignac like to be a barrister? That is a good idea. He must drudge for ten years, spend a thousand francs a month, keep a library and an office, go into society, kiss the hem of an attorney's gown to get some cases, and lick the law courts with his tongue. If the profession led to success, I would have nothing to say against it; but find me in Paris five lawyers who, at fifty, make more than fifty thousand francs a year. Pshaw! Rather than starve my soul in such a way, I would become a pirate. Besides, where could you get your money? It is not as easy as you think. You have the resource of marrying a rich woman. Do you think you would like that? It would be hanging a millstone about your neck; besides, if you marry for money, what is to become of your honorable high-minded sentiments? You may as well begin today with your revolt against human conventions. Do you think it would be nothing to crawl before a woman like a snake, to fawn at her mother's feet, and stoop to baseness that would disgust a pig? Faugh! If it could only bring you happiness!

But you would be as miserable as the stones in the sewer with a wife whom you had married in this way. It is better to fight with men than to quarrel with your wife.

"I have shown you the crossroads of life, young man; you must make your choice. But you have already chosen: you went to your cousin de Beauséant's and found out what luxury is. You went to the house of Mme. de Restaud, the daughter of père Goriot, and there you found what a Parisian woman is. That same day, you came back with an inscription on your forehead that I was able to read. It was, '*Success!* Success at any price.' 'Bravo,' I said, 'that is the kind of fellow I like!' You needed money; where could you get it? You bled your sisters. All brothers *dupe* their sisters more or less. The fifteen hundred francs that were scraped together for you, Heaven knows how, in a country where chestnuts are commoner than five-franc pieces, will soon slip away, like soldiers on a marauding expedition.

"What do you expect to do then? Work? Work, in your sense of the word, might bring to an old fellow of Poiret's stamp enough to live on at Mme. Vauquer's in his old age. A quick means of making a fortune is the problem that fifty thousand young men in your position are trying to solve today. You are a unit of that number, so judge of the efforts you will have to make, and the ferocity of the struggle. You must all kill one another like so many spiders in a pot if there aren't fifty thousand good places.

"Do you know how a man makes his way in this world? Either by the splendor of genius, or the adroitness of corruption. He must burst like a cannonball into the

ranks of his fellowmen, or he must glide in among them
like the pestilence. Honesty is of no use. Men yield to the
power of genius; they may hate it and try to calumniate
it because it refuses to share its spoils, but they yield to
it if it persists and kneel to it when they find that they
cannot suppress it. Corruption is general, but talent is
rare; therefore, corruption is the arm of mediocrity that
always abounds, and you may feel its sting everywhere.
You will find women whose husbands have a salary of
only six thousand francs in all, and yet who spend more
than ten thousand francs on their dress. You will find
clerks at twelve hundred francs a year buying land. You
will see women sell themselves to drive in the carriage of
the son of a peer of France who can race his horses on
the middle course at Longchamp. You saw the poor old
idiot Goriot forced to pay the bill of exchange that his
daughter had endorsed, and yet her husband has an income of fifty thousand francs. I defy you to take a step
in Paris without meeting with some infernal intrigue. I
lay my head to wager against a head of that lettuce that
you will put your foot in a hornet's nest in the house of
the first woman who happens to catch your fancy, though
she may be young, rich, and beautiful. The laws have
helped to corrupt them, and they are in a constant state
of warfare with their husbands. I would never come to
the end if I told you of the traffic they are engaged in
for the sake of their lovers, their clothes, their children,
their houses, or their vanity; rarely in the cause of virtue,
you may be sure.

"So, an honest man is a common enemy; but what do

you think an honest man is? In Paris, it is the man who holds his tongue and keeps his profits to himself. I am not talking of those poor slaves who are always toiling without receiving any reward for their labors and whom I call the confraternity of the poor of God. They realize virtue in all the flower of its folly, but they are miserable. I can see already the grimaces of those good people if God would play them the poor joke of absenting Himself from the Last Judgment. If you wish to succeed quickly, you must be rich or else appear so. To grow rich, you must play with big stakes, or else your game is a paltry one, and then, good-bye! If, in any of the hundred professions that are open to you, there are ten men who make a fortune quickly, the public calls them robbers.

"You may draw your own conclusions; I have shown you life as it is. It is no less ugly than a kitchen and quite as evil smelling; you must soil your hands if you mean to do the cooking. You must know how to wash off the stains, however; that is all that morality requires nowadays. If I speak in this way about the world, I have the right to do so, for I know it well. Do you think I am blaming it? Not in the least. It has always been the same, and moralists can never change it. Man is an imperfect being, and according as he is more or less hypocritical, fools say that he is or is not virtuous. I do not accuse the rich in favor of the poor: man is the same, whether in the upper, lower, or middle class. In every million of this higher kind of cattle, there are ten fellows who rise superior to everything, even the laws; I am one of them. If you are an intelligent man, you may walk in a straight line and carry your head erect. Still, you will have to fight against envy, calumny, mediocrity, and the whole world. Napoléon once fell in with a Minister of War who nearly sent him off to the colonies. Examine your own courage and see whether you can get up every morning with a better will than the day before.

"At this crisis, I am going to make you an offer that no man would refuse. Listen to me, for you see, I have an idea in my mind. I would like to live a patriarchal life on a large estate, say a hundred thousand acres, in the south of the United States. I want to be a planter with a gang of slaves, to make a few million by selling cattle, tobacco, and timber, and to live like a king, carrying out my own desires and leading a life that nobody dreams of here in this dungeon of bricks and mortar. I am a great poet, but I don't write my poems: they consist of deeds and feelings. I am, at this moment, in possession of fifty thousand francs, which could hardly buy me forty Negroes. I need two hundred thousand francs, because I want two hundred Negroes in order to satisfy my taste for patriarchal life. Negroes, you see, are like ready-made children that you can do what you choose with, without being afraid of having a crown solicitor after you to call you to account for them. With this black capital, in ten years I could make three or four million, and if I succeed, nobody will ask me who I am. I shall be simply M. Four-Million, citizen of the United States. I shall be fifty years old, still sound and well preserved, and I can amuse myself in my own way.

"Briefly, if I find a girl with a million for you, will you

give me two hundred thousand francs? Twenty percent commission, eh? Is that too expensive? You must make your little wife very fond of you, and once you are married, you will let her see that you are worried and remorseful, and pretend to be melancholy for a week or two. Then, some night, after a few caresses, you will kiss her, call her 'my love,' and confess to her that you are two hundred thousand francs in debt. This comedy is played every day by young men of the greatest distinction. A young wife never closes her purse to the man who has won her heart. Do you think you would lose by this transaction? No. You would find means in some speculation to make your two hundred thousand francs over again. With your money and your wits, you could amass as large a fortune as you wished. *Ergo*, in six months' time, you will have made yourself and a charming woman happy; and your friend Vautrin too, not to speak of your own family, who have to blow on their fingers all winter because they have no wood to keep them warm. Don't be surprised at what I offer you, or what I ask of you. Out of sixty fine marriages that take place in Paris, forty or fifty are the occasion of similar bargains. The Chamber of Notaries obliged Monsieur—"

"What do you want me to do?" Eugène broke in eagerly, interrupting Vautrin.

"Almost nothing at all," he rejoined, allowing a movement of joy to escape him, inexorable as the expression of the angler who feels a fish at the end of his line. "Pay attention to what I am going to say! The heart of a poor, unfortunate, unhappy girl is a sponge quick to fill itself with love, a dry sponge that swells as soon as a drop of sentiment falls upon it. To pay your court to a young woman buried in solitude, poverty, and despair, who has not the faintest suspicion of the fortune she is one day to inherit, is to hold the game in your own hand; it is like knowing the numbers of a lottery, or gambling in stocks when you are in possession of secret information. You would build a marriage upon indestructible foundations. When the girl comes into possession of her millions, she will cast them at your feet, as if they were so many pebbles. 'Take them, my darling! Take them, Adolphe! Take them, Alfred! Take them, Eugène,' she will say, if Adolphe, Alfred, or Eugène has been clever enough to make sacrifices for her. What I call making sacrifices for a girl is selling an old coat to take her to a supper of mushrooms on toast at the Cadran Bleu and from there to the play; it is pawning your watch to give her a new shawl. I need not tell you anything about scribbling love letters or any of the other nonsense so dear to a woman, such as, for instance, dropping water on a sheet of letter paper to make her think that you cry when you are away from her: you look to me as if you were perfectly familiar with the argot of the heart.

"Paris, you see, is like a forest in the New World swarming with twenty savage tribes—Illinois, Hurons, and others—who live on the prey offered them by the different classes of society. You are a hunter of millions, and to catch them, you must use traps, snares, and decoys. There are various ways of hunting. Some men hunt for a dowry, others pursue their quarry into bankruptcy;

there are those who fish for consciences, and those again who sell their victims bound hand and foot. The man who comes back with his game bag well filled is greeted with applause, entertained, and received in good society. Let us do justice to this hospitable soil, for you have to do with the most obliging city in the world. If the proud aristocracy of all the capitals of Europe refuse to admit to their ranks an infamous millionaire, Paris holds out its arms to him, rushes to his balls, eats his dinners, and drinks his health."

"But where shall I find a girl?" Eugène asked.

"She is yours, and right before you."

"Mlle. Victorine?"

"Exactly."

"What do you mean?"

"Your little Baroness de Rastignac is already in love with you."

"She doesn't have a penny," Eugène went on in surprise.

"Ah! There we are!" Vautrin said. "Allow me a few words, and everything will be clear to you. Father Taillefer is an old rascal who is supposed to have murdered one of his friends in the time of the Revolution. He is one of those fine fellows of mine who hold independent opinions. He is a banker, head partner in the house of Frédéric Taillefer and Company. He has an only son to whom he means to leave his property, to the detriment of Victorine. Now, I cannot bear such injustice, for I am like Don Quixote and love to take up the defense of the weak against the strong. If it were the will of God to deprive him of his son, Taillefer would take back his daughter; he would want an heir, for that is a folly engrained in human nature, and I know that he cannot have any more children. Victorine is sweet and attractive and will soon twist her father about, and she will make him spin like a top under the lash of his affection for her. She will be too grateful for your love to forget you, and you will marry her. I take upon myself to play the part of Providence, and I will direct the will of God. I have a friend to whom I am devoted, a colonel in the army of the Loire, who has just entered the Royal Guard. He has listened to my advice and become an ultra-Royalist, for he is not one of those fools who insist upon their own opinions.

"If I have another counsel to give you, my dear fellow, it is to care no more for your opinions than you do for your words. When you are asked for them, sell them. A man who boasts that he never changes his mind is a man who undertakes to walk forever along a straight line, a fool who believes in his own infallibility. There is no such thing as principle; emergency is everything. There are no laws, but only circumstances: a clever man unites himself to circumstances and emergencies in order to direct to them. If principles and fixed laws existed, nations would not change them as easily as we change our shirt. A man cannot be expected to be more virtuous than a nation. The man who has served France least is venerated as a fetish for having always held the same violent opinions; he is only fit to be put in the Conservatory, among the machines, and labeled La Fayette; whereas, the prince at whom everyone casts a stone and who

despises humanity enough to swear as many oaths as it
demands prevented the division of France at the Con-
gress of Vienna. He should be offered a crown, but he is
pelted with mud. Oh, I know about such things, for I
have the secrets of many men. That is enough; I shall
hold an unalterable opinion the day that I meet three
men who are agreed as to the working of a single principle, and I shall have a long time to wait! There aren't
three judges in the law courts who have the same opinion
concerning a point of law. I return to the man I was
speaking of. He would crucify Jesus Christ again if I told
him to do it. At a single word from his friend Vautrin,
he will pick a quarrel with that wretch, who doesn't even
send a five-franc piece to his poor sister, and . . . "

Here Vautrin rose, fell into guard, and made a motion,
like a fencing master, lunging with his rapier.

"He is a dead man," he added.

"How terrible!" Eugène exclaimed. "You are joking,
Monsieur Vautrin."

"There, there, please be calm," Vautrin returned.
"Don't behave like a child; still, if it amuses you, you
may be as angry and cross as you choose. Say that I am
an infamous rascal, a wretch, a ruffian, if you like; but
don't call me a cheat or a spy. Go ahead, and fire away!
I forgive you, for it is natural at your age. I was like that
once myself. Only reflect, for you will be sure to do worse
someday. You will flirt with a pretty woman and will take
money from her. You must have thought of it," said
Vautrin, "for how can you succeed if you don't turn your
love affairs to pecuniary account?

"Virtue, my dear fellow, cannot be divided; it either

exists, or it does not exist. People tell us we can do penance for our sins. That is a pretty system by which we can be absolved from a crime by an act of contrition. Do you think it is an act of faith, hope, and charity to seduce a woman for the sake of reaching a certain round in the social ladder, to sow dissension among the children of a family, or to have a hand in some of the other infamous practices that are carried on clandestinely or otherwise for pure pleasure or personal interests? Why should a dandy who robs a child of half his fortune in a single night get only two months in prison, and a poor devil who steals a thousand-franc note under aggravating circumstances be sent to the galleys? Such are the laws, and there is not one among them that is not absurd. The man who wears light gloves and uses fine words has committed murders in which blood is not shed, but where it is given; the assassin and the nobleman have opened the same door, and both at night! There is merely the difference of the shedding of blood between what I propose to you and what you will one day be guilty of. Do you believe in anything stable in such a world as this? I tell you to despise mankind and to observe the chinks you can slip through in the network of the law. The secret of a great fortune without apparent cause is a forgotten crime, because it was so neatly done."

"Silence, monsieur! I will hear no more; for you will make me doubt myself. Just now, I know nothing and can only feel."

"As you please, my pretty boy," Vautrin said. "I thought you had more character, I shall not say anything further. One last word, however."

He looked fixedly at the student, and added:
"You have my secret."

"A young man who can refuse your offer will know
how to forget it," Eugène said.

"That is well, and I am glad of it. Another man might
be less scrupulous, you see. Keep in mind what I wish
to do for you. I give you two weeks to consider my proposition, and you may take it or leave it, as you choose."

What a strong mind that man has! Eugène thought
as he watched Vautrin walking quietly away with his
cane under his arm. He has put bluntly to me what I
heard in polite language from Mme. de Beauséant. He
rent my heart with claws of steel. Why do I want to go
to Mme. de Nucingen? He guessed my motives as soon
as I conceived them. In short, the ruffian told me more
about virtue than I ever learned from men or books. If
virtue admits no compromise, I must have robbed my
sisters, he added, throwing the bags on the table.

He sat down and remained plunged in bewildered
meditation.

To be faithful to virtue and suffer sublime martyrdom!
Pooh! Everybody believes in virtue, but who is virtuous?
The nations of the earth have Liberty for their idol, but
what people is free? My youth is still as fresh as a cloud-
less sky: if I mean to be great or rich, musn't I make up
my mind to lie, to bow, to crawl, to play a part, to flatter
and dissimulate? Musn't I consent to be the servant of
those who have lied, bowed, and crawled? Before I can
be their accomplice, I must be their servant. No, I will
not. I wish to work uprightly and nobly; I wish to work
day and night and owe my success to my toil alone. It

will be a slow way of making a fortune, but every evening my head will rest upon my pillow without a remorseful thought. What could be better than to look back at one's life and see that it is as spotless as a lily? My life and I shall be like a young man and his sweetheart. Vautrin showed me what happens after ten years of married life. The devil! I am losing my head. I don't want to think of anything; my heart is the best guide.

Eugène was roused from his reverie by the voice of big Sylvie announcing his tailor, and he went in to meet him, still carrying his moneybags in his hand, a circumstance for which he was not sorry. After having tried his evening suit, he put on his new morning attire, which completely metamorphosed him.

I look quite as well as M. de Trailles, he thought. At last, I am dressed like a gentleman.

DIDN'T you ask me if I knew the houses where Mme. de Nucingen goes?" said père Goriot, coming into Eugène's room.

"Yes, I did."

"She is going next Monday to Maréchal Carigliano's

ball. If you can manage to be there, you will tell me if my daughters enjoy themselves, how they are dressed, and all about them."

"How did you find this out, my dear père Goriot?" Eugène asked, making him sit down beside his fire.

"Her maid told me. I know everything they do through Thérèse and Constance," he answered cheerfully.

The old man was like a lover, still young enough to exult in a stratagem that puts him in communication with his mistress without her suspecting it.

"You will see them," he added, artlessly expressing the painful sense of envy that possessed him.

"I can't tell," Eugène replied. "I am going to call on Mme. de Beauséant to ask her if she will present me to the Marshal's wife."

Eugène thought with secret joy of presenting himself at the Viscountess's, dressed as he meant to be in the future. What moralists call the mysteries of the human heart are merely the delusive thoughts and involuntary impulses of personal interest. Our waverings of mind and changes of purpose that are the subject of so much declamation are merely the calculations we make for the sake of our own pleasures. When Rastignac was well dressed and fitted out with new gloves and boots, he forgot his virtuous resolutions. Youth dares not survey itself in the mirror of conscience when it is tempted to wrongdoing, but middle age has seen itself reflected there; herein lies all the difference between these two phases of life.

For the last few days, Eugène and père Goriot, these two neighbors, had become good friends. Their secret friendship was due to the same psychological reasons that had engendered sentiments of a contrary nature between the student and Vautrin. The bold philosopher who wishes to verify the effect of our feelings upon the physical world will, no doubt, find more than one proof of their effective materiality in the relations they create between ourselves and animals. What physiognomist is quicker to divine a man's character than a dog is to find out whether a stranger likes him or not? The fact is that *atomes crochus*—mysterious elements of mutual sympathy—a proverbial expression in common use, remains in the language to give the lie to the philosophic twaddle, so interesting to those who like to sift the chaff of primitive words. When we are loved, we feel it. Feeling traverses space and imprints itself on everything. A letter is like a soul; it is so faithful an echo of the speaking voice that refined natures count it among the richest treasures of love. Père Goriot, whose unreasoned feeling raised him to the sublimity of the canine nature, had perceived the pity, the wondering affection, and young sympathy that had sprung up for him in the heart of the student. Their incipient friendship, however, had as yet brought about no confidences; for if Eugène had shown a desire to see Mme. de Nucingen, it was not because he expected her father to introduce him to her, but because he hoped the old man would inadvertently tell him something that would serve his turn. Père Goriot had spoken to him of his daughters only in reference to what Eugène had ventured to say of them publicly the day he had made his two calls.

"My dear monsieur," he had said to him next day, "how could you think that Mme. de Restaud was displeased with you for mentioning my name? My two daughters are very fond of me, and I am a happy father, except that my two sons-in-law have behaved badly to me. I was unwilling to bring suffering upon my dear girls by my quarrels with their husbands, and I preferred to see them privately. This secrecy gives me a thousand joys unknown to those fathers who can see their daughters when they like. I can't, you see, so when the weather is fine, I go to the Champs-Elysées, after making sure from my daughters' maids that their mistresses are to drive out. I wait along the way for them, and my heart beats when I see their carriages coming; they are charming in their pretty clothes and look at me with a smile that gilds the whole of nature for me like a sunbeam. Then I stay there till they come back, and when I see them again, their airing has done them good and given them a color in their cheeks. I hear somebody beside me saying, 'What a pretty woman,' and it makes my heart glad.

"Aren't they of my own blood? I love the horses that draw them, and I would like to be the little dog that lies on their knees. I live in their pleasures. Everybody has his own manner of loving, and as mine does no harm to anybody, why should people talk about me? I am happy in my own way. Is it against the law for me to go to see my daughters in the evening just as they are starting for a ball? I am dreadfully disappointed if I arrive too late and I am told, 'Madame has gone!' Once I waited till three o'clock in the morning for Nasie, because it was two days since I had seen her. I almost died of joy! Please don't speak to me again of my daughters, unless you have something pleasant to say about them. They want to overwhelm me with gifts of every kind, but I prevent them from doing it and say, 'Keep your money! What do you expect me to do with it? I don't need anything.' Really, my dear monsieur, what am I, after all? Nothing but a useless body, for my soul is always with my daughters. When you have seen Mme. de Nucingen, you must tell me which of the two you prefer," added the poor man after a moment's pause, as he saw that Eugène was getting ready for a walk in the Tuileries to pass the time before the proper hour for calling upon Mme. de Beau-séant.

This walk was fatal to the student. Some ladies observed him; he was so young and handsome and dressed with so much elegance and good taste! As he saw that he was the object of attention and possible admiration, he forgot his honorable scruples and the sisters and aunt whom he had robbed. He had seen flying aloft the demon who is so easily mistaken for an angel: Satan with his variegated wings, who scatters his rubies, shoots his golden shafts at the fronts of palaces, sheds a roseate light over women, and clothes with fictitious splendor the thrones of the earth, so unpretending in their origin; he had listened to the god of noisy vanity, whose glamor seems to us a symbol of power. Vautrin's words, cynical though they were, had lodged in his heart, just as there lies engraved in the memory of a maiden the ignoble profile of the old hag who has told her she may have "gold and love in plenty." Eugène sauntered indolently about and toward five o'clock presented himself at the house of Mme. de Beauséant, where he met with one of those cruel blows against which young hearts have no arms to defend themselves. Until then, he had found the Viscountess full of the polite amenity and the smooth grace inculcated by an aristocratic education but which is only complete when it comes from the heart.

As he entered, Mme. de Beauséant said to him shortly with an abrupt gesture:

"Monsieur de Rastignac, it is impossible for me to see you; at least at present! I am busy . . . "

To an observer, and Rastignac had not been slow to become one, her phrase, gesture, look, and inflection of voice were the history of the character and habits of her class. He felt the iron hand under the velvet glove, the personality, the egotism that lay beneath the polished exterior, the wood beneath the varnish. In short, he felt the sense of divine right that begins under the canopy of the throne and ends with the crest of the poorest gentleman. Eugène had allowed himself to be led too easily by the words of a woman to believe in the nobleness of her sex. Like other luckless mortals, he had signed in good faith the delightful compact that should bind a benefactor to the person he has obliged, the first article of which establishes a complete and consecrated equality between noble natures. The goodwill that unites two beings is a celestial passion as rare and as often misunderstood as true love. Both are born of the generosity of lofty souls. As Rastignac was anxious to get to the Duchess de Carigliano's ball, he pocketed the affront.

"Madame," he said, with emotion, "if it were not an important matter that is at stake, I would not have come to trouble you. If you are so kind as to allow me to see you later, I can wait."

"You may come and dine with me then," she said, somewhat confused by the harshness of her words, for she was a lady as good as she was great.

Rastignac was touched by her sudden change of manner, but as he went away he said to himself, I must cringe and bear every indignity. What can other women be if the best of them can, in a moment, forget her promises of friendship and cast me off like an old shoe? Each for himself then? Still it is true that her house is not a shop, and I am in the wrong for wanting anything of her. As Vautrin says, I must make myself into a cannonball.

The student's bitter reflections, however, were soon put to flight by the pleasure he felt in looking forward to dining with the Viscountess. Thus, by a kind of fatality, the most trivial circumstances of his life conspired to precipitate him into that career, in which, according to the remarks of the terrible sphinx of the Vauquer household, he was to be obliged, as if upon the field of battle, to kill to avoid being killed and to deceive to avoid being deceived; in which he was to separate himself from his heart and conscience, to wear a mask upon his face, to play with men without mercy, and as at Lacedemonia, to snatch at fortune, unperceived, in order to win the crown. When he returned to the Viscountess, she met him with the same gracious kindness that she had always shown him. They went in together to the dining room, where they found the Viscount waiting for his wife and the table spread with the luxury that, as everybody knows, reached its culminating point under the Restoration.

Like many other men satiated with enjoyment, M. de Beauséant had lost his interest in all pleasures except those of good living; as an epicure, he belonged to the school of Louis XVIII and the Duc d'Escars, so that his table was conspicuous for the luxury both of the service and the food. Eugène had never seen anything like it before, as it was the first time he had dined in a house in which social grandeur is hereditary. Fashion had just put an end to the suppers that used to wind up the balls of the Empire, at which the officers were obliged to summon all their strength in order to be prepared for all the combats that awaited them both within and without. Eugène had as yet been only to balls, but the assurance for which he was afterward so eminently distinguished and which he was already beginning to acquire prevented him from showing any foolish astonishment. Still, as he looked at the embossed silver and the thousand refinements of the sumptuous table, as he admired the noiseless way, quite new to him, in which the dinner was served; it would have been difficult for a man of such ardent imagination as his not to prefer a life of continual elegance to the privations he had been willing to embrace in the morning. His thoughts carried him back to his boardinghouse for a moment, and he was overcome with such profound disgust that he swore he would leave it in the month of January to live in a cleaner house and also to escape from Vautrin, whose heavy hand weighed upon his shoulder.

If a man of intelligence considers the myriad shapes that corruption, whether silent or loud tongued, assumes in Paris, he will marvel by what aberration the State establishes schools in which to assemble young men together, for what reason pretty women are respected, and why the gold displayed by the money changers does not fly off by magic from their tills. But if he comes to think how few examples of crime there are, particularly offenses committed by young men, he will feel real respect for the patient Tantaluses who struggle against themselves and are almost always victorious. If the poor student could be well described in his contest with Paris, he would furnish one of the most dramatic subjects of our modern civilization.

Mme. de Beauséant looked in vain at Eugène to urge him to speak, for he would say nothing before the Viscount.

"Are you going with me to the Opéra tonight?" the Viscountess asked of her husband.

"You cannot doubt how delighted I would be to obey you," he answered with a mocking courtesy that deceived Eugène, "but I am to meet a friend at the Variétés."

He means his mistress, she thought.

"Isn't D'Ajuda to be with you this evening?" the Viscount asked.

"No," she said, shortly.

"Very well, if you must have a companion, take M. de Rastignac."

The Viscountess looked at Eugène with a smile.

"It will be very compromising for you," she said.

"A Frenchman loves danger because it leads to glory, as M. de Chateaubriand has said," Rastignac answered with a bow.

A few moments later, he found himself at Mme. de Beauséant's side, in a coupé that was being rapidly driven to the fashionable theater, and he thought himself in fairyland as he entered a box opposite the stage and saw all the opera glasses in the house leveled at him as well as the Viscountess, whose dress was exquisite. He was passing from one enchantment to another.

"You have something to say to me," Mme. de Beauséant said. "Ah, look! There is Mme. de Nucingen in the third box from us. Her sister and M. de Trailles are on the other side."

While she was speaking, the Viscountess directed her eyes toward the box where she expected to see Mlle. de Rochefide, but as M. d'Ajuda was not there, her face lighted up wonderfully.

"She is charming," Eugène said, after looking at Mme. de Nucingen.

"She has white eyelashes."

"Yes, but what a pretty slender figure she has."

"Her hands are big."

"But she has lovely eyes."

"Her face is too long."

"Still, that is distinguished."

163

"It is lucky for her that it is so. See how she keeps taking up her opera glasses and dropping them again. Every motion shows that she is a Goriot," the Viscountess said to Eugène's great surprise.

Mme. de Beauséant was observing the house through her glasses and appeared not to be paying the slightest attention to Mme. de Nucingen, yet she did not lose a single gesture. The house was very brilliant, and Delphine de Nucingen was not a little flattered to find that she occupied the exclusive attention of Mme. de Beauséant's young, handsome, and well-dressed cousin. He would look at no one but her.

"If you keep on staring at her in this way, you will make a scandal, Monsieur de Rastignac. You will never succeed if you throw yourself at people's heads like that."

"Dear cousin," Eugène said, "you have already done much for me; if you are willing to complete the work you have undertaken, I only ask you to do me a favor that will cost you very little trouble and will be of great service to me. I am in love."

"Already?"

"Yes."

"And with this woman?"

"Would my pretensions be listened to in another quarter?" he said with an expressive glance toward his cousin. "The Duchesse de Carigliano is a great friend of the Duchesse de Berri," he went on after a pause. "You will see her; have the kindness to introduce me to her and to take me to the ball she is to give on Monday. I shall meet Mme. de Nucingen there and shall begin my first skirmish."

"With pleasure," she said. "If you have already taken a fancy to her, your affairs of the heart are progressing finely. There is De Marsay in the box of the Princesse Galathionne. Mme. de Nucingen is on the rack and looks spiteful. There is no better moment for approaching a woman, especially when she is a banker's wife. The ladies of the Chaussée-d'Antin are all fond of their revenge."

"What would you do in a similar case?"

"I would suffer in silence."

Just then, the Marquis d'Ajuda presented himself in Mme. de Beauséant's box.

"I neglected my business to come to you," he said, "and I tell you of it so that it may not be a sacrifice."

The brightness of the Viscountess's face taught Eugène to discriminate between the expression of true love and the affectations of Parisian coquetry. He was filled with admiration for his cousin and, saying nothing further, yielded his place to M. d'Ajuda with a sigh.

What a grand, noble creature a woman is when she loves like this, he thought. And this man is willing to betray her for a mere doll! How could one betray her?

He felt overcome with childish rage and would have liked to prostrate himself at Mme. de Beauséant's feet. He longed for the power of demons to transport her into his heart, as an eagle seizes a white sucking kid and carries it to his nest. He was humiliated to find himself in the great Museum of Beauty without owning a picture there—without a mistress of his own.

A mistress gives a man a position that is almost royal, he thought. It is the sign of power!

He looked at Mme. de Nucingen as a man who has received an insult looks at his enemy. The Viscountess turned toward him with a glance that expressed her gratitude for his discretion. The first act was at an end.

"I think you know Mme. de Nucingen well enough to introduce M. de Rastignac to her?" she said to the Marquis d'Ajuda.

"She will be delighted to make his acquaintance," he said.

The handsome Portuguese rose and took the student's arm, and in the twinkling of an eye, Eugène found himself in Mme. de Nucingen's box.

"Baroness," began the Marquis, "I have the honor of introducing to you the Chevalier Eugène de Rastignac, who is a cousin of the Vicomtesse de Beauséant. You have made so strong an impression upon him that I was anxious to complete his happiness by leading him to his idol."

He spoke in a mocking tone that helped to pass off the brutal significance of his words; but a woman never takes a speech such as his amiss, provided it be correct in form. Mme. de Nucingen smiled and offered Eugène her husband's seat, as he had just left her.

"I do not venture to ask you to stay with me," she said. "When a man is so fortunate as to be in Mme. de Beauséant's company, he remains there."

"But it seems to me," Eugène said in a low voice, "that if I want to please my cousin, I had better stay with you. Before the arrival of the Marquis, we were talking of you and your distinguished appearance," he added aloud.

M. d'Ajuda beat a retreat.

"Are you really going to stay with me?" the Baroness said. "We can make each other's acquaintance then; and Mme. de Restaud has given me a very strong desire to see you."

"She cannot be in earnest, for she has closed her doors against me."

"What do you mean?"

"I am conscientious enough to tell you the whole story; but I crave your indulgence, if I confide such a secret to you. I live in the same house with your father, but I did not know that Mme. de Restaud was his daughter. I was imprudent enough to speak of him quite innocently and so displeased your sister and her husband. The Duchesse de Langeais and my cousin were shocked by the bad taste of such filial apostasy; I told them the whole story, and they laughed like mad people over it. Afterward Mme. de Beauséant drew a parallel between you and your sister and, speaking of you in the most flattering terms, told me how kind you were to my neighbor, M. Goriot. Indeed, how could you help being fond of him? He adores you so passionately that I feel jealous of him already. We talked about you this morning for two whole hours, and this evening, as I was dining with my cousin, I was so full of what your father had told me of you that I said to her you could not be as beautiful as you were affectionate. Mme. de Beauséant was anxious to gratify my fervent admiration and invited me to come with her tonight, telling me with her usual grace that I would be sure to see you here."

"Then," the banker's wife said, "I am already indebted to you. At this rate, we shall soon be old friends."

"Though there would be nothing commonplace in a friendship with you," Rastignac said, "I can never wish to be your friend."

These foolish stereotyped phrases that beginners are so fond of using are sure to charm a woman, and it is only when they are read in cold blood that their meagerness is apparent. The gestures, accent, and look of a young man give them an incalculable value. Mme. de Nucingen was delighted with Rastignac, and then, like the rest of her sex, as she could find nothing to say in answer to his rapid questions, she reverted to something else.

"Yes, my sister does herself harm by the way in which she treats our poor father, who has really been all goodness to us. It was not until M. de Nucingen absolutely commanded me not to receive my father in the morning that I gave up the point to him; and I was very unhappy about it for a long time. I shed many tears. These violences coming after the brutalities of the marriage have been one of the chief causes that disturbed my domestic life. It is certain that I am thought to be the happiest woman in Paris, but in reality I am the unhappiest. You will think me crazy for talking in this way to you, but you know my father, and on that ground you cannot be a stranger to me."

"You have never found anybody yet," Eugène said, "who felt such a lively desire to place himself at your disposal. What are all women in search of? Happiness," he resumed in a voice that pierced her soul. "Then, if a woman's happiness lies in being loved and adored, in having a friend to whom she can confide her wishes and fancies, her joys and pains, to whom she can unveil her soul and show herself with all her fine qualities and pretty faults without fear of betrayal, you may be sure that this loving, devoted, constant heart can belong only to a young man who has kept his illusions, who is ready to die at a gesture from you, who knows nothing of the world and scorns to know anything of it, because you have become all the world to him.

"You will laugh at my ingenuousness, but I have come fresh from the provinces and have known none but noble souls. I thought that I could do without love. It has fallen to my lot to see my cousin and to read the secrets of her heart. I have learned from her the countless treasures of passion; and like Cherubino, I am in love with all women until I can devote myself to a single one among them. When I came in tonight and saw you, I felt drawn toward you by a strong current. I had already thought much about you, but I never dreamed that you were so beautiful. Mme. de Beauséant ordered me not to stare at you so hard, but she does not know the delight of looking at your pretty red lips, your white skin, and soft eyes—I know I am talking wildly too, but let me go on."

A woman likes nothing better than to hear such sweet speeches; the most rigid saint listens to them, even when she cannot answer. After this beginning, Rastignac continued with what he had to say in a low coquettish voice, and Mme. de Nucingen smiled encouragingly, glancing from time to time toward De Marsay, who never left the box of the Princesse Galathionne. Rastignac stayed with Mme. de Nucingen until her husband came in to take her home.

"I hope to have the pleasure of seeing you before the Duchesse de Carigliano's ball," Eugène said.

"Zinze my vife infites you," said the Baron, a thickset Alsatian whose round face suggested a dangerous amount of cunning, "you are zure of peing vell rezeived."

My affairs are progressing favorably, for she was not very angry when I asked her if she could love me. I have put a bit in the mare's mouth, and now I have but to jump on her back and guide her, Eugène said to himself as he went to say good night to Mme. de Beauséant, who was preparing to leave with D'Ajuda.

The poor fellow was quite unaware that the Baroness had paid no attention to him and was expecting a delusive and agonizing letter from De Marsay. In an elated frame of mind over what he supposed to be his success, he accompanied his cousin as far as the peristyle, where the people were waiting for their carriages.

"Your cousin is quite another man now," the Portuguese said with a laugh to the Viscountess, after Eugène had gone. "He means to break the bank, and as he is as supple as an eel, he is likely to succeed. You alone were clever enough to select for him a woman who is just looking about for consolation."

"We must first find out," Mme. de Beauséant said, "whether she still loves the man who has deserted her."

4

THE student walked home from the Opéra to the rue Neuve-Ste-Geneviève with his head full of the most flattering projects. He had observed the attentive scrutiny bestowed upon him by Mme. de Restaud when he was in the Viscountess's box and also in that of Mme. de Nucingen, and he inferred that her doors would no longer be closed against him. He was confident of winning the favor of the Marshal's wife, so he expected shortly to acquire four important protectors in the very heart of fashionable Parisian society. Without thinking too much of ways and means, he could see beforehand that in the complicated play of the world's interests he must cling to a wheel in order to mount to the top of the machine, and he thought himself strong enough to put in a spoke.

If Mme. de Nucingen takes an interest in me, he thought, I will teach her how to manage her husband. Her husband is very successful in business and might help me to make my fortune quickly.

He did not say this out bluntly, for he was not as yet shrewd enough to appreciate a situation, to sum it up, and to make his calculations. His ideas were floating along the horizon like light clouds, yet, though less fierce than Vautrin's, if they had been passed through the crucible of conscience, they would not have come out immaculate. It is by a series of such processes that men reach the lax morality in vogue at the present time. To-day more rarely than ever before are to be seen those upright men of determined will who never bend to evil and who consider the slightest deviation from a straight path a crime; those splendid examples of virtue that have suggested two masterpieces, the Alceste of Molière, and Jeanie Deans and her father in the more recent work of Walter Scott. Perhaps a work of the opposite description that would show the crooked ways through which an ambitious man of the world drives his conscience, when he tries to skirt along the edge of evil and succeeds in saving appearances and compassing his ends, might be quite as fine and dramatic.

By the time Rastignac had reached the door of his boardinghouse, he was in love with Mme. de Nucingen, who had struck him as being as light and delicate as a bird. He recalled the bewitching softness of her eyes, the exquisite silken texture of her skin, under which he could almost see the blood flowing, the enchanting tones of her voice, and her blond hair; he recalled everything. Perhaps too his walk, which had set his blood in motion, aided the fascination she exerted over him. He knocked loudly at père Goriot's door.

"I have seen Madame Delphine," he cried.

"Where?"

"At the *Italiens*."

"Was she enjoying herself? Come in."

The old man, who had got up in his nightshirt, opened the door and then went quickly back to bed.

"Tell me all about her," he begged.

It was the first time that Eugène had entered père Goriot's room, and as he was fresh from seeing the marvels of his daughter's dress, he could not repress a movement of astonishment on finding what a hole the old man lived in. There were no curtains on the windows, and the wallpaper, which was becoming unglued from the wall by the dampness, had shriveled up, disclosing bare patches of plaster discolored with smoke. The old man was lying on a wretched bed, with no covering but one thin blanket and a padded quilt made out of the good bits of Mme. Vauquer's old gowns. The floor was damp and very dusty. Opposite the window stood an old rosewood bureau with a rounded front and copper handles twisted in the shape of vine branches decorated with leaves and flowers; and a shabby wooden-top washstand, on which were placed a basin and pitcher and shaving utensils. Père Goriot's shoes lay in one corner, and beside the bed there was a little night table that had lost its door and marble top. In the chimney corner, which bore no trace of a fire, stood the square walnut table, whose bar père Goriot had used in crushing his silver dish. A forlorn desk on which the old man's hat was lying, a cane-bottomed armchair, and two other chairs completed the miserable furniture of the room. The canopy of the bed, which was attached to the ceiling by a rag, supported a dirty strip of red and white checked cotton. The poorest messenger would have been better lodged in his garret than was père Goriot in the house of Mme. Vauquer. The chilling aspect of his room was heartbreaking to Eugène and reminded him of the saddest prison cell. Fortunately, Goriot could not see the expression that Eugène's countenance portrayed as he put down the candle on the table beside the bed. The old man turned toward him, muffled to his chin in the bedclothes.

"Which do you like best, Mme. de Restaud or Mme. de Nucingen?"

"I like Mme. Delphine best," Eugène replied, "because she is fonder of you."

On hearing these words, which were spoken with fervor, the old man stretched his arm out of bed to press Eugène's hand.

"Thank you, thank you, he cried with emotion. "What did she say of me?"

The student repeated the Baroness's words, taking care to embellish them, and the old man listened to what he had to say as if it were the word of God.

"Dear child!" he said. "Yes, of course she loves me; but you must not believe what she told you of Anastasie. The two sisters are jealous of each other, don't you see, and that is another proof of their affection for me. Mme. de Restaud is fond of me too, I know, for a father sees into his children's hearts and judges their intentions just as God does ours. One is quite as affectionate as the other. Oh! If I had had good sons-in-law I would have been too happy. It is impossible that happiness should be perfect here below. If I could have lived with them and have been allowed only to hear their voices, to know they were near me, and to see them going and coming, as it used to be when they were at home, how my heart would have rejoiced! Were they well dressed?"

"Yes," Eugène said, "but, Monsieur Goriot, how does it happen that you are in such a garret, while your daughters are living in luxury?"

"Dear me," he answered, trying to look indifferent, "why should I need anything better? I cannot explain it to you very well, for I cannot put two words together in a proper way. It is all there," he added, laying his hand on his heart. "My whole life lies with those two girls. If they enjoy themselves and are happy, if they are prettily dressed and walk on soft carpets, what does it matter to me how I am dressed or where I sleep? I am never cold if they are warm nor in bad spirits if they are gay. I have no griefs but theirs. When you are a father and listen to your children's prattle, you will feel that they are your own, bone of your bone and flesh of your flesh, and the best part too. You will be bound up in their existence, and their footsteps will stir your very heartstrings. I hear their voices everywhere, and a single sad look of theirs chills my blood. One day you will know what it is to care more for your children's happiness than your own. I cannot explain how it is; it is an inward instinct that spreads joy through your whole being.

"So I really live three lives. Shall I tell you something very strange? When I became a father, I understood the nature of God. He exists everywhere, since all creation proceeded from Him, and so it is with me and my daughters. Only, I love my daughters better than God loves the world, because the world is not as beautiful as God, and my daughters are more beautiful than I. They are so near to my soul that I was sure you would see them this evening. Good heavens! I would black boots and run errands for any man who made my little Delphine as happy as a woman can be when she is truly loved. I heard through her maid that little De Marsay is nothing but a cur, and I felt like wringing his neck. What? Not love a pearl of a woman with a voice like a nightingale and a figure like a statue? Where were her eyes when she married that great Alsatian blockhead? They ought both to have chosen attractive, amiable, young men, but after all, they followed their own inclinations."

There was something sublime about père Goriot. Eugène had never till now seen him aflame with love for his daughters. It is worthy of remark that true feeling acts like an inspiration. No matter how ordinary a man may be, whenever he gives expression to a real and strong affection, he is wrapped in an impalpable essence that alters his countenance, animates his gestures, and lends a new inflection to his voice. Under the stress of passion, the dullest being may reach the highest degree of eloquence of thought, if not of language, and seems to be transfigured. At this moment, the old man's voice and gestures possessed the communicative power that marks a great actor. Aren't our fine feelings the poetry of the will?

"You may not be sorry to learn that she will probably break with De Marsay," Eugène said. "The fellow has left her for the Princesse Galathionne, but I fell in love with Mme. Delphine myself this evening."

"Pooh!" père Goriot exclaimed.

"I did indeed, and she did not dislike me either. We talked of love for a full hour, and I am to go to see her on Saturday, the day after tomorrow."

"Oh, how fond I would be of you, my dear boy, if she cared for you. You are good and would be kind to her, but if you betrayed her, I would cut your throat without more ado. A woman can't love twice, you know. Heavens! I am talking nonsense to you, Monsieur Eugène, and it must be cold for you here. My God, did you really hear her speak, and what message did she send to me?"

Nothing, Eugène said to himself. Then he added aloud, "She sent you a daughter's affectionate kiss."

"Good night, my boy! Sleep well, and may you have pleasant dreams, for your words have assured them to me. May God grant all your desires! You have been a good angel to me this evening and have brought my daughter near to me."

Poor old man, Eugène thought as he was going to bed. It is enough to touch a heart of stone. His daughter thought no more of him than she did of the Grand Turk.

After this conversation, père Goriot looked upon Eugène as an unexpected friend and confidant. They became attached to each other by the only tie that could ever bind the old man to another. Passion never makes a false calculation, and père Goriot foresaw that he would be nearer to his daughter and better received by her if she cared for Eugène. Moreover, he had confided to the young man one of his sorrows, which was that Mme. de Nucingen, whose happiness he prayed for a thousand times a day, had never known the sweetness of love. To use his own expression, Eugène was one of the most agreeable young men he had ever seen, and he thought he could be sure that his daughter would find in him the happiness that she had till now been deprived of. So it was that the old man felt for the student an ever-growing friendship, without which it would have been impossible to obtain the facts concerning the close of this history.

Next morning, at breakfast, the persistence with which père Goriot looked at Eugène, beside whom he had placed himself, the few words he addressed to him, and the change in his face, which usually presented the appearance of a plaster cast, surprised the boarders. It was the first time Vautrin had seen the student since their talk together, and he was evidently anxious to read his soul. Before going to sleep on the previous evening, Eugène had measured the vast field that opened in front of him, and now on recollecting Vautrin's project, he could not help thinking of Mlle. Taillefer's dowry and regarding her in the light in which even the most virtuous young man may regard a rich heiress. By chance their eyes met, and the poor girl was quick to observe how charming Eugène looked in his new attire. The glance they exchanged was expressive enough to assure Eugène that he was the object of the vague desires that fill a young girl's heart and are directed toward the first attractive man she meets. He heard a voice crying, "Eight hundred thousand francs!" but he suddenly plunged back into his memories of the night before, and it occurred to him that his ready-made passion for Mme. de Nucingen would prove an antidote to the evil thoughts he had involuntarily entertained.

"They sang Rossini's *Barber of Seville* at the *Italiens* last night," he said. "I never heard such delightful music! Heavens, how lucky a man would be to have a box at the Opéra!"

Père Goriot snapped up his words as eagerly as a dog watching for a movement of his master.

"You men live in clover," Mme. Vauquer said. "You can do anything you please."

"How did you come home?" Vautrin asked.

"On foot," replied Eugène.

"If it were I," the tempter went on, "I would not like any such halfway pleasures. I would go in my carriage to my box at the Opéra and come back comfortably. Everything or nothing! That is my motto."

"And a good one too," Mme. Vauquer added.

"Perhaps you are going to see Mme. de Nucingen," Eugène whispered to Goriot. "She will be sure to receive you with open arms, for she will want you to tell her a thousand little details about me. I have learned that she would do anything in the world to be received at the house of my cousin, the Vicomtesse de Beauséant. Don't forget that I love her too much not to try to procure her this gratification."

Rastignac made haste to set out for the law school, as he wanted to stay as short a time as possible in a house that was odious to him. He lounged about almost all day, a victim to the brain fever that besets a young man who has allowed his hopes to soar too high. He recalled Vautrin's arguments and was reflecting on society in general when he met his friend Bianchon in the Luxembourg Gardens.

"What makes you look so serious?" asked the medical student, taking his arm to walk up and down in front of the palace with him.

"I am bothered by troublesome thoughts."

"Of what kind are they? You know that thoughts can be cured."

"How?"

"By yielding to them."

"You are laughing at me without knowing what I mean. Have you read Rousseau?"

"Yes."

"Do you remember the place where he asks the reader what he would do if he could become rich by killing an old mandarin in China by the sole act of his will, without stirring from Paris?"

"Yes."

"Well?"

"Pooh! I have already come to my thirty-third mandarin."

"Don't joke. Come, suppose you knew it were possible and that a nod from you would do it, would you consent?"

"Is he a very old mandarin? But young or old, sick or well, my goodness—hell! No, I wouldn't."

"You are a good fellow, Bianchon. But, suppose you loved a woman enough to turn yourself inside out for her and that you needed lots of money for her dress, her carriage, and all her caprices?"

"You want me to be sensible and you take my senses away!"

"I am crazy, Bianchon; try to cure me. I have two sisters, beautiful and good as angels. How can I get together two hundred thousand francs for their marriage dowries five years from now? You see there are circumstances in life when a man must play for high stakes and not lose his chance of luck by betting pennies."

"You are putting the question that everybody has to solve at the entrance of life, and you want to cut the Gordian knot with your sword. If you mean to do it, my dear fellow, you must be an Alexander, or else you will be sent to the galleys. I am quite contented with the little round of existence I shall create for myself in the country, where I expect to succeed my father in the dullest way imaginable. A man's affections may be as perfectly satisfied in a small circle as in a vast sphere. Napoléon himself could not dine more than once, nor could he have more mistresses than a medical student who is a pupil at the Capucins'. Our happiness, my dear fellow, will always be bounded by our head and our heels; and whether it costs a million a year or only a hundred louis, the intrinsic perception we have of it is the same. I conclude in favor of the Chinaman's life."

"Thank you, Bianchon, you have done me good. I shall aways be your friend."

"I want to tell you," Bianchon went on, "that just as I was coming out of the Cuvier lecture in the Jardin des Plantes, I caught sight of Michonneau and Poiret sitting on a bench, talking with a man I saw hanging about the Chamber of Deputies in the disturbances of last year and who impressed me as a policeman disguised as a well-to-do bourgeois. We had better study that couple, and I shall tell you why later. Now, good-bye, for I must go and answer the roll call at four o'clock."

On returning to his boardinghouse, Eugène found père Goriot waiting for him.

"There is a letter from her," the old man said. "See how pretty her handwriting is!"

Eugène broke the seal and read as follows:

Monsieur:

My father has told me that you are fond of the Italian music, and I would be delighted if you would do me the honor to accept a seat in my box. We shall have Fodor and Pellegrini on Saturday, and I am sure that you cannot refuse. M. de Nucingen joins his entreaties to mine that you will come and dine quietly with us. If you accept, you will make him very happy by relieving him of the conjugal duty of accompanying me. You need not answer, only come, and be assured of my kind regards,

D. de N.

"Show it to me," père Goriot said to Eugène, after he had finished reading the note. "You will go, won't you?" he added, putting the paper to his nose. "How sweet it smells! Her fingers have touched it."

No woman throws herself at a man's head like this the student thought. She wants to make a dupe of me to bring back De Marsay. She does this only out of spite.

"Well," père Goriot inquired, "what are you thinking of now?"

Eugène knew nothing of the delirious vanity that possessed certain women of the day, nor was he aware that a banker's wife would make any sacrifice to open a door in the faubourg St-Germain. It was at the time when fashion exalted above all others those women who belonged to the society of the faubourg St-Germain and were known as the ladies of the Petit Château; among them Mme. de Beauséant, her friend the Duchesse de Langeais, and the Duchesse de Maufrigneuse occupied the most distinguished place. Rastignac had not as yet learned the mad desire of the ladies of the Chaussée-d'Antin to enter that upper sphere where the constellations of their sex were conspicuously shining. But his mistrust stood him in good stead, for it gave him self-possession and the baneful power of imposing conditions instead of accepting them.

"Yes, I will go," he replied.

So it was his curiosity that drew him to Mme. de Nucingen, whereas, if she had disdained him, he might have been impelled toward her by passion. However, he waited with impatience for the appointed hour next day, as there is perhaps as much charm for a young man in his first intrigue as there is in his first love. The certainty of success calls into existence a thousand joys that men will not acknowledge but that sometimes are the entire charm of some women. Desire is born no less of difficult than of facile triumph. All human passions are excited and kept alive by one or the other of these two causes that share the empire of love. Perhaps the division is in consequence of the difference of temperaments, that great question that dominates society, no matter what may be said to the contrary. If a man of a melancholy disposition needs the tonic of coquetry, a man of a nervous or sanguine nature might beat a retreat on encountering too persistent a resistance. To use other words, the elegy is as essentially lymphatic as the dithyramb is choleric. As he dressed himself, Eugène enjoyed to the full those trifling pleasures that a young man dares not mention, for fear of being laughed at, but that are so flattering to his vanity. As he brushed his hair, he recollected that a pretty woman's eyes would stray over his dark curls. He allowed himself, in short, all the childish folly of a young girl preparing for a ball. He looked complacently at his slender figure as he smoothed down his coat.

"It might be worse, certainly," he thought.

He went downstairs, where his fellow boarders were already seated at table, and bore good-naturedly the burst of ridicule excited by his elegant appearance. It is a feature peculiar to boardinghouses that an elaborate costume causes universal astonishment. Nobody can put on a new garment without everybody else remarking upon it.

"Kt, kt, kt, kt!" Bianchon said, clicking his tongue against his palate as if he were urging on a horse.

"You are dressed like a duke and peer of the realm!" Mme. Vauquer exclaimed.

"You are armed for conquest," observed Mlle. Michonneau.

"Cock-a-doodle-do!" the painter cried.

"My compliments to your wife," the museum employee said.

"Has the gentleman a wife?" Poiret inquired.

"A wife with compartments, watertight, guaranteed not to fade, and costing from twenty-five to forty francs, with the fashionable checked pattern, warranted to wash, will wear forever, half wool and half cotton, cures toothache and the other diseases, patronized by the Royal Academy of Medicine! It is excellent, besides, for children, and still better for headaches, plethora, and other maladies of the eyes, ears, and throat!" Vautrin cried, with the comic volubility and accent of a quack. " 'How much does this treasure cost?' you ask me gentlemen. 'Two sous?' No, nothing at all. It is left over from the belongings of the Great Mogul, and all the sovereigns of Europe, not excepting the Grrrrrand Duke of Baden, have wanted to see it. Walk straight in, and step into the little office. Come, strike up the band! Boom, boom, tra-la-la, boom, boom! M. Clarinet, you are out of tune," he went on hoarsely. "I will rap you over the knuckles."

"Dear me, how amusing that man is," Mme. Vauquer said to Mme. Couture. "I would never be tired of him."

In the midst of the jests and laughter that greeted Vautrin's comic speech, Eugène was able to catch a furtive glance from Mlle. Taillefer, who was leaning over to whisper something in Mme. Couture's ear.

"There is the cab," Sylvie announced.

"Where is he going to dine?" Bianchon asked.

"At Baroness de Nucingen's."

"She is père Goriot's daughter," the student added.

At this, all eyes were fixed upon the old man, who was gazing at Eugène with something like envy.

5

RASTIGNAC drove to the rue de St-Lazare and stopped at the door of an airily built house, with slender columns and narrow portico, that would be put in the category of what is called *pretty* in Paris; a true banker's house, full of expensive elegance, stuccowork, and stairways of marble mosaic. He found Mme. de Nucingen in a little drawing room decorated with Italian frescoes that gave it the air of a coffeehouse. The Baroness was in low spirits, and the efforts she made to conceal her annoyance interested Eugène the more, as they were evidently genuine. He had expected that his presence would make her happy, yet he found her in despair; and the disappointment piqued his vanity.

"I have small claim to your confidence," he said, after playfully alluding to her preoccupation, "but if I am in the way, I rely upon your good faith to tell me so frankly."

"Stay," she said, "for I would be alone if you went. My husband is to dine out, and I don't want to be left by myself, for I need to be distracted."

"What is the matter with you?"

"You are the last person to whom I could tell that!" she cried.

"I must know. Perhaps your secret has something to do with me."

"Perhaps! No, indeed," she continued, "it is one of those family quarrels that should be buried at the bottom of one's heart. As I told you the day before yesterday, I am not happy. Chains of gold are the heaviest of all."

When a woman tells a young man that she is unhappy, and the young man is clever, well dressed, and has fifteen hundred francs pin money in his pocket, he is apt to become conceited and think just as Eugène did.

"What more can you wish?" he returned. "You are young, beautiful, rich, and beloved."

"I don't want to talk of myself," she said with a perverse turn of her head. "We are to dine alone together and then are going out to hear some delightful music. Am I to your taste?" she asked, getting up to show her gown, which was made of white cashmere covered with costly Persian embroidery.

"Would that you were all mine!" Eugène exclaimed. "You look charming."

"You would have a very wretched piece of property," she said, smiling bitterly. "There is nothing here to show you how miserable I am, and yet, in spite of appearances, I am in despair. My troubles keep me awake at night, and I shall lose my good looks."

"That would be impossible," the student said. "But I am curious to hear of a sorrow that devoted love cannot put to flight."

"Ah, if I confided in you, you would leave me," she

replied. "Your love for me is, as yet, only the kind of pastime habitual with men; if you really loved me, you would be in absolute despair. You see I had better say nothing further. For heaven's sake, let us talk of something else. Come and let me show you my rooms."

"No, let us stay here," Eugène answered, sitting down on a sofa before the fire beside Mme. de Nucingen, whose hand he boldly took.

She let him keep it and even pressed it upon his with a concentrated energy that betrayed strong emotion.

"Listen to me," Eugène began. "If you are in trouble, you ought to take me into your confidence. I want to prove to you that I love you for your own sake. Either you must speak and tell me your worries, so that I may help you out of them, even at the cost of killing six men, or I shall go away and never come back."

"Then I shall put you to the test at once," she cried, striking her forehead in despair, as some sudden thought crossed her mind. Yes, she added to herself, there is no way left me but this.

She rang the bell.

"Is the Baron's carriage ready?" she asked of the servant.

"Yes, madame."

"I shall take it then, and you can give him my carriage and horses. Don't serve dinner till seven o'clock."

"Come, hurry," she continued, speaking to Eugène, who thought he must be dreaming when he found himself by her side in M. de Nucingen's coupé.

"Take us to the Palais Royal, near the Théatre Français," she said to the coachman.

During the drive, she appeared agitated and refused to answer the thousand questions showered upon her by Eugène, who did not know what to make of the firm, mute resistance he encountered.

She will escape me in a moment, he thought.

He almost lost his self-control, but as the carriage stopped, the Baroness looked at him in a way to silence his mad words.

"Do you really love me?" she asked.

"Yes," he answered, trying to hide his anxiety.

"You will think no harm of me, no matter what I ask of you?"

"No."

"Will you obey me?"

"Blindly."

"Have you ever gambled?" she inquired in a shaking voice.

"Never."

"Now, I breathe again. You will be lucky. There is my purse," she said. "Take it; it contains a hundred francs—all that I, who am such a happy woman, own. Find your way to a gambling house; there are plenty of them in the Palais Royal, though I do not know exactly where. Risk my hundred francs at a game called roulette, and lose them all or bring me back six thousand francs. I shall tell you my troubles on your return."

"The devil take me if I understand what you want me to do. Still, I will obey you," he said, and his heart thrilled as he thought, she will compromise herself with me, and then she can refuse me nothing.

He took the pretty purse, and after inquiring of a shop-keeper the way to the nearest gambling house, he turned in at Number 9. He ran upstairs, gave his hat to an attendant, then entered the room and asked where the roulette was. A servant led him in front of a long table, and to the surprise of the spectators who watched him closely, he inquired without embarrassment where he should place his stakes.

"If you put a louis on one of these thirty-six numbers and the number turns up you will have thirty-six louis," answered a respectable-looking old man with white hair.

Eugène deposited his hundred francs on the number of his age, twenty-one. A cry of astonishment was heard before he was aware of what had happened. He had won without knowing it.

"Take up your money," the old gentleman said. "You can't win twice on the same number."

Eugène took a rake that the old man handed him, drew in three thousand six hundred francs, and still in ignorance of the game, placed them on the red. The onlookers watched him enviously when they found he was going to play again. The wheel turned; he had won a second time, and the banker pushed him another three thousand, six hundred francs.

"You have now seven thousand two hundred francs," the old gentleman whispered in his ear. "If you follow my advice, you will take your leave, for the red was turned up eight times running. If you are charitably inclined, you will show your gratitude for this good counsel by relieving the needs of one of Napoléon's old prefects who is in great distress."

Rastignac, who was in a bewildered state of mind, allowed the old man with white hair to take ten louis from him and ran downstairs with his seven thousand francs, still understanding nothing about the game but stupefied by his good luck.

"Where are you going to take me next?" he said as he showed the seven thousand francs to Mme. de Nucingen after shutting the carriage door behind him.

Delphine folded him in a wild embrace and kissed him warmly, though without passion.

"You have saved me," she cried, as the tears of joy rained down her cheeks.

"I am going to tell you everything, my friend, for you will be my friend, won't you? As you see me, I am rich and prosperous and have everything I wish, or at least it appears so. You may as well know that M. de Nucingen will not allow me a penny of my own: he pays for the expenses of the house, of course, and for my carriages and boxes, but he gives me an entirely insufficient sum for my dress and keeps me in secret poverty, by the malice of forethought. I am too proud to entreat him, and wouldn't I be the lowest of all creatures if I bought his money at the price at which he is willing to sell it? I owned seven hundred thousand francs, and how is it that I allowed him to plunder me? Because of my pride and indignation. We girls are so young and innocent when we begin our married life! I could not bring myself to pronounce the words that were to ask my husband for money; I dared not. I used up my own savings and all that my poor father could give me; then I fell into debt. I was horribly deceived in my marriage, but I cannot speak of it to you; it is enough for you to know that I would rather jump out of the window than live with Nucingen on terms other than our each having separate apartments.

"When I was obliged to tell him of my foolish debts for jewels and such trinkets—for you know our poor father brought us up in luxury—I suffered martyrdom, but I had courage to tell him in the end. Didn't I have a fortune of my own? Nucingen flew into a passion and told me that I would ruin him, and other insulting things. I wished to be a hundred feet below the earth. As he had taken my dowry, he paid my debts, but he stipulated that I should afterward keep my personal expenses within a fixed sum, and I resigned myself for the sake of peace.

"Since then," she went on, "I have been foolish enough to minister to the vanity of someone whom you know. Though he has deceived me, it would be wrong for me to do injustice to the nobleness of his character. Still, it was shameful of him to desert me, for a man should never desert a woman to whom he has tossed a handful of gold in her hour of need. You dear, young, pure soul of twenty-one, you can't understand how a woman can take money from a man. Yet, heavens! Isn't it natural to share everything with the person to whom we owe our happiness? When everything has been given, who could mind a little more or less? Nobody thinks anything of money until love is dead. Aren't lovers bound for life? Who foresees a separation when he believes himself truly loved? You swear to us that your love is eternal; how, then, can our interests be distinct?

"You cannot imagine how much I suffered today when Nucingen refused to give me six thousand francs, and I know he squanders as much as that every month on his mistress, who is an opera dancer. I wanted to kill myself, and the maddest thoughts passed through my head. There were moments when I could have envied the lot of a servant, even that of my own maid. Could I ask help of my father? Impossible! Anastasie and I have drained him of everything. My poor father would have sold himself for six thousand francs if he could. I would have tortured him for nothing. I was mad with grief, but you have saved me from shame and death.

"I owed you this explanation, for I had behaved very unreasonably toward you. When you left me and I lost sight of you, I wanted to escape on foot, but where could I go? I don't know. This is the life of half the women of Paris; an outward show of luxury, and a heart full of cares. I know some poor creatures who are still more wretched than I. Some women are obliged to get false bills made out by their shopkeepers, and others are forced into robbing their husbands and making them believe that a cashmere shawl worth a hundred louis was sold for five hundred francs, or, if it cost five hundred francs, that it was sold for a hundred louis. There are even some poor women who starve their children and stoop to dishonest means in order to get a new gown. I am innocent of such odious deceptions. Listen to the worst of all. Some women sell themselves to their husbands in order to rule them, but I, at least, am free! I could make Nucingen cover me with gold, but I would rather suffer with my head resting on the heart of a man whom I can esteem. Ah! This evening, M. de Marsay will have no right to look at me as a woman whom he has paid."

She attempted to hide her tears from Eugène and dropped her face in her hands, but he drew them away, so that he might look at her, for her emotion made her beautiful.

"Isn't it horrible to mingle money with one's affections? You can't love me now," she said.

This mixture of good feeling that makes a woman great and the faults that the actual state of society obliges her to commit distracted Eugène; he admired this lovely woman, so artlessly indiscreet in her expressions of grief, and poured out a flood of sweet and soothing words.

"You won't use this as an arm against me," she said. "Promise me that you will not."

"Ah, I am incapable of such baseness," he exclaimed.

She took his hand, and in a charming impulse of gratitude, held it against her heart.

"Thanks to you," she said, "I am free and happy once more. I have been in the grasp of an iron hand. Now I wish to live simply and spend as little as possible. You will always like me, no matter how I am dressed, won't you? Keep this," she continued, taking only six of the banknotes from him. I really owe you three thousand francs, for I consider myself in partnership with you."

Eugène resisted manfully, but when the Baroness said that she would regard him as her enemy if he were not her accomplice, he accepted the money.

"It will be something put away against an evil day," he said.

"That is just what I was afraid of," she cried, turning pale. "If you wish me to be anything to you, swear to me that you will never gamble again. Good heavens! What if I would corrupt your morals? I would die of grief."

They stopped at her door. The contrast of such wealth and such poverty made Eugène giddy, and some of Vautrin's sinister words returned to echo in his ears.

"Sit down there," the Baroness said, as they entered the room, pointing to a sofa beside the fire. "I have a very difficult letter to write! Advise me."

"Don't write," Eugène said. "Put the banknotes in an envelope, address it, and send it to him by your maid."

"You are a perfectly delightful creature," she said. "That comes from your having been well brought up. You are a real De Beauséant," she added, smiling.

She is charming, thought Eugène, who was falling deeper and deeper in love.

He let his eyes wander over the room that was furnished with voluptuous elegance, like that of a rich courtesan.

"Now, have I pleased you?" she asked, ringing for her maid.

"Thérèse," she said, "take that yourself to M. de Marsay, and give it up only into his hands. If you don't find him at home, bring me back the letter."

Thérèse left the room, after darting a knowing look at Eugène. When dinner was announced, Rastignac offered his arm to Mme. de Nucingen, who led the way into a handsome dining room, where he found the same luxury in the appointments of the table that had delighted him at his cousin's.

"Whenever the Italian opera is sung," she said, "you must come and dine with me and be my escort in the evening."

"I would dearly like such a pleasant existence," he said, "if it could last, but I am only a poor student who has his fortune to make."

"It will be made for you," she answered with a laugh. "You see, things arrange themselves: I never expected to be so happy."

It is in a woman's nature to attempt to prove the impossible by the possible and to make presentiments take the place of facts. When Mme. de Nucingen and Rastignac entered her box at the Opéra Bouffons, she looked so pleased and handsome that her friends indulged in the petty calumnies against which a woman is defenseless, and which, though absolutely without foundation, are but too apt to influence public opinion. When a man knows Paris well, he believes nothing he hears and says nothing of what he sees. Eugène held the hand of the Baroness, and both, under the influence of an emotion more or less genuine, exchanged impressions on the sensations they received from the music. They passed an intoxicating evening, and when they went out together, Mme. de Nucingen insisted on taking Eugène in her carriage as far as the Pont Neuf, although she refused him a single one of those kisses she had so prodigally lavished upon him at the Palais Royal. Eugène reproached her for her inconsistency.

"That," she replied, "was the expression of my gratitude for your unexpected devotion, but now it would be a promise."

"And you are so ungrateful as not to be willing to make me one?" He was angry. With one of those impatient gestures that enraptures a lover, she gave him her hand to kiss, and he took it with a bad grace that delighted her.

"I shall see you at the ball on Monday," she said.

As Eugène walked home in the bright moonlight, he fell into a serious reverie. He was at once pleased and displeased: pleased with an adventure that would probably end by giving him possession of the object of his desires, one of the prettiest and best-dressed women in Paris, and displeased to find all his projects for the future impracticable. It was then that he understood the reality of those vague thoughts that had floated through his mind the night before, for failure invariably strengthens the sense of imaginary right. The deeper Eugène dipped into Parisian life, the less willing he was to remain poor and obscure. He fingered the thousand-franc banknote in his pocket and concocted a thousand plausible reasons for appropriating it. He finally reached the house in the rue Neuve-Ste-Geneviève, and as he went upstairs, he saw a light. Père Goriot had left his door open and his candle lighted, so that the student would not forget to come in and tell him about his daughter. Eugène concealed nothing from him.

"Then they think I am ruined," père Goriot cried in an agony of jealousy and despair, "but I have still thirteen hundred francs a year! Good God! Poor little girl, why didn't she come to me? I would have sold my stock; we could have used part of the capital, and I would have bought an annuity with the rest. Why didn't you come and tell me of her trouble, my boy? How could you have the heart to venture her poor little sum of a hundred francs? It's heartrending! This is what it means to have sons-in-law! If I had them here, I would wring their necks! Oh, God! Did she really cry?"

"Yes, with her head on my waistcoat," Eugène said.

"Oh, give it to me," père Goriot exclaimed. "Was it really wet with tears of my daughter, my dear Delphine, who never used to cry when she was little? I will buy you another, but don't wear that anymore; leave it to me. According to the marriage contract, she ought to have her own property. Tomorrow I am going to look up Derville, a lawyer, and I shall insist upon her fortune being invested for her. I know the law, and an old dog like me will find his teeth again."

"Look, here are a thousand francs she wanted to give me out of our winnings. Keep them for her in the waistcoat pocket."

Goriot gazed at Eugène and stretched out to take his hand, on which he dropped a tear.

"You will succeed in life," the old man said, "for God is just. You see I know something about honesty, and I can assure you that there are few men like you. Do you want me to love you too like a child of mine? Now, go to bed; you can sleep, for you are not yet a father. She cried, did she? And I must learn it now, I who was eating my dinner in peace like a blockhead while she was in trouble; I who would sell the Father, Son, and Holy Ghost to spare either of them a single tear!"

On my word, Eugène said to himself as he went to

bed, I think I shall be a good man all my life. There is some pleasure in following the dictates of conscience.

Perhaps only those who believe in God do good in secret, and Eugène believed in God.

6

NEXT day at the hour appointed for the ball, Rastignac went to Mme. de Beauséant's, who took him to introduce him to the Duchesse de Carigliano. He was most graciously received by the Marshal's wife and soon met with Mme. de Nucingen. Delphine had dressed herself to please everybody so that she might the better please Eugène, and she was eagerly awaiting the moment when she would catch his eye, though she believed that she was concealing her impatience. It was a blissful moment for a man who could read a woman's emotions. Who has not often taken pleasure in delaying the expression of his opinion, in fancifully disguising his approbation, or in eliciting a confession by the anxiety he causes? And who has not exulted in those fears that he knew a smile of his could dissipate? As the ball went on, it occurred to the student to take the measure of his position, and he saw that he had a place in the world as the acknowledged cousin of Mme. de Beauséant. The conquest of Mme. de Nucingen too, which was already attributed to him, brought him into such prominence that all the young men looked at him with envious eyes, and as he surprised the glances of some among them, he enjoyed the first fruits of vanity. As he walked from one room to another and passed through various groups of people, he heard them discussing his good luck; all the women foretold his success. Delphine was afraid of losing him and promised to give him that evening the kiss that she had so harshly refused the night before. During the ball, Rastignac received several invitations. His cousin presented him to several ladies of aristocratic pretensions, whose houses were said to be agreeable, and he found himself launched on the great world of fashionable Parisian society. This delightful evening made a brilliant beginning for him, and he was destined to remember it all his life, as a girl remembers the ball that was the scene of her triumphs.

At breakfast next morning, as he was talking about his success to père Goriot before the other boarders, Vautrin began to smile in a most diabolical manner.

"And so you think, do you," the fierce logician cried, "that a young man of fashion can live in the rue Neuve-Ste-Geneviève at the Vauquer establishment, in all ways a most respectable boardinghouse, no doubt, but anything rather than fashionable? It is substantial, the food is abundant, and it is proud of having been the transient abode of a Rastignac; but still it is in the rue Neuve-Ste-Geneviève and is blameless of luxury because it is purely *patriarchalorama.*

"My young friend," Vautrin went on, continuing to jest in a fatherly manner, "if you want to cut a figure in Paris, you must have three horses and a tilbury in the morning and a coupé in the evening; nine thousand francs in all for your carriages. You would be unworthy of your destiny if you spent less than three thousand francs at the tailor's, six hundred francs at the barber's, three hundred francs at the bootmaker's, and three hundred francs at the hatter's. Your laundry will cost you a thousand francs a year. Young men of fashion are obliged to be extremely particular about their linen, for it is more noticed than anything else. Love and the church require immaculate altar cloths. That makes fourteen thousand francs, and I don't mention what you will lose in gambling, betting, and giving presents, but you certainly need two thousand francs for pin money. I have led the kind of life, and I know the outlay. Add to these necessary expenses three hundred louis for your food and a thousand francs for your roost. Come, my boy, you must have twenty-five thousand a year in your pocket or you will stick in the mud, a laughingstock, shorn of your future, your success, and your mistresses! I have forgotten your valet and your groom. Can Christophe carry your love letters? And can you write them on the paper you are in the habit of using? That would be suicidal. Believe an old man of experience," he added in a louder tone of his base voice. "Either take yourself off to a virtuous attic with work as your spouse, or else choose another career."

Vautrin winked and leered in the direction of Mlle.

Taillefer in a way that recalled and recapitulated the be-
guiling arguments with which he had tried to corrupt the
student's heart. For some days after this, Rastignac led
the most dissipated kind of life. He dined almost daily
with Mme. de Nucingen and then went with her into
society. He came home at three or four in the morning,
rose and dressed at noon, and drove in the Bois with
Delphine when the weather was fine, wasting his time
without a notion of its value. He panted for the education of luxury and its fascinations with the impatient
ardor of the calyx of the female date, waiting for the
fertilizing pollen of its hymen. He played high, losing
and gaining great sums, and gradually accustomed himself to the extravagant life of the young men of Paris.
He had returned the fifteen hundred francs to his mother
and sisters out of his first winnings and had sent them
pretty gifts at the same time. Although he had already
announced his intention of leaving the Vauquer boardinghouse, he was still there at the end of January and did
not know how to leave.

Almost all young people are subject to a law apparently inexplicable, but whose cause is in their own youth
and in their mad onslaught upon pleasure. Whether rich
or poor, they never have enough money for the necessi-
ties of life, though they can always find enough to gratify
their caprices. They are lavish when they can succeed in
obtaining credit, but parsimonious about everything that
calls for cash, and they seem to make amends for what
they do not have by squandering whatever is within their
reach. To put it briefly, a student will take much better

care of his hat than of his coat. A tailor's large gains put him necessarily in the position of a creditor, whereas a hatter's modest profits make him one of the most stubborn shopkeepers toward those with whom he is forced to come to terms. If the young man who is sitting in the balcony at the theater presents a gorgeous waistcoat to the view of a pretty woman's opera glasses, it is doubtful whether he has a pair of socks; the hosier is peremptory in his demands for ready money.

So it was with Rastignac. His purse, which was always empty for Mme. Vauquer and always full for the requirements of his own vanity, had ill-regulated setbacks and successes that never allowed him to discharge his most natural debts. In order to leave the ignoble and foul-smelling boardinghouse where his pride suffered periodical humiliation, he would have been obliged to pay his hostess for a month in advance and buy furniture for a bachelor apartment. This was always impossible for him to accomplish. Though Rastignac knew how to raise money for gambling by purchasing gold watches and chains from his jeweler, dearly paid for out of his hoard of winnings, and then carrying them to the Mont-de-Piété, that somber and discreet friend of youth, he was without ingenuity or daring when it came to paying for his board and lodging or buying the tools that were indispensable in his profession of a man of fashion. He could not find his inspiration in vulgar necessity or in debts contracted for needs that had long been satisfied. Like most of those who live this happy-go-lucky life, he waited till the last moment before settling accounts that would have been sacred in the eyes of a bourgeois, just as Mirabeau never paid for his living except when it appeared under the compelling power of a bill of exchange.

Toward this time, Rastignac had spent his money and fallen into debt, and he began to understand that it would be impossible for him to continue his manner of existence without fixed resources. Still, though he kicked against the pricks of his precarious situation, he knew he was incapable of renouncing the great enjoyment of the life he was leading, and he determined to continue it at any price. The chances on which he had relied for making his fortune were growing chimerical, while the real obstacles in his way were increasing. On his initiation into the domestic secrets of M. and Mme. de Nucingen, he had learned that to turn his love into a money-making machine, a man must have sunk deep in shame and be willing to renounce the noble ideas that alone absolve the faults of youth. He had vowed himself to a life that was outwardly brilliant but inwardly consumed by secret remorse, a life whose fleeting pleasures were doomed to be dearly expiated by lasting anguish. He had plunged into it and, like the Absentminded Man of La Bruyère, had made his bed in the slime of the ditch, though, like him, he had as yet only contaminated his outermost garment.

PART FOUR

Shadows of Intrigue

 1

"HAVE you killed your mandarin?" Bianchon asked Rastignac one day, as they were getting up from the table.

"Not yet," he answered, "but he is at the death agony."

The medical student took this as a joke, and yet it was not. It was the first dinner Eugène had taken at the boardinghouse for some time, and he had been absorbed in thought during the course of the meal. Instead of going out at dessert, he remained in the dining room beside Mlle. Taillefer, toward whom he cast expressive glances from time to time. There were still a few boarders at the table eating nuts, and some of the others were walking up and down, finishing the discussions they were engaged in. As usual, they dropped off one by one, as each liked, according to the degree of interest he took in the conversation, or the relative excellence of his digestion. In winter, it was rare for the dining room to be entirely empty before eight o'clock, the hour when the four women were left together to take their revenge for the silence that the presence of so many men had imposed upon their sex.

Vautrin was struck by Eugène's preoccupation and remained in the dining room, although he had at first shown a disposition to leave it, keeping himself in the background in order to make Eugène think that he had gone. Then, instead of going off with the last of the boarders, he slyly stationed himself in the parlor. He had read the student's mind and foreseen a crisis.

It was true that Rastignac was involved in a perplexity known to many other young men of his kind, for whether Mme. de Nucingen loved him or was merely flirting with him, she had certainly made him suffer all the tortures of a genuine passion, bringing to bear against him the resources of a Parisian woman's diplomacy. After having compromised herself in the eyes of the world in order to obtain a firm hold of Mme. de Beauséant's cousin, she hesitated about actually giving him the rights that he was supposed to possess.

During the last month, she had so thoroughly inflamed his senses that she had succeeded in taking his heart by storm. Though in the early days of their acquaintance Rastignac had thought himself her master, Mme. de Nucingen had since become the stronger by dint of a maneuver that had set working in Eugène's heart all the good and evil sentiments of the three or four personalities existing in one young Parisian. Wasn't she therefore a calculator? No, for a woman is always true, even where she is most false, as she invariably yields to some natural impulse. It may be that when Delphine discovered the too-great power she had allowed this young man to gain over her and the too-great affection she had shown him, she was obeying some feeling of her own dignity that made her recall her concessions or amuse herself by holding them in suspense. It is so natural for a Parisian woman, even under the sway of passion, to waver in her fall and to try the heart of the man to whom she means to entrust the keeping of her future! All Mme. de Nucingen's early hopes had been betrayed, and the young egotist whom she had loved had scorned her devotion; it was with good reason that she was mistrustful. Eugène's quick success had made him conceited, and perhaps she observed in his manners toward her a mark of disrespect that was owing to the strangeness of their position. She was, no doubt, anxious to make an imposing impression on a young fellow of his age and to appear a great personage to him, after having so long played a small part in the eyes of the man who had deserted her. She could not bear to have Eugène think her an easy conquest, especially as he knew she had once belonged to De Marsay.

In short, after having submitted to the degrading yoke of that intolerable creature, a young libertine, she found so much pleasure in straying through the flowery paths of love that she lingered gladly to study all its charms, to feel its thrills, and to suffer herself to be caressed by its chaste breezes. True love was atoning for the sins of a false passion, and this mistake will frequently occur until men understand how many flowers are ruthlessly mowed down in a woman's soul by the first strokes of deception. Whatever her reasons, Delphine played with Rastignac and enjoyed playing with him, perhaps because she was sure that he loved her and that she had power to end her lover's woes if such were her royal pleasure.

For his own self-respect, Eugène was determined that his first combat would not end in defeat and persisted in his pursuit as a hunter is bent on killing his partridge the first time he shoots at the festival of Saint Hubert. His anxieties, his injured vanity, and his despair, whether true or fancied, bound him closer and closer to this woman, but although all Paris believed Mme. de Nucingen to be his, he had not advanced a step nearer her since the first day he had seen her. He was sometimes overcome with a blind rage, for he had not as yet learned that a woman's coquetry is sometimes more profitable than her love is pleasurable. The time of Delphine's hesitation allowed Rastignac to enjoy the first fruits of love, which, though delicious to the taste, were yet costly, half-ripe and bittersweet.

Sometimes when he saw himself penniless and without a future, in spite of the voice of conscience his thoughts would revert to the possible chances of fortune that Vautrin had pointed out to him in a marriage with Mlle. Taillefer. Now his needs were so peremptory that he yielded almost involuntarily to the artifices of the terrible sphinx whose eyes had so often fascinated him. When Poiret and Mlle. Michonneau went upstairs, Rastignac, believing himself to have no witnesses but Mme. Vauquer and Mme. Couture, who was knitting woolen wristlets and dozing beside the fire, turned to Mlle. Taillefer with a tender glance, under which her own fell.

"Are you in trouble, Monsieur Eugène?" Victorine asked after a moment's silence.

"Who is not in trouble?" Eugène answered. "Still, if we men could feel sure of being loved with devotion that would compensate us for the sacrifices we are always ready to make, perhaps we would never be in trouble."

Instead of answering him, Mlle. Taillefer gave him a look that was not in the least equivocal.

"You think yourself sure of your heart today, mademoiselle, but can you be sure of never changing?"

A smile that seemed to flash from her soul played over the poor girl's lips and illuminated her face so brightly that Eugène was alarmed at having provoked such a violent burst of feeling.

"Do you mean," he said, "that if you were rich and prosperous tomorrow, and a great fortune came to you unexpectedly, you would still love the poor young man whom you cared for in your adversity?"

She nodded prettily.

"Even if the young man is very unfortunate?"

She nodded again.

"What nonsense are you talking?" Mme. Vauquer cried.

"Leave us alone," Eugène said. "We understand each other."

"So there is an engagement between the Chevalier Eugène de Rastignac and Mlle. Taillefer?" Vautrin demanded in loud tones, as he suddenly appeared at the dining room door.

"How you frightened me!" Mme. Couture and Mme. Vauquer exclaimed in concert.

"I might have made a worse choice," Eugène said with

a laugh. Vautrin's voice had caused him the most disagreeable shock he had ever known.

"No more of these poor jokes, gentlemen!" Mme. Couture said. "Come upstairs with me, my dear."

Mme. Vauquer followed her two boarders for the purpose of economizing in fire and lights by spending the evening with them. Eugène found himself alone with Vautrin.

"I knew that you would come to it," Vautrin said, with his usual imperturbable coolness. "But listen to me, for I am delicate minded in my own way too. Don't decide at once, for you are not in your ordinary state of mind. You are in debt, and I want you to come to me out of pure reason and not out of passion or despair. Perhaps you need three thousand francs. Here they are, will you have them?"

The demon took a wallet from his pocket, and drawing out three banknotes, shook them in front of the student's eyes. Eugène was in a very difficult position. He owed debts of honor that amounted to a hundred louis to the Marquis d'Ajuda and the Comte de Trailles. He did not have the money and dared not go to spend the evening at Mme. de Restaud's, where he was expected. It was to be one of those informal gatherings where people drink tea and eat cake and run the risk of losing six thousand francs at whist.

"Monsieur," Eugène began, making an effort to control the convulsive trembling that took hold of him, "after what you have said to me, you must understand that it is impossible for me to place myself under an obligation to you."

"You would have pained me if you had answered in any other way," the tempter returned. "You are a handsome fellow of refined sensibilities, bold as a lion, and gentle as a young girl. You are a fit prey for the devil. I like young men of your stamp, and if you make a few more reflections, you will see the world as it really is. By playing a virtuous little comedy or two, a wise man may satisfy everybody's taste and receive loud applause from the fools who are looking on. Before many days are over, you will be one of us. Ah, if you would only consent to be my pupil, I would make you succeed in everything. Every wish you could frame would be instantly fulfilled, whether it were for honor, fortune, or woman. All civilization would be tinctured with ambrosia for your benefit. You would be our spoiled child, our Benjamin, and we would all gladly die for you. Every obstacle would be removed from your path. If you still have scruples, you take me then for a rascal? But let me tell you that a man who was quite as honest as you think yourself, M. de Turenne, condescended to a few trifling dealings with criminals without considering himself compromised in the least.

"You don't want to put yourself under obligation to me? You needn't mind that," continued Vautrin, who could not repress a smile. "Take this bit of paper," he said, producing a stamp for it, "and write across it: *Accepted for the sum of three thousand five hundred francs, payable in a year.* Then add the date. The interest is heavy enough to relieve you from your scruples, and you may call me a Jew, if you choose, and consider that you owe me no gratitude. I don't mind your despising me now, for I know that you will think a great deal of me later. You will find in me some of those yawning voids and great concentrated feelings that fools call vices; but you will never find me cowardly or ungrateful. I am neither a pawn nor a bishop, my dear fellow but, a castle."

"What kind of a man are you, at any rate?" Eugène cried. "You seem to be created for the express purpose of tormenting me."

"No, I am only an inoffensive person who is willing to bespatter himself so that you may walk immaculate for the rest of your days. I suppose you wonder at my devotion to you; and someday I will whisper to you the reason for it. I surprised you the other day when I showed you the springs of society and the working of the machine; but you will forget your alarm as quickly as a draftee on the field of battle forgets his, and you will accustom yourself to consider men as soldiers who are resolved to perish in the cause of their self-consecrated kings. Times have changed; once a man could say to an assassin, 'There are a hundred crowns; go and kill so and so for me,' and could dine with perfect ease after murdering a man for a trifle. Today, I propose to give you a large fortune in exchange for a little nod of assent that will in no way compromise you, and yet you hesitate. The age is effeminate."

Eugène signed the draft and gave it in return for the banknotes.

"Now, come, let us talk sense," Vautrin went on. "I want to go and plant tobacco in America a few months from now. I will send you some cigars from there in token of my goodwill. If I become rich, I will aid you. If I have no children, and it is likely, for I don't care about planting any little slips of myself, I will leave you my fortune. Isn't that a proof of my friendship? But I tell you I am fond of you. I have a passion for devoting myself to another. I have done it before now. Do you see, my boy, I live in a higher sphere than most people. I regard actions as a means to accomplishment and look only to the end. What is a man to me? No more than that," he said, clicking his fingernail against one of his front teeth.

"A man is all or nothing. He is less than nothing when his name is Poiret: you stamp on him as on a bedbug, and he flattens out and is foul smelling. But a man is a god when he is like you: he is no longer a machine covered with a skin, but a theater where the noblest feelings are brought into play, and I only live through my feelings. Aren't a man's feelings the whole world to him? Look at père Goriot: he has no thought in the universe but his two daughters; they are the thread by which he guides himself through creation.

"I have studied the whole of life and know there can be only one genuine feeling for me—that of friendship for another man. My passion is the same as that of Pierre and Jaffier, and I know *Venice Preserved* by heart. Have you seen many men who were so staunch that, when a comrade asked them to help in burying a corpse, they would lend a hand without saying a word or bothering about conscientious scruples? I have done that, myself.

I would not talk so to everybody, but you are a man of intelligence, and I can tell you everything because you can understand it. You can't paddle long in a swamp full of little reptiles like those you are living among here. Now, I have said my say. You are sure to marry; so let us each carry our points! Mine is iron and won't give way! Ha-ha!"

Vautrin went away without waiting to hear a refusal from the student, as he was anxious to put him at his ease. It was evident that he understood the secret of the faint resistance and half-hearted struggles with which men strive to cheat their consciences and justify their guilty deeds to themselves.

I shall never marry Mlle. Taillefer, no matter what he does! Eugène thought.

After a period of inward torture at the consciousness of having entered into a compact with a man who inspired him with horror and yet who had become magnified in his eyes by the cynicism of his ideas and the bold grasp he had of society, Rastignac dressed, called a cab, and drove to the house of Mme. de Restaud. For some days past, that lady had redoubled her attentions toward him, as she saw what rapid strides he was making in the great world and believed that his influence would one day be of value. He paid his debts to M. de Trailles and M. d'Ajuda and played whist part of the night, regaining all that he had lost. As he was superstitious, like most men who have their own way to make in the world and are more or less inclined toward fatalism, he persisted in regarding his good luck as a reward from Heaven for his perseverance in keeping to the right path. Next morning he made haste to ask Vautrin whether he still had his bill of exchange, and on receiving an affirmative answer, he returned the three thousand francs with a frank show of pleasure.

"That is right," Vautrin said.

"I am not your accomplice," Eugène said.

"I know, I know," Vautrin answered, interrupting him. "You are still behaving like a child who stops to watch the antics of a buffoon instead of going in to see the show."

TWO days later, Poiret and Mlle. Michonneau were sitting on a bench in the sun in a lonely alley of the Jardin des Plantes, talking with the gentleman who had already justly excited the suspicions of Bianchon.

"Mademoiselle," M. Gondureau was saying, "I can't see why you should feel any scruples. His Excellency, the Chief of the Police, in this kingdom—"

"Ah, His Excellency, the Chief of the Police, in this kingdom!" Poiret repeated.

"Yes, His Excellency is interested in this matter," Gondureau said.

It will seem improbable to most people that Poiret, who had once been a clerk in some office and who, though destitute of ideas, was probably possessed of the virtues of a good citizen, would continue to listen to a man who had made himself out to be a householder in the rue de Buffon and had then suddenly mentioned the police, dropping his mask of respectability and disclosing the countenance of an agent from the rue de Jerusalem. And yet, nothing could be more natural. The particular species of the great genus of fools to which Poiret belonged will be more easily understood after a remark that has been already made by certain keen observers, although, until now, it has never been published. There is a feathered tribe that occupies a position in the financial world between the first degree of latitude, which may be called an administrative Greenland admitting of salaries that run up to twelve hundred francs, and the third degree, a warmer and more temperate region where the salaries are from three to six thousand francs and where the system of gratuities takes root and flourishes in spite of the difficulties that attend its cultivation.

One of the most characteristic traits that mark the feeble narrow-mindedness of this subordinate race is the kind of involuntary, mechanical, and instinctive respect they feel for the grand lama at the head of any ministry, who is known to them by his illegible signature and by the name of His Excellency, Monseigneur the Minister, a title in all ways equal to *il Bondo Cani* of the Caliph of Bagdad and signifying in the eyes of this debased people sacred power without appeal. A minister is as infallible in his administrative capacity in the eyes of his employee as the Pope is in those of a Catholic; he throws a glamour over his acts, over his own words, and over those that are said in his name. The luster of his position covers everything and legalizes all his commands, and his title, which attests the purity of his intentions and the sanctity of his will, serves as a passport to the most inadmissible ideas. What a poor wretch of an employee would never do in his own interest he is eager to accomplish as soon as he hears the words *His Excellency* mentioned. Bureaucracy has its passive obedience just as the army has its: a system that stifles conscience and destroys its victims, who end by being fitted like screws into the great machine of government.

So it happened that M. Gondureau, evidently a good judge of men, was quick to recognize Poiret as a bureaucratic fool and brought out his *deus ex machina*, the magical title of His Excellency, at the very moment when he was obliged to unmask his batteries and overpower Poiret, who struck him as a male Michonneau, just as Michoneau gave him the impression of a female Poiret.

"As long as you say that His Excellency himself, His Excellency, Monseigneur le— Ah, that is quite a different thing," Poiret said.

"You hear what this gentleman says, and you seem to place confidence in his judgment," the pretended *rentier* continued, addressing Mlle. Michonneau. "Very well, His Excellency is now convinced that the fictitious Vautrin, who lives at Mme. Vauquer's house, is a convict who has escaped from the galleys of Toulon, where he was known as *Trompe-la-Mort*."

"Ah, *Trompe-la-Mort*," Poiret said. "He must be very fortunate to have earned that name."

"Of course he is," the agent returned. "He owes his nickname to his good luck in never losing his life in all the excessively daring enterprises that he has carried out. He is a dangerous man, I can tell you! He has qualities that are quite out of the common run. His conviction even did him great honor among his own set . . . "

"Is he, then, a man of honor?" Poiret asked.

"In his own way. He consented to take upon himself the crime of another, a forgery committed by a handsome young man to whom he was much attached, an Italian somewhat addicted to gambling, who has since entered the army, where his behavior has been irreproachable."

"But if His Excellency, the Chief of the Police, is sure that M. Vautrin is Trompe-la-Mort, why should he need my help?" put in Mlle. Michonneau.

"Yes, indeed," Poiret said, "if it is true that the Minister, as you have just done us the honor to tell us, is convinced . . . "

"Convinced is not the word for it; but he suspects. I will tell you how it is. Jacques Collin, surnamed Trompe-la-Mort, is in the confidence of three jails, whose prisoners have chosen him for their agent and banker. He finds great profit in this business, which naturally requires a man of mark."

"Ah, do you see the pun, mademoiselle?" Poiret cried. "This gentleman calls him a man of *mark*, because he has actually been marked."

"The fictitious Vautrin," the agent continued, "receives the convicts' capital, keeps it invested, and holds
it in readiness for those of them who escape, or for their
families, in case they bequeath it to them, or else for
their mistresses, when they draw upon him in their
favor."

"For their mistresses! You must mean their wives?"
Poiret observed.

"No, monsieur. The convicts have, almost always, ille-
gitimate wives whom we call concubines."

"So they live in a state of concubinage?"

"Necessarily so."

"Then," Poiret said, "that is an abomination that His
Excellency should not tolerate. Since you have the honor
of seeing him and appear to me to have philanthropic
ideas, it is your place to enlighten him on the immoral
conduct of these people, who set a very bad example to
the rest of society."

"Still, monsieur, the government does not put them
there as models of all virtue."

"That is true, monsieur, but just allow me—"

"Do let the gentleman speak, my dear," Mlle. Michonneau interposed.

"I want you to understand, mademoiselle," Gondureau
went on, "the government may be greatly interested in
laying hands upon an illicit fund, which is said to
amount to a large sum. Trompe-la-Mort receives into his
keeping not only the money of a few comrades but also
that belonging to the Society of the Ten Thousand—"

"Ten thousand thieves!" Poiret ejaculated, much
alarmed.

"No, the Society of the Ten Thousand is an association of aristocratic thieves who do work on a large scale and refuse to have a hand in an affair in which there are less than ten thousand francs at stake. This society is composed of the most distinguished among those who go safely through the Court of Assizes; they know the Code and never run the risk of being sentenced to death when they are caught. They confide in Collin, and he advises them. By the aid of his immense resources, he has been able to create a police of his own and to establish very extensive relations that are wrapped in impenetrable mystery. Though we have dogged him with spies for a year, we have not been able to see into his game. His coffer and his talents are therefore constantly used to serve the purposes of vice, defray the expenses of crime, and actually maintain an army of rascals who are in a state of perpetual warfare with society. If we can seize Trompe-la-Mort and get hold of his bank, we can destroy the evil, root and branch; therefore, this matter has become an affair of State and of government policy and will confer honor upon those who cooperate for its success. You, monsieur, may be employed again in the administration or become secretary to a commissary of the police, and neither office would interfere with your drawing your retirement pension."

"Why doesn't Trompe-la-Mort run off with the money?" inquired Mlle. Michonneau.

"Because," the agent said, "if he tried to steal the convicts' money, wherever he went he would be followed by a man who had instructions to kill him. A bank is not as easy to carry off as a young lady of good family, and besides, Collin is a fellow incapable of playing such a trick; he would think it dishonorable."

"You are right, monsieur," Poiret said. "It would be very dishonorable!"

"All this does not explain why you don't simply come and arrest him yourself," Mlle. Michonneau remarked.

"Well, mademoiselle, I am going to tell you. Only," he added in a whisper, "try to prevent your friend from interrupting me, or we shall never be done with this. He must be a fortunate old person, if he can induce anybody to listen to him. Trompe-la-Mort," he went on aloud, "came here disguised as a respectable man; he became outwardly a good citizen and lodged in an obscure boarding-house. He is a clever fellow, I tell you, and will never be taken asleep. Therefore, you may conclude that M. Vautrin is a man of consideration and is engaged in affairs of magnitude."

"Naturally," Poiret said to himself.

"In case there should be any mistake about arresting the real Vautrin, the Minister is anxious to avoid turning the commercial world and all public opinion against him. You see, the Prefect of the Police has his enemies and feels shaky in his position. If he should prove to be in the wrong, those who are watching for his place would take advantage of the universal brawling and squalling to get him ousted. We must proceed in this matter as we did in the case of Cogniard, the sham Comte de Sainte-Hélène; if he had been a real Comte de Sainte-

Hélène, we would not have come off cleanhanded. Therefore, we must make sure."

"Yes, but you need a pretty woman for that," Mlle. Michonneau said quickly.

"Trompe-la-Mort would not let a woman come near him," the agent said. "Let me tell you a secret: he doesn't like women."

"Then I can't see how I can be of use in making sure about him, even supposing that I consented to do so for two thousand francs."

"Nothing could be easier," the unknown man said. "I will give you a vial containing a dose of medicine prepared for the purpose of producing a rush of blood to the head that is very much like apoplexy in appearance but not in the least dangerous. The drug may be administered in either wine or coffee, and then, you must see that your man is immediately placed on a bed, and you must undress him, under the pretense of finding out whether he is dying or not. As soon as you are left alone, give him a slap on the shoulder and you will see the branded letters reappear."

"That is nothing at all," Poiret said.

"Then you consent?" Gondureau asked of the old maid.

"But, my dear monsieur," Mlle. Michonneau said, "in case there were no letters, would I have the two thousand francs?"

"No."

"What reward would I receive, then?"

"Five hundred francs."

"It is hard to do such a thing for so little money. The harm done my conscience is just the same, and I shall have to soothe my conscience, monsieur."

"I assure you," Poiret said, "that this lady has a great deal of conscience, besides being a very amiable and intelligent person."

"Well then," Mlle. Michonneau resumed, "give me three thousand francs if he turns out to be Trompe-la-Mort, and nothing at all if he is a respectable man."

"Agreed!" said Gondureau. "But on condition that it shall be all done by tomorrow."

"Not quite so soon, my dear monsieur; I must first consult my confessor."

"You are very sly," the agent said, rising. "Tomorrow, then, and if you should happen to want to see me, come to the petite rue Ste-Anne, at the end of the court of the Ste-Chapelle. There is only one door under the arch, and ask for M. Gondureau."

Bianchon was on his way home from the Cuvier lecture when the strange name Trompe-la-Mort struck on his ear, and he overheard the "Agreed" of the celebrated Chief of the Detective Police.

"Why can't you make up your mind? It would buy you a life annuity of three hundred francs," Poiret said to Mlle. Michonneau.

"Why?" she said. "I must think it over. If M. Vautrin were Trompe-la-Mort, I might make more by coming to terms with him. Yet if I asked him for money, I would be giving him warning, and he would be sure to get off scot-free. I would make an abominable mess of it."

"Even if you gave him warning," Poiret went on, "didn't the gentleman say he was watched? However, you would lose everything."

Besides, Mlle. Michonneau thought, I can't bear him! He has always said disagreeable things to me.

"It is much better for you to consent to this," Poiret continued. "As the gentleman said—and he seems to me a very respectable person and very neatly dressed—it is an act of obedience to the law to rid society of a criminal, however virtuous he may be. A drunkard once, always a drunkard. Suppose he took it into his head to murder all of us? The devil! We would be guilty of all the murders, without taking into consideration that we would be the first victims ourselves."

Mlle. Michonneau was too much preoccupied to listen to the sentences that fell one by one from Poiret's mouth, like drops of water dripping from a half-closed faucet. When the old man was once fairly launched on his series of phrases and Mlle. Michonneau did not interrupt him, he kept on talking like a machine that has been wound up. After he had begun on one subject, he was led by his digressions to make others of a quite opposite character, without arriving at any conclusion. By the time they reached the boardinghouse, he had become so involved in a succession of stories and the fugitive quotations they suggested that he was drawn on to relate his disposition in the case of M. Ragoulleau and Mme. Morin, in which he had appeared as witness for the defense. As they entered the house, his companion was quick to observe Eugène de Rastignac and Mlle. Taillefer absorbed in a close conversation of such thrilling interest that they paid no attention to the two old boarders crossing the dining room.

"It was sure to end like this," Mlle. Michonneau said to Poiret. "They have been exchanging killing glances for a week."

"Yes," Poiret answered, "so she was convicted."

"Who?"

"Mme. Morin."

"I am speaking to you of Mlle. Victorine," Mlle. Michonneau said, entering Poiret's room without paying any attention to where she was going, "and you say something about Mme. Morin. Who on earth is she, I would like to know?"

"What is Mlle. Victorine guilty of?" inquired Poiret.

"She is guilty of loving M. Eugène de Rastignac and is starting out without knowing where it will end, poor little fool!"

3

THAT morning Mme. de Nucingen had reduced Eugène to despair. In his heart he had entirely surrendered to Vautrin, although he was unwilling to sound the motives of that extraordinary man's friendship for him or the future of the union he had proposed to him. Nothing short of a miracle could extricate him now from the abyss into which he had fallen this last hour, in which he had exchanged the tenderest vows with Mlle. Taillefer. Victorine thought she heard the voice of an angel and that the skies were opening for her; Vauquer House shone with the fantastic hues that a scene painter gives to a theater. She loved and was loved in return, or at least she thought so! And what woman would not have thought like her if she had seen Rastignac and listened to him during that hour they had stolen from the Arguses of the house? As he struggled against his conscience, fully aware that he was doing wrong but meaning to do wrong, and trying to persuade himself that it would be easy to atone for a venial sin by making this girl happy, his despair lent him new charms and his face glowed with all the fires of hell that were aflame in his heart.

Fortunately for him, however, the miracle occurred: Vautrin came in in high spirits, and read the hearts of the two young people whom he had brought together by the machinations of his infernal genius. He suddenly disturbed their happiness by singing in a loud jeering voice:

> *"My Fannie's a charming girl,*
> *As simple as can be."*

Victorine rushed away, carrying with her enough bliss to make amends for the misfortunes of her whole life. Poor girl! The pressure of Rastignac's hand on hers, his hair that brushed her cheek, a word of his spoken so near her ear that she felt the warmth of his lips, his trembling arm passed round her waist, and his kiss upon her throat—these made up the ceremony of her betrothal, and the proximity of big Sylvie, who threatened to burst into the radiant dining room at any moment, rendered it more delightful, more real, and more rapturous than the fairest professions of devotion narrated in famous love stories. These *menus suffrages*—according to a neat expression of our ancestors—seemed crimes in the eyes of a pious girl like her, who confessed every two weeks! She had already lavished more of the treasures of her heart than she could have given, later on, when rich and prosperous, by entire self-surrender.

"It is all arranged," Vautrin said to Eugène. "Our two dandies are working hard. Everything was done according to rule. It was a difference of opinion. Our pigeon insulted my hawk. Tomorrow, then, at the fortifications of Clignancourt. At half past eight o'clock Mlle. Taillefer will inherit the love and fortune of her father, while she is sitting quietly dipping her buttered bread into her coffee. Isn't it amusing? Little Taillefer is a very good swordsman and is cocksure of success, but he will be killed by a thrust I invented myself, a way of raising a sword and hitting a man's forehead. I will show you the thrust, for it is tremendously useful."

Rastignac listened stupidly and could find nothing to say. At this moment, père Goriot, Bianchon, and some of the other boarders came in.

"You are just as I wanted you to be," Vautrin said. "You know what you are about. Well done, my little eagle! You will govern men, for you are strong, staunch, and robust; you have my respect."

He tried to take his hand, but Rastignac drew his away quickly and, turning pale, sank down on a chair; he thought he saw a lake of blood before him.

"Oh, we still have a few filthy rags of virtue left," Vautrin said in a low tone. "Papa Taillefer has three million; I know what his fortune is. The dowry will wash you white as a wedding gown, even in your own eyes."

Rastignac hesitated no longer. He resolved to go that evening to warn M. Taillefer and his son. At this moment, Vautrin having left him, père Goriot came up and whispered in his ear:

"You are in low spirits, my boy! I will cheer you up; come with me!"

The old man lighted his candle at one of the lamps and Eugène followed him, full of curiosity.

"Let us go into your room," said Goriot, who had asked Sylvie for the student's key. "This morning you thought she didn't love you, didn't you?" he went on. "She insisted upon your leaving her, and you went away angry and despairing. Foolish boy! She was expecting me. Now do you understand? We were to go together to complete the arrangements concerning a charming little apartment in which you are going to live three days from now. Don't let her know I told you; she wants to surprise you, but I don't think I have to keep the secret any longer. You will be in the rue d'Artois, two or three steps from the rue St-Lazare, and you will find yourself installed like a prince. We bought furniture fine enough for a bride and have been busy about many things this last month without saying a word to you. My lawyer opened the campaign; my daughter is going to have her thirty-six thousand francs a year, the interest of her dowry, and I shall insist upon her eight hundred thousand francs being invested in good landed property."

Eugène said nothing but kept walking up and down the mean, disordered room, with his arms folded. Père Goriot seized a moment when the student's back was turned to place upon the mantel piece a red morocco box stamped with the Rastignac coat of arms.

"My dear boy," the good man said, "I have done all I could in this matter, but you see there was some selfishness on my part, for I am interested in your change of lodgings. You won't refuse me a favor, if I ask it of you, will you?"

"What is it you want?"

"On the fifth floor, above your apartment, there is a room that belongs to it, and I would like to live there if you will allow me. I am growing old and think that I am too far from my daughters. I shall not be in your way at all, only I shall live there, and you can tell me about them every evening. You won't object to that, will you? When you come back at night and I am in bed, I shall say to myself, he has just seen my little Delphine; he has taken her to the ball and has made her happy. If I were ill, it would be like balm to my heart to hear your step, coming and going. You would seem like a part of my daughter! I shall only have a step to go to the Champs-Elysées where my daughters drive every day, and

I shall never miss seeing them, whereas, now I sometimes get there too late. Then, perhaps she will come to see you; I shall hear her and shall see her, the little darling, tripping along daintily in her morning cloak.

"This last month she has recovered her youth, her gaiety, and her freshness. The wounds in her heart have been healed, and she owes her happiness to you. Oh, I would do anything in the world for you! As we were coming home together a little while ago, she said to me, 'Papa, I am very happy!' They chill me when they call me Father ceremoniously; but when they say Papa, they revive all my old memories, and I imagine that they are little girls again. They seem more really my daughters, and I forget they belong to anybody else!" The poor man dried his eyes, for he was crying.

"It was a long time since I had heard the word *papa*, and a very long time since Delphine had taken my arm. Yes, it must be ten years since I last walked side by side with one of my daughters. How delightful it was to feel her dress brush against me, to suit my step to hers, and to feel her close beside me! I took Delphine everywhere this morning; we went shopping together, and then I took her home.

"Oh, do let me stay with you, and then, if you ever need anybody to do you a service, I shall be ready for it. If that big blockhead of an Alsatian died, if only good luck would send his gout to his stomach, how happy my poor girl would be! Then you could be my son-in-law and her avowed husband. The poor thing has been so cut off from all the pleasures of this world that I absolve her from everything, and God must be on the side of a loving father.

"She loves you too much," he continued, raising his head after a pause. "As we walked along together, she kept saying, 'Isn't it so, Papa? He is charming! He has a good heart! Does he speak of me?' She talked volumes about you, all the way from the rue d'Artois to the passage des Panoramas! She poured out her whole heart to me. All that beautiful morning, I was no longer old and felt as light as a feather. I told her that you had returned me the banknote of a thousand francs, and the dear child was moved to tears. What is that on your mantelpiece," he added at last, no longer able to control the impatience he felt at seeing Rastignac stand motionless before him.

Eugène, who was half-stunned, looked stupidly at Goriot. The news of the duel that Vautrin had announced to take place next day contrasted so violently with the realization of his fondest hopes that he experienced all the sensations of a nightmare. He turned toward the chimneypiece and, seeing the little square box, opened it and found inside a paper containing a Bréguet watch. On the paper was written:

I want you to think of me every hour, *because* . . .

Delphine

The last word alluded, no doubt, to something that had taken place between them, and Eugène was touched by it. His coat of arms was enameled on the gold lining of the box. This trinket, which he had so long coveted,

233

the chain, the key, the workmanship, and the design all fulfilled his desires. Père Goriot was radiant. He had, doubtless, promised to repeat to his daughter every detail of the surprise her gift would cause Eugène, for he shared in their young emotions and seemed as happy as they. He loved Rastignac already, both for his daughter's sake and for his own.

"You must go to see her this evening, for she expects you. Her great stupid husband is to have supper with his opera dancer. Oh, he looked so foolish when my lawyer told him what he must do. Doesn't he pretend to love my daughter to adoration? But if he touches her, I will kill him. The idea of my Delphine . . . " and with a sigh he continued, "would make me commit a crime; it would not be a homicide, however, for that imbecile is no better than a pig. You will take me with you, won't you?"

"Yes, dear père Goriot, you know how fond I am of you."

"I know it, and you are not ashamed of me either. Let me kiss you," he said.

He folded the student in his arms.

"You will be very good to her, promise me! You will go to her this evening, won't you?"

"Yes, certainly; I must go out at any rate for some business that is impossible to put off."

"Can I be useful to you in any way?"

"Yes, I think you can. While I am at M. de Nucingen's, you might go to the elder M. Taillefer and tell him to keep an hour for me this evening, as I must speak to him on a matter of the greatest importance."

"Is it true, then, young man?" père Goriot cried with a sudden change of expression. "Are you really courting his daughter as those fools downstairs say? Great heavens! You don't know what a blow I can give, and if you are deceiving us, the occasion would call for one. Oh, it isn't possible!"

"I swear to you that I love only one woman in the world," the student said. "I have only just found it out."

"You make me very happy," père Goriot exclaimed.

"But," the student resumed, "Taillefer's son is to fight a duel tomorrow, and I have heard it said that he will be killed."

"What difference does that make to you?" Goriot asked.

"I must tell him to keep his son at home—" Eugène cried.

Just then, he was interrupted by the voice of Vautrin, who was standing at the threshold of his door, singing:

"O, Richard, my king!
All the world forgets thee . . .
Broum! Broum! Broum! Broum! Broum!
Long have I wandered, far and near,
And I've been seen . . .
Tra la la la la . . ."

"Gentlemen," Christophe called, "the soup is waiting, and everybody is at the table."

"Come," Vautrin said, "I want you to try a bottle of my Bordeaux."

"So you think the watch is pretty, do you?" père Goriot asked. "She has good taste, hasn't she?"

Vautrin, père Goriot, and Rastignac went downstairs together and, in consequence of coming late, found themselves placed next to each other at the table.

Eugène showed the most marked coldness to Vautrin during dinner, although the latter, always agreeable in Mme. Vauquer's eyes, quite outdid himself on this occasion. His sallies were so sparkling that he put all the guests into good humor. His coolness and assurance threw Eugène into consternation.

"What is the matter with you today?" Mme. Vauquer asked. "You are as gay as a lark."

"I am always gay when I have done a good stroke of business."

"Business?" Eugène inquired.

"Yes, business. I have delivered a parcel of merchandise that will bring me in a good commission. Mademoiselle Michonneau," he said, perceiving that the old maid was studying him, "is any one of my features displeasing to you, that you are scrutinizing me with the *American* eye? You must tell me and I will change it to oblige you. Poiret, we couldn't be angry for such a trifle as that, could we?" he added, winking at the old man.

"By Jove, you ought to pose for a comic Hercules," the young painter said to Vautrin.

"I am quite willing, provided that Mlle. Michonneau will pose as a Venus of Père-Lachaise," Vautrin replied.

"And Poiret?" Bianchon asked.

"Oh, Poiret must pose as Poiret."

"He will make the god of the garden," Vautrin cried, "for he is derived from *poire*."

"An overripe pear then," Bianchon went on. "You will find yourself at dessert then, between the pear and the cheese."

"They are all talking nonsense," Mme. Vauquer said, "and it would be much better for you to give us some of your Bordeaux, for I have just caught sight of a bottle of it. It will keep up our spirits, not to speak of its being good for the stomach."

"Gentlemen," Vautrin began, "the President calls us to order. Mme. Couture and Mlle. Victorine will not be shocked at your jests, but you must respect père Goriot's innocence. I propose a little *bottleorama* of Bordeaux, doubly well known on account of the name of Lafite, though I speak without political allusion. Come, blockhead!" said he, looking at Christophe, who had not budged. "Here, blockhead! What, don't you understand your name? Blockhead, bring the wine."

"Here, monsieur," Christophe said, presenting the bottle to him.

After filling the glasses of Eugène and père Goriot, Vautrin slowly poured a few drops in his own, which he tasted while his two neighbors were drinking. Suddenly he made a wry face.

"The devil! The devil!" he cried. "It tastes of the cork. Take it yourself, Christophe, and go and get us some more; you know where it is, don't you? On the right. We are sixteen, so bring us down eight bottles."

"Since you are treating the crowd," the painter said, "I will pay for a hundred chestnuts."

"Oh! Oh!"

"Booououh!"

"Prrrr!"

These exclamations exploded on every side like the fuses of so many fireworks.

"Come, Mamma Vauquer, give us two bottles of champagne," Vautrin cried.

"Is that all?" she said. "Why don't you ask for the whole house? Two bottles of champagne! That would cost twelve francs, and I don't have them. But, if M. Eugène will pay for the champagne, I will give you some cherry cordial."

"You might as well take a dose of senna as her cordial," the medical student said in a low voice.

"Will you be quiet, Bianchon," Rastignac cried. "I can't hear senna mentioned without being nauseated. I will pay for the champagne," he added.

"Sylvie," said Mme. Vauquer, "bring us the biscuits and the little cakes."

"Your little cakes are too big," Vautrin said. "They have grown a beard, but we'll have the biscuits."

The Bordeaux was soon circulating freely; the guests grew animated and were twice as gay as before. It was a scene of mad laughter, in the middle of which were to be heard imitations of the sounds made by various animals. The museum employee tried to reproduce a Paris street cry that bore much resemblance to the mewing of an amorous cat, and then eight voices immediately bellowed the following calls:

"Knives to grind!"

"Chickweed for your birds!"

"A bargain, ladies! A bargain!"

"China to mend!"

"Boats to let!"

"Clothes-beaters, wife-beaters!"

"Old clothes, old hats, old lace to sell!"

"Sweet syrups, cherry syrup!"

Bianchon received the palm for the nasal accent with which he called:

"Umbrellas to sell!"

A little later this absurd conversation had reached a pitch of deafening clamor; it was like an opera whose orchestra was conducted by Vautrin. He kept a careful eye on Eugène and père Goriot, who seemed already tipsy. They drank little and leaned back in their chairs contemplating the unusual disorder before them with great seriousness; they were both preoccupied with what they knew they had to do during the evening, and yet they felt incapable of rising from their seats. Vautrin watched them with sidelong glances and seized the moment when their unsteady eyes were on the point of closing to lean over and whisper in Rastignac's ear:

"My little fellow, you are not clever enough to struggle with your old friend Vautrin, and he likes you too well to let you do a foolish thing. When I have resolved on anything, nobody but God is strong enough to bar my way. Ah, you were going to tell Father Taillefer and behave like a little schoolboy! The furnace is heated, the dough kneaded, and the bread is on the baker's shovel; tomorrow when we bite it, the crumbs will fly over our heads; and do you want to prevent it from being put in the furnace now? No, no, it shall be baked! If you have any slight remorse, your digestion will carry it off. While you are sleeping your little sleep, Colonel Comte Franchessini will open the estate of Michel Taillefer with the point of his sword. Victorine will inherit fifteen thousand francs a year from her brother. I have informed myself thoroughly, and I know that the mother's property amounts to more than three hundred thousand . . . "

Eugène heard these words without having the power of answering them; his tongue was glued to his palate, and he felt overcome by irresistible drowsiness. He saw the table and the faces of the guests through a luminous mist. Soon the noise ceased, and the boarders went out one by one. Then, when there was no one left but Mme. Vauquer, Mme. Couture, Mlle. Victorine, Vautrin, and père Goriot, Rastignac saw, as if in a dream, Mme. Vauquer pouring together the heeltaps in order to fill some other bottles.

"Ah, how young and foolish they are!" the widow was saying.

These were the last words that Eugène was able to understand.

"There is nobody like M. Vautrin for playing such jokes," Sylvie said. "Just look at Christophe there, sound asleep like a top, and snoring."

"Good-bye Mamma," Vautrin said. "I am going to the Boulevard to see M. Marty in the *Desert Mountain*, a great play that has been adapted from *The Solitary*. If you like, I will take you and both these ladies."

"No, thank you," Mme. Couture said.

"What," cried Mme. Vauquer, "do you refuse to go and see a play that has been taken from *The Solitary*, a work that was written by Atala de Chateaubriand and that we all liked reading so much? It is so pretty that we cried like so many Magdalens of Elodie under the lime trees last summer, and it is moral too and might furnish a useful lesson for your young lady."

"We are not allowed to go to the theater," Victorine answered.

"Look how those two have gone off," Vautrin said, moving père Goriot's and Eugène's heads up and down in a ludicrous manner.

He placed the student's head upon a chair so that he might sleep more comfortably and kissed him warmly on the forehead, singing:

> "Sleep, my loves, forever sleep,
> While for you my watch I keep."

"I am afraid he is ill," Victorine said.

"Then stay and take care of him," Vautrin rejoined. "That is your duty as a submissive wife," he whispered in her ear. "The young man adores you, and I promise you that you shall be his little wife. It will be said of you," he continued aloud, " 'They were much honored through all the land; they lived happily and had many children.' That is the way all love stories end. Come, Mamma," said he, turning toward Mme. Vauquer and passing his arm around her waist. "Put on the Countess's hat, her handsome flowered gown, and her scarf. I will go and get you a cab myself."

He left the room, singing:

"Sunlight, sunlight, divine sunlight,
That mak'st the mellow pumpkins bright . . ."

"Dear me, Madame Couture," Mme. Vauquer said, "I could live happily in a garret with that man. Look," she added, turning toward père Goriot, "the old fellow has quite gone off. That old skinflint never thought of taking me anywhere! Oh, goodness! He is going to fall on the ground! It is indecent for an old man to lose his wits like this! I suppose you will say that he can't lose what he has never had. Sylvie, help him to get upstairs."

Sylvie took the old man under the arm, made him walk along, and threw him, all dressed, on his bed, like a bundle.

"Poor young man," Mme. Couture said, pushing aside Eugène's hair, which was falling about his eyes. "He is like a young girl and doesn't know what excess means."

"I have kept a boardinghouse for thirty-one years," Mme. Vauquer said, "and I can say that, though I have had many young men under my hands, as they say, I never saw one so gentlemanlike and distinguished as M. Eugène. How handsome he looks asleep! Let him rest his head on your shoulder, Madame Couture. Ah, he has fallen against Mlle. Victorine's: there is a Providence for children. A little more, and he would have cut his head on the knob of the chair. They make a very pretty couple together."

"Will you be quiet!" Mme. Couture exclaimed. "You are saying extraordinary things . . ."

"Oh, pooh!" Mme. Vauquer said. "He doesn't hear anything. Come, Sylvie; come and dress me. I am going to put on my long stays."

"Your long stays, after having dined?" Sylvie said. "No, you must find somebody else to lace you, for I do not wish to help to kill you. An imprudence like that might cost you your life."

"I don't care; I must do honor to M. Vautrin."

"Then you must be very fond of your heirs, no?"

"Come, Sylvie, no more objections," the widow said, turning to go.

"At her age too," the cook said to Victorine, pointing to her mistress.

Mme. Couture and her ward, upon whose shoulder Eugène was sleeping, were left alone in the dining room. Christophe's snoring, which resounded through the silent house, called attention to the peaceful slumber of Eugène, who was sleeping as sweetly as a child.

Victorine was happy to find herself in a position to perform a charitable act that allowed free scope to her womanly affections and permitted her to feel, in all innocence, that the young man's heart was beating against hers. There was a proud expression on Victorine's face that was almost maternal in its solicitude, and above the many thoughts of her heart, there rose supreme a tumultuous impulse of joy, kindled by the exchange of pure young love.

"Poor dear girl!" Mme. Couture said, pressing her hand.

The old lady looked with admiration at the pure, delicate face, now illuminated with an aureola of happiness. Victorine was like an artless picture of the Middle Ages, in which the artist has neglected the accessories to lavish the calm and noble magic of his brush upon the yellow tints of the face, which seems to have caught the golden hues of heaven.

"He didn't drink more than two glasses, Mamma," Victorine said, running her fingers through Eugène's hair.

"If he were a dissipated man, my dear, he would have stood the wine as well as the others. It is very much to his credit that so little affected him."

A carriage was heard driving up to the door.

"Mamma," the young girl said, "there is M. Vautrin. Please take hold of M. Eugène. I would not like that man to see me in this position; he uses the most humiliating expressions, and his looks are as embarrassing to me as if I were being stripped of my gown."

"No, you are mistaken," Mme. Couture said. "M. Vautrin is a worthy man, something like my poor husband; he is abrupt but good-hearted, rough but of a kindly disposition."

Vautrin came in quietly and looked at the picture made by the two people in the encircling light of the lamp.

"There," he said, crossing his arms, "is a scene that would have inspired that good Bernardin de Saint-Pierre, the author of *Paul and Virginie*. Youth is very beautiful, Madame Couture! Sleep, my poor boy," he said to Eugène. "Fortune comes sometimes while we are sleeping.

Madame," he resumed, addressing the widow, "what I find so attaching and so attractive in this young man is the knowledge that his soul is as beautiful as his face. See, isn't he like a cherub, leaning on the shoulder of an angel? He is really worthy of being loved! If I were a woman, I would be willing to die for him. No, that's nonsense! I mean I would be willing to live for him.

"When I see them thus, madame," he said in a whisper in the widow's ear, "I cannot help believing that God created them so that they might belong to each other. Providence has secret ways; it searches the heart and the inward parts," he exclaimed aloud. "When I see you, my children, united by your innocence and by all human affections, it seems to me impossible that you should ever be separated in the future. God is just.

"But," he added, speaking to the young girl, "I think I have seen lines of prosperity in your hand. Let me have it, Mademoiselle Victorine, for I know all about palmistry and have often told fortunes. Don't be afraid. Oh! What do I see? On my honor, you will soon be one of the richest heiresses in Paris. You will make the man who loves you perfectly happy. Your father will call you back to him, and you will marry a handsome young man with a title who adores you."

At that moment, the heavy steps of the coquettish widow, who was approaching, interrupted Vautrin's prophecies.

"Here is Mme. Vauquerre, beautiful as a star-r-r, and looking as gay as a carrot. Aren't you a little bit uncomfortable?" he said, touching the top of her corset. "You are pretty well squeezed, Mamma! If you cry, there will be an explosion, but I will pick up the fragments with the zeal of an antiquarian."

"He really understands how to make French compliments!" the widow said, leaning over to Mme. Couture's ear.

"Good-bye, my children," Vautrin went on, turning toward Eugène and Victorine. "I bless you," he said, placing his hands upon their heads. "Believe me, mademoiselle, an honest man's prayers are worth something; they must bring good fortune, for God listens to them."

"Good-bye, my dear," Mme. Vauquer said to her boarder. "Do you think," she added in a low tone, "that he has any further designs upon me?"

"Him! How can I tell?"

"Ah, dear mother," Victorine said with a sigh, looking at her hands when the others were gone, "if that good M. Vautrin were telling the truth!"

"Only one thing is necessary for that," the old lady replied. "If only your monster of a brother could fall from his horse."

"Oh, Mamma!"

"Good heavens, is it a sin to wish bad luck to your enemy?" rejoined the widow. "Very well, I would do penance for it. Yes, really, I would be willing to put flowers on his grave. The cowardly fellow hasn't the courage to say a word for his mother, and yet he manages by some underhand means to keep her property and cheat you out of it. My cousin had a large fortune, but unfortunately for you, there was nothing said about it in the marriage contract."

"I would find my happiness very hard to bear if it cost anybody's life," Victorine said. "If my brother had to die to make me happy, I would rather stay here always."

"Good heavens, as that good M. Vautrin says, who, you see, is very religious," rejoined Mme. Couture. "I was so pleased to find out that he is not as incredulous as the others, who speak of God with less respect than the devil would dare to do. Well, well! Who can tell through what paths it will please Providence to lead us?"

With Sylvie's help, the two ladies finally succeeded in taking Eugène to his room, where they laid him on the bed, and the cook loosened his clothes so that he might sleep more comfortably. Before leaving the room, when her aunt's back was turned, Victorine imprinted a kiss upon Eugène's forehead, with the blissful consciousness of stolen joy. She looked about his room and focusing, as it were, the many pleasures of the day in a single thought, she made a lasting picture of it for herself and went off to sleep, the happiest creature in Paris.

The orgies that had enabled Vautrin to administer a narcotic in their wine to Eugène and père Goriot were also the cause of his own undoing. Bianchon, who was half-tipsy, forgot to question Mlle. Michonneau on Trompe-la-Mort; if he had pronounced the name, he would certainly have aroused the suspicions of Vautrin, or to give him his real name, Jacques Collin, one of the celebrities of the galleys. Then, also, the epithet of a Père-Lachaise Venus decided Mlle. Michonneau in favor of delivering over the convict to the law at the very moment when, trusting to his generosity, she was deliberating whether she would not find more advantage in warning him and helping him to escape by night. Now she sallied forth, with Poiret as her companion, in quest of the famous Chief of the Detective Police in petite rue Ste-Anne, still under the impression that he was merely a superior officer named Gondureau. The Director of the Judiciary Police received her politely. After a conversation in which everything was discussed at length, Mlle. Michonneau asked for the potion by means of which she was to make the discovery of the branded letters. By the evident satisfaction with which the great man of the petite rue Ste-Anne set to work to find a vial in the drawer of his desk, Mlle. Michonneau guessed that the projected seizure of Vautrin meant something more important than the arrest of a mere convict. By dint of beating her brains, it occurred to her that, owing to information obtained from certain convicts who had betrayed the secrets of their comrades, the police hoped there would still be time for them to lay hands on a treasure of considerable value. She explained her conjectures to the old fox, but he only smiled and tried to divert her suspicions.

"You are mistaken," he replied. "Collin is the most dangerous *sorbonne* the thieves have ever had on their side. That is all. The scamps know it; he is their standard, their support, in short, their Buonaparte; they all love him. The rascal will never leave his *tronche* on the place de Grève."

As Mlle. Michonneau could not understand, Gondureau explained to her the two slang words that he had used. *Sorbonne* and *tronche* are energetic expressions in the language of thieves, who have been the first to feel the necessity of considering the human head under two aspects. *Sorbonne* means the head of a living man, with his power of thought and counsel; *tronche* is a scornful term used to indicate the worthlessness of a head, after it has been severed from the body.

"Collin is playing a game with us," he resumed. "When we are to encounter men of his stamp that are like bars of English tempered steel, we reserve to ourselves the resource of killing them if they show the slightest resistance while being arrested. We count upon some violence on his part tomorrow morning that will allow us to make an end of him. In that way we would avoid a trial and all the expense of his food and custody, and we would rid society of him. The legal proceedings, the subpoenas for the witnesses, their pay, and all the machinery that frees us legitimately from such rogues as he cost more than the three thousand francs you are to receive. Time is economized too. A good bayonet-thrust in the stomach would save Trompe-la-Mort from a hundred crimes and prevent his example from leading on fifty wretches who are now prudently confining themselves to petty offenses. That is the proper method for the police to pursue, and a true philanthropist would call it warding off crime."

"And serving the country," put in Poiret.

"There, you are really talking sense this evening," the

Chief of the Police replied. "Yes, indeed, we are serving our country, but the world is very unjust toward us. We are rendering society great services that are utterly ignored. Still, it is the part of an intelligent man to rise above prejudice, and the part of a Christian to accept those evils that accompany right-doing when it is not accomplished according to received ideas. Paris is Paris, you see. This remark explains my life. I have the honor to wish you good morning, mademoiselle. I shall be in the Jardin du Roi tomorrow. Send Christophe to M. Gondureau in the rue de Buffon, to the house where I used to be. Monsieur, I am your servant; if anything is ever stolen from you, you may make use of me to get it back for you, for I shall be quite at your service."

"Only think," Poiret said to Mlle. Michonneau, "that there are some fools who are entirely upset by hearing the police mentioned. That gentleman is extremely amiable, and what he asks of you is as plain as day."

THE next day was destined to take an extraordinary place in the annals of the Vauquer establishment. Until then, the most marked event that broke the peaceful current of the life there had been the meteoric apparition of the pretended Comtesse de l'Ambermesnil, but that incident paled before the occurrences of this great day, which was from then on to furnish a subject for all Mme. Vauquer's conversations.

In the first place, Goriot and Eugène de Rastignac slept until eleven o'clock, and Mme. Vauquer, who had come in from the Gaieté at midnight, stayed in bed until half past ten. The prolonged slumbers of Christophe, who had consumed the wine that Vautrin gave him, retarded the service of the house, but Poiret and Mlle. Michonneau had no objection to the breakfast being less punctual than usual. Victorine and Mme. Couture slept until late in the morning, and Vautrin, who had gone out before eight o'clock, returned at the very moment that breakfast was put upon the table. So it was that nobody protested when, at a quarter past eleven, Sylvie and Christophe knocked at all the doors and announced that breakfast was served. During the absence of Sylvie and the servant, Mlle. Michonneau, who was the first person to go downstairs, poured her drug in Vautrin's silver cup, which held the milk for his coffee and was warming in the double boiler together with the cups of the other boarders. The old maid had counted upon this particular arrangement of the boardinghouse for carrying out her design.

It was with some difficulty that the seven boarders were gathered together, and just as Eugène was coming downstairs last of all, stretching himself, a messenger handed him a letter from Mme. de Nucingen. It ran as follows:

I am moved by no false vanity, nor am I angry with you, my dear friend. I waited for you until two hours past midnight. Fancy what it is to wait for anyone whom you love! Whoever has once known this torture can never inflict it upon another, so I see that you are in love for the first time. What can have happened? I was overcome with anxiety, and if I had not feared to betray the secrets of my heart, I would have hastened to find what was keeping you, good or bad. But if I had gone out at that hour, whether on foot or in a carriage, I knew I would be ruined, and I felt the misery of being a woman. I beseech you to reassure me and to explain why it was that you did not come, after what you said to my father. I may be angry with you, but I shall forgive you. Are you ill? Why do you live so far away from me? Send me a line, for heaven's sake. I will see you soon, won't I? One word will do, if you are busy. Say, "I am coming," or "I am ill." Yet, if you were not well, surely my father would have come to tell me of it! What can have happened then?

"Yes, what has happened?" Eugène cried, as he hastened into the dining room, crumpling the letter that he had not finished. "What time is it?"

"Half past eleven," Vautrin said, putting the sugar into his coffee.

The escaped convict turned upon Eugène the cold and fascinating gaze that is the gift of certain men of eminently magnetic temperament and is said to have the power of calming madmen in insane asylums. Eugène trembled in every limb. The sound of a cab was heard in the street and a servant in M. Taillefer's livery, who was immediately recognized by Mme. Couture, rushed wildly in.

"Mademoiselle," he cried, "your father asks for you. A terrible thing has happened. M. Frédéric has fought a duel and has been wounded in the forehead. The doctors despair of his life, and you will hardly have time to say good-bye to him, for he has lost consciousness."

"Poor young man!" Vautrin exclaimed. "How could he get into a quarrel when he had a good thirty thousand francs a year? Young people have no idea how to behave themselves."

"Monsieur!" Eugène cried.

"Well, what is it, you big baby?" Vautrin said, tranquilly drinking his coffee, an operation that Mlle. Michonneau watched too closely to be able to share in the prevailing excitement over the extraordinary event that had just occurred.

"Aren't there duels every morning in Paris?" he went on.

"I am going with you, Victorine," Mme. Couture said, and the two ladies flew off without hat or shawl.

Before leaving the room, Victorine looked at Eugène with tears in her eyes that seemed to say she had never dreamed that their happiness could cost her so much sorrow.

"Then you must be a prophet, Monsieur Vautrin!" Mme. Vauquer said.

"I am everything," said Jacques Collin.

"It is very singular!" Mme. Vauquer resumed, stringing together a series of insignificant phrases upon the event. "Death comes without consulting our plans. The young often go before the old; we women are lucky not to have to fight duels, but then we have illnesses that men haven't. We bring children into the world and not without a great deal of trouble too. What a prize for Victorine! Her father will be forced to adopt her."

"Think of it!" Vautrin said to Eugène. "Yesterday she was without a penny and this morning she has several million."

"I am sure you have played your cards well, Monsieur Eugène," Mme. Vauquer exclaimed.

At this interpellation, père Goriot turned toward Eugène and caught sight of the crumpled note in his hand.

"You haven't even finished it! What does that mean? Are you like all the others?" he asked.

"Madame, I shall never marry Mlle. Victorine," Eugène said to Mme. Vauquer with an intensity of horror and disgust that surprised the boarders.

Père Goriot seized the student's hand and pressed it. He would have liked to kiss it.

"Oh, indeed!" Vautrin said. "The Italians have a good expression: *col tempo.*"

"I am waiting for your answer," Mme. de Nucingen's messenger said to Rastignac.

"Tell her I will come," he replied, and the man went off. Eugène was in a state of violent excitement that did not admit of self-control.

"What shall I do?" he said, speaking to himself aloud. "I have no proof against him!"

Vautrin smiled. The drug had been absorbed by his stomach and was beginning to take effect, but he was so robust that he was still able to rise from his chair and say to Rastignac in a hollow voice:

"Fortune comes to us while we are asleep, my boy."

Then he fell flat upon the floor as if he were dead.

"Then there is such a thing as Divine Justice!" Eugène ejaculated.

"What has happened to poor dear M. Vautrin?" Mme. Vauquer cried.

"Apoplexy!" Mlle. Michonneau suggested.

"Go, Sylvie, my girl, and call the doctor," the widow said. "Oh, Monsieur de Rastignac, run quickly after M. Bianchon, for Sylvie may not find our doctor, M. Grimprel, at home!"

Rastignac was happy to have a pretext for leaving such a horrible den and started off at top speed.

"Christophe, run to the apothecary and ask for some remedy for apoplexy."

Christophe obeyed.

"Now, père Goriot, help us to carry him up to his room."

They lifted Vautrin and managed to get him upstairs and put him on his bed.

"I am no use here and am going to see my daughter," père Goriot said.

"Selfish old man," Mme. Vauquer screamed. "Go. I hope that you die like a dog yourself."

"Go and see if you have any ether," M. Michonneau said to Mme. Vauquer, when she and Poiret had loosened Vautrin's clothes.

Mme. Vauquer went down to her room, leaving Mlle. Michonneau mistress of the field.

"Come, take off his shirt, and turn him over quickly!" she said to Poiret. "Try to spare my feelings by uncovering as little of his body as possible. You stand there like a sheep!"

Vautrin was turned over, and when Mademoiselle Michonneau slapped his shoulder smartly, the two fatal letters appeared in white against the red.

"There, you have gained your reward of three thousand francs very easily," Poiret exclaimed as he held Vautrin in bed while Mlle. Michonneau put on his shirt. "Oh, how heavy he is," he continued as he laid him down again.

"Do be quiet. Suppose he had his strongbox here?" the old maid said hastily, and her eyes seemed to look right through the walls, so great was the eagerness with which she examined every bit of furniture in the room. "Suppose we opened his desk under some pretext or other?" she went on.

"It might be wrong," rejoined Poiret.

"No," she insisted. "Stolen money that once belonged to everybody is nobody's property any longer. But we have no time, for I hear Mme. Vauquer coming."

"Here is the ether," Mme. Vauquer said. "Goodness me, what a day of adventures we are having! Heavens! That man can't have apoplexy; he's white as a chicken."

"White as a chicken?" Poiret repeated.

"His heart beats regularly," the widow said, putting her hand to his heart.

"Regularly?" Poiret asked in surprise.

"He is doing very well."

"Do you think so?" Poiret inquired.

"Bless me! He looks as if he were sleeping. Sylvie has gone for a doctor. Just see, Mademoiselle Michonneau, he is inhaling the ether. Pooh! It is nothing but a passing spasm; his pulse is good. He's as strong as a giant. Look at his shaggy chest, mademoiselle; he is sure to live a hundred years! His wig stays on well; see it's glued and isn't the right color, for he is red-haired by nature. They say that red-haired people are either all good or all bad; he must be good, don't you think so?"

"Good to hang," Poiret said.

"On the neck of a pretty woman, you mean," cried Mlle. Michonneau quickly. "Go away, Monsieur Poiret. It is for us women to nurse the men when they are ill. Besides, you may as well take yourself off, for any help you are," she added. "Mme. Vauquer and I will care for dear M. Vautrin."

Poiret went away meekly without a murmur, like a dog that has been kicked by his master.

Rastignac had gone out to walk and breathe the air, for he felt stifled. The evening before, he had meant to prevent the crime that had now taken place at the appointed hour. What had happened, and what was he to do? He trembled for fear that he was already the accomplice of Vautrin. The composure of Vautrin awed him even yet.

"Suppose that he would die without confessing?" he thought.

He rushed through the paths of the Luxembourg Gardens as if a pack of hounds were pursuing him; he could almost hear their barking.

"Well," Bianchon cried as he met him, "have you read *Le Pilote?*"

Le Pilote was a radical paper, under the direction of M. Tissot, that carried the news of the day to the provinces only a few hours later than it came out in the morning papers and was consequently twenty-four hours in advance of any other newspaper outside of Paris.

"There is a fine story in it," the medical student said. "Taillefer's son has fought a duel with Comte Franchessini, of the old guard, and has received a cut two inches deep in the forehead. Little Victorine has become one of the richest heiresses in Paris. Oh, dear! If we had only known it! What a lottery death is! Is it true that Victorine looked at you favorably?"

"Stop, Bianchon; I shall never marry her. I love a charming woman, and I am loved by her in return—"

"You talk as if you were lashing yourself up to keep true to her. Show me a woman worth the sacrifice of M. Taillefer's fortune."

"All the demons are after me then!" Rastignac cried.

"With whom are you angry? Are you mad? Give me your hand so I may feel your pulse," Bianchon said. "You are feverish."

"Go to Mamma Vauquer," Eugène said. "That wretch Vautrin has fallen down as if he were dead."

"Ah," Bianchon said as he left Rastignac, "you confirm some suspicions of mine that I am very anxious to verify."

Rastignac's long walk was a very solemn one. He made a thorough investigation of his conscience, and if he ever hesitated or faltered in his self-examination, at least his virtue emerged from this fierce and terrible ordeal, tried like a bar of iron that is proof against every shock. He recollected the confidences père Goriot had made him the night before and the apartment that had been rented for him near Delphine in the rue d'Artois. He took out her letter, read it over again, and kissed it.

"Such love as hers shall be my anchor of safety," he said. "The poor old man has bitterly suffered; he says nothing of his griefs, but it is easy to see that he has had them. I shall take care of him as if he were my father and shall make him as happy as I can. If she loves me, she will often come and spend the day with him. The great Comtesse de Restaud is a wicked woman; she would be willing to make a porter of her father. Dear Delphine! She is kinder to the old man; she is worthy of being loved! Ah, this evening I shall be happy!"

He drew out his watch and looked at it admiringly.

"All has gone well with me! When two people love each other eternally, then can help each other, and there is no harm in my taking this. Besides, I am certain to succeed, and then I can return it all a hundredfold. There will be no crime in this connection with Delphine; nothing to call a frown from the most austere virtue. How many honorable people are united in the same way! We are deceiving nobody; it is only deception that is de-grading. Wouldn't it be hypocritical of us to renounce each other? She has long been separated from her husband, and, moreover, I will tell the Alsatian brute that he must yield his wife to me, because it is not in his power to make her happy."

Rastignac's struggle lasted long. His youth and virtue were to gain the victory; nevertheless, toward half past four, as the evening was closing in, he was impelled by irresistible curiosity to return to his boardinghouse, which he swore he would leave forever. He was anxious to find out whether Vautrin were dead. After administering an emetic to Vautrin, Bianchon had ordered the contents of his stomach to be carried to the hospital, where they could be chemically analyzed, and the insistence with which Mlle. Michonneau tried to have them thrown away only strengthened his suspicions. Moreover, Vautrin's recovery was too rapid for Bianchon not to mistrust some plot against the gay fellow who was the life of the boardinghouse. When Rastignac returned, he found Vautrin up and standing near the dining-room stove. The news of young Taillefer's duel had drawn the boarders together earlier than usual; they were all curious to know the details of the affair and the influence it had upon Victorine's fate, so all of them except père Goriot were assembled and occupied in discussing the morning's adventure. When Eugène entered the room, his eyes met those of the imperturbable Vautrin, whose look searched his heart, stirring some evil chords there so strongly that he shuddered.

"Well, my boy," the convict said, "death will have a quarrel of long standing with me. According to the testimony of these ladies, I have held my own against a rush of blood to the head that might have killed an ox."

"You might as well say a bull," Mme. Vauquer cried.

"Perhaps you are sorry to see me alive?" Vautrin whispered to Rastignac, whose thoughts he believed he could guess. "I must be a damned strong man!"

"Yes, indeed," Bianchon said. "The day before yesterday, Mlle. Michonneau was talking of a gentleman surnamed Trompe-la-Mort; that name would suit you very well."

Vautrin appeared thunderstruck by this name; he turned pale and tottered, and his magnetic glance flashed like a ray of sunlight upon Mlle. Michonneau, whose strength failed her under the intensity of his will. The old maid sank back on a chair, and Poiret stepped quickly between her and Vautrin; he understood that she was in danger, as he saw the ferocious meaning in the convict's face, now no longer covered by the benignant mask that had concealed his real nature. The boarders stared in amazement at this drama that they could not understand. At that moment were heard the footsteps of several men, and the clink of soldiers' muskets against the pavement of the street. Just as Collin was mechanically looking about at the walls and windows for some means of escape, four men appeared at the parlor door. The first one was the Chief of the Detective Police, and the three others officers of the peace.

"In the name of the law and the King!" said one of the officers, whose voice was drowned by a universal murmur of astonishment.

Silence was soon established, and the boarders separated to give passage to three of the men, who kept their hands in their side pockets, in which they carried loaded pistols. Two guards followed the police agents and took possession of the parlor door; two others held the door that led to the staircase. The steps and guns of several soldiers echoed on the pebbled way that ran along the front of the house. Thus all hope was cut off from Trompe-la-Mort, toward whom all eyes were irresistibly drawn. The Chief of the Police walked straight up to him and began by giving him a violent blow on the head that sent his wig flying and disclosed his head in all its repulsiveness. His short, brick-red hair was in keeping with his head and face, whose fearful features of blended cunning and strength, in harmony with his body, were clearly illuminated as if by the fires of Hell. Everybody understood Vautrin, his past, his present, his future, his inexorable doctrines, his religion of selfish pleasure, the kind of royalty conferred upon him by the cynicism of his thoughts and acts, and the power of his organization inured to everything. The blood mounted to his face, and his eyes glowed like a panther's. He bounded into the air with such fierce energy and gave so loud a roar that the boarders shrieked with terror. At this leonine gesture, the police agents took advantage of the general clamor to seize their pistols. Collin understood his danger as he saw the arms cocked and glittering in the men's hands, and he suddenly exhibited the highest of human faculties. It was a horrible and majestic spectacle! His countenance presented a phenomenon that can be compared only to a boiler full of dense steam, powerful enough to upheave mountains but which may be instantly dissipated by a single drop of cold water. The drop of water that cooled his rage was the lightninglike rapidity of reflection. He smiled and looked at his wig.

"You are not very polite today," he said to the Chief of the Police.

He stretched out his hands to the guards, nodding to them to come on.

"Gentlemen," he said, "put on the manacles or the handcuffs. I take those present to witness that I offer no resistance."

The dining room resounded with a murmur of applause, extorted by the promptness with which the lava and flame had burst forth from this human volcano and had rushed back into it again.

"This is something you didn't bargain for, you swaggering housebreaker," the convict continued, addressing the celebrated Director of the Detective Police.

"Come, undress him!" the gentleman from the petite rue Ste-Anne ordered, with much scorn.

"Why?" Collin asked. "There are ladies present. I deny nothing and give myself up."

He paused and surveyed the assembly with the air of an orator who is about to make startling revelations.

"Write down what I say, Papa Lachapelle," he said, speaking to a little old man with white hair who was sitting at the end of the table and had drawn from his portfolio a paper on which to put down a report of the proceedings.

"I confess to being Jacques Collin, called Trompe-la-Mort, who was sentenced to twenty years' imprisonment, and I have just proved to you that I have come lawfully by my surname. If I had merely raised my hand," he said to the boarders, "those three police spies would have covered Mamma Vauquer's floor with my blood. The wretches have caught me in a pretty trap!"

Mme. Vauquer turned sick at these words.

"My God! It is enough to make me ill; and to think that I went with him to the Gaieté last night!" she said to Sylvie.

"You must be philosophical, Mamma," rejoined Collin. "Are you any worse off for sitting in my box last night at the Gaieté? Are you any better than we are?" he cried. "There is less infamy in the branding of our shoulders than there is in your hearts; limp members of a corrupt society that you are! Even the best among you could not resist me." He fixed his eyes upon Rastignac with an engaging smile that contrasted oddly with the fierce expression of his face. "Our little bargain holds good just the same, my boy, in case you care to accept it! You know what I mean!"

He sang:

> "My Fanny's a charming girl,
> As simple as may be."

"Don't be embarrassed," he went on. "I shall be able to get my share. I am much too feared to be *tricked!*"

The manners and language of the galleys, their abrupt transitions from the ludicrous to the horrible, the appalling greatness, the good-fellowship, and the baseness that belong there were suddenly represented in this episode and by this man, who was no longer a single man, but the epitome of a degenerate nation, of a people at once savage, logical, brutal, and facile. In a moment, Collin had become a poet of infernal genius, who gave expression to every human sentiment save that of repentance. He wore the look of a fallen archangel resolved for war. Rastignac lowered his eyes and accepted this kinship of crime in expiation of his evil thoughts.

"Who betrayed me?" Collin asked, letting his terrible eyes wander over the people present.

"It was you, you mercenary hag," he said, fixing his eyes on Mlle. Michonneau. "You brought on that pretended stroke of apoplexy, you inquisitive creature. With one word I could have your throat cut in a week, but I forgive you, for I am a Christian. Besides, it was not you who sold me. But who could it have been? Aha, you are searching upstairs, are you?" he exclaimed, as he heard the police officers opening his wardrobes and seizing his effects. "The nests are empty, for the birds flew away yesterday. And you can never find out anything, because I keep my books here," he added, tapping his forehead. "Now I know who it was who sold me. It must have been that rogue Fil-de-Soie, wasn't it, old nab'em?" he asked, turning to the Chief of the Police. "It agrees too well with the time of my having our banknotes upstairs. There is nothing more to be found, little spies. As to Fil-de-Soie, he shall be dead and buried within two weeks, even if you set all your gendarmes to guard him.

"How much did you give to this Michonnette?" he said, turning to the police agents. "Three thousand francs? I was worth more than that, you decrepit Ninon, you tattered Pompadour, you Venus of Père-Lachaise! If you had warned me, you would have had six thousand francs, but you didn't guess that, you old seller of human flesh, or you would have given me the preference. Yes, I would have parted with them gladly to avoid a journey that is inconvenient to me and makes me lose money," he continued, as the men were putting on the handcuffs. "These people take pleasure in dragging me about forever to torment me. If they would only send me directly to the galleys, I would soon return to my occupations in spite of our little simpletons on the quai des Orfèvres. At the galleys, they will all turn themselves inside out to help their general, the good Trompe-la-Mort, to escape! Has any one of you more than ten thousand brothers ready to do everything for him?" he asked proudly. Then striking his heart he added, "There is some virtue there; I have never betrayed anybody. See them, you sordid hussy," he said to the old maid. "They look at me in terror, but you make them sick with disgust. Take your reward."

He paused as he turned his gaze upon the boarders.

"What fools you are!" he said. "Have you never seen a convict? A convict of the stamp of Jacques Collin here present is less cowardly than other men and protests against the deep deception of the social contract, as it has been called by Jean-Jacques, whose disciple I boast myself. In short, I stand alone against the government, with all its courts, its gendarmes, and its resources, and I can evade them all."

"The devil!" the painter said. "He would make a splendid model!"

"Tell me, you who are the lackey of my lord the Executioner, Master of the Widow (poetic and terrible name that the convicts give the guillotine)," he continued, turning to the head of the Detective Police, "be a good fellow and tell me if it is Fil-de-Soie who sold me. I would not like him to pay the penalty for another, for it would be unjust."

At that moment, the police officers who had opened and inventoried everything in his room reappeared and spoke in a low voice to their chief.

The official report had been made.

"Gentlemen," Jacques Collin said, addressing the boarders, "they are about to take me away. You have all been very polite to me during my stay here, and I shall remember it with gratitude. I wish you good-bye and hope you will allow me to send you some figs from Provence."

He made a few steps toward the door and turned to look at Rastignac.

"Farewell, Eugène," he said in a sad, sweet tone that contrasted singularly with the harsh tones in which he had till now spoken. "If you are in trouble, I have left you a devoted friend."

In spite of his handcuffs, he was able to fall into guard, and making a beat with his right foot he cried, "One, two!" and went through the motions of fencing.

"In case of distress, address yourself to him. You can dispose of the man and his money."

These last words were said with so much buffoonery that no one could understand them except Rastignac and the extraordinary man himself. After all the gendarmes, soldiers, and police agents had left the house, Sylvie, who was rubbing her mistress's temples with vinegar, looked up at the astonished boarders.

"Well," she said, "he was a man all the same!"

Her speech broke the spell thrown over the assembled company by the diversity and multiplicity of feelings that the foregoing scene had excited. It was then that the boarders, after exchanging glances, turned to Mlle. Michonneau, who was cowering near the stove, thin, cold, and dried up as a mummy, with her eyes cast down as if she feared that the green shade she wore was not sufficient to hide their expression. The antipathy with which her face had so long inspired them was now suddenly explained. A low murmur whose perfect uniformity betrayed unanimous disgust made itself heard. It reached Mlle. Michonneau's ears, but she did not stir. Bianchon was the first; he leaned toward his neighbor and whispered:

"I shall take myself off, if that woman continues to dine with us."

In the twinkling of an eye, everybody except Poiret showed his acquiescence in the suggestion of the medical student, who, armed with the universal approval, advanced toward the old man.

"You who know Mlle. Michonneau so well," he said, "speak to her and make her understand that she must leave here instantly."

"Instantly?" Poiret repeated in amazement.

Then he stepped up to the old maid and whispered a few words in her ear.

"But I have paid for my quarter, and I can stay here for my money as well as anybody else," she said, looking round upon the boarders with her viper's eyes.

"That is no matter; we can all club together to pay it back to you," Rastignac said.

"You are upholding Collin, monsieur," she said to the student with a venomous and questioning glance. "It is not difficult to know why."

At this, Eugène gave a bound as if he were going to rush upon the old maid and strangle her. He understood all the treachery of her look, which threw a horrible light into his soul.

"Leave her alone," the boarders cried.

Rastignac crossed his arms and remained silent.

"Let us finish with Mlle. Judas," the painter said to Mme. Vauquer. "Madame, if you do not turn Mlle. Michonneau out-of-doors, we shall leave your barrack in a body and shall tell everybody that all your boarders are spies and convicts. In case you comply with our request, we shall observe silence concerning this event, which after all, might happen in the best society, until convicts are branded upon the forehead and prevented from masquerading as repectable citizens and playing the foolish pranks they are so fond of."

On hearing this, Mme. Vauquer recovered her strength in a miraculous manner, rose up, crossed her arms, and opened her eyes that were clear of all traces of tears.

"But, my dear monsieur, do you wish to ruin my house? There is M. Vautrin. Oh, good heavens!" she said. "I can't help calling him by his respectable name! There is one room empty already," she resumed, "and you want me to have two more on my hands to rent, at a season when everybody is provided for."

"Come, gentlemen, let us get our hats and go and dine at Flicoteaux's, in the place Sorbonne," Bianchon said.

Mme. Vauquer saw at once the course most advantageous to herself and moved toward Mlle. Michonneau.

"Come, my dear little woman," she said, "you can't wish to give the deathblow to my establishment, hey? See to what extremity these gentlemen are driving me; go up to your room for this evening."

"That won't do at all," the boarders cried. "We want her to leave the house this instant."

"But the poor lady has not dined yet," Poiret said piteously.

"She can go and dine wherever she wants," several voices exclaimed.

"Turn the spy out-of-doors!"

"Turn the spies out-of-doors!"

"Gentlemen," Poiret cried, suddenly rising to the courage of a lovesick ram, "respect one of the fair sex."

"Spies have no sex," the painter answered.

"Precious *sexorama!*"

"Out at the *doororama!*"

"Gentlemen, this is unseemly. When people are sent away, formalities must be observed. We have paid our money, and we intend to stay," Poiret said, putting on his cap and taking a seat beside Mlle. Michonneau, whom Mme. Vauquer was still lecturing.

"Naughty little man," the painter said with a ludicrous expression, "go away, naughty little man."

"Come, if you don't go away, we shall go ourselves," Bianchon said.

The boarders moved simultaneously toward the parlor.

"Mademoiselle, what can you expect of me?" Mme. Vauquer screamed. "I shall be ruined. You can't stay; they are going to use violence."

Mlle. Michonneau rose.

"She will go! She won't go! She will! She won't!"

These alternate cries and the hostile nature of what was said about her constrained Mlle. Michonneau to take her departure, after concluding some stipulations with the hostess in a low voice.

"I shall go to Mme. Buneaud's," she said with a threatening air.

"Go where you wish, mademoiselle," Mme. Vauquer said, who understood the cruel insult implied in the choice of a rival establishment that she hated. "Go to Mme. Buneaud's, and you'll get wine that would make a goat wince and dinners bought secondhand."

The boarders placed themselves in two ranks in deep silence. Poiret gazed at Mlle. Michonneau so tenderly and showed himself so naively uncertain as to whether he would follow her or remain that the boarders, happy at the departure of Mlle. Michonneau, burst out laughing at the sight of him.

"Get up, Poiret," the painter cried. "Come on there! Come on!"

The museum man sang, in an exaggerated manner, the beginning of a familiar song:

> "*Partant pour la Syrie,*
> *The young and brave Dunois.*"

"Go with her, for you are dying to do it; *trahit sua quemque voluptas!*" Bianchon said.

"Everybody follows his own fancy—a free translation from Virgil," said the tutor.

Mlle. Michonneau looked at Poiret and made a gesture as if to take his arm; he could not resist this appeal and stepped forward to offer his escort to the old maid. There was a burst of applause and laughter.

"Bravo, Poiret! Old Poiret! Apollo-Poiret! Mars-Poiret! Courageous Poiret!"

At that moment, a commissioner entered and handed a letter to Madame Vauquer, who read it and then sank back into her chair.

"I may as well burn down my house, for the lightning has struck it!" she cried. "Young Taillefer died at three o'clock. I am well punished for having wished those ladies good luck at the expense of that poor young man. Mme. Couture and Victorine ask me to send their things, for they are going to live with Victorine's father. M. Taillefer allows his daughter to keep Mme. Couture with her as a companion. Four apartments vacant, and five boarders lost!"

She sat down, apparently on the brink of tears.

"Bad luck has come to me!" she moaned.

The noise of a carriage stopping before the door resounded in the street.

"Another windfall!" Sylvie exclaimed.

Goriot appeared with a countenance so flushed and radiant with happiness that he looked like another man.

"Goriot in a cab?" the boarders said. "The world must be coming to an end!"

The old man went straight up to Eugène, who was moping in a corner, and took him by the arm.

"Come," he said gayly.

"You don't know what has happened," Eugène said. "Vautrin turned out to be a convict, and they have just arrested him. Young Taillefer is dead."

"Well, what difference does that make to us?" père Goriot replied. "I am going to dine with my daughter at your house, do you understand? She is waiting for you; come along!"

He pulled Rastignac so violently by the arm that he forced him to go with him and carried him off as a man might carry off his mistress.

"Let us have dinner," the painter cried, after which everyone took a chair and sat down at the table.

"Everything has gone wrong today," big Sylvie remarked. "I forgot to stir the mutton stew, and you will have to eat it burned; so much the worse for you."

Mme. Vauquer did not have the heart to say a word as she counted only ten persons instead of eighteen round her table; but everybody did his best to cheer and console her. Though the talk first turned upon Vautrin and the events of the day, the boarders were insensibly led in the wandering course of conversation to speak of duels, the galleys, prisons, the administration of justice, and the laws that needed reform, so they soon found themselves a thousand miles from Jacques Collin, Victorine, and her brother. Although there were only ten of them, they made noise enough for twenty and seemed to be more numerous than ever; this was the only difference between today's and yesterday's dinner. The habitual thoughtlessness of that selfish world that seeks for a new prey to devour in the daily events of Paris took the upper hand, and Mme. Vauquer allowed herself to be soothed by hope, which stemmed from the voice of big Sylvie.

5

THIS whole day was destined to affect Eugène like a series of phantasmagoria, and in spite of his strong character and clear head, he was unable to bring his ideas into order when he found himself seated in a cab beside père Goriot, whose words betrayed unwonted happiness and resounded in the student's ears, after the many emotions through which he had passed as if they were the words of a dream.

"It was all arranged this morning. We three are to dine together, together! Do you hear? It is four years since I have dined with Delphine, my little Delphine. Now I am going to have her beside me for a whole evening. We have been in your new apartment all day; I worked like a drudge in my shirt-sleeves. I helped to carry the furniture. Oh, you don't know how sweet she is at dinner; she will be so thoughtful of me and say, 'Here, Papa, take some of this, it is very good.' And then I won't be able to eat at all. Oh, it is so long since I have seen her in peace, as I hope to see her tonight!"

"Everything is upside down today," Eugène said.

"Upside down?" père Goriot said. "No, the world was never so happy before. I see only gay faces in the streets and people who shake hands and kiss one another; they all look as joyful as if they were going to dine with a daughter and eat a delicious little dinner, such as Delphine ordered this morning before me from the chief cook of the Café des Anglais. But it makes no difference what the dinner is, for aloes would be sweet as honey to me if I were with her."

"I believe I am beginning to live again," Eugène said.

"Hurry, driver!" père Goriot cried, opening the front window. "Drive faster and I will give you five francs extra if you take me where I told you in ten minutes."

On hearing this promise, the coachman drove them through Paris like lightning.

"He is just crawling," père Goriot kept saying.

"Where are you taking me?" Rastignac inquired.

"To your own house," père Goriot answered.

The cab stopped in the rue d'Artois. The old man got out first and flung ten francs to the coachman with the lavishness of a widower who forgets everything in his frenzy of excitement.

"Come, let us go upstairs," he said to Rastignac, traversing the courtyard with him and leading him up to the door of an apartment on the third story at the back of a fine new house. Père Goriot had no need to ring, for Thérèse, Mme. de Nucingen's maid, opened the door for them. Eugène found himself in a charming little bachelor apartment consisting of an antechamber, a little parlor, a bedroom, and a study looking out over a garden. In the little parlor, whose furniture and decorations could bear comparison with all he had ever seen that was prettiest and most attractive, by the gleam of the lighted candles he saw Delphine. She rose from a sofa by the fireside and, putting the hand screen she held on the mantelpiece, said to him in a tone of voice that was full of tenderness:

"So I had to send in search of you, monsieur—you who will not understand."

Thérèse left the room; the student clasped Delphine closely in his arms and shed tears of joy. The contrast between what he saw about him and what he had been seeing through the course of this day, whose many excitements had wearied his heart and head, brought on an attack of nervous emotion.

"I knew he loved you," père Goriot said in a low voice to his daughter, while Eugène, quite overcome, lay back on the sofa unable to say a word or to explain anything yet as to how this last tap of a magic wand had been given.

"Come and see everything," Mme. de Nucingen said, taking him by the hand and leading him into a room whose carpet, furniture, and least details recalled Delphine's in miniature.

"There is no bed," Rastignac said.

"No," she said blushing and pressing his hand.

Eugène looked at her and, though still young, understood the treasure of true modesty in the heart of a loving woman.

"You are one of those beings whom a man must always adore," he whispered in her ear. "Yes, I dare say it now that we understand each other so well: the warmer and truer love is, the more hidden and mysterious it should be. We shall not let anybody into our secret."

"I shall not be anybody," père Goriot said discontentedly.

"You know very well that you are part of *us*, you . . . "

"Oh, that is what I wanted. You will pay no attention to me, will you? I shall go and come like a good spirit that is always near you, although you do not see it. Now, Delphinette, Ninette, Dedel, wasn't I right to tell you that there was a pretty apartment in the rue d'Artois and that we had better furnish it for him? You did not want to do it. Oh, I am the author of your happiness, just as I am the author of your days. Fathers must always give to be blessed. Being a father means to be eternally giving."

"What do you mean?" Eugène asked.

"Yes, she hung back and was afraid of gossip, just as if the world were worth her happiness! And yet all women dream of doing what she is doing . . . "

Père Goriot was talking to himself, for Mme. de Nucingen had drawn Eugène into the study, from which there echoed the sound of a kiss, however lightly given. The room was quite in accordance with the elegance of the rest of the apartment, and no comfort was lacking.

"Have we guessed your wishes right?" she asked as they walked back to the parlor to sit down to table.

"Yes," he said, "too well. I appreciate this perfect luxury, this realization of a beautiful dream, and all the romance of a life of youth and elegance too thoroughly to be unworthy of them; but I cannot accept them from you, and I am still too poor to . . . "

"Ah, indeed! Are you resisting me already?" she said with a little air of mocking authority and one of those pretty little grimaces that women make when they try to laugh away a man's scruples.

Eugène had been questioning himself very solemnly that day, and the arrest of Vautrin, which showed him the depths of the abyss into which he had so nearly fallen, had strengthened his delicacy and better feelings so powerfully that it was impossible for him to yield to this caressing refutation of his generous impulse. Profound sadness took possession of him.

"What!" Mme. de Nucingen said. "Do you refuse? Do you know what the meaning of such a refusal would be? You mistrust the future and dare not bind yourself to me. It must be that you are afraid of betraying my affection. If you love me, if I—love you, why should you recoil before such a slight obligation? If you only knew the pleasure I have had in furnishing this little apartment, you would not hesitate, and you would beg my pardon. I had some money of yours, and I put it to a good use, that is all. You think yourself great, but you are only little after all. You ask a great deal more . . . Ah," she cried, as she caught the passionate look upon Eugène's face, "and yet you make so much ado about mere trifles. If you don't love me, then you are right not to accept. My fate lies in a word from you. Speak! Father," she added, turning toward her father after a pause, "tell him some good reasons. Does he think that I am less jealous of our honor than he?"

Père Goriot had been watching this lover's dispute with a fixed smile like that of an opium eater.

"My child, you are at the beginning of life," she continued, taking Eugène's hand in hers. "You meet with a barrier insurmountable to most men; a woman's hand opens it for you, yet you draw back! You are certain to make your way and achieve a brilliant fortune; success is written on your handsome forehead. Then can't you return me what I am lending you today? In old times, ladies gave their knights armor and swords, helmets, coats of mail, and horses, so that they might go and fight in their name in a tournament. Now, Eugène, the things I offer you are only the arms of our own time, the implements necessary to a man who means to rise. The garret you are now living in must be pretty if it looks like Papa's room! Come, aren't we going to dine? Do you want to make me unhappy? Answer me," she insisted, shaking his hand.

"Good heavens, Papa, make him decide, or I shall leave this place and never see him again."

"I am going to make you decide," père Goriot said, waking up from his ecstasy. "Dear Monsieur Eugène, you are ready to borrow money from the Jews, aren't you?"

"I must," Eugène answered.

"Good! I have you then," rejoined the old man, taking out a worn and wretched leather wallet. "I have turned Jew; I have paid all the bills, and here they are. You don't owe a penny for all this. It does not amount to a large sum—only five thousand francs at the most. I lend them to you! You cannot refuse me, for I am not a woman. You may write me an acknowledgment on a scrap of paper, and you can repay me by and by."

Tears rushed into Eugène's and Delphine's eyes, and they looked at each other in astonishment. Rastignac took the old man's hand and pressed it.

"Why not? Aren't you my children?" Goriot said.

"But my dear father," Mme. de Nucingen said, "how did you manage this?"

"I will tell you," he answered. "When I found that you had made up your mind to bring him to live near you and saw you buying an outfit like a bride's, I thought to myself that you would soon get into trouble. The lawyer says that a suit brought against your husband to oblige him to return your property will last more than six months. Good. So I sold my government stock, which brought me an income of thirteen hundred and fifty francs, and with fifteen thousand francs I bought a life annuity of twelve hundred francs, well secured by mortgage; then I paid your shopkeepers with the rest of the capital, my children. I have a room upstairs for a hundred and fifty francs a year, I can live like a king on two francs a day, and I shall have something left over. I never wear out anything and shall hardly ever have to buy new clothes. For two weeks I have been laughing in my sleeve and thinking how happy you both will be. You are happy, aren't you?"

"Oh, Papa, Papa!" Mme. de Nucingen cried, running to her father and springing upon his lap.

She covered him with kisses, and letting her blond hair stray over his cheeks, dropped tears on his old face now so bright with happiness.

"Dear Father, you are a father! No, there is not one like you on the earth. Eugène was already very fond of you, but now, what will it be?"

"But, my children," said père Goriot, who, for ten years had not felt his daughter's heart beating against his, "Delphinette, are you going to make me die of joy? My poor heart is breaking. Now, Monsieur Eugène, we are already quits!"

The old man clasped his daughter in such a wild and frantic embrace that she exclaimed:

"Oh, how you hurt me!"

"I hurt you?" he said, turning pale.

He looked at her with a sorrow that seemed more than human. In order to describe the expression of this Christ among fathers, it is necessary to seek a comparison in those pictures in which the princes of the palette have represented the suffering endured by the Savior of men for the salvation of the world.

"No, no, I can't have hurt you," he went on, questioning her with a smile. "It was I who was hurt by your cry. The cost was greater than I said," he continued, whispering in his daughter's ear, which he kissed with great circumspection, "but we must deceive him about it, or he would be angry."

Eugène was petrified by this man's inexhaustible devotion and, as he looked at him, gave expression to the artless admiration that is faith in the young.

"I shall be worthy of all this," he cried.

"Oh, Eugène, you have said something very noble," Mme. de Nucingen exclaimed as she kissed the student on the forehead.

"He refused Mlle. Taillefer and her millions for your sake," père Goriot said. "Yes, the little girl loved you, and now that her brother is dead, she is as rich as Croesus."

"Oh, why do you tell her this?" Eugène cried.

"Eugène," Delphine said in a low voice, "now I have one regret this evening. Ah, I shall love you well and love you always."

"This is the happiest day I have spent since you and your sister married," père Goriot said. "God may make me suffer as much as may be His will, provided it not be through you, and I shall be able to say to myself, in February of this year, for a moment, I was happier than

other men can be in the whole course of their lives. Look at me, Fifine," he said to his daughter. "She is very pretty, isn't she? Tell me, have you met many women with such a beautiful complexion as hers, or such a little dimple? No, I don't think you have; and yet I am the father of this lovely creature. From now on, when she is happy with you, she will be a thousand times more charming. If you need my share of Paradise, I am ready to give it up to you and to descend into Hell myself. Now let us eat," he went on, not knowing what he said. "Our dinner is before us."

"Poor Father!" Delphine said.

"If you only knew, my child," he said as he rose and walked over to her and, taking her head in his hands, kissed her braids of hair, "how happy you can make me at very little cost to yourself. Come and see me sometimes; I shall be right above here, and you will only have a step to go. Promise me that you will, promise!"

"Yes, dear Father."

"Say it again."

"Yes, my dear Father."

"That is enough, for I would make you say it a hundred times if I followed my own inclination. Let us eat our dinner."

They behaved like children all through the evening, and père Goriot was not the most sensible of the three. He sat at his daughter's feet and kissed them; he gazed long into her eyes, rubbed his head against her dress and in short, was as foolish as the youngest and most tender lover could be.

"You see," Delphine said to Eugène, "when my father is with us, I am obliged to give him all my attention. It will be a bore sometimes."

Eugène, who had already been conscious of several impulses of jealousy, could not blame her speech, though it contained the germ of all ingratitude.

"When will the apartment be ready?" Eugène asked, looking round the room. "Must we part tonight?"

"Yes, but tomorrow you must come and dine with me,' she answered slyly. "There is the opera tomorrow evening."

"I shall go and sit in the pit," père Goriot said.

It was midnight and Mme. de Nucingen's carriage was waiting. Père Goriot and the student returned to their boardinghouse, talking of Delphine with a growing enthusiasm that gave rise to a curious rivalry of expression between their two violent passions. Eugène could not hide from himself that the father's love, which lay outside of any personal interest, surpassed his in depth and persistence. The idol was always pure and beautiful in the eyes of her father, whose adoration fed upon all the past as well as the future. They found Mme. Vauquer sitting beside her stove between Sylvie and Christophe; the old landlady was like Marius on the ruins of Carthage. She was waiting for the only two boarders she had left and was bemoaning herself with Sylvie. Lord Byron has put some very fine lamentations into the mouth of Tasso, but they are far from equaling the profound truth of those uttered by Mme. Vauquer.

"Then there will be only three cups of coffee to make

tomorrow morning, Sylvie. Dear me! My deserted house, it is enough to break one's heart. What is life to me without my boarders? Nothing at all. Here is my house dismantled of all the men that made up its furniture, and my life was in them. What have I done to draw down all these misfortunes upon me? I have laid in provisions of beans and potatoes for twenty persons. And the police in my house! We shall eat nothing but potatoes, and I shall send away Christophe."

The servant, who was sleeping, woke up with a start, saying:

"Madame?"

"Poor fellow! He is like a watchdog," Sylvie said.

"The season is over, and everybody is settled now. Where shall I find new boarders? I shall lose my senses. And that hag of a Michonneau took away Poiret from me! What did she do to attach that man to her so closely? He follows her like a little poodle."

"Ah, bless me!" Sylvie said, tossing her head. "Those old maids know all kinds of tricks."

"And that poor M. Vautrin of whom they have made a convict," the widow continued. "I tell you, Sylvie, I can't believe it yet. Such a good-natured man, who took fifteen francs' worth of coffee and brandy a month and who paid up to the last penny!"

"And generous too," put in Christophe.

"There may be some mistake," Sylvie suggested.

"No, he confessed it himself," Mme. Vauquer replied. "And to think of all these things happening to me, in a part of the city where not even a cat passes! On my faith as an honest woman, I am dreaming. You know, we saw Louis XVI come to grief, we saw the downfall of the Emperor, and then we saw his return and his second fall; it was all in the range of possibilities. But there are no chances against a boardinghouse. People can do without a king, but they can't do without eating; and when an honest woman, born a De Conflans, furnishes dinners with all sorts of good things, unless the end of the world comes . . . But that is it, it must be the end of the world!"

"Only think that Mlle. Michonneau, who did you all this wrong, is to receive three thousand francs, they say," Sylvie cried.

"Don't mention her; she is a wretch," Mme. Vauquer said. "And she is going to Mme. Buneaud's in the bargain! But she is capable of everything; she must be guilty of horrors. No doubt she murdered and stole in her time. She ought to go to the galleys instead of that poor dear man . . ."

Eugène and Père Goriot rang at that moment.

"Ah, there are my two faithful ones," the widow sighed.

The two faithful ones, who had only preserved a very slight memory of the disasters of the boardinghouse, announced without preface to their hostess that they were going to live in the Chaussée-d'Antin.

"Oh, Sylvie," the widow said, "this is the last straw. You have given me my deathblow, gentlemen! It has struck me in the stomach; I have a pain there. This day has made me ten years older. I shall go crazy; upon my honor I shall! What shall I do with the beans? Since I am alone here, you must go off tomorrow, Christophe. Good night, gentlemen, sleep well."

"What is the matter with her?' Eugène asked of Sylvie.

"Oh, dear me! All the boarders have left because of what has happened, and it has turned her head. I hear her crying now, and it will do her good to blubber. This is the first time she has shed a tear since I have been in her service."

The next day Mme. Vauquer had become rational, as she called it. Though she looked distressed like a woman who had lost all her boarders and the whole course of whose life had changed, she still kept her head and showed herself an example of true, deep sorrow—sorrow caused by injured interests and interrupted customs. Certainly, the look cast by a lover on the dwelling of his mistress as he leaves the spot forever is no sadder than that of Mme. Vauquer as she sat at her empty table. Eugène tried to cheer her by assuring her that Bianchon, whose term at the hospital was approaching its conclusion, would doubtless come to take his place, that the museum employee had often spoken of his desire to have Mme. Couture's apartment, and that in a few days all vacancies would be filled.

"God grant it may be so, dear monsieur, but misfortune has come here. Death too will come in less than ten days, you shall see," she said, looking lugubriously round the dining room. "Which one will death take?"

"It is a good thing to get out of here," Eugène whispered to père Goriot.

"Madame," Sylvie said, running in with a frightened expression, "it is three days since I have seen Mistigris."

"Oh, if my cat is dead, or if he has run away, I—"

The poor widow could not finish her sentence; she clasped her hands and threw herself back in her arm-chair, overpowered by this terrible omen.

PART FIVE

Confrontation

1

TOWARD noon, the hour of the postman's arrival in the quarter of Paris near the Panthéon, Eugène received a letter in a handsome envelope sealed with the arms of De Beauséant. It contained an invitation to M. and Mme. de Nucingen for the great ball that was to be given by the Viscountess and had been announced a month ago. There was also a little note enclosed for Eugène:

I thought, monsieur, that you would take pleasure in delivering my greetings to Mme. de Nucingen; I send you the invitation you asked for and, I shall be charmed to make the acquaintance of Mme. de Restaud's sister. Bring me your pretty friend then, and try not to give her all your affection, for you owe much to me in return for what I feel for you.

Vicomtesse de Beauséant

"I see," Eugène said, as he reread the note, "Mme. de Beauséant tells me clearly enough that she does not want Baron de Nucingen."

He hastened to Delphine, happy to be able to offer her

a pleasure for which he would no doubt receive his reward. Mme. de Nucingen was taking her bath, so Rastignac waited in the boudoir, a prey to the natural impatience of an eager young man wild to take possession of the mistress whom he has loved for a whole year. There are some emotions that do not occur twice in the life of young people. The first true woman a man loves—that is to say, the woman who appears to him surrounded by the splendid accessories required by Parisian society—never has a rival. Love in Paris bears no resemblance to love elsewhere. Neither men nor women are the dupes of the glittering commonplaces that everyone parades, out of decency, concerning affections that pretend to be disinterested. In Paris, it is not enough for a woman to satisfy the heart and the senses, for she knows perfectly that she has still greater obligations to fulfill toward the thousand vanities that go to make up life. There, above all, love is essentially boastful, brazen, prodigal, charlatanical, and ostentatious. If all the ladies of the court of Louis XIV envied Mlle. de la Vallière the ardent passion that made the great king forget that his cuffs had cost a thousand crowns apiece when he tore them to facilitate the Duc de Vermandois's entrance into the world, what can be expected of the rest of humanity? You may be young, rich, and titled, still better if possible; the more incense you bring to burn before your idol—if you have an idol—the more she will smile upon you. Love is a religion, and its worship is more costly than that of other religions; its presence is transient, and its path is strewn with devastation like that of a wanton boy. The luxury of sentiment is the poetry of the attic; without this treasure, what would become of love in such a place? If there are exceptions to the Draconian laws of the Parisian code, they are to be met with in solitude in those souls who have not allowed themselves to be carried away by the teachings of society, who dwell beside some fountain of clear water, ever flowing and ever springing up anew, and who, faithful to their own green shade and happy to listen to the language of the infinite, which they find written in all that surrounds them and within themselves, wait patiently for their wings to grow and look down upon those who are of the earth.

But Rastignac, like most young men who have had a foretaste of the splendors of life, wished to enter the arena of the world in full armor; he had caught its fever and felt perhaps that he had the strength to subdue it, although still ignorant of the means or end of his ambition. In default of a pure and sacred love that fills a man's life, this thirst for power may become a fine thing if all personal interest is laid aside and the greatness of a country is proposed as an aim. But the student had not yet reached the point from which a man can contemplate and judge the course of life. Until then, he had not even completely shaken off the charm of those fresh sweet thoughts, which, like a grateful shade, shelter the youth of children brought up in the country. He had always hesitated to cross the Parisian Rubicon, and in spite of his eager curiosity, he had preserved some secret notions of the happy life of a true gentleman in his château.

Nevertheless, his last scruples had vanished on the

previous evening when he found himself in his new apartment, and upon actually enjoying the material advantages of fortune, after having so long enjoyed the moral advantages of noble birth, he had cast away the skin of a provincial and had established himself in a position from which he could descry a bright future. So as he waited for Delphine, luxuriously ensconced in the pretty boudoir that now belonged partly to him, he saw himself so far away from the Rastignac who had come to Paris the year before that as he looked at himself through mental opera glasses, he doubted whether he now bore the slightest resemblance to his former self.

"Mme. de Nucingen is waiting for you in her room," said Thérèse, whose voice made him start.

He found Delphine stretched out upon her sofa, beside the fire, blooming and refreshed. As he saw her lying among clouds of muslin, he could not help comparing her to those beautiful Indian plants, whose fruit comes with the flower.

"At last we are together," she said with emotion.

"Guess what I brought you," Eugène said, sitting down beside her and taking her hand to kiss it.

Mme. de Nucingen thrilled with joy as she read the invitation. She turned toward Eugène with moist eyes and threw her arms round his neck to draw him close to her in an access of satisfied vanity.

"And it is to you," she said, then whispered in his ear, "—to you, dear. Thérèse is in my dressing room and we must be prudent." And aloud again, "—to you that I owe this joy? Yes, I dare call it a joy, for as you obtained it for

me, isn't it more than a triumph of vanity? Nobody has
been good enough to introduce me into this society. Perhaps you will think me petty, frivolous, and light-minded
like a true Parisian; but think, my friend, that I am ready
to sacrifice everything to you and that, if I desire more
ardently than ever to enter the faubourg St-Germain, it
is because you are there yourself."

"Don't you think,' Eugène asked, "that Mme. de
Beauséant is evidently telling us that she does not expect
the Baron de Nucingen at her ball?"

"Yes," the Baroness said, returning the letter to Eugène. "Those women have a genius for impertinence; but
never mind, I shall go. My sister is to be there, for I
know she is preparing an exquisite gown for the occasion.
Eugène," she went on in a low voice, "she is going there
to dispel some horrid suspicions. You don't know the reports about her! Nucingen came to tell me this morning
that they are talking of her at the club without any re-
straint. Good heavens, on what does the honor of a
woman and her family depend? I feel myself assailed
and wounded in the person of my poor sister. According
to what certain people say, M. de Trailles signed bills of
exchange amounting to a hundred thousand francs, almost all of which have now fallen due and for which he
was about to be prosecuted. In this extremity, my sister
is supposed to have sold her diamonds to a Jew—those
beautiful diamonds you must have seen her wear and
which came to her from her husband's mother. Nothing
else has been talked of for two days, so I can understand
why Anastasie has ordered a gorgeous gown and wants to

attract all eyes at Mme. de Beauséant's, where she means to appear in her diamonds and all her glory. But I don't wish to be behind her. She has always tried to get the better of me and has never been kind to me, though I was always doing something for her and was ready to lend her money when she had none. Let's not talk of other people now; today I would like to be quite happy."

At one o'clock in the morning Rastignac was still with Mme. de Nucingen, who bade him a lover's adieu that promised future joys and said with a melancholy expression:

"I am so timid, so superstitious even—for you may give my presentiments any name you please—that I tremble for fear that I pay for my happiness by some frightful calamity."

"Child!" Eugène exclaimed.

"Ah, it is I who am a child this evening," she said, laughing.

Eugène returned to his boardinghouse with the certainty of leaving it the next day, and on the way there he gave himself up to the dreams of a young man who still has the taste of happiness on his lips.

"Well?" père Goriot asked as Rastignac passed in front of his door.

"Well," Eugène answered, "I shall tell you everything tomorrow."

"Everything, won't you?" the old man called. "Now go to bed, and tomorrow we shall begin our happy life."

2

THE next day Goriot and Rastignac were waiting only for the goodwill of a porter to enable them to leave their boardinghouse, when toward noon the noise of a carriage stopping at Mme. Vauquer's door resounded through the rue Neuve-Ste-Geneviève. Mme. de Nucingen alighted from the equipage and asked if her father were still in the house. Upon an affirmative answer from Sylvie, she ran lightly up the stairs. It happened that Eugène was in his room, although his neighbor was unaware of it. At breakfast, he had begged père Goriot to take away his things, telling him they should meet at four o'clock in the rue d'Artois. But, while the old man was out in search of porters, Eugène had promptly answered the roll call at college and had returned to the boardinghouse without anyone's knowledge in order to settle with Mme. Vauquer, being anxious to spare this expense to père Goriot, who in his fanaticism would doubtless have paid for him too.

The landlady was out, so Eugène ran up to his room to see whether he had forgotten anything and congratulated himself on his forethought as he saw in his table drawer the IOU that he had signed for Vautrin and had carelessly thrown there on the day that he had paid it off. Not having any fire, he was about to tear the paper into bits, when he recognized Delphine's voice and, without making any more noise, stopped to hear what she said, for he thought she could have no secrets from him. Then, after the first words, he found the conversation between the father and daughter too interesting for him to stop listening.

"Oh, Father!" she cried. "Heaven grant that it occurred to you to demand an account of my fortune in time to prevent my being ruined! May I speak?"

"Yes, the house is empty," père Goriot answered in a strange voice.

"What is the matter, Father?" Mme. de Nucingen asked.

"You have come," the old man replied, "to plunge a dagger into my heart. God forgive you, my child! You do not know how much I love you, for if you had known it, you would not have said such things without preparing me for them, especially if there is nothing desperate. What has happened that is so pressing as to oblige you to come here for me when we were to be in the rue d'Artois a few minutes later?"

"Oh, Father, could I be mistress of my first impulse in a catastrophe? I am driven crazy! Your lawyer has brought to our knowledge a little earlier the misfortune that will probably overtake us later. Your experience in business will be necessary to us, and I have rushed in pursuit of you as a drowning man clings to the last straw. When M. Derville found that Nucingen met him with all sorts of quibbles, he threatened him with a lawsuit, telling him that the authority of the president of the tribunal came to me this morning to ask if I desired his ruin and mine. I answered that I knew nothing of all this, but that I had a fortune of which I should now be in possession, that it was for my lawyer to attend to this dispute, that I was densely ignorant and incapable of understanding anything about the matter. Is not that what you advised me to say?"

"You were quite right," père Goriot replied.

"Very well," Delphine continued, "he then enlightened me concerning his affairs. He has invested his capital and mine in enterprises that are as yet hardly begun, for which he has been forced to disburse large sums. If I constrain him to produce my dowry, he will be ogliged to file his petition of bankruptcy; whereas, if I consent to wait a year, he pledges himself upon his honor to double or triple my fortune for me by investing my capital in operations of real estate, at whose completion I shall be mistress of all the property.

"Dear Father, he was in earnest and he frightened me. He asked my pardon for his conduct, returned me my liberty, gave me permission to behave as I choose, on the condition that I give him the power of carrying on the business in my name. In order to prove his good faith, he promised to call M. Derville every time I desire it, to decide whether the deeds, in virtue of which I am made the owner of the property, are drawn up in due form. In short, he gave himself over to me, bound hand and foot. He asked me to allow him to keep the house for two years more and entreated me not to spend any more upon myself than the allowance he gives me. He showed me that all he can do is to preserve appearances, that he has dismissed his opera girl, and is compelled to use the most rigid and secret economy to carry out his speculations to the end without injuring his credit. I scolded him and pretended to doubt all he said, so that I might drive him to extremes and get more information from him: he showed me his books and really wept. I never saw a man in such a state. He lost his head, raved, and talked of killing himself. He made me pity him."

"And you believe in all that nonsense?" père Goriot cried. "He is an actor! I have met with Germans in business before, and they all have the appearance of candor and good faith; but when they use their frankness and good nature to hide their trickiness and charlatanism, they are worse than anybody else to deal with. Your husband is deceiving you. He feels himself hard pressed and is acting a part; he means to remain more the master under your name than he is under his own. He is going to profit by this circumstance to shelter himself from the risks of his business. He is as sly as he is treacherous; he is a very bad fellow.

"No, no, I won't go to Père-Lachaise, leaving my daughters stripped of everything. I know something about business still. He says he has invested his funds in various enterprises; very well, his interests must be represented by actual values, receipts, and contracts! Let him show them and settle with you. We shall choose the most profitable investments and take the chances; we shall have the titles acknowledging liability, made out in your name, 'Delphine Goriot, wife of Baron de Nucingen, having property in her own right.'

"Does the man take us for fools? Does he think I can bear for two days the thought of leaving you without money and without bread? I could not bear it a day, not a night, not even two hours! If it were true, I could not survive it. What! Have I sweated and toiled for forty years and carried sacks upon my back, have I stinted myself all through my life for you, my darlings, who made all my labors and burdens light to me; and today shall my fortune, my whole life, vanish in smoke? I would go mad and die. By all that is most sacred in earth and Heaven, we are going to clear up this thing and examine the books, funds, and speculations! I shall not eat until I convince myself that your fortune is intact. Thank God, your property is in your own right, and you will have for your lawyer M. Derville, who is fortunately an honest man. Heavenly powers! You shall keep your snug little million and your income of fifty thousand francs to the end of your days, or I shall make a disturbance in Paris, I tell you. I shall address myself to the Chambers if the courts are against us.

"To know that you were peaceful and happy as far as regarded money was the thought that softened all my ills and soothed my sorrows. Money is life; money accomplishes everything. What nonsense is that great idiot of an Alsatian talking to us! Delphine, don't concede a quarter of a penny to that big fool, who has put a chain round you and made you miserable. Since he requires your help, we shall have the whiphand and shall make him walk straight. My God, my head is on fire; there is something in my brain that burns me. My Delphine in need! Oh, my Fifine, you! The devil! Where are my gloves? Come, let us go; I want to see everything, the books, the business, the funds, the correspondence, immediately. I shall not be calm until I prove that your fortune is safe and see it with my own eyes."

"Dear Father, do go about it prudently! If you carry the slightest desire for revenge into this affair or show too-hostile intentions, I am lost. He knows you and thought it natural that at your instigation I would be uneasy about my money, but I swear to you that he holds it in his hands and is determined to hold it. He is the man to run off with all the capital and leave us in the lurch, the scamp! He knows that I would not be willing to dishonor the name I bear by prosecuting him. He is weak and strong at the same time. I have thought it all over; if we drive him into a corner, I am ruined."

"Then he is a rogue?"

"Yes, Father," she said, throwing herself weeping into a chair. "I didn't like to acknowledge it, for I wished to spare you the grief of having married me to a man of his stamp. His secret habits and his conscience, his soul and his body all agree! It is appalling; I hate and despise him. Yes, I can no longer esteem that vile Nucingen after what he said to me; a man capable as he is of undertaking the commercial transactions of which he spoke to me has not the slighest delicacy, and I am frightened because I could read his soul. He, my husband, offered me my freedom, and you know what that means? Provided I am willing, in case of trouble, to be a tool in his hands; in short, if I consent to lend him my name."

"But the laws exist, and there is a place de Grève for sons-in-law like him!" père Goriot cried. "I would guillotine him myself if there were no executioner."

"No, Father, no laws can reach him. I am going to repeat to you briefly what he told me, divested of all the circumlocutions in which he wrapped his meaning. He said, 'Either all is lost, and you are ruined and penniless, for I cannot choose any other person except yourself for an accomplice, or you must allow me to carry out my speculations.' Is that clear? He still depends upon me; my integrity as a woman reassures him; he knows that I shall content myself with my own fortune and leave him his. It is a wicked and dishonest partnership to which I must agree on pain of being ruined. He buys my conscience and pays me for it by leaving me free to be Eugène's wife. 'I allow you to commit faults; let me perpetrate crimes by ruining poor people.'

"Is that plain enough yet? Do you know what it is he calls his speculations? He buys unimproved lots in his own name and then has the houses built upon them by straw men. These men make a bargain for the buildings with the contractors, pay with bills at long term, and consent, for the consideration of a small sum, to give a receipt to my husband, who is then in possession of the houses; whereas the men themselves settle with the duped contractors by going into bankruptcy. The name of the house of Nucingen was enough to dazzle the poor builders. I understood it all, and I also understood that in order to prove, in case of need, that he had made enormous payments, Nucingen has sent considerable sums to Amsterdam, London, Naples, and Vienna. How shall we get hold of them?"

Eugène heard a sound as if père Goriot had fallen heavily on his knees upon the floor of his room.

"My God, what have I done? My daughter is in the power of this wretch who will exact anything he chooses from her. Forgive me, my girl!" the old man cried.

"Yes, if I am in trouble, you are perhaps responsible," Delphine said. "We have so little sense when we marry; we know nothing of the world, of business, or of men and their ways. Our fathers ought to think for us. Dear Father, I am not reproaching you; forgive me what I have said. In this I only am to blame. No, don't cry, Papa," she said, kissing her father on the forehead.

"Don't cry anymore, my little Delphine. Let me kiss away the tears from your eyes. I am going to gather my wits together and unravel the tangled skein of your husband's affairs."

"No, let me do it; I can manage him. He loves me, and I can use my influence to induce him to invest some capital for me at once in real estate. Perhaps I can make him buy back Nucingen, in Alsatia, in my name, for he thinks much of it. Only, come tomorrow to examine his books and affairs. M. Derville knows nothing about business. No, don't come tomorrow, I don't want to upset myself. Mme. de Beauséant's ball comes off the day after tomorrow, and I wish to take care of myself so I can look fresh and pretty and do honor to my dear Eugène! Come and let us look at his room." At that moment, a carriage stopped in the rue Neuve-Ste-Geneviève, and Mme. de Restaud's voice was heard on the staircase saying to Sylvie:

"Is my father at home?"

This circumstance was most fortunate for Eugène, who was on the point of throwing himself on the bed and feigning to be asleep.

"Oh, have you heard of Anastasie, Father?" Delphine said as she recognized her sister's voice. "It seems that strange things are happening in her household too."

"What?" père Goriot exclaimed. "Then it will be the end of me. My poor head cannot stand another misfortune."

"Good morning, Father," the Countess said, entering. "Oh, Delphine, are you here?"

Mme. de Restaud appeared to be embarrassed at meeting her sister.

"How do you do?" the Baroness said. "Do you think my presence here extraordinary? I see my father every day."

"Since when?"

"If you came to see him, you would know."

"Don't tease me, Delphine," the Countess said in a mournful tone. "I am very unhappy. I am lost, my poor father; oh, quite lost this time!"

"What is the matter, Nasie?" père Goriot cried. "Tell us everything, my child. She is turning pale! Delphine, come, help her, be kind to her, and I shall love you still better if I can."

"Poor Nasie," Mme. de Nucingen said, making her

sister sit down, "speak, for we are the only two people who will always love you enough to pardon everything. The tie of blood is always the strongest, you know."

She held the salts for her sister to inhale, and the Countess recovered.

"It will kill me!" père Goriot said. "Do come nearer, both of you," he went on as he stirred the turf fire. "I am cold. What is it, Nasie? Tell me quickly or I shall die."

"Very well," the poor woman said, "my husband knows everything. Just imagine, Father, do you remember that bill of exchange of Maxime's some time ago? It was not the first; I had already paid many of them. Toward the beginning of January, M. de Trailles looked to me distressed. He did not say anything, but it is so easy to read people's hearts when you love them; a mere nothing tells you so much, and besides I had presentiments. He was more loving, more tender than I had ever known him, and I was very happy. Poor Maxime! He has told me that he was then secretly bidding me farewell and meant to blow his brains out. At last I tormented and entreated him so much, spending two hours on my knees before him, that he told me he owed a hundred thousand francs. Oh, Papa, a hundred thousand francs! I was crazy, for I knew that you could not have them, and I had spent everything . . ."

"No," père Goriot said. "I could not have raised them, unless I had gone out and stolen them. But I would have been willing to go, Nasie! I will go now!"

At these words, that were mournful as the last groan

of a dying man and that betrayed the agony of a father's love grown powerless to help, the two sisters paused. What egotism could have remained unmoved at this cry that revealed the depths of his despair, as a stone sounds the abyss into which it is cast?

"I raised the money by disposing of what did not belong to me, Father," the Countess said, bursting into tears.

Delphine was moved and wept with her head on her sister's shoulder.

"It is all true then," she said.

Anastasie's head drooped; Mme. de Nucingen clasped her sister in her arms, kissed her tenderly, and held her against her heart.

"Here you may always be sure of being loved and not judged," she said.

"My darlings," père Goriot said, faintly, "why is it only trouble that has brought you together?"

"To save Maxime's life and to save my own happiness," the Countess continued, encouraged by these proofs of warm and lively affection, "I took to M. Gobseck, the usurer whom you know, a man of truly diabolical nature whom nothing can move, the family diamonds that M. de Restaud thinks so much of, and I sold them all, his and mine. I sold them! Do you understand? Maxime was saved, but I am lost. Restaud has found out everything."

"Through whom? How could he? Let me kill him!" père Goriot cried.

"Yesterday he sent for me to come into his room, so

I went. 'Anastasie,' he said in a voice—oh, his voice was enough, and I knew what was to follow—'where are your diamonds?' 'In my room,' I said. 'No,' he said, looking at me, 'they are here, on my bureau.' He pointed to the case that he had covered with a handkerchief. 'You know where they have come from?' he asked. I fell down at his feet and wept. I asked him by what death he wished me to die."

"You said that," père Goriot exclaimed. "By heavens, as long as I am alive, I will burn by a slow fire the man who dares to hurt either of you! Yes, I will slash him to pieces, like—"

Père Goriot stopped and the words died in his throat.

"And then, my dear," the Countess went on, "he asked of me something more difficult than dying. Heaven grant that no other woman may ever hear what I heard!"

"I shall murder the man," père Goriot said quietly. "But he has only one life, and he owes me two. Go on, what did he say?" he added, looking at Anastasie.

The Countess continued:

"After a pause he fixed his eyes on me and said, 'Anastasie, I am ready to bury everything in silence, and we shall remain together, for we have children. I shall not try to kill M. de Trailles, for I might not hit him, and if I tried to dispose of him in some other way, I might come into collision with the law. If I killed him in your arms, I would dishonor the children. In order that you may save from destruction your children, their father, and me, I shall impose two conditions. Answer me: is one of your children mine?' I said, 'Yes.' 'Which one?' he demanded. 'Ernest, our eldest boy,' I answered. 'Very well,' he said, 'now swear to obey me from now on, on one point.' I swore. 'You will sign your consent to the sale of your property when I ask it of you.' "

"Don't sign," père Goriot cried. "Never sign that. Oh, Monsieur de Restaud, you can't succeed in making a woman happy, and if she goes elsewhere in search of happiness, do you punish her for your own impotence? I am there, me! Stop there; he will find me in his path. Rest easy, Nasie. He cares about his heir; very well. I can kidnap his son, who is my grandson too, by God! I shall be able to get possession of the little fellow and shall put him in my own village; you need not be alarmed, for I shall take very good care of him. I shall make the monster come to terms when I say to him, 'It is between us two. If you want to have your son, give back your wife's property to her, and let her conduct herself as she pleases.' "

"Father!"

"Yes, I am your father; a true father, and that wretched aristocrat shall not maltreat my daughter. By thunder! I don't know what is in my veins. I have the blood of a tiger there, for I would like to murder these two men! Oh, my children, is this then your life? But it is my death. What will become of you, then, when I am no longer with you? Fathers should live as long as their children. My God, how badly arranged the world is! And yet they say God has a Son; He should save us from suffering through our children. My darlings, do I owe your presence here to your troubles alone? You only bring me your tears. Yet I know you love me; I see it. Come to me and pour out your complaints! My heart is large; it has room for everything. Yes, you may rend it if you choose; and out of the fragments the hearts of many fathers may be made. I would like to bear your sorrows and suffer for you. Oh, when you were little, you were very happy . . . "

"That was our only good time," Delphine said. "Where are the delightful hours we spent sliding down the sacks in the granary?"

"I have not told you all, Father," Anastasie whispered to Goriot, who gave a start. "The diamonds were not sold for a hundred thousand francs, and Maxime is being prosecuted. We have only twelve thousand francs more to pay. He has promised me to be good and not to gamble anymore. I have nothing left in this world except his love, and I have paid for it too dearly not to die if I lost him. I have sacrificed my fortune, my honor, my peace of mind, and my children for his sake. Oh, do what is necessary so Maxime may be at least free and respected, so that he may remain in the world where he will surely make a position for himself. Now he owes me more than my happiness alone, for we have children who would be left penniless. We shall all be ruined if he is put in Ste-Pélagie."

"I don't have the money, Nasie. I have nothing, nothing! It is the end of the world. I am sure the world is going to pieces. Go and save yourselves before it happens! Oh, I still have my silver buckles and six spoons and forks, the first I ever had in my life. But I have only my annuity of twelve hundred francs . . . "

"What did you do with your government stock?"

"I sold it, reserving this remnant of income for my needs. I required twelve thousand francs to fit up an apartment for Fifine."

"At your house, Delphine?" Mme. de Restaud asked of her sister.

"What difference does that make," interrupted père Goriot. "The twelve thousand francs have all been used."

"I can guess," the Countess said. "It was for M. de Rastignac. Oh, poor Delphine, stop where you are. You see what I have come to."

"My dear, M. de Rastignac is incapable of ruining his mistress."

"Thanks, Delphine. In my distress, I expected better things of you, but you never loved me."

"Yes, she loves you, Nasie!" père Goriot cried. "She was just telling me so a moment ago. We were speaking of you, and she was insisting that you were beautiful, and she only pretty!"

"She!" the Countess repeated. "She is a splendid but cold creature."

"And even if I were," Delphine said, flushing, "how have you behaved toward me? You have disowned me, closed against me the doors of all the houses where I wanted to go, and you have never missed the slightest opportunity of causing me pain. And did I ever come, like you, to get one thousand francs after another out of our poor father and reduce him to his present condition?

It is all your work, sister. I have seen my father as much as I could. I never turned him out of my doors and then came to fawn upon him when I needed him. I didn't even know that he had used his twelve thousand francs for me. I have been reasonable, and you know it. Besides, when Papa has made me presents, I never asked him for them."

"You have been luckier than I. M. de Marsay was rich, and you know something about it. You have always been as mean as dirt. Good-bye, I have neither sister nor—"

"Stop, Nasie!" père Goriot screamed.

"Only a sister like you could repeat what even the world no longer believes; you are a monster!" Delphine said.

"My children, my children, be quiet, or I shall kill myself before you."

"Go, I forgive you, Nasie," Mme. de Nucingen continued, "you are unfortunate. But I am kinder than you. To tell me that, just as I was ready to do anything to help you, even to entering my husband's chamber, which I would not do for myself or for . . . This is worthy of all the evil you have done me for nine years."

"My children, my dear children, make up your quarrel," their father said. "You are both angels."

"No, let me alone," the Countess cried, shaking off her father, who had taken her by the arm. "She has less pity for me than my husband would have. Wouldn't you say that she is the image of all virtue?"

"I would rather have it supposed that I owe money to

M. de Marsay than confess that M. de Trailles costs me over two hundred thousand francs," Mme. de Nucingen replied.

"Delphine!" the Countess cried, making a step toward her sister.

"I tell you the truth, when you are slandering me," the Baroness returned coldly.

"Delphine, you are a—"

Père Goriot rushed forward, seized the Countess, and prevented her from speaking by covering her mouth with his hand.

"Heavens, Father, what have you been taking this morning?" Anastasie said.

"It is true, I am to blame," her poor father said, rubbing his hands on his trousers. "But I didn't know you were coming, and I was packing."

He was happy to incur a reproach that turned his daughter's wrath upon him.

"Ah," he went on as he sat down, "you have broken my heart. I am dying, my children. My brain is burning as if it were on fire. Do be kind and affectionate to each other, or you will kill me. Come, Delphine and Nasie, you were both in the right and both in the wrong. Dedel," and he turned his eyes brimming with tears upon the Baroness, "your sister needs twelve thousand francs; let us try to get them for her. Don't look at each other like that." He knelt down before Delphine. "Ask her pardon for my sake; she is more unfortunate than you."

"Poor Nasie," Delphine said, terrified by the strange

wild expression that grief had lent her father's countenance, "I have been in the wrong; kiss me . . ."

"Ah, you are pouring balm into my heart," père Goriot cried. "But how shall we find the twelve thousand francs? Suppose that I offered myself as a substitute?"

"Oh, Father!" the two daughters exclaimed, throwing their arms around him. "No, never."

"God will reward you for such a thought, for our lives would be too short to show our gratitude, don't you think so, Nasie?" Delphine said.

"And then, poor Father, it would only be a drop in the bucket," the Countess observed.

"Can't a man do anything with his heart's blood?" the despairing father cried. "I will devote myself to whoever saves you, Nasie. I will kill a man for him. I will do like Vautrin; I will go to the galleys! I—"

He stopped as if struck by lightning.

"Nothing," he said, tearing his hair. "If I only knew where I could go to steal, but it is hard too to commit a robbery. Then I would need time and assistance to break into the bank. I must die; there is nothing left for me but to die. Yes, I am good for nothing; I am no longer a father! She asks me to help her, she is in need, and wretch that I am, I have nothing to give her. Oh, you old rascal, you bought an annuity for yourself and yet you had daughters! Didn't you love them then? Die, die like the dog that you are. Yes, I am less than a dog, for a dog wouldn't have behaved like me! Oh, my head, it's getting cloudy!"

"Papa," the two young women screamed, supporting him on both sides to prevent him from beating his head against the walls, "do be sensible."

He was sobbing. Eugène was appalled and took up the bill of exchange that he had signed for Vautrin; its stamp allowed a larger sum. He changed the figures and made a bill of exchange, in due form, for twelve thousand francs, to the order of Goriot.

"Here is your money, Countess," he said, entering père Goriot's room and presenting the bill. "I was sleeping till your conversation awoke me, and I discovered what I owed to M. Goriot; here is the bill that you can negotiate and that I will discharge faithfully."

The Countess stood motionless, holding the paper.

"Delphine," she said, pale and quivering with anger, rage, and fury, "I was ready to forgive you everything, God be my witness. But this! What! This gentleman was in his room and you knew it? You had the meanness to revenge yourself by allowing me to give into his hands my secrets, my own life and my children's, my honor, and my shame! Go, you are nothing to me from now on. I hate you and shall do you all the harm in my power, I—"

Anger stopped her speech, and the words stuck in her throat.

"He is my son, our child, your brother, your savior!" père Goriot cried. "Embrace him, Nasie! I will embrace him myself," he added, clasping Eugène madly. "Oh, my child! I would like to be more than a father to you; I want to take the place of your whole family. Would that

I were God Himself, that I might throw the whole universe at your feet. Kiss him, Nasie, he is not a man, he is an angel, a real angel."

"Let her alone, Father; she is beside herself," Delphine said.

"Beside myself indeed! And what are you?" Mme. de Restaud demanded.

"My children, I shall die if you keep this up," the old man said, falling upon his bed as if he were shot. "They are killing me!" he added to himself.

The Countess looked at Eugène, who stood like a statue, dazed by the violence of the scene before him.

"Monsieur?" she said, questioning him with her gesture, voice, and eye without paying attention to her father, whose waistcoat Delphine was rapidly unbuttoning.

"Madame, I shall pay the money and shall hold my tongue," he replied without waiting for her to finish.

"You have killed our father, Nasie!" Delphine said, pointing to the old man, who had fainted. Her sister rushed from the room.

"I forgive her," said the poor man, opening his eyes, "for her situation is terrible and would turn a stronger head than hers. Try to comfort Nasie and be kind to her; promise your poor father, who is dying," he entreated of Delphine as he pressed her hand.

"What is the matter with you?" she asked in alarm.

"Nothing, nothing," her father replied. "It will soon pass. Something is pressing against my forehead; it is a headache. Poor Nasie, what a future!"

The Countess returned at that moment and flung herself beside her father's knees.

"Forgive me!" she cried.

"Don't," père Goriot said. "Now you are giving me still more pain."

"Monsieur," the Countess said to Rastignac, her eyes bathed in tears, "grief has made me unjust. You will be a brother to me, won't you?" she continued, putting out her hand to him.

"Nasie," Delphine said, taking it in hers, "little Nasie, let us forget everything."

"No," Anastasie said, "I shall remember it."

"My darlings," père Goriot called, "you have drawn aside the curtain that was in front of my eyes, and your voices give me new life. Kiss each other once again. Tell me, Nasie, will this bill of exchange save you?"

"I hope so. Will you add your signature to it, Papa?"

"Oh, how stupid I was to forget it! But I was ill, Nasie, and you must not be angry with me. Send me word that your trouble is over. No, I will go myself. Yet, no, I cannot see your husband, for I would kill him at once. As to his converting your fortune into personal property, I shall be there to prevent it. Go quickly, my child, and see that Maxime behaves himself."

Eugène was stupefied.

"Poor Anastasie always had a violent temper," Mme. de Nucingen said, "but she has a good heart."

"She came back to get the bill endorsed," Eugène whispered in Delphine's ear.

"Do you think so?"

"I would like not to believe it. You must not trust her," he returned, lifting his eyes to Heaven, as if to confide in God the thoughts he dared not express.

"Yes, she has been always something of an actress, and my poor father is taken in by her wiles."

"How are you, dear père Goriot?" Rastignac asked of the old man.

"I would like to sleep," was the answer.

Eugène helped Goriot to get to bed and, when the poor man had fallen asleep with Delphine's hand in his, his daughter withdrew.

"We shall meet at the Opéra tonight," she said to Eugène, "and you will tell me how he is. Tomorrow, you shall change your abode, monsieur. Let me see your room. Oh, how horrid," she exclaimed as she entered it. "You are worse off here than my father. Eugène, you have behaved nobly, and I shall love you still better if it is possible; but my child, if you want to make your fortune, you must not throw twelve thousand francs out of the window like that again. The Comte de Trailles is a gambler, though my sister does not want to believe it. He must have been trying to make his twelve thousand francs in the place where he loses and wins his heaps of gold."

A groan from Goriot called them to his bedside; he seemed to be asleep, but as the two lovers drew near, they heard him say:

"My daughters are not happy!"

Whether he was asleep or awake, the accent of his words moved his daughter's heart so deeply that she went up to the bed where her father was lying and kissed his forehead. He opened his eyes, saying:

"It is Delphine."

"Yes, how are you?" she inquired.

"Very well," he said, "don't be anxious, I shall soon go out. Go, my children, and be happy."

Eugène took Delphine home, but he was so troubled about the state in which they had left Goriot that he refused to dine with her and returned to the boarding-house. He found that père Goriot had risen and was about to sit down at the table. Bianchon took up a position from which he could get a good view of the old man, and when he saw him take up his bread and sniff it to find out what flour it was made from, the student observed a total absence of consciousness in the action and made an inauspicious gesture.

"Come and sit by me, M. Physician from the Cochin hospital," Eugène said.

Bianchon went to him the more readily because the move brought him nearer the old boarder.

"What is the matter with him?" Rastignac inquired.

"Unless I am much mistaken, he is done for! Some extraordinary change must have taken place in him, and he looks to me as if he were threatened with an imminent attack of serous apoplexy. Though the lower half of his face is calm enough, the features of the upper half are drawn toward his forehead, in spite of all he can do. Do you see? Then his eyes have the particular appearance that shows that the serum has penetrated the brain. They look as if they were full of fine dust, don't they? Tomorrow morning I shall know more about it."

"Is there any remedy for it?"

"None. His death might be delayed if it were possible

to bring on a reaction in the lower extremities; but if these symptoms do not disappear by tomorrow evening, the poor old man is gone. Do you know what circumstance it was that caused his illness? He must have received a violent blow, under which his mind has succumbed."

"Yes," Rastignac said as he remembered how the old man's two daughters had worked upon their father's heart without mercy.

At least Delphine loves her father, Eugène thought.

THAT same evening at the Opéra, Rastignac took some precautions to avoid alarming Mme. de Nucingen.

"You need not be anxious," she said, in reply to Eugène's first words. "My father is strong. We disturbed him a little this morning. Our fortunes are at stake; can you understand the extent of such a misfortune? I could not live if your affection had not made me insensible to what I would have formerly considered mortal anguish. Now there is only one fear or one misfortune possible for me—that of losing the love that has made me experience the pleasure of living. Outside of this one feeling, everything is indifferent to me, and I care for nothing else in the world. You are everything to me. If I am aware of the advantage of money, it is so that I may better please you. To my shame, my lover is more to me than my father. Why? I do not know. All my life is in you. My father gave me a heart, but you have taught it to beat. The whole world may blame me, but what difference does it make to me, if only you, who have no right to be displeased with me, absolve me from the faults into which I am driven by an irresistible passion? Do you think me an unnatural daughter? Oh, no; it is impossible not to love a father as good as ours. Could I prevent his finding out the inevitable consequences of our unfortunate marriages? Why did he allow them to take place? He should have reflected for us. I know that today he suffers as much as we, but how can we help that? Can we comfort him? We could never succeed. Our resignation caused him more pain than our reproaches and complaints did him harm. There are some situations in life in which all is bitterness."

Eugène remained silent, filled with tenderness at this candid expression of true feeling. If Parisian women are often false and mad with vanity, if they are sometimes selfish, cold coquettes, it is certain that when they truly love, they sacrifice more sentiment to their passion than other women; their very littleness makes them great and they are sublime. Moreover, Eugène was struck by the profound justice with which a woman estimates her natural feelings when she is separated and removed from them by a more privileged affection.

Mme. de Nucingen was hurt by Eugène's silence.

"What are you thinking of?" she asked.

"I am considering what you have said to me. Until now, I believed that I loved you better than you loved me."

She smiled and armed herself against the pleasure she felt in order to keep their conversation within the bounds of conventionality. She had never before heard the stirring words of young, true love. A little more, and she could no longer have contained herself.

"Eugène," she began, changing the subject, "do you know what is going on? All Paris will be at Mme. de Beauséant's tomorrow evening. The Rochefide family and the Marquis d'Ajuda have arranged to keep everything secret, but the King is to sign the marriage contract tomorrow, and your poor cousin has heard nothing as yet. She will not be able to avoid receiving her guests, and the Marquis will not be at her ball. There is nothing talked of but this affair."

"The world laughs and delights in such infamy, but don't you know that Mme. de Beauséant will die of it?"

"No," Delphine said with a smile, "you do not understand women of her class. All Paris will go to her house, and I shall be there too. I owe the pleasure to you, however."

"Don't you think," Rastignac said, "this is one of those absurd reports so frequent in Paris?"

"We shall know the truth tomorrow," she replied.

PART SIX

The End Approaches

1

E UGÈNE did not return to his boardinghouse, for he could not resist the joy of establishing himself in his new apartment. If, the night before, he had been obliged to leave Delphine at an hour after midnight, this time it was Delphine who left him at two o'clock to go home.

He slept late the next morning and toward noon looked for Mme. de Nucingen, who came to breakfast with him. It is so natural to the young to be eager in the pursuit of gay pleasures that he had nearly forgotten père Goriot. It was a perpetual delight to him to accustom himself to his new and elegant belongings, and Mme. de Nucingen was with him lending a fresh charm to everything. However, toward four o'clock, he recollected the old man and the happiness that he had anticipated in coming to live in the house in which they were. Eugène observed that père Goriot should be moved at once if he were going to be ill, and he left Delphine to rush back to the boardinghouse.

Neither père Goriot nor Bianchon was at the table.

"Père Goriot has gone to pieces," the painter said to him. "Bianchon is upstairs with him. The old man saw one of his daughters, the Comtesse de Restaurama, and then insisted upon going out and became much worse. Our society is to be deprived of one of its most brilliant ornaments."

Rastignac hastened toward the stairs.

"Monsieur Eugène!"

"Monsieur Eugène, Mme. Vauquer is calling you," Sylvie cried.

"Monsieur Eugène," the widow said, "you and M. Goriot were to leave here on the fifteenth of February. The fifteenth was three days ago, for it is now the eighteenth, so you must pay me a month's board for both of you; but if you are willing to pledge yourself for père Goriot, your word will be enough."

"Why? Don't you trust him?"

"Trust him? If the old man lost his senses and died, his daughters would not give me a penny, and his effects are not worth ten francs. He carried off his last bit of silver this morning; I can't tell why. He was dressed like a young man, and God forgive me, but I think he had rouge on, for he looked so much younger."

"I answer for everything," Eugène said, who feared a catastrophe and shuddered with horror.

He went up to père Goriot. He found the old man lying on his bed with Bianchon sitting beside him.

"Hello, Father," Eugène said.

The old man smiled sweetly and, turning his glassy eyes toward him, asked:

"How is she?"

"Well; and you?"

"I am doing well."

"Don't tire him," Bianchon said, drawing Eugène into a corner of the room.

"Well?" Eugène inquired.

"He can only be saved by a miracle. Serous congestion has taken place. I have applied mustard plasters; fortunately he feels them and they are acting."

"Can he be moved?"

"Impossible. He must be left where he is and spared all emotion and physical fatigue."

"Dear Bianchon," Eugène said, "we must take care of him together."

"I have already had the chief doctor of my hospital here."

"What did he say?"

"He will give his opinion tomorrow evening. He promised to come after his day's work is over. Unluckily, this poor old man committed an imprudence this morning and refuses to explain it. He is as obstinate as a mule; when I speak to him, he pretends not to hear and feigns sleep to avoid answering; or if his eyes are open, he begins to moan. He went out in the morning and walked about on foot, nobody knows where. He took out with him everything he possessed of value and exhausted his strength in making some damned bargain or other. One of his daughters came here."

"The Countess?" Eugène asked. "A tall brunette with bright, handsome eyes, pretty ankles, and a lithe figure?"

"Yes."

"Leave me alone with him a moment," Rastignac said.

"I shall make him confess, and he will tell me the whole truth."

"Then I shall go and have dinner in the meantime; only try not to excite him, for we have still some slight hope."

"Don't worry."

"They will enjoy themselves very much tomorrow," père Goriot said to Eugène when they were alone. "They are going to a great ball."

"What did you do this morning, Papa, to make you so ill this afternoon that you have to stay in bed?"

"Nothing."

"Was Anastasie here?" Rastignac asked.

"Yes," père Goriot answered.

"Good! Don't hide anything from me; what did she ask of you?"

"Ah," he said, collecting his strength to speak, "she was very unhappy. Oh, my child! Nasie has not had a penny since the affair of the diamonds. She had ordered for the ball a dress embroidered with gold that was to suit her to perfection. Her dressmaker turned out to be a wretch who refused her credit, so her maid paid a thousand francs on account for the gown. Poor Nasie! To think she had to come to that! It tore my heartstrings. When the maid saw that Restaud was estranged from Nasie, she was afraid of losing her money and made an agreement with the dressmaker not to have the gown sent home until the thousand francs are returned. The ball is tomorrow, the gown is ready, and Nasie is in despair. She wanted to borrow my pieces of silver and pawn them. Her husband insists upon her going to the ball to show all Paris the diamonds she is reported to have sold. Can she say to the monster, 'I owe a thousand francs; pay them for me.' No, I understood that. Her sister, Delphine, will go in a superb gown and Anastasie should not be behind her younger sister. My poor girl was drowned in tears, and I was mortified not to have the twelve thousand francs yesterday that I would give the rest of my wretched life to redeem that wrong. You see I had strength to bear everything, but this last want of money has broken my heart.

"Oh, I did not stop to think about it, but I plucked up courage and spruced myself up, sold my buckles and the silver for six hundred francs, and pledged my annuity for one year to Papa Gobseck for four hundred francs, cash down. I can live on dry bread; it used to be enough for me when I was young, and I can still get along with it. At least my Nasie will have a delightful evening and be beautifully dressed. I have the bill of a thousand francs under my pillow, and it keeps me warm to know that I have beneath my head something that is to give pleasure to poor Nasie. Now she can turn that wicked Victoire out-of-doors. Think of a servant not trusting her mistress!

"I shall be well again tomorrow; Nasie is coming at ten o'clock. I don't want my daughters to think me ill, for they would not go to the ball but would stay to take care of me. Nasie will kiss me tomorrow as if I were her child, and her caresses will cure me. After all, I might have spent a thousand francs at the apothecary's, and I like better to give it to my Nasie, my cure-all. At least, I shall help her in her embarrassment, and that absolves me from my selfishness in buying an annuity. She is in the depths of trouble, and I am not strong enough to draw her out of it. I am going to return to business. I shall go to Odessa to buy grain, for there corn costs one-third of the price of ours at home. Although the importation of cereals in their natural state is forbidden, it never occurred to the good people who make the laws to prohibit products whose principal part is wheat. Eh, eh! I have found that out this morning. There are some fine speculations to be made in starch."

He is crazy, Eugène thought, looking at the old man. "Try to keep quiet, and don't talk," he added aloud.

When Bianchon came upstairs, Eugène went down to dinner. The two spent the night watching the old man by turns, one of them reading medical books and the other writing to his mother and sisters.

Next day, according to Bianchon, the symptoms were more favorable, but they required constant care, which the two students alone were capable of and which it would be impossible to describe in the reticent language of the present day. The students applied leeches and mustard plasters to the exhausted body of the old man; they tried footbaths and medical devices that called for all their strength and devotion to attend to. Mme. de Restaud did not come but sent a messenger for the sum she wanted.

"I thought she would come herself; but it is no matter for she would have been worried," said the old man, who seemed pleased with the circumstance.

At seven o'clock in the evening, Thérèse arrived with a letter from Delphine to Eugène. It ran:

What are you up to my dear friend? You have hardly begun to love me and are you neglecting me already? In the confidences you poured into my heart, you showed me too noble a nature for me not to place you among those who understand the many different shades of sentiment and always remain faithful. As you said, when we were listening to the *Prayer of Moses*, "For some people, it is an ordinary note, but for others, it is the infinity of music." Remember that I am expecting you this evening to go with me to Mme. de Beauséant's ball.

It is certain that M. d'Ajuda's contract was signed at court this morning, and the poor Viscountess never knew of it till two o'clock. All Paris will rush to her house, just as the mob collects on the place de Grève when an execution is to take place. Isn't it horrible to go to see whether she succeeds in hiding her sorrow and knows how to die nobly? I would not go myself if I had ever been at her house before, but she will probably not receive again, and all the efforts I have made would be in vain. My situation is quite different from that of the others. Besides, I am going for your sake too. I am waiting for you, and if you are not with me in two hours, it will be a crime that I may not be able to forgive.

Rastignac seized a pen and answered thus:

I am expecting a doctor to know whether your father has yet some time to live. He is dying. I shall go to you to carry you the decision, and I fear it may be a sentence of death. You will decide whether you can go to the ball. I send much love.

The doctor came at half past eight and, without giving a favorable opinion, did not think that death would be immediate. He predicted alternate rallies and relapses, upon which the old man's life and reason would depend.

"It will be better for him if he dies quickly," was the doctor's last word.

Eugène entrusted père Goriot to Bianchon's care and went to carry Mme. de Nucingen the sad news, which he, who was still influenced by ideas of filial duty, believed would put an end to all amusement.

"Tell her to enjoy herself all the same," called père Goriot, who had appeared to be asleep but sat up in bed as Rastignac went out.

The young man was in deep distress as he presented himself before Delphine. He found her with her hair already dressed and her slippers on, waiting only to add her ball dress, but like the finishing strokes of a painter's brush, so here the last touches were to demand more time than the background of the canvas.

"What, aren't you dressed?" she asked.

"But, madame, your father—'

"Still my father!" she cried, interrupting him. "You can't teach me what I owe my father. I have known my father a long time. Not a word, Eugène; I shall not listen to you until you have dressed yourself. Thérèse has prepared everything for you at your apartment. My carriage is waiting; take it, and come back again. We can talk about my father on the way to the ball. We must go early, for if we are caught in the file of carriages, we shall be very lucky if we make our entrance at eleven o'clock."

"Madame—"

"Go, not a word," she said, running into her boudoir in search of her necklace.

"Go, Monsieur Eugène, or you will displease Madame," Thérèse said, hastening the young man's exit.

He was appalled by the fashionable parricide. While dressing, he was occupied with the saddest and most discouraging reflections. To him the world appeared like an ocean of mud into which if a man merely dipped his foot, he would sink to the neck.

There are only petty crimes committed in the social world, he thought. Vautrin is greater.

He had seen the three great expressions of human society: Obedience, Struggle, and Revolt; or the Family, the World, and Vautrin. He dared ally himself with none of them. Obedience was wearisome; Revolt, impossible; and Struggle, uncertain. His thoughts carried him back to the bosom of his family; he remembered the pure emotions of his peaceful life and recalled the days passed among his fond relations. By conforming to the natural laws of the domestic hearth, those dear people lived in an atmosphere of ample, constant, and untroubled happiness. But in spite of his better thoughts, he could not summon courage to confess the faith of a pure soul to Delphine and to enjoin upon her virtue in the name of affection. The education he had begun had already borne its fruits, and his love was already selfish. His tact had enabled him to read the nature of Delphine's heart, and he foresaw that she was capable of treading over her father's body to the ball, yet he did not have the strength of mind to reason with her, the courage to displease her, or the virtue to leave her.

She would never forgive me for being right when she was wrong, he thought.

Then he began to weigh the doctor's words and indulged himself with thinking that père Goriot was not as dangerously ill as he had supposed; in short, he accumulated many unrighteous reasons for justifying Delphine. She did not know her father's condition, and even if she went to see him, he would be sure to send her to the ball. The implacable formula of social law often condemns an apparent crime that is excusable through the innumerable modifications introduced into family life by the difference of characters and the diversity of interests and situations. Eugène was anxious to deceive himself and ready to sacrifice his conscience to his mistress. Within two days, everything in his life had changed. A woman had come to disturb his existence; she had effaced his family and confiscated all for her own good. Rastignac and Delphine had met under conditions qualified to give each of them the most perfect enjoyment of the other. Their passion, for which the way had been so well prepared, had thrived upon what kills most passions —its own gratification. Now that his mistress belonged to him, Eugène understood that up to this time he had felt nothing stronger than desire; he had not loved her until his happiness was already in his grasp; love is perhaps only the acknowledgment of the pleasure. Whether she was base or noble, he adored this woman for the joy he had brought her as a dowry, and for all that she had given him; and Delphine loved Rastignac as Tantalus would have loved an angel who came to him to satisfy his hunger or to quench the thirst of his parched throat.

"Now tell me, how is my father?" Mme. de Nucingen said when Eugène came back, dressed for the ball.

"Very ill!" he answered. "If you are willing to give me a proof of your affection, you will go there with me at once."

"Yes, she said, "but not till after the ball. Dear Eugène, be kind and don't lecture me; come."

They started, and Eugène was silent for part of the way.

"What is the matter?" she asked.

"I can hear your father's last groan," he said, in a tone of vexation.

Then he related, with the passionate eloquence of youth, the cruel behavior to which vanity had impelled Mme. de Restaud, the fatal consequences of her father's last act of devotion and the cost of Anastasie's embroidered robe. Delphine wept.

I shall spoil my looks, she thought, and her tears stopped flowing.

"I shall go and take care of my father and shall not leave his bedside," she assured Eugène.

"Ah, that is what I wished to hear from you," he cried.

The lanterns of five hundred carriages lighted the approach to the De Beauséant mansion, and on each side of the illuminated portal stood a magnificent gendarme. The fashionable world was arriving in such numbers, and everybody pressed forward so eagerly to see a great lady at the moment of her fall, that the apartments on the ground floor of the house were already full when Mme. de Nucingen and Rastignac presented themselves. From the time when all the courtiers flocked to see La Grande Mademoiselle whom Louis XIV had robbed of her lover, there had been no more signal disaster of the heart than that of Mme. de Beauséant. In such circumstances, the last daughter of the almost royal house of Bourgogne rose superior to her calamity and up to the last moment dominated the world, whose vanities she had accepted only to minister to the triumph of her passion.

The rooms were resplendent with the gowns and smiles of the most beautiful women of Paris. The most distinguished men at court, ambassadors, ministers, and noted persons of every description, decked with crosses, stars, and many-colored ribbons, thronged about the Viscountess. The notes of the orchestra resounded under the gilded ceilings of this palace, which was empty in the eyes of its queen. Mme. de Beauséant was standing by the door of the first drawing room to receive her treacherous friends. Dressed all in white and with no ornament in her simply braided hair, she seemed calm and made no show of sorrow, pride, or pretended joy. No one could read her soul; she looked like a marble Niobe. There was a shade of mockery in the smiles she gave her intimate friends, but to everyone she appeared like herself and looked so much the way she had when she wore the aureola of happiness that even the most insensible admired her, just as the young Roman women used to applaud the gladiator who smiled as he died. It was as if the world had adorned itself to bid farewell to one of its sovereigns.

"I feared that you would not come," she said to Rastignac.

Her words seemed to him to convey a reproach, and with a voice full of emotion, he answered:

"I have come to stay last of all."

"That is well," she said, shaking hands with him. "Perhaps you are the only person here whom I can trust. Oh, my friend, love a woman whom you can always love. Never desert her!"

She took Rastignac's arm and led him to the sofa in the room where the card tables were.

"Go to the Marquis," she said. "My servant Jacques will take you there and will hand you a letter for him. I ask him to return my correspondence, and I fondly believe that he will give it all to you. If you come back with the letters, go up into my room. They will bring me word."

She rose to receive the Duchesse de Langeais, her best friend, who had just arrived. Rastignac went to the Rochefide mansion, where he knew the Marquis d'Ajuda was to spend the evening, asked for him, and saw him. The Marquis took him to his own house and gave a box into his charge, saying:

"The letters are all here."

He evidently wished to speak to Eugène, either to question him concerning the ball and the Viscountess, or to confess perhaps that he was already in despair about his marriage, as he was destined to be later; but the light of pride burned in his eyes and he had the miserable courage of keeping his better feelings to himself.

"Say nothing about me, my dear Eugène."

He pressed Rastignac's hand with wistful affection and gave him a sign of dismissal. Eugène returned to the Hôtel de Beauséant and was conducted to the room of the Viscountess, which he found full of preparations for departure. He sat down beside the fire, looking at the cedar box, and fell into a profound melancholy. To him, Mme. de Beauséant assumed the proportions of one of the goddesses in the *Iliad*.

"Ah, my friend," the Viscountess said, entering the room and leaning her hand upon Rastignac's shoulder.

He saw his cousin in tears, her eyes raised toward Heaven. One hand was trembling, and the other lifted toward the box. Suddenly she took it, threw it in the fire, and watched it burn.

"They are dancing! They all came at the required time, whereas death will come late! Hush! my friend," she said, placing her finger on Eugène's lips, as he was about to speak. "I shall never see Paris or the world again. At five o'clock in the morning I am to leave here, to bury myself in the depths of Normandy. Since three o'clock I have been obliged to make preparations, sign deeds, and attend to my affairs; I could send no one to him . . . "

She paused.

"I was sure that he would be found at . . . "

She paused again, overwhelmed with her sorrow. There are moments in life so miserable that certain words are impossible to pronounce.

"In short," she resumed, "I counted upon you this evening to do me this last favor. I wished to give you a proof of my friendship. I shall often think of you, for you have seemed to me good, noble, young, and truthful, in a world in which such qualities are rare. I hope that you will sometimes think of me. Here," she said, looking about her, "here is the case in which I have always kept my gloves. Every time I took out a pair before going to a ball or to a play, I knew that I was beautiful because I was happy, and every time I touched the case, I dropped into it some joyous thought: it holds a great part of myself, an entire Mme. de Beauséant who is now no more. Please accept it from me, and I shall have it sent to your apartment in the rue d'Artois. Mme. de Nucingen is looking very well this evening; try to love her well: If we never see each other again, my friend, be sure that I shall pray for you who have been so kind to me. Now, let us go downstairs, for I don't want anybody to think that I am weeping. Eternity lies before me, and as I shall live in it alone, no one will call me to account for my tears. One last look at this room."

She stopped, then after hiding her eyes in her hand

for a moment, she dried them, bathed them with fresh water, and took the student's arm.

"Let us go," she said.

Rastignac had never as yet experienced so powerful an emotion as he now felt at being brought into contact with a grief so nobly restrained. On their return to the ball, Mme. de Beauséant made Eugène walk about the rooms with her—a last and delicate attention paid him by that gracious lady. He soon caught sight of the two sisters, Mme. de Restaud and Mme. de Nucingen. Mme. de Restaud was magnificent in her display of diamonds, which must have been scorching to her as she was wearing them for the last time. However strong her love and pride, she could barely endure her husband's gaze. The sight of her was not cheering to Rastignac, for behind the diamonds he saw the miserable bed on which père Goriot was lying. The Viscountess misunderstood the melancholy of his expression and withdrew her arm from his.

"Go," she said, "I would not deprive you of your pleasure."

Eugène was soon claimed by Delphine, who was exulting in the effect she produced and was anxious to place at her lover's feet the homage she received from a society into which she hoped soon to be adopted.

"What do you think of Nasie?" she asked.

"She has turned everything to money, even her father's death," Rastignac replied.

Toward four o'clock in the morning, the crowded rooms began to clear, and soon the music stopped entirely. The Duchesse de Langeais and Rastignac found themselves alone in the great drawing room, when the Viscountess entered it, expecting to find the student there alone. She had just bade goodbye to M. de Beauséant, who kept repeating to her as he left her to go to bed:

"You are wrong, my dear, to go and shut yourself up at your age. Stay with us!"

As she saw the Duchess, Mme. de Beauséant could not restrain an exclamation.

"I have guessed your plans, Clara," Mme. de Langeais said. "You are leaving us forever, but you shall not go without listening to me and without our understanding each other."

She took her friend's arm, drew her into the next room, and there, looking at her with tears in her eyes, she clasped her in her arms and kissed her on both cheeks.

"I cannot part from you coldly, my dear," she said. "I would feel too remorseful about it. You can count upon me as upon yourself. You have been great this evening; I have felt myself worthy of you and am anxious to prove it to you. I have done you wrong and have not always been kind; forgive me, my dear. I disclaim all that I have said to wound you and would like to take back my words. One and the same sorrow has brought us together, and I cannot say which of us two is the more unhappy. M. de Montriveau was not here this evening, do you understand? Whoever has seen you at this ball, Clara, will never forget you. I am going to make one last effort, and if I fail, I shall enter a convent. Where are you going?"

"To Courcelles, in Normandy, to love and pray until the day when God takes me out of this world. Come, Monsieur de Rastignac," she added with emotion, believing that the young man was waiting for her.

The student bent his knee, took his cousin's hand, and kissed it.

"Farewell, Antoinette," continued Madame de Beauséant. "I hope that you may be happy. As to you," she said as she turned to the student, "you are young and happy and can still have faith in life. In my departure from the world, like nuns and others privileged in death, I know there are hearts that feel for me sincerely."

Rastignac left about five o'clock, after having seen Mme. de Beauséant in her traveling carriage and after receiving her tearful farewell that showed him how those of the highest rank are not free from sorrow or exempt from the laws of the heart, as certain demagogues have tried to make the lower classes believe. It was cold and damp as he made his way on foot toward the boarding-house. His education was approaching its completion.

"We shall not be able to save poor père Goriot," Bianchon said, as Rastignac entered the old man's room.

"Dear père Goriot," Eugène said, looking at the old man, who appeared to be asleep, "go on and follow the modest destiny to which your desires are restricted. I am in hell and must stay there. Believe all the evil you hear of the world! Juvenal himself could not paint its ghastliness, covered up with gold and precious stones."

2

THE next day Rastignac was awakened about two o'clock by Bianchon, who was obliged to go out and who begged him to assume the charge of père Goriot, whose condition had grown much more alarming during the morning.

"The poor man doesn't have two days, perhaps not six hours to live," the medical student said, "yet we must continue to combat the disease. He will need some expensive treatment. We can take care of him, but I don't have a penny. I have turned his pockets inside out and searched his bureau drawers, but the result was zero. I questioned him in one of his lucid moments, but he told me he didn't have a single penny. How much have you?"

"I have twenty francs left," Rastignac answered. "I shall go and play with them and win."

"What if you should lose?"

"I would ask his sons-in-law and his daughters for money."

"Suppose they don't give you any?" rejoined Bianchon. "But raising money is not the most urgent necessity at present; the old man must be covered with burning mustard plasters from his feet to halfway up his thighs. If he cries out, we may have some means of helping him. You know how to do it, and besides, Christophe will help you. I am going to the apothecary's to answer for all the medicines we shall buy there. It is unfortunate that the poor man was not moved to our hospital, for he would be better off there. Come and let me place you in charge, and don't leave him till I come back."

The two young men entered the room in which the old man was lying. Eugène was shocked by the change in his face, which had grown white and contracted and indicated extreme weakness.

"How is it, Papa?" he said, leaning over the bed.

Goriot raised his dull eyes and looked at him very attentively without recognizing him. This was more than Eugène could stand, and his eyes filled with tears.

"Bianchon, shouldn't there be curtains on the windows?"

"No, he is beyond being affected by atmospheric conditions; it would be too much good luck if he could feel heat or cold. Still, we need a fire to heat his beverages and to prepare many things for him. I shall send in some sticks that will last till we can get some more wood. Yesterday and last night I burned all yours and all the poor man's own turf. It was damp, and the water dripped from the walls. I could hardly dry the room. Christophe swept it, for it was just like a stable. I burned some juniper, it smelt so badly."

"My God," Rastignac exclaimed, "and think of his daughters!"

"If he asks for anything to drink, give him this," the hospital student said, showing Rastignac a large white jar. "If he moans and his stomach is hot and hard, you must get Christophe to help you give him—you understand. If he is excited and talks a great deal, even if he is a little delirious, you may let him alone, for it would not be a bad sign. Send Christophe to the Cochin hospital, and either our doctor, my comrade, or I will come to apply the caustic. While you were sleeping this morning, we had a great consultation with a pupil of Dr. Gall, a head doctor of the Hôtel Dieu, and our own. As these gentlemen thought they discovered some curious symptoms, we are going to watch the progress of the illness to see if it can throw light upon certain important scientific points. One of the doctors claims that if the pressure of the serum were exerted upon one part of the brain more than upon another, particular symptoms would develop. So be careful to listen to him if he speaks, in order to find out what sort of ideas he is dwelling upon: whether they are the result of memory, insight, or judgment; whether he is busied with facts or feelings; whether he is making calculations or recalling past events; in short, you must be prepared to give us an exact account of what he says. It is possible that the attack may affect all parts of the brain alike, and then he will die in the imbecile condition he is in at the present moment. In a disease like his, everything is very strange.

"Suppose the bomb burst here, for instance," Bianchon continued, pointing to the back of the patient's head, "there have been examples of extraordinary phenomena in similar cases: the brain recovers some of its faculties, and death is delayed. Again, the serum may be deflected from the brain and mark out for itself other courses that can be discovered only by an autopsy. At the Hospital for Incurables, there is an idiotic old man in whom the effusion followed the spinal column; he suffers horribly, but he lives."

"Did they enjoy themselves?" père Goriot asked, recognizing Eugène.

"Oh, he thinks of nothing but his daughters," Bianchon said. "He said to me more than a hundred times last night, 'They are dancing! She has her gown.' He called them by name, and may the devil take me, but he made me cry by his intonations when he said, 'Delphine, my little Delphine! Nasie!' I give you my word of honor, it was enough to make anybody burst into tears," the medical student said.

"Delphine," the old man said, "she is there, isn't she? I was sure of it."

His eyes had recovered their power of motion and rolled wildly about as he looked at the walls and door.

"I am going downstairs to tell Sylvie to make the mustard plasters," Bianchon cried. "It is the proper moment for them."

Rastignac stayed alone in the room, sitting at the foot of the bed, with his eyes fixed upon the old man's head that was both terrible and pitiful to look at.

Mme. de Beauséant has taken flight, and this old man is dying, he thought. Great souls cannot stay long in this world. How indeed should noble feelings exist in harmony with a petty, paltry, and superficial society?

Recollections of the ball of the night before crowded back into his mind and made a strange contrast with the deathbed scene before his eyes. Bianchon suddenly reappeared.

"Look here, Eugène, I have just seen our head doctor," he said. "I have come back, running all the way. If he should show any signs of returning sense or speech, wrap him in a mustard plaster long enough to cover him from his neck to the lower part of his back; and send for us."

"Dear Bianchon," Eugène exclaimed.

"Oh, a scientific fact is at stake," the medical student replied with all the ardor of a neophyte.

"Then," Eugène said, "I am the only one who takes care of the poor old man out of affection."

"If you had seen me this morning, you would not say that," Bianchon answered without taking offense. "Doctors who have been in practice for a long time think of nothing but the case, but I still think of the patient, my dear boy."

He went out, leaving Eugène alone with the old man, in expectation of a crisis that very soon declared itself.

"Ah, it is you, my dear child," père Goriot said, recognizing Eugène.

"Are you better?" the student asked, taking his hand.

"Yes, my head felt as if it were squeezed tight in a vice, but it is freer now. Have you seen my daughters? They will be here before long and will hasten here as soon as they know I am ill, for they used to take such good care of me in the rue de la Jussienne. Good heavens! I wish my room were clean enough to receive them in. There was a young man who burned all my turf."

"I hear Christophe now," Eugène said. "He is bringing up some wood that the young man sends you."

"That is well, but how shall I pay for the wood? I don't have a penny left, my boy. I have given everything away, everything. I am living on charity. At least I hope the embroidered gown was beautiful. Oh! I am in such pain! Thank you, Christophe; God will reward you, my good fellow, for I have nothing!"

"I will pay both you and Sylvie well," Eugène whispered in the servant's ear.

"My daughters told you they were coming, didn't they, Christophe? Go to them again and I will give you five francs. Tell them that I am not well, and that I long to see them and kiss them again before I die. Say that to them, but don't frighten them too much."

Christophe left at a sign from Rastignac.

"They will come," the old man resumed. "I know them. If I die, how much I shall pain my kind Delphine, and Nasie too. I would like not to die, so that I could spare them their tears. Dying, dear Eugène, means that I shall not see them anymore. I shall find the place where people go after death very dreary. It is like hell for a father to be separated from his children, and I have served my apprenticeship ever since my daughters married. My paradise was in the rue de la Jussienne. Tell me, if I go to Heaven, do you think I could come back and live near them as a spirit? I have heard of such things; are they true?

"I think I can see my girls now as they were in the rue de la Jussienne. They came downstairs in the morning and said, 'How do you do, Papa?' Then I took them on my knees, caressed them a thousand times, and played little tricks upon them. They kissed me so sweetly in return. We breakfasted and dined together every day; I knew what it was to be a father and to enjoy my children. When they lived in the rue de la Jussienne, they were simple and docile; they knew nothing of the world, but they loved me. Oh, God! Why could they not be always little girls?

"Oh, I am in pain; my head is drawn so tight. Oh, oh, forgive me, my children, for I am suffering horribly, and it must be agony indeed, because you have accustomed me to pain. My God, if I had only their hands in mine, I would not feel this torture. Do you think they will come? Christophe is so stupid; I should have gone myself. He will have the pleasure of seeing them.

"Were you at the ball last night? Tell me about them; they knew nothing of my illness, did they? If they had known, they would not have danced, poor little things. Oh, I don't want to be ill any longer, for they still need my help too much. Their fortunes are in danger, and what brutes their husbands are! Cure me, cure me! Oh, I suffer! Ah ah ah! You see you must cure me, because they want money, and I know where to go to gain some. I shall go to manufacture starch at Odessa. I am clever and shall make millions. Oh, I am in torment!"

Goriot was silent for a moment, apparently making a mighty effort to gather strength to bear the pain.

"If they were here, I would not complain," he said. "Then why should I complain now?"

A slight drowsiness overcame him and lasted for some time. Christophe returned. Rastignac, thinking that père Goriot was asleep, let the man speak aloud as he gave the account of his errand.

"I went first to the Countess," he said, "and it was impossible for me to speak with her, because she was deeply engaged in business with her husband. As I persisted, M. de Restaud came himself and said to me quite indifferently, 'So M. Goriot is dying? It is the best thing he can do. I need Mme. de Restaud to finish some important business; she can go when that is done.' He looked as if he were angry. I was going away when the Countess came into the antechamber by a door I had not noticed before and said, 'Christophe, tell my father that I am occupied with my husband and that I cannot leave him; it is a question of life or death for my children, but as soon as we have finished, I shall go to my father.' As to the Baroness, that is another story. I could not even see or speak with her. 'My mistress came in at quarter past five from the ball,' the maid said to me. 'She is sleeping, and she will scold me if I wake her before noon. As soon as she rings, I shall tell her that her father is worse. There is always time to tell bad news.' All my entreaties were in vain, I can tell you. I asked to see the Baron, but he had gone out."

"Neither of his daughters will come!" Rastignac cried. "I am going to write to both of them."

"Neither of them!" the old man repeated, sitting up

in bed. "They are busy, they are sleeping and will not come. I knew it. A man must die to find out what his children are. Ah, my friend, never marry and never have children! You give them life, and they give you death. You help them into this world, and they drive you out of it. No, they will not come! I have known it for ten years and have sometimes said it to myself, but I dared not believe it."

A tear gathered upon the red rims of his eyes, but did not fall.

"Ah, if I were rich and had kept my fortune, if I had not given it to them, they would be here and would cover my cheeks with kisses. I would live in a fine house, with handsome rooms and servants and a fire of my own; they would be beside me, in tears, with their husbands and children. I would have all that. But now, I have nothing. Money buys everything, even daughters. Oh, where is my money? If I had riches to leave, they would tend me and care for me, and I would hear their voices and would see them. Ah, my dear child, my only child, I prefer my poverty and abandonment, for at least when a poor man is loved, he is sure that he is truly loved.

"No, I would rather be rich, for then I would see them. But who knows? Both their hearts are hard as rocks; I loved them too much for them to love me. A father should be always rich and should rein in his children as if they were vicious horses. And I was on my knees to them. The wretches! This is a worthy end of what their conduct has been for the last ten years. If you knew how attentive they were to me in the early part of

351

their married life. Oh, I am suffering a cruel martyrdom! I had just given them nearly eight hundred thousand francs apiece, and neither they nor their husbands could be disagreeable to me. They received me at their houses, and it was 'my dear Father' here, and 'my good Father' there! My place was always set at their tables, and I dined with their husbands who treated me with politeness. They thought I still had something left. Why was it so? I had not told them anything of my affairs, and a man who gives eight hundred thousand francs to his daughters is a man to make much of. They were devoted to me, but it was for my money. The world is an ugly place; I have learned that. They took me to the theater in a carriage, and I stayed at their parties if I chose. They called themselves my daughters and acknowledged me as their father. I have kept my wits, I tell you, and nothing escaped me. Everything hit the mark and cut me to the heart. I knew it was all a sham, but the evil was past remedy. I was not as much at my ease in my daughters' houses as at the table downstairs; I could think of nothing to say. When some fashionable guest whispered in the ear of one of my sons-in-law, 'Who is that gentleman?' he would answer, 'He is very rich; he is made of money.' 'The devil he is!' the guest would answer and then would look at me with the respect my money called for.

"But though I was in the way sometimes, I made handsome amends for my failings. Besides, who is perfect? My head is in torture! I am suffering enough pain now to kill me, my dear Monsieur Eugène, but it is nothing in comparison with the pain I felt at the first look from Anastasie that told me I had mortified her by some foolish speech of mine; that look of hers chilled my blood. I would have liked to know everything; but one thing I knew, and that was that I had no place on the earth. The next day I went to find comfort with Delphine, and I made another blunder that displeased her too. I was almost crazy, and for a week I could not tell what I ought to do. I dared not go and see them for fear of their reproaches, so there I was with the doors of both my daughters shut against me.

"Oh, my God, Thou knowest the misery and suffering I have endured; since Thou hast counted the dagger-thrusts I have received in this time that has so aged and changed me, that has whitened my hair and sapped my life, why dost Thou make me suffer now? I have expiated my sin of loving them too well. They have revenged themselves upon my affection and have tortured me like executioners. Fathers are so foolish, and I loved them so much that I went back to them again as a gambler to his game. My love for my daughters was my vice; they were my mistresses, my everything. They often wanted jewelry or something else; their maids used to tell me, and I gave the things to buy a kind reception from them. But all the same, they would lecture me about my manners in society; they never even waited until the next day. They began to blush for me. That's what it is to give your children a good education. Still, I could not go to school at my age.

"My God! I am in horrible anguish! Those doctors,

those doctors! If they opened my head, I would suffer less. My daughters, my daughters! Anastasie, Delphine! I want to see them. Send the gendarmes for them and bring them by force! Justice is on my side, everything is on my side, nature and the civil code. I protest, for the country will be ruined if fathers are trampled under foot. That is clear, for society and the world rest upon the relation between parents and their children, and everything will crumble away if children stop loving their fathers.

"Oh, if I could see them and hear them, no matter what they said; if I could only hear their voices, it would soothe my pain, especially if it were Delphine who came. But tell them when they are here not to look at me as coldly as they do. Ah, my good friend, Monsieur Eugène, you don't know what it is to see a loving look changed suddenly to a frown. Since the day when they ceased to smile upon me, I have been in perpetual winter; I have had only sorrows to bear, and I have borne them! I have lived to be humiliated and insulted; I love them so much that I pocketed the affronts with which they sold me every poor little timid pleasure. Think of a father seeing his daughters only in secret! I have given them my life, and they will not give me an hour today! I am thirsty and hungry and my heart is on fire; they will not come to ease my deathbed, for I am dying, I feel it. They don't know what it is to tread their father's body under foot! There is a God in Heaven, and He avenges us fathers, in spite of ourselves.

"Oh, they will come! Come, my darlings, come and give me a kiss, a last kiss, that shall be the last sacrament of your father, who will pray God for you, who will tell Him that you have been good girls, who will plead for you. After all, you are innocent. They are innocent, my friend. Tell it to all the world, and let no one trouble them on my account. It is all my fault; I accustomed them to trample upon me. I liked it. It concerns no one else, neither human nor divine justice. God would be unjust if He condemned them because of me. I have not known how to behave and was so foolish as to abdicate my rights. I was willing to degrade myself for them. What can you expect? The finest natures and noblest souls would have succumbed to the corruption of my fatherly indulgence. I am a wretch and am justly punished. I alone am responsible for my daughters' sins, for I spoiled them. Now they long for pleasure as they used to long for sweets. When they were young girls, I always allowed them to satisfy their whims; at fifteen they had a carriage—nothing was denied them. I alone am guilty, but guilty through my love. Their voice loosened my heartstrings.

"I hear them, they are coming. Oh, yes, they will come. The law requires that children shall come to the bedside of their father; the law is on my side. It will only cost them one trip in a cab; I will pay for it. Write them that I have millions to leave them. It is true, upon my honor. I am going to manufacture macaroni at Odessa; I know how, and with my scheme I shall make millions. Nobody has thought of it yet, and it will not be injured by transportation like wheat or flour. Oh, there will be millions in starch! It is not a lie; tell them millions, and even if they come out of avarice, I would rather be deceived, for I would see them. I want my daughters; I am their father, and they belong to me!"

He sat up in bed confronting Eugène, his head with its thin white hair wearing a most threatening appearance.

"Come," Eugène said, "lie down again, dear père Goriot; I will write to them. As soon as Bianchon returns, I will go myself if they do not come."

"If they don't come?" the old man repeated, sobbing. "But I shall die, die in an attack of rage, rage, I say. I am very angry! At this moment, I see my entire life. I am a dupe, they do not love me, they have never loved me; it is plain enough. Since they have not come already, they will not come at all. The longer they delay, the less they will care about giving me this joy; I know them. Since they have never been able to understand my griefs, my pains, and my needs, so they will not understand my death; they are not even in the secret of my affection for them. Yes, I can see now that my habit of draining my lifeblood for them took away the value of all I did. They might have asked me to put out my eyes, and I would have allowed them to put them out; I am too stupid. They think all fathers are like theirs.

"A man ought to maintain his own rights. Their children will avenge me. It is in their own interest to come here; warn them that they are preparing misery for their own deathbeds by what they are doing now. They are committing all possible crimes in this one. But go and tell them that not to come is parricide! They have sinned enough without adding this to what they have done. Shout like me, 'Come, Nasie! Delphine! Come to your father who has been so good to you and who is suffering.' Nothing, nobody! Shall I die, then, like a dog? Desertion is my reward. They are infamous and wicked; I hate them, I curse them. I shall rise from my coffin at night to curse them again; for, after all, my friends, am I wrong? They are behaving very badly, are they not? What am I saying? Didn't you say that Delphine was there? She is the kinder of the two. You are my son, Eugène; love her and be a father to her. Her sister is very unhappy. And their fortunes! Oh, my God! I am dying; I am suffering more than I can bear! Cut off my head, and leave me only my heart."

"Christophe, go and bring Bianchon," Eugène cried, terrified by the character the old man's cries and complaints were taking, "and call a cab for me. I am going for your daughters, dear père Goriot and shall bring them back to you."

"Use force, force. Ask for a guard and soldiers of the line; do all you can," he said, turning upon Eugène a last look with a glimmering of sense. "Tell the government and the attorney general that they must bring them to me, for I wish it."

"But you have cursed them."

"Who said that?" the old man asked in amazement. "You know that I love and adore them. I shall be cured if I see them. Go, my dear fellow, my beloved child, go. You are good to me; I would like to thank you, but I have nothing to give you but the blessings of a dying man. Oh, I would like to see Delphine, at least, to ask her to pay my debts toward you. If her sister cannot come, bring Delphine. Tell her that you will not love her if she does not come. She loves you so much that she will come. Give me something to drink; I am burning up inside. Put something on my head. If I could feel but the hand of one of my daughters, it would save me, I am sure. My God, who will restore their fortunes if I die? I want to go to Odessa for them and make macaroni there."

"Drink this," Eugène said, raising the dying man and holding him with his left arm while with his right hand he held a full cup of medicinal drink.

"You must love your father and your mother," the old man said, pressing Eugène's hand in his own failing ones. "Do you know that I am going to die without seeing my daughters? To be always thirsty and never able to drink, that is how I have lived for ten years. . . . My two sons-in-law have killed my daughters. Yes, I have had no daughters ever since they married. Fathers, tell the Chambers to make a law about marriage, and don't let your daughters marry if you love them. A son-in-law is a scoundrel who spoils and corrupts your daughter. No more marriages, I say! It is marriage that robs us of our daughters, so that we cannot have them with us when we are dying. Make a law on the death of fathers. It is frightful, this! Vengeance! It is my sons-in-law who prevent them from coming. Kill them! Kill Restaud, kill the Alsatian; they are my murderers! Death or my daughters! Ah, it is over, and I am dying without them! Without them! Nasie, Filfine! Come, why don't you come? Your father is going . . . "

"Dear père Goriot, be calm, try to keep quiet. Don't excite yourself, and don't think."

"Not to see them, that is the pang of death!"

"You shall see them."

"Is it true?" the old man asked, bewildered. "Oh, I shall see them, see them, and hear their voices. I shall die happy. Yes, I do not ask to live longer; I do not care about it, for my sorrows were always growing greater. If I could only see them and touch their gowns, nothing but their gowns; that is very little to ask. If I could only, only feel something belonging to them! Let me put my hands on their hair . . . their hair . . . "

His head fell back on the pillow as if struck by a blow, and he groped about the coverlet with his hands, as if he were trying to touch his daughters' hair.

"I bless them," he said, making an effort, "bless them."

Suddenly he subsided, and just then Bianchon entered.

"I have seen Christophe," he said. "He is to bring you a cab."

Then he looked at the sick man and forced back the eyelids. The two students saw that the eyes were dull and lifeless.

"I don't think he will revive," Bianchon said.

He felt the old man's pulse and laid his hand upon his heart.

"The machine is still running, but in his case, it is to be regretted, for it would be better for him to die."

"It would indeed," Rastignac said.

"What is the matter with you? You are pale as death."

"I have been listening to his moans and cries. There is a God! Oh, yes, there must be a God, and He has made a better world for us, or our earth is meaningless. If it had not been so tragic, I would burst into tears, but my heart and stomach are terribly oppressed."

"We shall need a great many things, you know; where shall we get the money from?"

Rastignac drew out his watch.

"There," he said, "you can pawn that. I don't want to stop on the way, for I am afraid to lose an instant, and I am expecting Christophe. I don't have a penny. I shall have to pay for my coachman when I return."

R ASTIGNAC rushed downstairs and started for Mme. de Restaud's, in the rue du Helder. His imagination, which was excited by the horrible scene he had witnessed, stimulated his anger. When he was shown into the antechamber and asked to see Mme. de Restaud, he was told that she was not to be seen.

"But I am sent by her father, who is dying," he said to the servant.

"We have the strictest orders from the Count, monsieur."

"If M. de Restaud is at home, let him know his father-in-law's condition and tell him that I must see him at once."

Eugène waited for a long time.

Perhaps he is dying at this very instant, he thought.

The servant conducted him to the first drawingroom, where he was received by M. de Restaud, standing before a fireplace in which there was no fire. The Count did not ask him to sit down.

"Monsieur," Rastignac said, "your father-in-law is dying in a wretched hole and without a penny to buy wood; he is at the point of death and begs to see his daughter . . ."

"Monsieur," the Comte de Restaud answered very coldly, "you may have observed that I am not fond of M. Goriot. He has injured himself in my eyes by his behavior toward Mme. de Restaud. He has been the bane of my life, and I regard him as the enemy of my peace. It is perfectly indifferent to me whether he lives or dies. Such are my feelings in relation to him. The world may blame me; I scorn its opinion. I have business to accomplish more important than troubling myself about what fools or outsiders may think of me. As to Mme. de Restaud, she is not in a state to go out, and besides, I do not wish her to leave the house. Tell her father that as soon as she has fulfilled her duties toward me and my child, she will go to see him. If she loves her father, she can be free in a few moments."

"It is not for me to judge your conduct, monsieur; you are master of your wife. But may I rely upon your word? Promise me only to tell her that her father hasn't a day to live and that he has already cursed her for not coming to his bedside."

"Tell her yourself," M. de Restaud answered, struck by the indignation that Eugène's tone betrayed.

Rastignac followed the Count into the drawingroom, where the Countess was in the habit of sitting, and where he now saw her drowned in tears and lying back in an armchair as if she were weary of life. He felt sorry for her. Before turning to Rastignac, her timid glance at her husband told of the prostration of a will, crushed by moral and physical tyranny.

The Count nodded, and she thought she had his permission to speak.

"I have overheard everything, monsieur," she said. "Tell my father that if he knew the condition in which I am, he would forgive me. I did not expect this torture; it is more than I can bear, monsieur! But I shall resist to the end," she added to her husband. "I am a mother. Tell my father that in spite of appearances I am not to be blamed for my conduct toward him!" she cried in despair to Rastignac.

Eugène bowed to the Count and Countess and left the room bewildered, guessing the terrible crisis in Mme. de Restaud's life. M. de Restaud's tone had convinced him of the uselessness of the step he had taken, and he understood that Anastasie was no longer free. He hurried to Mme. de Nucingen, whom he found in bed.

"I am ill, my dear friend," she said. "I caught a cold

coming from the ball, and I am afraid of inflammation of the lungs. I am expecting the doctor."

"If the hand of death were already upon you," Eugène said, interrupting her, "you would have to drag yourself to your father. He is calling for you, and if you could hear only the least of his cries, you would forget your own illness."

"Perhaps my father is not as ill as you think, Eugène; but as I would be in despair to have you consider me in the wrong, I shall do as you wish. I know he would die of grief if my illness became fatal in consequence of my going to him now. I shall go as soon as I have seen my doctor. Oh, why don't you have your watch?" she exclaimed, observing that the chain was missing.

Eugène blushed.

"Eugène, Eugène, if you have already sold it or lost it. Oh, that would be unfortunate!"

Rastignac bent over Delphine's bed and whispered in her ear:

"Do you wish to know? Very well, I will tell you. Your father didn't have a penny to buy the shroud in which he will lie tonight. I pawned your watch because I had nothing left."

Delphine sprang suddenly out of bed and, running to her desk, took out her purse and handed it to Rastignac. She rang the bell, exclaiming:

"I am going, I am going, Eugène. I would be a monster if I didn't. Let me dress myself; go, but I shall get there before you. Thérèse," she called to her maid, "tell M. de Nucingen to come up and speak with me directly."

Eugène was so glad to be able to tell the dying man

that one of his daughters was coming to him that he was almost in good spirits when he reached the rue Neuve-Ste-Geneviève. He opened the purse in order to pay his coachman at once, but though it was the purse of a young, rich, and fashionable woman, it contained but seventy francs. Upon going upstairs, he found Bianchon attending père Goriot, who was being operated upon by the surgeon of the hospital, under the supervision of the doctor. They were burning his back with caustic—the last and useless remedy of science.

"Can you feel it?" the doctor inquired.

Père Goriot, who had caught sight of the student, answered:

"They are coming, aren't they?"

"He may revive," the surgeon said. "He is speaking."

"Yes," Eugène replied, "Delphine is to follow me."

"Oh," Bianchon said, "he is only talking of his daughters, whom he has been crying for, as they say a man impaled on a stake cries for water."

"Stop," the doctor said to the surgeon. "There is nothing more to be done; we can't save him."

Bianchon and the surgeon laid back the dying man upon his foul bed.

"We must change the sheets," the doctor said, "for though there is no more hope, we must respect human nature. I shall come back, Bianchon," he said to the medical student. "If he complains again, put some opium on the diaphragm."

The surgeon and the doctor left the room.

"Come, Eugène, courage, my boy!" Bianchon said to Rastignac when they were alone together. "We must put a clean nightshirt on him and change his sheets. Go and tell Sylvie to bring up some and to come and help us."

Eugène went downstairs, where he found Sylvie busied in helping Mme. Vauquer set the table. At Eugène's first words to her, the widow came up to him with the acrid politeness of a suspicious shopkeeper who is anxious neither to lose her money nor to displease her customer.

"Dear Monsieur Eugène," she said, "you know as well as I do that père Goriot doesn't have a penny. Giving sheets to a man who is about to turn up his toes means losing them, especially as one of them must be sacrificed for the shroud. You already owe me a hundred and forty-four francs; add to that forty francs for sheets, a few other little things, and the candle that Sylvie will bring you, and it will all mount up to two hundred francs at least—a sum that a poor widow like me cannot afford to lose. Well, be fair, Monsieur Eugène; I have lost quite enough in these last five days since bad luck has come to me. I would have given thirty francs to have that old man go away then, as you said he was going to do. This has a bad effect upon my boarders, and for a song I am ready to have him taken to the hospital. Put yourself in my place. My house stands first with me; it is my life."

Eugène rushed up to père Goriot's room.

"Bianchon, where is the money for the watch?" he asked.

"There, on the table; there are still three hundred and sixty-odd francs remaining. I have paid all we owe out of what they gave me. The receipt from the Mont-de-Piété is underneath the money."

"There, madame," Rastignac said loathingly, after

coming downstairs, "let us square our accounts. M. Goriot has not long to stay with you, and I—"

"Yes, poor man, he will be carried out feet first," she said, counting over the two hundred francs, with an expression half-pleased and half-melancholy.

"Be quick," Rastignac said.

"Sylvie, get the sheets and go and help the gentlemen upstairs. Don't forget Sylvie," she added in Eugène's ear. "She has been sitting up for two nights."

As soon as Eugène's back was turned, the old lady hurried to her cook.

"Take the turned sheets from Number 7. Goodness me, they are plenty good enough for a dead man," she whispered.

Eugène, who was already partway upstairs, did not hear the old landlady's words.

"Now," Bianchon said to him, "let us put on his nightshirt. Hold him up."

Eugène went to the head of the bed and supported the dying man, while Bianchon drew off his shirt. Père Goriot made a gesture as if to clutch something upon his breast and uttered plaintive, inarticulate cries like those of an animal in pain.

"Oh," Bianchon said, "he wants a little hair chain and a locket that we took off a few minutes ago when we applied the caustic. Poor man, we must give it back to him. It is on the mantelpiece."

Eugène took up the chain made of braided pale blond hair that had no doubt been Mme. Goriot's. On one side of the locket he read: ANASTASIE, and on the other:

DELPHINE. It was the image of his heart on which it had always lain. The curls it contained were of such very fine hair that they must have been cut off in his daughters' early childhood. When the old man felt the locket again on his breast, he heaved a prolonged sigh that evinced a satisfaction very painful to witness. It was one of the last echoes of sensation that seemed to withdraw itself to the unknown center from which our sympathies arise and toward which they flow. There was an expression of sickly content on his face. The two students, struck by this manifestation of the strength of a feeling that survived the power of thought, each dropped warm tears upon the dying man, who uttered a shrill cry of joy.

"Nasie, Fifine!" he said.

"He is still alive," Bianchon said.

"What good is that to him?" Sylvie asked.

"Only to help him to suffer," Rastignac replied.

After motioning to his companion to imitate his example, Bianchon knelt down and passed his arms under the sick man's knees, while Rastignac did the same thing on the other side to support his back. Sylvie stood ready to pull away the sheets as soon as père Goriot would be lifted and to replace them by those she brought. Misled, no doubt, by the tears, the old man made a last effort to stretch out his hands and, feeling the heads of the young men on each side of his bed, seized them violently by the hair and muttered feebly:

"My darlings!"

These two words bore the accents of the soul that fled even as he spoke.

"Poor dear man," Sylvie said, moved by the exclamation that revealed the supreme sentiment of his life, now aroused for the last time by this ghastly and involuntary deception.

So père Goriot's last sigh was a sigh of joy. It was the expression of his whole existence, and he was still deceived. They laid him reverently back upon his bed. From that moment, his countenance retained the painful imprint of the struggle between life and death in a machine that had already lost the mental consciousness that is the source of all sense of pleasure and pain in a human being. Death was now only a matter of time.

"He will last this way for some hours and will die without anybody knowing it. There will not even be any hoarse breathing. The attack must have spread all over the brain."

At that moment, the step of a young woman who was panting violently was heard upon the stairs.

"She is too late," Rastignac said.

It was not Delphine, but Thérèse, her maid.

"Monsieur Eugène," she said, "there has been a violent scene between my mistress and her husband about some money the poor Baroness begged for her father. She fainted, and when the doctor came, he had to bleed her. She screamed, 'My father is dying; I want to see Papa!' Her cries were heartbreaking."

"Enough, Thérèse. She might come, but it would now be superfluous, for M. Goriot has lost consciousness."

"Poor, dear gentleman, is it as bad as that?" Thérèse said.

"You don't need me anymore, so I must go down to attend to dinner, for it is half past four o'clock," Sylvie said, as she came near jostling against Mme. de Restaud on the stairlanding outside.

The appearance of the Countess was tragic and solemn. She looked at the deathbed, badly lighted by a single candle, and burst into tears as she saw the mask-like face of her father still quivering with the last vibrations of life. Bianchon retired discreetly.

"I could not get away soon enough," the Countess said to Rastignac.

The student nodded sadly in the affirmative. Mme. de Restaud took her father's hand and kissed it.

"Forgive me, Father! You used to say that my voice would call you from the grave; then come back to life for one moment to bless your repentant daughter. Hear me! This is terrible, for your blessing is the only one that I can ever receive here below. Everybody hates me, and you alone loved me. Even my own children will hate me. Take me with you, and I will love you and care for you. He does not hear. I am mad."

She fell upon her knees, and looked wildly upon the ruin before her.

"Nothing is missing in my sorrow," she said to Eugène. "M. de Trailles has gone off, leaving enormous debts, and I have found out that he deceived me. My husband will never forgive me, and I have made him master of my fortune. I have lost all my illusions. Alas, for whom have I betrayed the only heart that truly loved me?" She pointed to her father. "I misunderstood him,

I repulsed him, I did him a thousand unkindnesses, wretch that I am!"

"He knew it," Rastignac said.

Just then père Goriot opened his eyes, but the action was merely convulsive. A gesture from the Countess that showed the hope she felt was as dreadful to look at as the eyes of the dying man.

"Can he hear me?" the Countess cried. "No," she said, sitting down beside the bed.

As Mme. de Restaud expressed her desire to watch over her father, Eugène went downstairs to have a little food. The boarders were already assembled.

"Well?" the painter asked. "I hear you have a little *deathorama* upstairs?"

"Charles," Eugène replied, "I think you should find some less mournful subject to crack jokes about."

"Can't we laugh here anymore, then?" the painter said. "What difference does it make, as long as Bianchon says the good man has lost consciousness?"

"Well, well," the museum employee said, "he will die as he has lived."

"My father is dead!" the Countess screamed.

At this terrible cry, Sylvie, Rastignac, and Bianchon rushed upstairs and found Mme. de Restaud unconscious. They revived her and helped her down to the carriage that was waiting for her. Eugène placed her in the care of Thérèse, whom he ordered to take her to Mme. de Nucingen's.

"He is certainly dead," Bianchon said, coming downstairs again.

"Come, gentlemen, sit down at the table," Mme. Vauquer said. "The soup is growing cold."

The two students took their places, side by side.

"What must we do now?" Eugène asked of Bianchon.

"I have closed his eyes and arranged him decently. When the physician of the district has confirmed the death, which we are to declare, we must sew the body in a shroud and bury it. What else could we do with it?"

"He will never sniff his bread again like this," one of the boarders said imitating the old man's familiar trick.

"Good God, gentlemen," the tutor said, "leave père Goriot alone, and don't dine off him anymore, for we have had him served with every sauce for the last hour. One of the privileges of the good city of Paris is that a man can be born, live, and die here without calling any attention to himself. Let us profit, therefore, by the advantages of civilization. There are sixty deaths today, and do you want to mourn over all the deaths in Paris? Père Goriot has died, and so much the better for him. If you love him, go and stay with him, and let the rest of us eat our dinner in peace."

"Oh, yes," the widow said, "it is much better for him that he is dead. He must have had many sorrows in his life."

This was the sole funeral oration pronounced over a being who, in Eugène's eyes, represented the epitome of Fatherhood. The fifteen boarders began to talk as usual, and when Eugène and Bianchon had finished eating, they were chilled with horror by the clatter of the knives and forks, the laughter and conversation, the various expressions of these gluttonous, indifferent faces, and their utter unconcern. They went out to find a priest to watch and pray all night beside the dead man and were forced to measure the last duties paid him by the small sum of money of which they could dispose. Toward nine o'clock at night, the body was placed on a stretcher between two candles in the bare room, and a priest came to sit beside it. Before going to bed, Rastignac, having informed himself from the priest of the price for the service and the burial, wrote a few words to the Baron de Nucingen and the Comte de Restaud, begging them to send their businessmen to provide for the expenses of the interment. He sent his note by Christophe and then went to bed and slept, overpowered by fatigue.

Next morning Bianchon and Rastignac were obliged to go in person to declare the death, which was confirmed about twelve o'clock. Two hours later, as neither of the two sons-in-law had sent any money and as nobody had come in their name, Rastignac was forced to pay the priest. Sylvie asked ten francs for sewing the body in a shroud, and Bianchon and Eugène calculated that if the deadman's relations were unwilling to contribute, they would find it difficult to meet the expenses. So the medical student took it upon himself to lay the body in a pauper's coffin, which he had brought from his hospital, where he had been able to buy it cheaper.

"Play a trick upon those scoundrels," he said to Eugène. "Go and buy a lot for five years at Père-Lachaise, and order a third-class funeral at the church and at the undertaker's. If the daughters and sons-in-law refuse to reimburse you, you can have engraved upon the tomb-stone: 'Here lies M. Goriot, father of the Comtesse de Restaud and the Baronne de Nucingen, who was buried at the expense of two students.'"

Eugène followed his friend's advice, only after having been in vain to the houses of M. and Mme. de Nucingen and M. and Mme. de Restaud. At neither house could he get farther than the door, for both porters had received strict orders not to admit anybody.

"My master and mistress," they both said, "can see nobody. Their father is dead and they are in deep mourning."

Eugène had enough experience in Parisian society not to insist. His heart was oppressed when he recognized the impossibility of reaching Delphine.

Sell some of your jewels, he wrote to her from the porter's lodge, *and see that your father is decently carried to his last resting place.*

He sealed the note and begged the Baron's porter to give it to Thérèse for her mistress; but the porter gave it to the Baron de Nucingen, who threw it in the fire. After Eugène had made his arrangements, he returned to the boardinghouse about two o'clock and could not restrain his tears as he saw by the back door, resting upon two chairs in the deserted street, the coffin, scantily covered with a black cloth. Beside it was a silver-plated copper vessel full of holy water, and a wretched sprinkler that nobody had as yet touched. The door was not even draped with black; it was the funeral of a pauper, with neither display, followers, friends, nor relations. Bianchon, who had been obliged to return to the hospital, had left a line for Rastignac to tell him what he had done about the church. He said he had found that a mass would cost too much, that they must content themselves with a vesper service that would be less expensive, and that he had sent Christophe with a note to the undertaker. As Eugène finished reading Bianchon's scrawl, he saw in Mme. Vauquer's hands the locket set in gold that held the hair of the old man's daughters.

"How did you dare touch that?" he demanded.

"What? Should we have allowed it to be buried with him?" Sylvie said in answer. "It is gold."

"Certainly," Eugène said indignantly, "let him at least take away with him the only thing that represents his two daughters."

When the hearse arrived, Eugène had the coffin placed in it, unscrewed the lid, and placed religiously on the old man's breast the little image of that happy time in which Delphine and Anastasie were young and pure virgins, docile and simple, as he had said in his dying moments. Rastignac and Christophe alone, with two undertaker's men, followed the hearse that bore the poor man to St-Etienne du Mont, a church not far from the rue Neuve-Ste-Geneviève. On reaching there, the coffin was laid down before a little low somber chapel, near which Rastignac looked in vain for père Goriot's two daughters or their husbands. He was alone with Christophe, who thought himself obliged to pay his last tribute of respect to a man who had helped him with some good tips. While they were waiting for the two priests, the choirboy, and the beadle, Rastignac pressed Christophe's hand, without being able to say a word.

"Yes, Monsieur Eugène," Christophe said, "he was a good, kind man, who never said an angry word, never hurt anybody, or did any harm."

The two priests, the choirboy, and the beadle came and gave all that can be had for seventy francs, at a time when religion is not rich enough to pray for nothing; they sang a psalm, the *Libera*, and the *De Profundis*, and the service lasted twenty minutes. There was one single mourning carriage for one of the priests and a choirboy, who allowed Eugène and Christophe to get in with them.

"There is no following," the priest said, "and we had better drive quickly and not delay, for it is half past five."

As the body was replaced in the hearse, two empty carriages emblazoned with armorial bearings, belonging to the Comte de Restaud and the Baron de Nucingen, appeared and followed the funeral to Père-Lachaise. At six o'clock, père Goriot's body was lowered into the grave, around which his daughters' servants were standing, who left with the priest at the end of the short prayer due the old man in return for the student's money. When the gravediggers had thrown a few shovelfuls of earth upon the coffin to cover it, they stood up, and one of them, addressing Rastignac, asked for their fee. Eugène fumbled in his pockets and, not finding anything, was forced to borrow a franc from Christophe. This circumstance, so trivial in itself, brought upon Eugène a fit of intense sadness. The evening was closing in, and the damp twilight irritated his nerves; as he looked at the grave, he dropped into it the last tear of his youth—a tear wrung by sacred emotions from a pure heart, such a tear as rises to Heaven from the earth on which it is shed. He folded his arms and looked up into the clouds, and, seeing him thus, Christophe went home.

Rastignac, now alone, advanced a few steps toward the upper part of the cemetery and saw beneath him Paris, lying tortuously along both banks of the Seine where the lights were beginning to twinkle. His eyes fixed themselves almost eagerly upon the space between the place Vendôme and the dôme des Invalides, upon the home of the great world he had longed to penetrate. The glance he darted on this buzzing hive seemed in advance to drink its honey, while he said proudly:

"Now for our turn—hers and mine."

Then, as a first challenge offered to Society, Rastignac went to dine with Mme. de Nucingen.

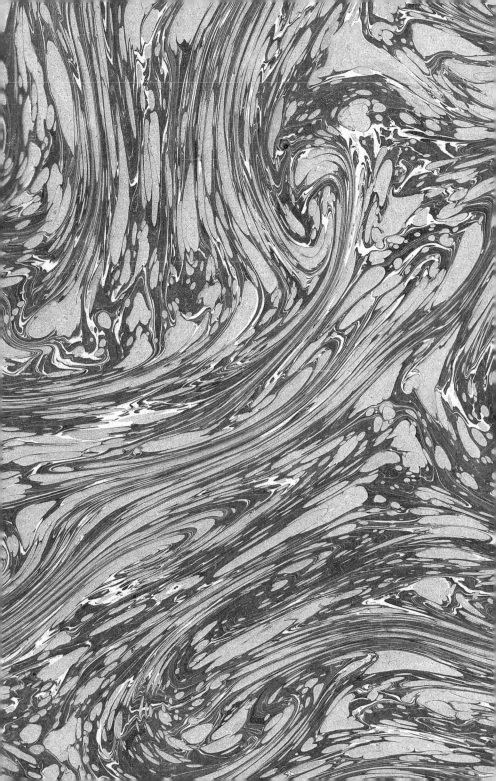